I've travelled the world twice over,
Met the famous: saints and sinners,
Poets and artists, kings and queens,
Old stars and hopeful beginners,
I've been where no-one's been before,
Learned secrets from writers and cooks
All with one library ticket
To the wonderful world of books.

MARIAN

In this enchanting blend of myth, legend, history, and imagination, the Robin Hood story is related from the viewpoint of Lady Marian Fitz Walter. The turbulence and excitement of twelfth-century Britain and France form the backdrop for Marian's adventures. They span her childhood at Blidworth in Sherwood Forest; her quest for the answer to a dangerous family secret in France; and her return to England in the service of Queen Eleanor, leading to her disastrous involvement with Guy of Gisbourne.

CATHERINE J. TODD

MARIAN

Complete and Unabridged

ULVERSCROFT
Leicester

First published in Great Britain in 1991 by
Robert Hale Limited
London

First Large Print Edition
published November 1993
by arrangement with
Robert Hale Limited
London

British Library CIP Data

Todd Catherine J.
 Marian.—Large print ed.—
 Ulverscroft large print series: general fiction
 I. Title
 823.914 [F]

ISBN 0–7089–2978–8

Published by
F. A. Thorpe (Publishing) Ltd.
Anstey, Leicestershire

Set by Words & Graphics Ltd.
Anstey, Leicestershire
Printed and bound in Great Britain by
T. J. Press (Padstow) Ltd., Padstow, Cornwall

This book is printed on acid-free paper

For H.E.J. and C.A.J.

THE FAMILY TREE (simplified)*†

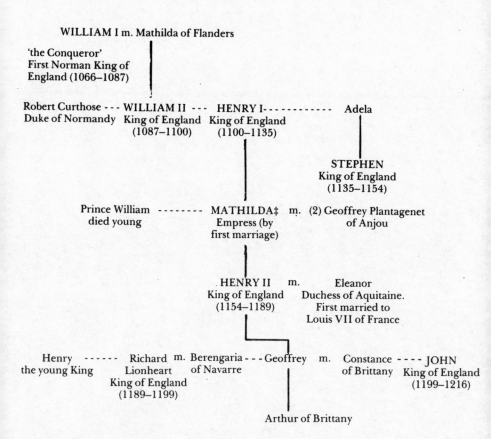

WILLIAM I m. Mathilda of Flanders

'the Conqueror'
First Norman King of
England (1066–1087)

Robert Curthose - - - WILLIAM II - - - HENRY I - - - - - - - - - - - - Adela
Duke of Normandy   King of England   King of England
                    (1087–1100)   (1100–1135)

STEPHEN
King of England
(1135–1154)

Prince William - - - - - - - - MATHILDA‡ m. (2) Geoffrey Plantagenet
died young   Empress (by   of Anjou
                                  first marriage)

HENRY II   m.   Eleanor
King of England   Duchess of Aquitaine.
(1154–1189)   First married to
                   Louis VII of France

Henry - - - - - - Richard m. Berengaria - - - Geoffrey   m.   Constance - - - - JOHN
the young King   Lionheart   of Navarre   of Brittany   King of England
                    King of England   (1199–1216)
                    (1189–1199)

Arthur of Brittany

* Only legitimate children are included.
† Not all children of any union are included.
‡ Also known as Maud.

Acknowledgements

Selections from *The Art of Courtly Love* by Andreas Cappellanus are reprinted by permission of Columbia University Press (translated by J. J. Parry, NY, 1941).

Richard the Lion Heart's prison song was translated by Henry Adams in *Mont St Michel and Chartres* (Constable & Co., London, 1904).

Prologue

MEN say that time stands still in the forest, but I know better. Nature has its own cadence, though the stones blacken with age and the paths creep small into dim glades; I know this because I lived in Sherwood nearly a year's turning. When daffodils make yellow stars on the green grass and the wind is sweetest in the oaks, the seeds of autumn's death have already taken hold, just as it is the winter sleet that brings forth the green again. Nothing abides. Even the stars move, in the dome of heaven.

Time, too, has its rhythm. Of course, I am old now, and the old always give gold's weight to their yesterdays. I am no exception, but that is not what I mean. The past cannot begin again. The bards sing and the children remember, but the man is gone. In the songs there are men in the forest still, and women too; they will be there to the last, seeking the trust stronger than love and the hope that brightened even the darkest hours of that doomed life. That is the legend. Those who lived it, saving only myself, sleep in the dust.

I think of him often, now that the wall that divides us will soon be broken down. Memory is cruel. Last night, as I had not done in years, I turned in the bed, expecting to find human warmth at my back, in the hollow of his body. I met only the cold linen and shut my eyes tightly, trying to hover in the shadows between waking and sleep. I almost succeeded. I could feel the touch of his hand on my cheek, could almost see — remember — his face again. His eyes were grey, their depths stirring like the sea. I called his name and stretched out my arms, but he went sifting through my hands, impalpable and wavering, like a dream.

Those shadows hold more pain than the daylight world, with its commonplaces and small comforts. Pain, yes. I rose from my cold cot to open a window, though the chill of night was sharp enough to raise the flesh on my arms. The moon rode high and full, and the breeze carried the bitter tang of the surrounding marshes. As I looked out I seemed to see the dark, clotted masses of the great oaks huddled at the edge of sight, though there are none within miles of here. The treacherous air was full of the scent of the forest, spicy like the wild grasses and dead leaves, heavy beneath the canopy of branches.

I shrank from it bodily, as if it were a ghost. Oh God, will a breeze never be just a breeze again, a tree only a tree, instead of a burning spike of memory? Sherwood kept its hold on us, even in our bed. It is fifteen years since I have touched a man, but the vision is so clear I could reach out even now, awake, and caress the curved, white scar on his shoulder where an arrow once pierced his flesh. It was life he sought in the act of love, the antithesis of all the death and suffering not even he could prevent.

The wind, tugging at the window covers, almost drowned out the banging of my heart.

I didn't know it was possible to so desire something which death has taken away from me.

Book One

Blidworth

THERE is bad blood in the family. That is true of a great many families these days, but there are few who claim descent from the Devil, or, worse, give credence to the story by circulating it themselves. Certainly Richard embraced it with bizarre enthusiasm and was fond of using the family tree as an excuse for his unnatural affections and worse.

Around the Millennium, Black Fulk, a Count of Anjou, had married a lady of whom he knew nothing but 'the fairness of her body'. That sounds likely enough; the Angevin appetites have always been decidedly carnal. When the Countess displayed a reluctance to attend church and positively refused to stay for the Consecration of the Host, her husband, scenting scandal, ordered his knights to compel her to remain. She eluded them and promptly flew out of the window, never to be seen again — not, however, before she had provided Anjou with several heirs, the foundation of the present dynasty.

That was Melusine, the Devil's spawn. I never heard what became of her afterward (though Black Fulk went on to have another wife burned at the stake and, as an old man on pilgrimage to the Holy Land, had himself dragged about Jerusalem with a halter round his neck while a servant flogged his naked back and he howled to Heaven for mercy). I can guess what she must have looked like — beautiful, of course; that much may be deduced from Fulk's attraction. Her hair, I think, was red. Not the ruddy, sunburnt hue of her descendants, but the red of new fire, febrile and intemperate. That red is in the blood, and formed her true legacy: immoderation is as much the family standard as a sprig of broom, the *planta genista*.

When I first met Henry Plantagenet, King Henry II of England and lord of all the lands from the Aquitaine to Normandy, I was still a child in my parents' care, living in our manor house in Blidworth, near the town of Nottingham.

My father had a number of properties in the shire, but his richest holdings were in Normandy, so we saw him seldom. My mother, though Breton by birth, preferred living in England. There was some mystery in this. Blidworth was a profitable estate, but it stood on a lonely hill in the midst of Sherwood forest, far from the society and amusements she might have known on the Continent. If she had been happy in her isolation her choice might have made sense, but she was not. I was too young to understand the reasons for this, though I felt the burden of it. I thought it must have something to do with me, and with my parents' desperation to have a son who would supplant me.

It seems I was scarce out of swaddling bands before I knew what it meant that my father had no male heir. In the beginning, he would return oftener from France, and when he departed would leave instructions that a messenger be sent in the case of pregnancy. I lived in the weather of my mother's moods, and at those times the sky grew black. Once, I think, there was a baby, but my mother lost it. Naturally I heard none of this directly, but my nurse told me, through her tears, that my mother had suffered a tragedy and must not be disturbed. My father left on one of his visits to Normandy soon after. The tension in the house eased, so I did not miss him, but my mother must have feared what would happen if she did not eventually conceive.

After my father left she would turn her attention to me. As much as I craved her approval, I felt uncomfortable under her relentless scrutiny and possessiveness. She would hold me in her arms, but vehemently, as if we might have few embraces left. The slightest childhood scrape had to be concealed from her panicked fuss. I was learning to appease and watch out for her, without really understanding what it was she expected. She hinted at my 'specialness' and intimated that she had quarrelled with my father over my future. "He would like you to go into the church," she told me. "But I have other ideas. I have . . . friends who will help me make a good marriage for you. Better than *he* suspects!"

If I had been a little older, I might have made more of this, but my childhood seemed etched in stone, and the time at which I would be sent away (no more than a few years distant) to some great house to learn the skills of a lady, or to study in a convent school, seemed as remote as grey hair and the grave. As it was, my mother was my security and my whole world, and every other feeling an unwelcome complication.

One year, St John's Eve, or Midsummer as it was called of old, fell during my father's absence, and my mother decided to hold our celebrations at home. I was very disappointed because the year before we had all gone to the castle at Nottingham. Then they had had a really big bonfire, hot and enormous, so that some of the boys singed their hair and clothing as they bent to light their sticks. Long after I was sent to bed sulking and unsleepy, the fire continued to flash and crackle while the unmarried youths and girls encircled it in a dance. I lay awake as long as I could, but I never heard when the dancing stopped. This year I had determined to stay up.

There was another reason I wanted to go to Nottingham, one I had not confided even to my friend Janet, the cook's daughter. The castle was full of older boys and girls who were being polished through service to the Sheriff or his lady, as well as a host of the less exalted in rank. There was someone there I hoped to see again, though he was not well-born and was older besides, which made him unlikely to view me as a suitable playmate or to win my mother's approval if he did. I was too young to regard any male with the undoubted seniority of four or five years with anything more than hero-worship, but this Rob (I knew no more of him than that) had inspired my childish loyalty.

It had been hot for weeks before last year's Midsummer's Eve, and the grass was already yellow and dry. You could see the heat shimmer in waves above it, and even the shade of the great trees was not cool enough. Some of the local children had dammed up a small stream near the castle for a swimming hole, but the ranking castle visitors — mostly the older boys and girls — had taken it over and would go there to splash and play every afternoon. I was mad to go too, but my mother said we had not come to Nottingham so I could run wild like a village hoyden and kept me close to her. When she and my father had their own amusements, she would send me off to 'practise my riding' with some other luckless small children and a guard. We would often ride by the swimming hole and watch the more favoured splashing and pushing each other under, their bodies white as fish beneath the water and their hair dark and stuck to their cheeks with wet. Without their castle finery, they might have been peasants, rowdy and blithe.

One afternoon, probably the fourth or fifth of our visit to Nottingham, we were taking our usual ride along the water meadows when we came again to the little pond. A cloud of insects buzzed over it; a group of boys stood at the edge, their backs to us, jeering and calling out to something in the water. There was splashing and laughter too, but it was no longer light-hearted.

Even though I couldn't see what was

13

happening, for some reason I was sure they were drowning a cat. When I was younger some of the Blidworth boys had stoned a kitten, first tentatively and then with enthusiasm, and there was about this circle some of that same mixture of shame and excitement. "Make them stop!" I called to the guard, who was leading us on.

He halted and turned around on his horse. He was sensible of his responsibilities, but he was a reluctant nursemaid and spoke to us no more than he had to. He looked at me with disbelief. "Best let it be," he said. "It's only boys."

I thought that was the whole point. I slid from my pony and ran over to the group yelling "stop!" at the top of my voice. It occurred to me, briefly, that I was in fact acting like the village hoyden my mother had railed against, but it was too late to stop now. What I saw at the pond's edge checked me momentarily. It was no kitten they were tormenting but another boy. I had already noticed him at the castle because he was delicate and pretty as a girl, his blond hair curling, his skin pale and fresh. His father was one of the Sheriff's knights, a big bluff man who mocked his son's effeminate ways. He certainly did not look pretty now. He was trying to laugh, but his eyes were red and his soft mouth crumpled in an effort not to cry. Every time he would try to get up from the pond someone would step forward from the circle and push him down, especially one boy, big and black-haired, who seemed, unlike the others, whole-hearted in his bullying.

Inflamed beyond sense by righteous wrath, I grabbed the bully's arm and said, "Stop it. Can't you see he doesn't like it?"

The bully shook off my arm like a bear baited by dogs. I could see him considering whether to throw *me* in, but he glanced at the guard, who was rounding up our wide-eyed riding party preparatory to coming over, and thought better of it. "Leave us alone, you little brat," he said, with disgust. "It's nothing to you."

The object of my would-be rescue lay there snivelling, looking no more grateful for my intervention than his tormentors did. How long we might have stood at an impasse I don't know, for just then a voice asked, "What's this then?"

I had not seen him come up. He had a bow slung casually over his shoulder, so he must have been practising archery nearby. His clothes were good, but not fine. He looked sturdy, and his face was pleasant, though not open. He was only a boy, but he moved like a prince, or at least the way I imagined a prince would. The group gave way for him, even Bully. Such is the mystery of command.

"It's naught to do with you, Rob," Bully repeated, though with less certainty. The other boys looked frankly relieved to have the game broken up and started clouting each other playfully.

The newcomer shrugged and smiled a little, extending his hand to help the downed victim to his feet. But the victim was having none of it. "I don't need any help," he said, his lower lip stuck out and quite ruining his looks. "Not from the likes of you." He glanced contemptuously in my direction. "Not from a girl, either." He shoved himself up and Bully gave him a hand out of

16

the water. I will never understand boys.

Rob's expression froze on his face like a mask, and slowly he brushed the brown hair back from his forehead with the hand he had extended. "As you like," he said, with apparent indifference, and picked up his bow again.

The guard, who had come trotting up, touched my arm impatiently. "Let's go, Lady Marian. The other children are waiting. You boys stop fighting now, or I'll give each of you a clout you won't soon forget."

Rob looked at me then, a shared moment between co-conspirators. Then he smiled, a real one this time, and bent to kiss my hand, just like a grown-up knight.

"Who was that?" I asked the guard, when he was helping me mount my pony.

"Who was who?" he said gruffly. He was quite put out by my 'mucking about with the boys' as he put it, and would not stop grumbling.

"That boy. Rob, I think they called him."

He rolled his eyes dismissively. "Him?

No one fit for you to know, my lady. He's the bastard son of a minor forest official hereabouts. He rides along with his father sometimes, so a few of the boys know him." I was not too clear on what a bastard was, but I knew it was shameful and a mysterious disadvantage. Still, I was intrigued. Throughout the rest of the ride I kept remembering the boy and my small adventure.

It would be a long time before I saw him again.

* * *

A year later, an eternity in childhood, I could scarcely remember his name or face. Memory was vague and alternated between embarrassment and a grand drama of which I was the undoubted heroine. I thought it would be fun to see my accomplice again, who would regard me with admiration and affection. I was bored with Blidworth and longed for the adventure of Midsummer at Nottingham. I whined to go.

My mother was not sympathetic. I suppose, in retrospect, that she was

18

concerned for her reputation; St John's Eve is not given to the abandon of May Day, but the heat of the fire can melt resolution, and a woman whose lord is away cannot afford to be talked about. "Never mind," she told me, pursing her lips and shaking her head in annoyance over the mistake in her weaving for which I was, no doubt, to blame. She was easily distracted and had trouble concentrating on two things at once. "I've already spoken to Geron. Everything's arranged. We'll have our own fire wheel, and the boys can collect old bones and rubbish for the bonfire. It'll be fun, you'll see. Besides," she glanced at me sidelong and smiled slightly — she had a kind of brittle prettiness which softened into beauty when she smiled — "wait till you taste what Cook is preparing — frumenty and currant tarts and cherry wine . . . " I stooped shamelessly to the bait, a hawk to the lure. In those days I was always greedy for sweets.

The day dawned fair and clear, as the summer solstice often does. The warm air carried the scent of damp earth and of the ripening hay grass, ready for the next day's mowing. The last, lingering traces of spring hung on; it was six weeks until the stifling blast of Lammas, and the Feast of First Fruits.

By dusk we were quite giddy with excitement. Janet, the cook's daughter, and I had already been thrown out of the kitchen, and even Geron, my father's steward, lost patience and shooed us away. We sat in the hot, walled garden all afternoon amid the hyssop and summer savory, playing with our dolls and eating the sweet cakes Janet had wheedled from her mother. Between bites she told me how, a few days before, she had seen a White Lady beckoning from the forest path. The spectre moaned and wrung its bony hands. Just as it had been about to point and call her by name, Janet assured me, she clapped her hands over her ears and called on the Holy Mother to save her. When she looked again, the path was empty except for a small white bird.

I would have believed her if she had told me she met a dragon as big as Nottingham Castle. There is a different nobility in childhood; by rank Janet should have been trailing after me, showing me the deference and attention I gave her instead. She had the sharpness of a quick mind, and a kind of edge to her teasing that I shrank from. Her mother adored her, spoiling her dreadfully with sweets from the kitchen, though *she* never suffered from awkwardness, or fat. She was a vivid companion and an inspired storyteller, and though we passed for friends, she held me in thrall as surely as the King did my father.

By the time Geron took the small wheel to the clearing I was already feeling sick. The air seemed to ferment about us like bad wine. The boys were running along the edges of the fields, screaming and waving their flaming brands. In the half-light they looked strange and frightening. Geron took the wheel to the edge of the slope and shouted to everyone to stand clear. Then he lifted his own wand from the bonfire to the wheel, and it burst into bright circles of sparks. The scent of pitch engulfed me in sticky sweetness.

I put a hand to my mouth.

"What's the matter?" Janet was watching me quizzically.

"I feel sick."

She rolled her eyes, with a hint of superiority. Her illnesses were much more interesting, and they were rarely inconvenient. "I'll tell Geron."

"No, don't." I would rather have died on the spot than make myself the object of sympathetic, exasperated attention. "I'll be all right."

She shrugged and turned away. She would have told him anyway, no matter what I said, but the wheel was already lighted and about to begin its descent. The steward manoeuvred it with two sticks and then shoved it hard down the small hill. The red-gold ribbon of flame raced round and round in the near darkness. The sun's disc had reached its highest point of the year and was turning south again.

At the bottom of the slope the wheel began to slow down, wobbling and lurching till it collapsed in on itself in a smouldering heap. For some reason everyone cheered. My concentration was broken and I felt my forehead erupt in a chilly sweat, a sure sign I had little time to lose.

Janet had also recovered her train of thought. "Geron," she bawled.

I summoned what remained to me of dignity and strength and fled the light, running as far as I could beyond the walls into the road. A small stream, part of our water supply, chattered along the walls and by the roadside a few steps from where I stood, a safe distance to go. Beyond that was the forest, and I would not go there in the dark. Men of property no longer had to live in armed fortresses like Nottingham Castle just to sleep the night in safety, as they had in the days before Henry Plantagenet took the crown and imposed harsh justice on the lawless, or so my father said. Still, the forest was the forest. The road to Blidworth was scarcely more than a track off the main highway, and the green darkness held many secrets. No one knew for sure what manner of creature dwelt there with the wolves and foxes, and the Blidworth folk, my nurse among them, were full of tales of things glimpsed in the shadows or heard in the wind. I remembered Janet's White Lady and felt my skin prickle. I plunged my hand quickly into the clear, cold water and splashed my face, spilling some down my front as I did so. I felt much better now and straightened, ready to run full tilt for home. Then I heard the horseman.

The road was a silvery slash in the darkness; a bend prevented me from seeing too far ahead. Beside it the grass was tussocky over the broken ground and the trees drew together in black masses. Down the wind, slow and clear, came the sound of hooves on the lane. Whatever *it* was, I was sure *it* was coming for me. No rider with legitimate business in Blidworth would be travelling the forest paths alone at night. I went scurrying for my mother, and safety.

Fear, like grief, reorders the universe. Small obstacles loomed large in the path, the undergrowth clawed at my feet, the stairs were slippery and the doors resisted my frantic pressure. Inside the hall, dark and cool under the blackened timbers, the tables cleared, the servants talking in quiet voices, the world suddenly righted itself again. But outside there was still the horseman. "Geron," I called.

He came over, half scowling. "Where

have you been, Lady Marian? Your mother — "

"There's someone coming. I heard him."

Deflected, Geron went off to see. I started to cross the room to join my mother, remembered that my clothes were dirty and damp, and stopped in the shadows behind her. There was a stir at the door, then shouting. One voice, harsher and louder than the rest: "For God's sake! Let me go. Don't you — "

The voice broke in anger, and its owner came into the hall, throwing off restraint as easily as an unwanted cloak. He planted his legs in the middle of the room and from this secure base glared at all of us. His eyes, in the glow of the fire, were shot with red, which seemed to be the colour of the rest of his body as well. I was very glad I had not met him in the road.

Ahead of me my mother stiffened and gave a little cry. Then she said in a voice I scarcely recognized: "It's the King."

I stared at the Red Man in disbelief. Mud and something dried and yellow caked his boots, and he smelled of sweat and horses, even from a distance. He was neither tall nor handsome, and to my eyes he was old as well. I was baffled by my mother's joke. No one so unmajestic could be Great Henry, master of two-thirds of the territory of France, whose crowning as King of England had put an end to the bitter wars of succession between his mother Mathilda and King Stephen, both heirs of Henry I. I looked at his hands, in which, my father said, the King held all our lives. They were freckled and hairy. I was doubly certain.

My mother insisted. She beckoned me to her side with a sharp gesture — I had not, after all, escaped her notice, which should not have surprised me but always did — and pulled me down with her in a deep curtsey. Her neck was arched in newfound consequence and she had a half-smile on her lips. "Your Grace."

The Red Man threw back his large head and laughed. "I see they don't believe you, Lady. Well, it's what I get for coming on alone. They warned me, but they're always complaining about something. Besides, you can't imagine how long it takes a whole court to move anywhere. I doubt they'll be here before morning."

You could have heard an acorn's fall to the forest floor. Nowadays the Plantagenet eccentricities are not only well known but colourfully embroidered, but at Blidworth Henry had outrun his reputation.

"My lord is not at home, Your Grace," my mother said, in the same peculiar tone of voice. I must say, my mother was behaving very oddly. Her eyes were downcast and her voice low, but it seemed to me she could barely suppress her elation. Her hand trembled on my shoulder.

"I'm sorry to hear it," the Red Man, or, as I should say, the King said formally. "But it's of no consequence. He could hardly have known I was coming. Is there anything to eat?"

Life returned to the room. Geron and the servants had realized that some portion of the court of England would be descending on the household within hours and that, in the meantime, the King was hungry. The servants went scuttling.

I tried to disengage myself from my mother's grip but she caught my arm and held me tighter so that the folds of her skirt almost covered my face. The movement caught the King's attention and he looked down at me with eyes that had faded from red to clear blue-grey. "Who is this?"

"My daughter Marian, sir." Her tug on my elbow reminded me to curtsey again. He smiled at me, and the look was full of interest instead of the half-attention adults usually accord children. But I would not be easily wooed. I was embarrassed and tongue-tied before strangers, and I was confused as well. For the first time in my life I was confronting the difference between truth and legend, in the person of the King. What had I expected? Someone tall and glorious as an angel, I suppose; certainly not this rough and stocky man with dirty clothing. Of course it was silly; if a ruler's royalty were stamped so plainly on his human exterior, what would be the need for crowns and imperial purple?

I expected to be dismissed at once and saw that my nurse expected it too, since she crept up quietly to lead me off to bed.

"Come here," said the King.

I heard my mother's breath hiss, like a goose. She put a hand flat on my back and pushed me forward.

He touched a rough finger under my chin and smiled at me again. The torches in the hall must have flared then, for the room seemed lighter. He looked at my mother. "She has the look of you, and not of her father." He laughed shortly. "It's just as well."

I didn't know what he meant by this because I had always heard it said that my father was a handsome man. My mother, however, did not take offence and seemed to relax. She raised her eyes to meet the King's, and smiled.

"Come and talk to me while I eat, Marian," he said jovially. "Even a king can use good company." Over my head, he winked at my mother and extended one of the hands I had already scrutinized for special markings. I still saw nothing to distinguish it but took it anyway, while my mother came fluttering after.

★ ★ ★

His place at the table was set with my father's finest service and his own cup. The linen was dazzling white, and a wonderful array of dishes — some left over from the day's festivities and some that had been set aside for future banquets — steamed and sizzled in their bowls and platters. The basin of water was presented so that the King could wash, but he only half dipped his hands into the bowl and shook them, so that the water ran in brown rivulets down his wrists and disappeared into his sleeves. Then he brought out his knife, wiped it on the table cloth, and cut off a joint of meat. This he waved about in the air, not even remaining seated while he ate from it, talking as he paced up and down. The rich dishes cooled on the table, untouched.

To me, wrung out by the day's pleasures and excesses, and the lateness of the hour, it seemed more a performance than a conversation, a mummer's prancing and capering around the hall. He spoke to everyone and no one, and though

I remember little of what was said, it did not seem to matter. A king, I was learning, made his own rules, and did not have to be faithful even to those. This was certainly true of his table manners, which I could see my mother was shocked at. In the middle of an enthusiastic and detailed recital of the virtues of all the royal hunting birds in Nottingham mews (on which topic he appeared most boringly thorough, and, according to Geron's later appraisal, quite accurate), he suddenly turned to me and asked, as if it were somehow part of the earlier conversation, "You're what now? Eight? Nine? Can you read?"

My mother answered for me, as she often did. "Of course not." I thought she sounded a bit defensive, which was only natural. I wanted to please her by impressing the King, but I wasn't sure what attitude to embrace. I had the feeling, as I often did when adults conversed, of an undercurrent of the unsaid from which I was excluded by want of understanding.

The King swirled the dregs in the wine cup, watching them settle with great attention. "What's it to be, then? Weaving? Running the household? The convent, possibly." He fixed me with a bright gaze there was no escaping. "What are you good at, Marian?"

It was a question I had already considered without success. My hands were clumsy with the shuttle, and while I was made to untangle warp and woof and begin again, I fared little better with repetition. Janet was much quicker in domestic arts, and though I should have been learning how to direct the servants and the manor people, for the most part I let them intimidate me. Knowing no other touchstone for achievement, I said simply, "I don't know, sir."

"She is well-behaved and will make a very good wife," my mother said in an exasperated tone. "Provided, of course, that a worthy husband is found for her."

"Meek and mild, eh?" He laughed. "I suppose it's possible, but I wouldn't want to make any bets."

I had been thinking. I almost tugged at his sleeve, but thought better of it. "Please, Your Grace," I said to him, "I don't know how to read, but I would like to learn."

"Would you? Would you, by God?" This did seem to please him. "If you would like to learn I'll see that you do. You have the King's solemn promise. So then," he continued, facing me as he sat on the bench, knees wide and hands between them still cradling the forgotten wine cup, "let's see what we can make of this poppet. Look at me, Marian."

I obeyed him.

"Do you know where the road goes, the one outside your door?"

I nodded. "To Nottingham. And the other villages."

"That's true. And after? Where does it lead?" He spoke without a trace of condescension, and I did not wonder at a king's interest in my small affairs. His lack of fuss made it seem quite natural. Henry's rapport with children was, historically speaking, not without its ironies. At that very moment, his sons were engaged in their nearly ceaseless manoeuvring to possess themselves of his power, his person, and his crown.

I named the farthest plausible place I could think of, the city whose towers and spires shone magically in the imagination, on a bend in a river that ran to a silvery sea.

He smiled. "Yes, but this is a sweet country, and even London is not its centre, nor its end. Imagine hills green with rain or lakes still and slick as church glass, and high moors and woods where the rowans roar in autumn gales, and you'll still not know half of it. And that is only England. The road unwinds before you like a piece of string, and even when you reach land's end you can pick it up again on the other side of the sea, in some far distant country . . . " He spoke then of his travels and of wanderers of other times and places, for he could read. He was like a minstrel, and the music he made touched me with both pleasure and sadness. There are no words to rekindle it now, but at the time, warmed by his sense of adventure, I could have turned gladly from the rushlights and the voices and passed through the gates as easily as a rustle of wind in the meadowgrass.

I don't know what he meant to 'make

of me', as he had told my mother, or whether he simply enjoyed having a rapt audience (which extended far beyond my own ears in the hall) for his tales. Certainly Henry was full of energy, but in those days — after Becket and Rosamund Clifford — like as not it was mad and misdirected. His courtiers, strung out between Nottingham and Blidworth, had cause to think so, especially since he left our house early next morning.

Later, when I succumbed to my nurse's pinching and prodding and went finally to bed — my mother being too occupied to see to it herself — I held off sleep, as I did on my Saint's Day or the Eve of the Three Kings' visit. Beside me, Nurse pierced the warm darkness with her snores, while I pondered King Henry's asking me what I was good at, as if I were a boy in knight's training. Memory of my own thick tongue and slow wits made me squirm in the bed, but reflection brought no better answer to mind, as it is supposed to do. Besides, I would be punished on the next day for being singled out as the object of King Henry's brief attention. Janet would find a way to mock me and turn the experience to my disadvantage; I was as certain of that as I was of her envy. Still, for whatever reason, a King had come to Blidworth, and the world seemed alive with possibilities. I fell asleep dreaming of a white road stretching through clumps of trees, until it melted away in the distance into a shimmering haze, at the very edge of untravelled realms.

Some time after this, my mother died in childbirth, and I was sent to live at the Abbey of Fontevrault, on the threshold of Anjou in France.

Book Two

Fontevrault

1

I N the Abbey of Fontevrault, in the closed garden that is her symbol, is a statue of the Blessed Mother, the work of an artist from the south. It bears, like the songs of a troubadour, the unmistakable stamp of its maker, the craft of a certainty of hand and soul. The child in her arms looks out on the world, already a little apart from it: gracious, forgiving, radiant, far-seeing. But it is her face, in the overlay of years, I remember best; beneath the shadowy pleats of her veil, her eyes see only Him. Here was none of the sticky sweetness of children's tales but only the double-edged gift of knowledge, and with it, inevitably, acceptance. The message was as clear and stripped-down as the plain chant, and well suited to stone. Human eyes, beside the carved ones, looked as shallow as glass.

It is not true, as some people think, that Fontevrault (bluntly speaking) was a 'chicken coop ruled by hens'. It is a double monastery (men and women) under the oversight of Lady Abbess, whose authority in administrative matters is more or less supreme. Still, I lived there a long time and had little traffic with any men outside the priests who confessed us and said Mass. The monks were, if anything, more claustrated than the nuns, with their own refectory, dormitory, and enclosure. In after years people were always amazed when I told them this. Everyone likes to quote Abbot Bernard ('To be always with a woman and not to have intercourse with her is more difficult than to raise the dead'), or to cite the Premonstratensians, who expelled women from all their mixed settlements, promising to 'avoid them like poisonous animals' henceforth. I don't know where Bernard got his information, but I can't believe, from all I have heard, that it was based on first-hand experience. You will think me impious, now that he has been canonized, but the Abbot of Clairvaux had not been popular at Fontevrault, whose very foundation he deplored as pernicious and diabolical. He was, if you understand me, a man who loved the Holy Mother and scorned women.

There was little even Bernard could have faulted in the plan for my upbringing. Fontevrault nurtured and cosseted its charges with all the stringency the first families of the duchies of France demanded for their daughters. We were destined, presumably, for advantageous marriages or careers in the Church, and the very least the parents could expect in return for the enormous sums the abbey received as endowments was that the girls should emerge with reputations and options intact. The nuns themselves (and we through them) were governed in strict accordance with the Rule of St Benedict. I succumbed to the rituals — obeying the bells that were the abbey's voice, observing the silences, eating and sleeping and praying and studying in a rhythm which rose and fell with the seasons. Obedience, the nuns said, was the mother of monastic virtues, but I know only that for me, for a while, it was as restful and time-effacing as a warm bath. So, then, all that is as it should be. And yet . . .

41

The abbey was founded, nearly a hundred years before I arrived, as a place of shelter and retirement for those determined to leave the World. But the World found its way to Fontevrault after all. Troubadours came there, and kings and queens, soldiers and harlots (reformed, of course), the hungry and the rich, and lepers, who, like the harlots, had their own foundation within the abbey grounds. The goal of the Religious Life — the end of the long hours of enforced silence, subduing the flesh through fasting and deprivation, and the discipline of the Rule — is the suppression of the self and the renunciation of human passion. And yet it was at Fontevrault that I discovered my self, and where I first began to learn about love.

One day, when I had been there more than four years, it fell to the girls at the Abbey School to decorate St Mary's church, the Great Minster, for Christmas. I have seldom seen so many stone buildings in one place as there were at Fontevrault, and St Mary's was the abbey's pinnacle. In contrast to the dark intimacy of English churches, the slender pillars seemed to soar to enormous heights which ended in great, luminous domes. The building's beauty was bare, pointed, and unsoftened. Above all it was very clean, clean of the litter and impurities of the world and of the soul.

It was also, on that long ago winter's day, extremely cold. We had on our warmest clothing and cloaks, even indoors, but still my hands shook as I laid out the candles around the altar and festooned the columns with the holly and mistletoe we had gathered in the surrounding forest. We were enjoined from speaking in the Great Minster, but our breath made frosty puffs in the air. The mists curled and drifted round the doorway. Around the vaulted arches a sheltering bird flitted from perch to perch, chattering as it went.

And I found myself at my mother's funeral. Strange, how a detail like the swooping bird could bring it all back: the two coffins, one so tiny, the frozen ground which had to be broken with an axe, my father's face, grim and closed off to everyone, to me. The bird in the Blidworth church had sung joyously, as if it were spring. Everything came back to me, as real as the scent of evergreens on the altar, except the memory of how I felt. Already, on the day of the funeral, my nurse was packing my things for the trip to Fontevrault. "It's all been arranged," she said soothingly. But the person who had always arranged my life was gone, and I was rudderless and numb.

Without these spells of unwanted memory, I could almost believe my mother was waiting for me in another country, waiting to see how I would turn out, if I would justify her care and cajoling and her mysterious expectations. I suppose death *is* another country. And I felt guilty, because I was still drifting, and I had no idea how I would turn out at all.

The scores of candles were set out, and the arch of holly, evergreens and mistletoe where the Abbess would stand to lead the Christmas chant was finished at last. (*What shall I cry? All flesh is grass, and all its beauty is like the flower of the field* . . .). We gathered up our ribbons and baskets and passed shivering through the Great Cloisters into the kitchen gardens.

Or where the gardens would be when spring came round again. Now the earth was bare and bleak, like the skeletons of the trees in the orchards. But some of the warmth from the five huge fireplaces — already hung with blackened cauldrons and spits of meat for the feast to come — seeped out from the kitchen, and we huddled in the shelter of the wall, bursting with talk. It spilled from us in a flood, as if someone had uncorked a wine jar. Sometimes the Holy Quiet was just too much to bear.

"I have news," Hildegarde said triumphantly, hugging herself and jumping up and down with excitement, or cold. Hildegarde always had more news than anyone else, most of it surprisingly accurate. She dished it out with less *oblige* than *noblesse*, and she had a penchant for finding out information that could discomfit or embarrass.

"What is it?" we asked, with a mixture of anticipation and dread.

"She's back! The Countess of Champagne! Sister Louise told me she was coming, and then I saw her at the Abbey guesthouse. She brought three of her ladies and a *mountain* of baggage. Wait till you see!"

"Who is that?" asked Lucy. Lucy was promised to the abbey, and rather dim. Lately she had appointed herself the guardian of its virtue as well. Her seraphic smile showed bad teeth.

Hildegarde was happy to enlighten her. "Marie of Champagne? Only the daughter of Eleanor of Aquitaine and her first husband, King Louis of France! The half-sister of King Philip! And, mind you, one of the chief patronesses of the abbey where you are soon to become a nun."

"I knew it," Lucy said miserably. "I just forgot."

"Of course you did. Did you forget about the Courts of Love, too?" She lowered her voice conspiratorially. "Maybe this time we can get her to tell us about them."

"The nuns may not like it, Hildegarde," Lucy said.

Hildegarde threw her arms over her head but remembered to keep her voice

46

down. "Oh *bother* what the nuns think. If it weren't for the Countess and the rest of the family, Fontevrault wouldn't be half as famous or half as rich. Think of it! This is the woman who brought Andreas the Chaplain to Eleanor's court at Poitiers to formulate the Rules of the Courts of Love. If we can get her to talk to us, she can tell us what they are. We may never get another chance. It's already been three years since she was here last time."

I had never heard of the Courts of Love in England, where the Queen was out of favour, but in France even a monastery could not keep out the stories. Of course the Courts were over by then, routed with Eleanor from her refuge in Poitiers. Since then she had been in prison in England for aiding her sons in their wars against their father King Henry. Presumably one has more weighty things to consider when accused of virtual treason. Still, the surviving fragments of rumour were exciting: tribunals of women sat in judgement on knotty problems of love and duty, made rulings, and ordered the knights whose cases came before them to submit to the whims of their ladies. It was all deliciously improbable and very appealing to convent-bred girls, who were more used to stories of St Jerome, and the constant sermons he made to the holy ladies who followed him, about the dangers of female company and the contributions of Eve to the world's evils. No wonder we were so eager to talk with the Countess.

"I have a plan," said Hildegarde. She always did. She looked at me. "Marian, I think you should be the one to approach her. You're from England. Eleanor's your Queen. You can tell the Countess how much you admire her mother and how you'd like to learn more about court life in Poitiers. That should sweeten her up. Tell her you can't learn anything about the real world by living at Fontevrault. The Lord knows that's the truth."

"Oh, Hildegarde," Lucy protested.

Hildegarde turned on her fiercely. "Do you have a better idea?"

"She'll see right through it," said Cecily, the abbey's newest entrant. "But I think it will work. She'll be flattered we asked."

"You sound as if you know her," Hildegarde said suspiciously.

Cecily shrugged. "She visited my family once or twice, when the Count was still alive."

"Then shouldn't *you* be the one to talk to her?" I asked hopefully.

She shook her head. "She wouldn't remember me. And besides, I don't think she's on very good terms with us right now. My family doesn't stay on good terms with anyone very long." Like Lucy, Cecily was promised to the abbey. The Lusignans were one of the richest (and wildest) families in the Aquitaine, and it would need the prayers of more than one daughter 'In the Life' to ensure their salvation. Sometimes the outright gift of a future was a matter of great bitterness; 'not good enough for a man, so given to God', was the way Cook had described the plight of some poor, plain girl I had known in Blidworth. Cecily, however, was neither plain nor poor, and she showed no indication that her position disturbed her.

"It's settled then," Hildegarde said. "Talk to her today, Marian, after Lady

Abbess leads the nuns into the Great Minster. There won't be many of us left in the refectory — "

"Excuse me, I have to go," Cecily interrupted. "I promised Sister Domitilla I would help her mend the bedding. Good luck, Marian."

"She's deceitful," Hildegarde declared, when she had gone. "Imagine not even saying that she knows the Countess."

"Not deceitful, reserved." I had a fellow feeling with Cecily. I didn't like prodding and prying either. Besides, only a fool would tell Hildegarde everything.

"No, it's more than that. She could tell us *lots* of things. Her mother was a cradle friend of Lady Abbess. Did you see the reliquary the Abbess gave her? It has a bone of St Cecilia's. It must be worth a *fortune*. And she won't talk about Lady Abbess, or her life at home, or anything."

"Well, do we want to know about her wonderful past?" sniffed Lucy, nettled by the Abbess's partiality for Cecily. "I'm sure I don't."

2

THE first rule of the refectory is never to think of it until you are there. An obsession with food, like other forms of morbid self-absorption, is one of the undesirable passions to be rooted out of monastic life. Still, even the wild-eyed hermits of the deep forest, for all their nuts and acorns, could not have encountered the Great Feast of Christmas with indifference. The refectory was like a stage set for a mystic drama. The room was long and narrow, the windows shuttered against the winter's spite. The burnished candlesticks caught the glow of the guttering flames, and huge shadows leaped and huddled across the walls.

Beneath a large crucifix of polished olive wood, Lady Abbess sat at the head table with the guests, some of whom were noble women who resided more or less permanently at Fontevrault, without taking any vows. There was a guest house for pilgrims and travellers as well, but these women found sanctuary in the abbey while continuing to live — with servants, finery, and private incomes — much as they had in the houses of their parents or husbands. I was young enough to think this shameful. Nothing worse than the death of my mother had yet come my way, and I was hard in the manner of those who have everything before them.

Lady Abbess intoned the Blessing, and, making the deep bow to both the crucifix and her reverend presence, we took our seats. Our distance from the salt effectively reinforced the Virtue of Humility, as did the greasy water in the washing ewers, when they finally came our way. But there were sweet cakes, warm and crumbling, and hot marrow broth, chicken with cardamon and almonds, tarts with fruit and custard, and a litany of wonderful dishes ladled by the refectorian. The words of the Christmas Message, in the reader's sweet cadence, lapped at the silence and coaxed more flame from the candles and cressets.

Even across the entire length of the

refectory, the Countess cut a striking figure, the more so in such company because she looked about her forthrightly, as people did on the Outside, with eyes blue as the sapphire adorning her finger. The dim light flattered her and made her look much younger, like the slim blonde girl she must once have been. She was now well past her youth, but in the shadows the echo of beauty was still there.

The reading and the feasting continued in the manner set down by custom and the Rule. Some of the older nuns began to nod openly, with eyes shut and jaws slack, for which they would later have to confess at the Chapter of Faults. Now that I have reached the age where I regularly succumb to the somnolent effects of wine and a full stomach I am more sympathetic, but then such peccadillos were the object of ill-concealed mirth. At last, Lady Abbess arose and gave the Benediction, which brought the celebrations to a close.

We kept our places while the nuns filed past us in a stately procession, two by two, sweeping the rushes with trailing hems. Each person made the reverence for Lady Abbess as she passed, and if I had kept custody of the eyes as is proper I would not have seen what happened next. Cecily, lowest in seniority even among our humble group, was seated along the bench from me, at the very edge of the table. Almost without pausing the Abbess reached out and put a hand to Cecily's bowed head, drawing her palm down softly across her face from cheek to chin. Cecily kept her eyes downcast and the Abbess smiled. The affectionate gesture surprised me. I was quite in terror of Lady Abbess, more because of her reputation and position than because she had ever done anything to frighten me personally. My lady's wrath could scare the lichen off the Abbey walls, and few entered her chambers without at least an inward tremble as she pronounced the 'Benedicite'. I could never understand how the nuns could call her 'Mother'.

As Hildegarde had predicted, the Countess stayed behind after the nuns filed into the church. I had my orders. I approached the head table, where she sat talking with the other guests. Now that

I was closer I could see the age lines, and that the hair was grey, not golden. I bowed so low my sleeves swept the floor. "Excuse me, Your Grace. I was . . . that is, we were . . . we wondered whether . . . "

Was there the smallest twitch in her lips, a suppressed smile? "Yes?"

I took a deep breath. "We'd like permission to . . . to visit you, Your Grace. We were hoping you'd tell us about your court — "

"I am only the dowager duchess now, my child. I lead a much simpler life than I used to."

" — at Poitiers, Your Grace."

"Ah." She folded her long fingers together on the table and leaned back. "Then it's my mother's court you'd like to hear about, not mine. How many of you are there?"

I gestured toward the remainder of our group, doing their best to look modestly hopeful.

"So few? I'm used to a larger audience! Where are you from, child?"

"England, ma'am. But the others come from the demesne of France."

"England?" She wrinkled her nose as if she smelled something bad. "I do not much care for England. It's an uncouth country whose King has the manners of a barbarian."

"Where your mother is Queen," said one of her companions teasingly.

"Much good has it done her! You can't rule from confinement, however gilded the cage. Well, should I tell these children about the Courts of Love?" she asked her friends. "That's what this is all about, of course."

"Oh, do it, Your Grace," said one of the women with surprising vehemence. "I love Fontevrault, I really do. No place gives me a greater sense of peace. But think of living here all the time! Look at these 'children', as you call them. What do you see?"

Now the Countess did smile. "The sap is rising."

"Exactly. Is it any wonder they want to know something about men and love and the real world? And who could tell them any better than you?"

"My own thought precisely," said Countess Marie.

So it was as easy as that. At the time we thought her friends and our importunings had overcome her reluctance to entertain us, but now I understand her better. She was probably as eager to share her stories as we were to hear them, a result of that didactic urge that afflicts us all in old age. It causes us to babble on about our experiences in the often futile hope that we will get recognition and respect from the young. This book is a product of it.

"Well, this isn't a lecture," said the Countess, when we were gathered at her feet in the guest house. "What do you want to know?" The hard part about being in the Countess's quarters was keeping my hands off her possessions. The colours! The clothes pole was staggering beneath a pile of brocaded purples and spun gold. The hangings were sky-blue, the coverlet silver samite in a fleur-de-lys pattern. It was as if someone had cracked a window to let in a rift of sunlight on a cloudy day.

"About the C-C-Courts of Love, please, Your Grace," said Hildegarde, stammering with nerves. "And the Rules."

The Countess frowned a little and pursed her lips. "Perhaps we'd better start at the beginning. Do you know what 'love' is? Love is suffering."

"S–Suffering?"

"Yes. Preferably a man's suffering, but it goes either way. The suffering comes from seeing and thinking about the beauty of the opposite sex, which makes you want to, ah, enjoy the embraces of that person. Now, this love is a dangerous state. It can make men act like brute beasts, or it can ennoble them and be the source of all their virtue."

She sighed and looked down at her hands. "My mother's court at Poitiers was full of young men. A lot of them didn't have enough land or money or anything much to do. There's talk now of sending men to reinforce the Holy Land — you'll see the sort I mean if there should be another Crusade. In Poitiers, they mostly got into trouble. So my mother had the idea of writing up a code of manners which would make them into civilized beings and, not incidentally, encourage them to show more respect for women." She lifted her head and smiled. "And that is how we came to write the Rules of Love."

Her blue eyes looked into the distance, lost in memory. "I brought my chaplain, Andreas, from Champagne, and we had him write down our doctrine. He wasn't very willing." Her lips twitched again. "He thinks women are vain, greedy, gluttonous, and deceitful, among other things, so he wasn't very happy about putting his name to a document that says that we hold the power to accept or reject a man, and that no matter how difficult the trials we set for him, he must treat us with humility and respect."

The Rules were simple enough once you accepted the idea behind them — *That which a lover takes against the will of his beloved has no relish* or *A true lover considers nothing good except what he thinks will please his beloved* — but the concept was manna from Heaven after such a long diet of the disobedience of Eve and the weakness of female flesh.

"Do you mean to say," I asked her, shedding my shyness in my pleasure and excitement, "that the man has to do whatever the woman asks him to, in order to prove his love?"

"Well, it isn't the law of the land," she said, with a smile. "I don't believe my brother King Philip or King Henry of England would consider themselves bound by our Rules. And remember, the woman must behave with seemliness too. One assumes that." She shook her head ruefully. "We had our own courts at Poitiers, and the men felt bound by our judgements *then*. We would sit on a raised dais in the Great Hall — sometimes as many as sixty of us — and the men would submit their cases or questions like this: 'A certain knight was in love with a woman who loved someone else. She promised him that if she ever lost the love of her beloved then her love would go to this man. A short while later she married her lover. The first knight then demanded the, ah, fruits of her promised love. She refused, saying she had not lost the love of her lover.' We talked about this one for hours. I gave the opinion that love could not exist between married people.' She paused. "My mother said she thought it would be nice if it could, but that in her experience it was impossible. So we recommended that the lady grant the knight the love she had promised."

"So this love exists only outside of marriage?" Cecily asked her.

Countess Marie sat up straight in her chair. "I had forgotten this is Fontevrault, not Champagne," she said in the voice of one who is resuming control of a situation allowed the briefest momentary lapse. "But some of you girls will be married soon, and you are old enough to know the truth. If you are not very powerful or lucky, some man will make every important decision in your life. First your father, then your husband, then, if you live long enough, your son. Love — the kind we've been talking about — can give you a kind of power, if you withold your favour until you exact your will. Marriage — where love is a sacrament and a duty — removes the source of that power. The Courts of Love were just games, really. But I promise you, this is not."

"What do you think *it's* like?" Hildegarde asked furtively, when we had left the Countess's quarters. "Do you think it hurts?"

"I'm sure it does," I told her, though I wasn't. "But what I can't believe is that wanting what the Countess kept calling a woman's 'ah, embraces' is enough to turn a man into her slave."

"But wouldn't it be wonderful if it's true," she said wistfully. "I suppose we'll find out sooner or later."

"I won't," said Lucy.

Cecily shuddered and said nothing.

★ ★ ★

I discovered that thinking at length about Love created unusual sensations in my body, which lately had itself become a stranger I could no longer make predictions about. As always, the nuns had a plan for meeting this contingency: Sister Helen, who supervised us in the dormitory, told us one should take the scourge lightly, under her supervision. A bath — in which we poured a bucket of water over our shivering flesh (washing head to foot; at Fontevrault nothing was done by halves) — seemed to work just as well.

3

"I HEAR you've been visiting the Countess," Sister Beatrice said, in the scriptorium.

The sun shone thin and yellow as spun gold through the window, and one of the abbey cats stretched and bared his stomach cosily. In an hour or two the clouds would come back, but for now you could believe in spring. The stripped-down skeletons of the orchard outside cast intricate shadows through the openings in the wall, and in the silence you could hear the scratch-scratching of pens on vellum and the dry rattle of turning pages.

I loved the scriptorium. Just as the abbey church retained a gloss of prayer and meditation, like gilt on a statue, this place was marked by the mind's labour. The King of England had once asked me what I was good at, and if he ever inquired again I would be able to answer him after all. I could read. I was enamoured of words on the page, the way they fit together into a visible pattern to make up meaning layer by layer, sentence by sentence. I loved the precision of grammar and the permanence — both exhilarating and terrifying — of putting pen to parchment.

You will say this should not have been news to me, but in Blidworth it was not the fashion, and I had been accustomed all my life to the slippery, sliding, transitory qualities of speech. The idea that words might live beyond not only the moment but the man, that speech or song might be snatched from the air and penned, preserved independent of memory or judgement (or even truth), seemed to me a wonderful thing.

(Of course, it was this same graven quality that did not appeal to troubadours; much later, when I had occasion to know one well, I asked him why he had never written down any of his words. "I can't imagine anything more dull than a song that's identical every time," Alan told me. "I vary my words according to my mood, my audience, and my inspiration. That's what art is." Nevertheless, he was wrong. Now that he is gone, his work will vanish when the last man dies who heard him sing.) I found that Aristotle, Ptolemy, Virgil, and the Church Fathers would yield up their sense in the end, if one said the words over often enough. What to do with this knowledge was another problem. Sister Beatrice, who taught us our lessons, wanted me to stay at Fontevrault. "The only true happiness for a woman of learning," she told us, "is to be found in the Church." At this she would look at me meaningfully. It is natural among such nuns as Sister Beatrice — for whom the Church is not a comfortable second best but a choice embraced with the zeal of the apostles — to proselytize, and as a competent pupil I attracted her notice. For all her fervour, she was quite realistic, and though she had clearly made up her mind on the subject thirty years earlier, she might even have been right. Beatrice believed, as many others did not, that the path of learning led straight to God; she wielded her formidable intelligence like a siege engine, demolishing any obstacles or distractions in its path.

The cat, an irredeemably unmonastic tom named 'Hector', paid homage to the tone of Sister's voice by removing himself on soft feet to another basking place. The scratching stopped; pens and brushes were laid down. In the warmth of the afternoon, the slightly musty smell of the calfskin and the sweet scent of wax tickled the nose.

"Well?" she asked, raising one silvery eyebrow with all the dangerous poise of a catapult.

Lucy began to puddle up over her tablet. Her eyes were always turning moist with sympathy, most of which was directed towards herself. I sensed that a needlessly detailed confession was imminent, so I pinched her. Poor Lucy. She was prey to a particular kind of conventual Hell: a false humility which led her into an almost perpetual burning shame over the stigma of her sins, real or imagined. The pinch was a momentary cure at best.

Sister's mouth twitched and then set itself again in granite. She tapped her shoes on the hard tiles. The sound seemed to fill the room. Like hawks, we began to get nervous under her stare. Lucy sniffled.

"We've just been hearing stories and things," said Hildegarde bravely. "We meant no harm."

That was true enough, but we could hardly protest that we thought the nuns would like it. The Countess had begun telling us stories which she said illustrated and embodied the Rules of Love. Most of them were by her bard Chrétien de Troyes, whom she called 'the greatest poet in the world'. "It will be your duty," she told us seriously, "to patronize poets, even the humblest travelling minstrel. You never know where you'll find greatness. I hope it will be your pleasure, too." The Countess, or Chrétien, seemed to favour stories in which the hero must be humiliated in order to prove his love for his lady. One of our favourites was 'The Knight and the Cart' (*The Lover should be Humble, Love will root out Pride*, and *Love can deny nothing to Love*), in which Lancelot abases himself by riding in a hangman's cart in pursuit of the kidnapped Queen Guinevere and later allows himself to be driven off the tournament field in disgrace because she has ordered him to fight badly as a test of his devotion.

"No harm?" Sister Beatrice encompassed all of us in her glare. "Child, you have no notion of what harm is. What do you think your parents would say about your listening to all those stories — that nonsense about men and women who can't control their passions? You can't have failed to notice that all these Great Loves you've been hearing about are based on adultery! Why do you think they all have sad endings? Lancelot and Guinevere, Tristan and Iseult! If you fan the coals in secret, you shouldn't be surprised when the flames break out and burn you up." She stopped and surveyed us. "Did you really expect we wouldn't have heard of these stories? Oh, I can see by your faces that you did." She shook her head, muttering. "The Good Lord give me strength.

"Now, listen, ladies: I'm going to tell you again. Virtue takes repetition and practice. You can't expect to say 'just this once' to God, or talk yourself into believing you couldn't help giving way, and then hope you won't fall into error and sin. You've all been drifting toward temptation, and you knew very well what we would say about it. You too," she said pointedly to Lucy, whose face was streaked with tears. "Crying doesn't absolve you."

Temptation, I remember thinking, was something Sister Beatrice could know little about. What could *she* be tempted by, old as she was, and protected by the Rule and her habit and the Abbey walls?

"Now of course we will not forbid you to go on seeing the Countess, but I think you will find yourselves without much leisure time in the near future. Her Grace deserves our highest respect, and naturally we hold her blameless. She is a grown woman of indisputable faith and virtue, a patroness of great renown. Besides, you must remember — " She frowned and shook her head, visibly clamping down on her own frank tongue. "Remember who she is, that's all, if you must consider the stories she's told you. It would be best if you could forget them altogether. And now, let's get down to the matter of your penance."

Afterwards I asked Cecily if she understood the remark. She shrugged. "I think she just meant that if the Countess had been born a man instead of a woman she would be King of France as well as heir to the Aquitaine, and her mother would be Louis' widow instead of Henry's wife. Now *that's* frustrating. Is it any wonder she loves stories about men enslaved by women or knights riding in carts?"

★ ★ ★

Next day, for our penance, we began a month's work in the infirmary, performing the tasks usually carried out by servants or the reformed harlots who sought sanctuary at the abbey. We had already studied the sunny side of the healing arts — how to gather herbs and dry them and use them in medicines, how to cleanse and dress a wound, how to splint a broken bone — but now I saw that we had been protected.

We were excused only for Mass and the Offices, and from duty in the leprosarium.

We spooned porridge into toothless gums and wiped it off the linens afterward. Worst was changing bandages, because we had to clean them for another use. The juices of life, turned sour and fermented, clung to the hands and coated the basin with putrid slime. I remembered that I had shuddered at the thought of washing beggars' feet on Maundy Thursday and wondered how Lady Abbess could do it with such composure. I was old enough then to have begun to take pleasure in my own body's ripening, in flesh that was smooth and soft and fresh. But in my self-absorption I had not yet discovered that the body could humiliate as well. One blind, aged sister, her flesh yellow and loose on her bones, rocked in agony in a bed that stank of excrement. "Jesus has forgotten me," she moaned. "He never reached my age. He never had just to rot away, to pray every hour for a quick death. So how could He actually have shared all human experience?"

What could I say to her, young and healthy as I was, while I stood at her bedside rigid and ashamed of my loathing? Her pain seemed to me a betrayal, her bitterness beyond my capacity to heal. Sister Beatrice and Lady Abbess had thought only that we needed reminding that while any light-minded fool worships beauty and youth, He loves even (or especially) these afflicted, and in the face of that, any other love is second best.

We were all very glad when the month was over.

4

AFTER a month in the infirmary, it is small wonder if one is quiet for a while. Still, something more than this seemed to be troubling Cecily. She grew pale and silent and took to slipping off alone more often than usual. I thought it might be homesickness, a malady we all caught sooner or later, or some more private grief. I did not like to ask her.

One spring day, when a clear green dusk was falling and the evening star could just be seen through the soft air, I went walking in the orchards, taking the remoter path that skirted the wall. The way was sheltered, and you sometimes met someone from the community there, in search of a privacy impossible indoors. So, when I saw two figures, one seated and the other kneeling as if in supplication or confession, I slowed to quietness and tried to fade unnoticed in the deepening twilight.

"Marian." It was a cry for help. Cecily stood up, her face wild and distraught.

The other person, who remained immobile, was Lady Abbess. I made the deep reverence. The Abbess rose, straight-backed and forbidding, but her voice sounded weary. "Come here, child, and sit with your friend awhile. But mind you're both inside in time for Vespers."

We stood in silence, watching her proceed along the orchard path as if she were followed by a hundred courtiers. I don't think she meant to give herself airs; it was the nature she was born with, coupled with a consciousness of the respect owed to one from whom so much is demanded. Her powers, moreover, were buttressed by Heaven, and few queens could really say the same. Still, of the person, of the woman behind the veil, I knew next to nothing. I had not yet learned that people were not like paintings on a wall, fixed forever in one position.

Cecily had not spoken. "What's the matter?" I asked her, still thinking about the Abbess. "Are you homesick?"

She gave me a long look that told me

I had disappointed her. Her eyes, under the headpiece, were the colour of winter midnight. "No," she said at last, turning her head away. "Are you?"

To give her time, and because it was something I had thought about, I answered her. "Well, yes, sometimes. But now it's more like a pain I remember than one I really feel. I can just barely summon up a picture of Blidworth, but I know I can't really go back to the way things were. That all changed for me when my mother died."

Cecily pressed me. "Will you stay here, then? Will you become a nun?"

I shrugged. At that time I believe I still considered it possible. "I'll have to see what my father has in mind, since he has no other heir. I'm happy enough here now, but I don't think I have the Calling."

This was something we awaited with mingled complacency and dread all during the years at Fontevrault. We were taught that God would let us know — doubtless in some suitably dramatic fashion — if one or any of us was among the chosen few. So far He had not spoken to me or singled me out. Still, there was an excitement to those days when I thought it could happen, that I might awaken one morning bathed in a pool of unearthly light, or be visited by an angel too bright to look upon, or receive a nod from the Holy Mother's statue. Sister Beatrice went out of her way to discourage such notions, but they persisted.

"I don't have the Calling either," Cecily said with surprising firmness, "but I begged my mother to let me be sent here."

"Why? I thought . . . " I thought it was arranged for her from birth as part of the blood-price for Lusignan sins, but I could not say this, so I broke off.

"I had to get away from my uncle."

"Oh." I waited for more. Nothing.

"He tried to have me," she said at last.

I almost cried 'What?', but her tone, as dry and matter-of-fact as if she found the subject tedious, saved me. I remembered how tormented she had looked kneeling by Lady Abbess and was silent.

She told me something of her family life.

I had heard tales about the Lusignans; they are as colourful, if that is the word, as the Plantagenets. It was even said that one of the women turned into a serpent from the waist down every Saturday night, but from what I can tell it is the men who are the snakes. Her uncle had tried to force her into an impiety with no more shame or conscience than a beast. It began with hands under her tunic, importunate knocking against her when no one was looking, wet kisses whenever he greeted her. When he started to come into her room, she saw that trying to avoid a confrontation was only encouraging him, and she threatened to go to her mother.

"What did he say?" I asked, no doubt breathlessly. I was horrified, of course, but in the rapt, excited way suitable to hearing about the martyrdom of canonized virgins. The story wasn't real for me yet, and Cecily's flat, dispassionate telling didn't bring it to life.

"He laughed, and told me to go ahead. He said it was likely she knew anyway and kept quiet because he had promised to arrange a good marriage for me. He said if I let him . . . if I let him do what he wanted I would be better for it afterward. Then he clapped a hand over my mouth and pulled out his . . . He forced me to put my hand on it." She shuddered. "He . . . he didn't even seem to like it. Then he pinched my nipple as hard as he could, until my eyes watered. Can you imagine? He said I could see he would do what he wanted in any case. Then he went away. I just stood there, feeling like a piece of beef hung up on a butcher's hook."

"What did your mother say when you told her?"

She looked at me.

"Oh, Cecily, you must have told her! You can't believe she knew and did nothing. Of course he'd say that to frighten you off." I was thinking of my own mother and her concern for the proprieties. Sometimes, lately, memory gave her Sister Beatrice's face, which was absurd, and when I tried to sort it out, denied me her real one. Still, I was sure she would not have let this happen to *me*.

Somewhere in the tree above an owl

79

screeched, startling us both. It was near the hour of Vespers. Neither of us made a move to go.

"I thought of telling her, I even planned to. But then I considered: my uncle had never behaved in an unseemly way in front of anyone but the lower servants, who were too much in fear of him to say anything but what he told them. If he said I was making the whole thing up, my mother would be in a different position. So would I, for that matter, since my father was gone. While I was working this out in my mind, she sent for me to say that my uncle had arranged a marriage for me, the very one he had promised. My father had given his consent. You can imagine what I thought."

"Yes, but . . . " I'm not sure what I could have told her. I was nothing loath to give advice, as a reward for her confidence and a measure of my interest, but would she have wanted to hear that her mother might have saved her after all? Whatever the truth of it, she was at Fontevrault now. In any case, she overrode me.

"It was arranged that I would go

to that family's household on my next birthday, in three month's time. I knew nothing against my future husband — for all I know it was as advantageous a match as my uncle claimed, and the parents might have been kind to me while I lived in their house. Certainly I would have had a year before the wedding took place. There was nothing against it, except that my mother was so obviously pleased it seemed a betrayal. And then there was the way my uncle looked at me when he knew I had heard the news. So I went to my mother and told her I had had a vision, and that I wanted to come here. It was easy enough to arrange, because of Lady Abbess."

She did not sound particularly glad or relieved. I would have reached out to touch her, till I remembered how she shrank from it. "Did he — did your uncle leave you alone then?" I asked her.

"Oh, yes. He was even rather kind, as he had been all my childhood. I've thought about it a lot," she said, unnecessarily, "and I wonder if he really meant to do as he said. Look at me — I'm not the type to have men pushing against me out of lust, am I? And a year ago I had no breasts — my body looked just like my brother's under a tunic. So why would he do it? It could be that he just enjoyed seeing me afraid."

She looked at me hopefully, as if I could give her some answer. I did not say the obvious, that either way her uncle's motives did him little credit. Even then I could see something of what lay behind the rest — shame at having been the object of her uncle's lechery, and a measure of worry that she might somehow have provoked it. Stumbling after comfort, all I could do was pick up the thread she had given me and spin it out as if I knew all about it.

"There are lots of reasons why he might have done it," I told her. "As you say, it might have been to put you in fear, or because he was jealous of your father" — I saw by her expression, this was near the mark — "or just because he is a rutting pig. Whyever, it's a sin. *His* sin. And you've put yourself beyond his reach here. I'm sure Lady Abbess told you that."

"Lady Abbess?" She recoiled as if I'd struck her. "Do you think I told *her* all this?" Her calm had disappeared and she looked almost as distracted as she had when I had come upon her on the path.

"She obviously holds you in affection. And I'm sure she wouldn't tell your mother if you asked her not to."

She shook her head vehemently. "She won't, because she won't find out. Promise me you'll never tell anyone what I've told you, especially not her."

I promised, flattered to be the guardian of such a secret. But if she refused to share this trouble with Lady Abbess, I didn't see how I could help her.

She seemed to have read my thoughts. "I've been having dreams lately about what he did to me, what he almost did. I can't stop thinking about it. So I thought it might help if I told someone. I — "

Just then the Angelus tolled. The habit of obedience and the Abbess's admonition made me rise, but Cecily put a hand on my arm. "I came here to keep my pride," she said in a lower voice. "Do you remember what the Countess said, about men making all the decisions in our lives? Fontevrault was the only thing I could choose for myself, even though our lives are no more our own here than they would have been at home. I've thwarted my uncle, I've punished my mother if she was involved, but most of all I changed my whole life for that one moment of freedom and revenge. Now I have to face up to the consequences. I won't have children, or a husband, I won't even" — she laughed a little — "have the pleasure or the 'suffering' of what Her Grace calls 'Love'. My whole life is different, because of what my uncle did. What kind of power is that, to have over somebody else?"

She sighed. "Lady Abbess has been after me" — she gave the words a stress I wondered at — "to tell her what's wrong. I told her I was troubled about my vocation. I could scarcely admit I lied about it altogether."

I shivered. "What did she say?"

Cecily shrugged. "That it was enough to obey God's will without demanding the additional grace of liking your choice."

There was no answer to this. "We have to go," I said, gesturing toward the church. Cecily shrugged again and got to her feet, and we moved with apparent reverence toward St Mary's, the Great Minster, where, stretching out like the sea, voices chanted the Gregorian rhythm of the Vespers. My friend had recovered her composure, but I knew I had not really helped her. I was surprised to find that I envied her a little; all my life had been lived at the direction of others, and now, I began to suspect, even whether I stayed on at Fontevrault would result from an accumulation of inevitabilities or my father's express intervention. Cecily had taken her life into her hands like a river and altered its channel by her own will. And that, however painful the consequences, is something.

5

JERUSALEM had fallen, which from the world's dawn has been its holiest city.

Saladin, the terrible Saracen lord, had wrested Jerusalem from Christian hands; the King (another of Cecily's uncles, Guy of Lusignan) was captured and the citizens massacred. The Infidels held the True Cross and the Holy Sepulchre. At Fontevrault we remembered Zion, singing, as the Psalmist has it, the Lord's song in a strange land. We put on sackcloth and rent it, and the smell of incense clung to our skin and hair. It was Christ himself who had been struck at and humiliated, the Bishop told us, when he came to the pulpit of the abbey church, and He who summoned Christians to his aid.

Within the month, the Holy Father appealed for a new Crusade. The armies of God would restore Jerusalem and avenge its capture. The first to answer the call was Richard of Poitou, called *coeur de lion*, heir to the Aquitaine and the oldest surviving son of Henry and Eleanor of England. The others followed like the flood tide in spring.

Despite the fever of the outside world, salvation by crusade did not enjoy universal popularity at Fontevrault. Sister Beatrice said that grand gestures of revenge were unmonastic, and that a crusade was the only way some men could get into Paradise without having to renounce fine clothes or the pleasures of the flesh. The last Crusade, forty years before, had been an unmitigated disaster. Countess Marie, whose husband, father, and mother had all participated, told us that at one point in the journey the desperate marchers had to bleed the horses and roast their carcasses in order to satisfy their thirst and hunger. There were hideous slaughters and dreadful quarrels. King Louis found the pleasure-loving Syrian Franks indistinguishable from the Saracens and, moreover, in much less danger than they had represented. He returned disappointed and embittered and shortly thereafter he and Queen

Eleanor were divorced, reportedly because of her scandalous behaviour with her uncle in Antioch.

All the same, this one seemed a great undertaking which, though subject to misunderstandings and distortions, promised to be a fine adventure. I will not live to see the city restored. As much darkness and blood and barbarity went into the attempt to get it back as into its loss, and all for nothing. But then, closed in by abbey walls and seething beneath our rituals and submissions, how could we not be moved by the spectacle of merchants leaving their shops, kings their governments, and fathers their wives and children, to traverse strange lands? Joy was a bubble, beauty a withering flower, life itself a sparrow's flight across a lighted hall beside the timeless sweep of eternity and salvation.

I wondered if my father would take the cross. I had seen him only rarely since my mother died and he sent me on the ship to France in the company of his steward. Of course, Geron visited me now and then to see how I was getting along and bring me news of England.

The Blidworth house, he informed me, was nearly closed down; he kept it up just enough for the customary rituals and feast days in the village, which was the duty of an absent lord. There were new taxes to finance the Crusade, and my father wanted to keep expenses down.

Every time Geron visited, I expected he would bring me news of my father's remarriage. It was the prudent thing for him, having no male heir, and I'm sure he intended it. In that case, whatever my own feelings, I would certainly have been encouraged to stay on at Fontevrault. Once he had a legitimate son to inherit the properties, my father might see my becoming a nun as the most efficient and desirable disposition of my future.

Perhaps I wronged him. I see him still through a child's eyes, imbued with authority and — fairly or unfairly — possessed of the power to alter my life. I never had the chance to discover his shades and nuances. I made such a point of expecting the worst, I lost sight of what the worst could be. So when Geron came to see me, looking whey-faced and solemn, I guessed only that the dreaded marriage had taken place at last, or, failing that, that he had decided to embark on the Crusade. My relief at Geron's quick denial was only momentary. What he brought was news of my father's death.

There was nothing moving or momentous about it, except to me. He was riding after a stag when he suddenly clawed at his throat, gasping for air. A few minutes later, despite his companions' frantic ministrations, his soul left his body lying in the muck beside the horse. He was not granted the grace of premonition and died in the full meat of his sins.

It made me furious. I found I was most angry at my father. I am ashamed to confess this, even now. He was gone; he had died as he had lived, with no thought of me. *You never loved me*, my mind told him accusingly, *and now it's too late.*

Masses were said for the repose of his soul; I put on mourning and went through the rituals of grief with exactitude. I did not confess that I felt bitter and as empty of sorrow as a squeezed cloth. Everyone was very kind.

Geron assured me the rites had been properly attended to, so all that remained, after the Masses, was to offer rosemary at the shrine of the Blessed Mother. The herb grew more plentifully in the cloister garden than it had at Blidworth. I remembered my father's laugh when Mother told him what she had heard from Cook: in England, the plant only grows where a woman rules the house. In France, they put it on the grave, that the dead might not be forgotten. I laid a sprig of it at the foot of the statue and said a prayer for my mother as well.

I soon perceived that Geron's manner toward me had changed, that he was at the same time less friendly and more polite. I should have expected this, since I was my father's sole heir so far as anyone knew (there are many unpleasant surprises in such cases, so one can never be certain until the matter is settled at law), and Geron was now my steward. Still, his deference startled me, and I was abrupt and rude-sounding out of embarrassment. That he appeared to take no notice I took as further indication of my new standing.

A short time later I was summoned to Lady Abbess, to discuss my future.

The abbatial chambers were next to the guest house and were as spare as the other was luxurious and comfortable. The Rule was strict about private possessions, and the parlour in which Lady Abbess received visitors and conducted Fontevrault's business was stripped-down and scrubbed, outfitted only with a highbacked chair, a trestle, and two stools. I have heard of many in religious life who live better than kings (St Bernard, to do him justice, found this particularly abhorrent), but if Lady Abbess was vain, it was not about her personal furnishings.

The hangings slapped and swished as I entered.

"*Deo Gratias*."

"*Benedicite*, my lady."

"Sit down." She gestured toward a stool as I came up from my bow. I resisted the profound interest I had suddenly taken in the floor and raised my eyes to her face. I think it must have been the first time I ever really looked at it.

Abbesses are seldom young, and of course to me she would have seemed venerable in any case. But I believe in fact she did look older than her years; her face was stamped with the responsibility she had borne for her sons and daughters in Christ, for pilgrims and penitents, and for those like me who had been entrusted to her care. Something about her demeanour indicated that the burden deepened her self-regard, not that she had swollen notions of her importance but that she knew precisely what she was worth.

Memory, coloured by youth and fear, shows me a large woman, tall but slim as an arrow, and with its straightness as well. Her gaze was dark and piercing. She had heavy brows which could shadow her eyes in disapproval or lift almost mockingly in surprise. Of course, under the veil, it is the eyes one notices first, and I saw — or thought I saw — a look that wanted something of me. I shifted uncomfortably on my stool.

"Well, child," she began at last, "how are you getting on?"

I said that everyone had been very

kind. I was as incapable of parading my pent-up feelings before the imperturbable façade of her authority as I was of pitching offal at the Queen.

She nodded. "If you think you are up to it, I think we must talk now about your future. Unsettling times are coming to Fontevrault. The Crusade will mean a number of interruptions in our work — visitors, dispensations, blessings, manuscripts, not to mention the outcome of the enterprise itself. It could be years before — God willing — Jerusalem is recaptured and those who have taken the cross are safely home again. This is no time to be — well — unsettled, and frankly I may not be able to give you as much attention later on. So, then," she said briskly, arranging objects on the trestle top into some kind of order, "Sister Beatrice has said you would be an asset to the abbey, and particularly to her in the scriptorium." She leaned forward. "Do you have a vocation?"

It is not fair to say I was surprised by the question. I had anticipated something of the sort sooner or later, though I would have preferred later, and had tried to plan my response. I had hoped, if I entered, that the decision would be made for me by divine intercession, but the Abbess's pallid praise offered me a watered-down version of a Calling: the abbey would be glad to have me, and who was I to disoblige Our Lord's representative on earth? Still, when pressed, I saw that I was not yet ready to commit myself to Fontevrault; I wanted to leave the choice open, not realizing that choices have a lifespan of their own.

I murmured my gratitude to Sister Beatrice. I recalled how happy I had been during my years at the abbey. I began to prattle, filling up what had become an embarrassing silence. Lady Abbess seemed amused and in no hurry to help me out.

Finally she took pity on both of us. "Let's just say you don't know yet." She folded her hands in front of her. "I have spoken with your steward, the one who brought you the news," she said. "He says it is arranged that, in default of any male relative to act as guardian, you will become the King's ward until you enter the Order or, failing that, King Henry arranges a marriage for you."

This pleased me well enough. Wardship, as everyone knows, is one of the crown's chief sources of revenue, and it is only in the case of great heiresses or heirs under age that the King would personally intervene in marriages or other matters. Permission was almost always given after the preliminary arrangements were made. I was about to say that I was content when I remembered that, so long as I was the King's ward, the fees and knights owed by the estate would revert to the royal purse, but that once I had taken Simple Vows the income would all belong to Fontevrault. Instead, mindful of a conversation I had had with the Countess, I asked whether or not, given the limited extent of my father's holdings, my dowry would even be acceptable to the abbey.

I don't think the Countess meant to put this into my head, but her surprise, when she asked me who my family was, was so genuine I was taken aback. "It's just that I had expected to know them," she told me soothingly. "There are so few spaces for pupils at Fontevrault that only certain families are usually considered. And then there is the cost, and the amount of the dowry if one joins the Order." She had stared at me shrewdly. "I think you are luckier than you realize."

Lady Abbess seemed to find nothing amiss. "Why of course the dowry would be sufficient. Under the circumstances . . . well, it's true that the lands aren't all that much, but even if you decide not to stay a handsome contribution will come to the abbey. It was all arranged years ago. And then there's the chalice, after all."

It was my turn to be surprised. "The chalice?"

She lifted one great eyebrow like a bird's wing. "The one your father sent with you. That by itself would be the beginning of a dowry." She cast this down like a glove and watched me expectantly, waiting for me to pick it up. I could not. I knew nothing of any chalice among the family possessions, let alone one of such value.

She continued to stare at me, her eyes dark in a face like carved ivory. Then, visibly, she came to some decision, shifting her posture in the chair. Her laugh was unexpected. "No matter, then. You can see it some other time, but not now." The tone was all cool efficiency. "After you've made your decision you can ask the Sacristan to show it to you. Yes," she said, nodding to herself, "I'm sure that's best . . ."

I half rose from my stool, expecting dismissal. "Sit," she commanded, with just a hint of malice. "I am not finished."

I sat.

"Touching Cecily Lusignan . . ." She began moving the objects on the trestle top again, destroying the order she had created. She seemed uneasy, a mood I found it easy to catch. I did not want to discuss Cecily's problems with Lady Abbess.

"I would like to know what she said to you that day on the orchard path. Something is troubling her. She won't tell me what it is and I need to know if I'm to help her."

"I'm sure she's told you she is concerned about her vocation."

Lady Abbess sighed. "I'm not a fool, Marian. I know there is more to it than that. She was in distress. I asked you to speak with her. I would like to know the outcome of that conversation."

From lack of wit or imagination I told her the truth. "I'm very sorry, Lady Abbess, but Cecily asked me not to tell anyone."

When I was very young, my mother had told me I would never be punished for being honest. Probably no one over the age of five believes that, but nevertheless I received a vivid refutation. Her Ladyship was quite put out. Who was I, she asked me, to decide such a matter? Cecily was her spiritual daughter, her soul was the Abbess's responsibility; surely, short of the secrets of the confessional, she had a right to know anything pertaining to that custodianship. She cajoled me, she bullied me, and she even frightened me a little, but from an early age I had received such treatment from my mother and sooner or later I always passed from obedience to stubborn resistance. I reached that point now. I knew it would cost me dear. The room was as chill as the abbey crypt.

In fact she was angrier than I realized, ice masking the whirlpool. "Keep your confidence, then. But in view of this discussion I think it would be just as well if you kept away from Cecily in the future. Of course, you will see her," she said, raising a hand to stifle my half-uttered protestation, "but I expect you to keep strictly to the Silences, in your mind as well as in outward observance. After all, Cecily will be clothed soon, a bride of Christ, and she should not be distracted from that by anyone. If you choose to join the Order, that will be another matter. You already know," she added, almost casually, "what the Rule says about special friendships."

I thought I must not have heard her correctly. Then I saw her watching me, calculating the effect of her words, and knew that I had not misunderstood.

I was near tears at the injustice of it, and only my anger saved my dignity. *Amitiés particulières* are forbidden by the Rule because they are seen as stumbling blocks, earth-bound attachments which hinder the seeker from the true task: stripping the self of passion and becoming a vessel for the Love and Will of God. Nothing and no one must be clung to.

That is fair enough, but anyone 'In the Life' can tell you the injunction implies much more than that.

There are things of which one does not speak openly — at least, not in such a place as Fontevrault — but which are acknowledged in the effort made to avoid even their appearance. It is an ancient story, as old as David and Jonathan, and I dare say the older members of the community could confront the suggestion with a quieter mind. But I was young, on the brink of womanhood, and the very idea made my skin crawl in horror and revulsion. I must have recoiled visibly. Even knowing that I was innocent even of the thought, that Lady Abbess had spoken in anger and with an unbecoming degree of spite, and that staying away from my friend would be a desertion and give credence to the accusation, I could not shake off the feeling of taint. The Abbess could not have found a more effective way of keeping me from Cecily.

I don't remember the brief words that closed the interview. I have the impression the Abbess retreated a little and said more gently that she had only warned me for my own good and Cecily's. I don't know what I replied. Some seed of knowledge, sharp as a thorn, had worked itself into my mind, and it was too late for retreat. Once the rain has fallen, you can't put it back into the sky.

Some time after this I began sleeping badly and imagining intruders stealing toward my cot to slit my throat, as outlaws do. Rigid with anxiety, I listened for what seemed like hours to sounds in the darkness, but all I ever heard was the soft breathing and occasional stirrings of less troubled dreamers. Occasionally I would awaken suddenly, startled, to find myself standing far from my bedside, intent on some dimly remembered purpose. Lucy confided that I talked in my sleep.

I kept my distance from Cecily.

6

GEOFFREY OF MONMOUTH, that chronicler of Britain whose tales sometimes sound as if he had imbibed too much home-brewed Communion wine before cutting his quills, was a favourite of King Henry. The King was especially partial to the stories of Arthur, an ancient British ruler, and his followers. In an acute fit of Arthur fever, he even had the bodies of the hero and his queen dug up from their alleged resting place and reinterred in a site of honour at Glastonbury Abbey. I'm not sure why he found these figures so fascinating. In Geoffrey's stories, Arthur galloped endlessly around the English countryside in search of someone to kill, until *he* was finally killed by a treacherous nephew. (Chrétien de Troyes did it much better, I think). Wales being the land of Calamity as well as of fermented imagination, it is no surprise that few of the rulers of Britain in the *Chronicle* came to happy ends. Perhaps that is what attracted King Henry. In any event, I only mention it because, in the course of my studies, I found one of Geoffrey's stories which might have proven much more useful to the King if he had attended to it instead.

This was the tale of a king near his dotage, who, looking to his succession, divided his patrimony between his married daughters. One daughter, his favourite, he left portionless because she refused to flatter him with exaggerated pronouncements of love. Though she continued loyal, her sisters rewarded their father's favour by stripping him of his remaining estate and dignity, and harassing him finally into despair and humiliation.

Anyone can see that Henry, Lear-like, was the architect of his own misfortunes. His sons were hardly models of filial piety, but his arrangements for them seemed almost calculated to create jealousy and bad feeling. The King gave with one hand and took away with the other. He set them up like pieces on a chess-board and could not keep from moving them around. The game had other players — Henry's estranged Queen Eleanor and King Philip of France, among others — but it was Henry himself who had set it in motion. Even when Death deprived him of two of his pawns (his sons the young King Henry and Geoffrey of Brittany), he tried to play it out with Richard and John. There is a term, *shah mat*, for the last, winning play of a chess game. It is Arabic, and it means 'the King is dead'.

But that was still to come. It is all one cloth for me now and hard to pick out the threads as they were woven. For a time, it seemed as if the Crusade would end the rivalries and feuding. The two Kings — of France and England — and the Count of Flanders vowed to set out together for Jerusalem at Easter twelvemonth. Count Richard, as I have said, had already taken the cross months before; it appeared that the formidable family energy would be unleashed against the Infidel instead of each other.

However, the uneasy truce was short-lived. King Henry's partiality for his son John and his efforts to secure the Aquitaine for him (now that Richard had succeeded his dead brother as heir to England) caused Richard to suspect that his lands might be given to John as soon as his back was turned in Jerusalem. He therefore asked his father to confirm him as heir to the Aquitaine before he set out. Henry refused, and also denied his request for money to finance his expedition.

Richard, never a man to swerve aside from what he began, set about trying to pawn Poitou and his other secure inheritances for whatever they would bring. In later years, when he needed to fund some scheme or other, this was the means he used, no matter how detrimental the result or unfair the process. I myself was a victim of it. But this was the first time, and the lands were his own, not someone else's. Just then, rebellion broke out in Poitou, spearheaded by the Lusignans. Count Richard, whose departure was necessarily delayed, laid waste to the Lusignan estates and destroyed their castles (one of which was the property promised to Fontevrault as Cecily's dowry). It was widely rumoured that the revolt had been instigated by King Henry himself.

As I have suggested, the rights and wrongs of the situation were complicated. Anyone — even someone whose heart and fortune were not interwoven in the complexities — would have trouble unravelling the mutual injustices and slights. But it is the unseemliness of it all that still moves me. I write this now, when so much worse came after, but it is no less true for all that. Men on either side of the sea will tell you it is no small thing to be left alone, in peace, no matter who is in power. This very sentiment had made Henry king, and popular. But one can dip from the well only so long until it runs dry.

Meanwhile, whatever its private inconvenience, Fontevrault opened its gates in the cause of the Crusade. The Saladin tithe had been levied throughout the Plantagenet possessions, and the Abbey was a natural collection point (as well as a substantial contributor). After the taxmen came the bards, eager to make songs about such a Great Undertaking. Some sang from the soul, some because their stomachs were empty, some because their patrons instructed them to. In the end it didn't matter; it is the artist's gift that the semblance of feeling can be truer than the feeling itself.

One evening, we had permission to hear Bertrand de Born, who was staying at the abbey. It was a crisp autumn night; the yellow moon cast a sweet light even on Bertrand's brooding features. The collection of riches to finance the Crusade had begun to overflow our storage area; there were chests and boxes stacked within the courtyards, livestock spilled out from the stables, chickens clucked from unlikely places. It was no longer such a quiet place. Bertrand had to pitch his famous voice louder to be understood.

If there is anyone now who doesn't remember Bertrand de Born, let me say that first of all he was a spoiler. Despite his talent and his noble birth, his real passion was stirring up trouble. He required a constant stream of objects for his wrathful indignation, and so he made the causes of others his own. For reasons best known to himself, he had taken against King Henry, so now his efforts were directed at setting Henry's sons against him.

However, when he sang, you forgot everything else (proving that great artists do not, in fact, need great souls). His verses made me restless as the dry leaves that drifted in the riffling air. Troubadours are wanderers by nature and soon find other work if they are not. The call to leave home and love for the adventure of a lifetime is a subject even a villain like Bertrand can breathe life into. If I could, I would have taken the cross on the spot. As it was, I was left feeling immured and dissatisfied, as if all the small discontents of the past months had come to a head like some dreadful pox.

I was still in spiritual Limbo; I had told Sister Beatrice I needed more time with, I'm sure, an air of self-importance, since she replied she was sure the abbey could bear the suspense. In fact, for the moment I had no place to go, but it wasn't just that. Countess Marie had taught me to think well of Love, to yearn for it with all my pent-up feelings and fantasies. Fontevrault counselled acceptance, humility, and suppression in exchange for a life of the mind and the spirit, in the service of God. In truth, I was of two minds, and I hardly knew which way to turn.

By chance I saw more of Cecily, but she offered no more confidences. I had begun to convince myself I had imagined the Abbess's implications, that she had meant no more than that I should allow Cecily her privacy and a tactful period of seclusion. It was far easier to undermine my own understanding than to believe the Abbess capable of deliberate cruelty. But time had passed, Cecily was preparing to be clothed as a novice, and the basis of our friendship had eroded.

I looked round for her now, thinking, in view of my own restlessness, of what she must be feeling. She was standing very still, hands folded in her sleeves and locked against her chest. Bertrand had just finished a song about St Agnes and was bowing to Lady Abbess. Soon the bell for Compline would ring and we would go into the church. I touched Cecily's elbow. She shrank back as if my fingers had burned her.

Her eyes, which had been watching the singer, met mine. "Oh, sorry," she murmured.

"What's the matter?"

She made a barely perceptible gesture at the bard. "He gave me this."

I took the small scroll from her and turned into the dim light of the cressets to read: *Meet me in the orchard when the nuns have gone to bed.*

I gave it back to her. "Well, what does he want?"

"What do you think he wants? He said he knew my father and had a message to give me from him. Then he handed me this. That's all."

"That was cruel."

"Yes." She still stood hugging herself and shivering a little. Why didn't the bell ring so we could be safe? Cecily was vulnerable, and Bertrand de Born could be spiteful when spurned. No doubt he did know her father and hoped, at the very least, to make more trouble with the Plantagenets. And then, I realized suddenly, Cecily had become very attractive, the more so to a man like Bertrand because she was promised to the Church. Trouble was meat and drink to him.

Cecily seemed to be thinking along these lines herself. "What is he really after, do you think?" She spoke in the assumption of shared calamitous experience, but I had no answer to give her. I held to what I knew.

"Don't try to find out." I took her arm. "Come away. It's almost Compline."

She nodded, lifting up her skirt and leading the way into the abbey church, crushing the dead leaves beneath her slippers as she went.

* * *

Of course he stalked her; I see that now.

He could do nothing as base as make himself obvious to the community, but like an incubus or a watcher in the hills he interrupted her solitude and haunted the edges of her life. He could put on seeming virtue like a cloak in front of the sisters and drop it again just as quickly. There was no honour in it, or passion either, most likely, but Cecily's attention was caught as the hare's is by the hunter.

It is easy to understand why she did not report Bertrand's behaviour to the Mistress of Novices or Lady Abbess. There were no improprieties one could put a name to, only insinuations and an embarrassing fixity of attention. He could easily make her look silly and hysterical at the very least. Besides, he would be gone soon, and after all, she asked me, what could happen in the Abbey?

It is less easy to explain why she didn't simply stop going out. I told her, in as many ways as I could think of, that to walk out alone clearly encouraged his attentions. I reminded her gently that her position at Fontevrault was difficult just then, thanks to the rebellion of her family and the loss of her dowry. She replied that she would not allow herself to be imprisoned by an abbey guest, and that to seem to be hiding would only give Bertrand the power he obviously craved, that of directing or affecting her course of action. I could see, after what she had been through, why she did not like being left to the mercies of others, and that is why I did not go to Sister Beatrice or someone in the abbey myself. But I did point out that being right in principle did not necessitate abandoning common sense. When she grew stubborn and silent, I did not insist further; I still had a measure of freedom not permitted her, and I didn't like to remind her of it.

One day soon after that I was sent early to bed with a fevered disorder of the stomach. The infirmarian mixed me a poppy potion and set a basin beside my bed, on the floor of the dormitory. The nuns had curtained cells in rows along the walls to allow them privacy, but we had cots in the centre. A nun slept at each end of our row, like guardian angels. But the dormitory was empty when I slid beneath the covers. The linen felt cool and smooth, the blanket prickly. I pulled it up to my ears and sank swiftly to the edge of sleep.

At first I thought I was dreaming. I opened my eyes blearily, and then I heard the sound again. Few noises could have roused me from my drugged sleep, but I pushed myself up and swung my feet over the edge of the bed. The floor was cold and hard. I staggered over to the cell and drew back the curtain as softly as I could. I grasped the cloth in my hands and peered around it.

The penitent was bent over one of the chests the sisters used to store their habits and personal belongings, her breasts bare against its metal studs. Her gown was pulled down about her feet, her arm upraised to bring down the whip against her back. It was not an ordinary whip but a small ring with five knotted thongs suspended from it. It came down on her bare flesh with a crack, followed by a sharp little gasp of pain. I watched, as if my wits had left me, as the dreadful instrument came up again. "For you, for you," she murmured, rocking back on her knees and thrashing herself again.

The blood dripped down her back, which was already slicked with sweat, onto her shift. "Help me, help me," she moaned, and raised her hand, twitching, to scourge herself again.

I found my tongue, which was thick in my mouth, at last. "Stop it!" I shrieked, dropping the curtain and catching her arm before it fell again.

Cecily looked up at me and wobbled a little as if she were about to faint. I didn't feel very steady either. I dropped down beside her and leaned panting against the chest. "Why?" I asked her.

People outside the monastery walls usually misunderstand the flagellum or hair shirts or spiked arm bands or any of the other means by which the person in religious life offers up his physical pain for the sins of the world. The Discipline is not meant to be a punishment but a kind of self-crucifixion so that the spiritual side of your nature can take greater effect. But at Fontevrault, self-scourging, like everything else, was meant to be done with moderation, whatever the frenzy of ecstasy or despair.

She shook her head mournfully. "Don't ask me."

"Then talk to Father Confessor, or Sister Beatrice."

"I can't tell anyone." Her withdrawal extended even to her eyes. Her body was twisted into a distorted posture, as if she had been seized and wrung out. I had lost mother and father, been uprooted from my home and sent to live among strangers, but watching her I felt that I still had not suffered greatly. It was something to fear, evidently.

Her shift was down about her waist, unregarded. I moved to pull it up, but when I touched the material she cried out in pain. "You'll have to have someone see to your back, at least," I told her. "The cloth will stick to the blood and the wounds could fester." The sweat broke out on my forehead and I thought I might be sick.

Cecily looked at me and said, sounding more like her old self, "What were you doing here?"

"The ague." I was beginning to shiver a little. "I got sick in the refectory and they sent me to bed."

"Then go back to it." The tone was firm, shutting me out again. "I'll be all right."

"How can you? It's all right not to tell me what's wrong if you don't want to, but what are you going to say to the community? Lady Abbess will demand a reason, you know that." I did not add that I thought that was all for the best. It was clear that Cecily needed more help than I could give her.

"It's all right," she insisted, pulling up the front of her shift and getting to her feet. "I know who to go to."

I spoke the suspicion that was in my mind. "Does this have anything to do with . . . with *him*?"

She winced. No doubt her back throbbed and smarted, for her voice was tight. "Even if it did, he'll be leaving tomorrow. So you see, you can go to bed and leave it to me. I'm not in danger."

In spite of what I had just seen, she made me feel silly and officious. "I only wanted to help," I said, knowing I sounded sulky but unable to prevent it.

"I know," she soothed me as if I were a child. "You might like to know that my family and Count Richard have made it up, and my father and uncles have all taken the cross. Lady Abbess had the news today. It appears my vocation is safe."

I heard the sarcasm, but I thought it was directed at her family. "That's wonderful," I told her. I had reached the point where all I wanted to do was lie down. I am ashamed to say that what I felt more than anything was relief that she did not want my help, that she had not dragged me into her nightmare. So I left her to cope as she could, and by the time the illness had purged itself and my head was clearer, it was already too late.

7

THE walls of Fontevrault had been built to shut the world out, and they were absurdly ineffective even at that. The life of the abbey flowed on inexorably like the Loire, and many lives were swept up in its stream or touched by what happened along its shores. Stone and mortar are powerless against such a current.

They are still less of a barrier if someone wants to make her way into the world again. It must have seemed like a ballad: the pleached path through the orchards, the air frosty and brittle with starlight prickling on the skin, the white horse tethered outside the wall, waiting. She would have had her heavy cloak, pulled close around her neck against the evening chill and covering the plain tunic we all wore.

Bertrand de Born, however, was no hero out of song or legend. I can't imagine what she expected of him, beyond her ruin. His flirtations were notorious and he was already on bad terms with the Lusignans and half the other continental lords. He had some personal wealth, but his best assets were his talent, which was considerable, and his colubrine charm, which was not, at least to me. Besides, he was middle-aged and going to flesh. Their future together, however brief, is impossible to imagine; it is only the aftermath — of degradation, scandal, and personal torment — that is certain.

In the event, speculation proved unnecessary. A monk making a private prayer in the garden after Lauds (the brothers' rules were more lax in this respect) saw the couple and alerted his Superior, who in turn got a sister to awaken Lady Abbess. Bertrand was summarily dispatched from Fontevrault (if he had been less famous, he might have been excommunicated) to ply his trade in some other court. In time, no doubt, he would make a song of it.

The wind had risen, banging and clattering the shutters against the dormitory walls when Hildegarde woke me with the story. I could scarcely hear her over the din, and my head was still fuzzy with sleep and sickness, so it was several minutes before I understood. To my surprise she seemed neither triumphant nor envious, only concerned, a little outraged, and just slightly self-important at being the bearer of bad news.

"What have they done with Cecily?" I asked her.

"I heard they took her to the infirmary first, probably to see whether she is still 'intacta'."

I shook my head but said nothing about her bloody, beaten back. There was no need to fuel gossip with Cecily's private agonies. But I hoped, when they saw it, they would realize how hard she had struggled with temptation.

"Afterwards they — Lady Abbess, Father Confessor, and the Novice Mistress — shut her up in a room near the Abbess's chambers," Hildegarde went on. "Everyone is forbidden entrance, and only fully professed nuns can bring her food. That's all I know."

"Will they send her away, do you think?"

She paused to consider, without gloating. It might have been that true extremes of circumstance and emotion brought out her better nature. It might also be that she, like the rest of us, was simply growing up. "Probably not," she said at length. "Think how it makes Fontevrault look, for one thing. No one will want to do anything over-hasty. Besides, the Rule permits it, if the sinner repents and wishes to return. My guess is they'll bring her to repentance, which shouldn't be too difficult, since she's half way there already. How else did she manage to get herself caught?"

That was true enough. But, I thought, it would certainly be better for Cecily if they sent her away from temptation and from memory, too. Fontevrault had a foundation in England, which would serve very well. I said as much to Hildegarde, who laughed.

"Marian, how many years have you been here now? Haven't you been listening? 'Humility, Submission, Obedience'. Cecily will have to submit to staying here in the community with everyone knowing and pitying or despising or even envying her

123

but all the while saying nothing. *That* will be her real penance, and it will make or break her. Besides, there is something else, something you must have seen. Lady Abbess wants her."

My mind went back to the conversation in the Abbess's room, to the hands moving nervously over the table top. "Yes, I suppose she does."

"Oh, not like that, I don't think." Hildegarde could be remarkably frank. "She has far too much esteem for herself even to consider it. If she wants anything at all, I'd say it's a protegée. Or maybe a child. My father used to say their barrenness sometimes drove nuns to madness."

"And mine used to say that convent cemeteries were full of dead babies," I lied. My father, on any of his rare visits home, would never have said such a thing in my presence. In fact I'd once overheard Cook say it to someone when she didn't know I was listening. I don't know what made *me* say it, except that I was upset.

"Well, in any case, Cecily's mother is Lady Abbess's friend," Hildegarde said smoothly. "I'm sure she'll be allowed to stay on as a novice." She shivered a little. "Better her than me. Why should anyone want to marry Jesus when she could have a flesh and blood man?"

★ ★ ★

The trees were naked now, swept bare by the wind whistling and moaning among the branches and along the walls. The sea, which I had not seen for several years, would be pounding the shore in rhythmic rage. The chill crept under even the heaviest mantle, and frost slaughtered the plantings with a crusader's zeal. No one could remember a year's ending more wretched and spiteful.

As it was, the bitter weather was only meet. Outside the abbey walls, the world was crumbling.

The fighting — between father and son, Plantagenet and Capet, and various other combinations — had exhausted the funds collected for the Crusade and proven so embarrassing in view of that Sacred Enterprise that a conference was called so that the three principal antagonists could settle their differences before further damage was done. King Philip and Count Richard demanded, as their settlement price, that King Henry officially acknowledge Richard as his heir. Further, they asked for an immediate marriage between Richard and Alais Capet, Philip's sister, who had been living at the English court since her childhood in expectation of a match with a Plantagenet prince.

Henry, for reasons best known to himself, refused.

From that moment Alais's fate was changed, and not for the better. Poor Alais. It was widely rumoured that she was King Henry's mistress, in spite of having been reared in the Queen's household, and now Richard gave this out as the reason behind his father's refusal. If it was true, she got little enough in return for her favours, and her brother was only too eager to blacken her name in order to fan the embers of Richard's resentment. Later, when he was crowned, Richard repudiated Alais as damaged goods, so Philip got what he deserved. It was only Alais, who married a lesser count and drifted into obscurity when she could have been Queen, who might be pitied.

Richard's public accusation, along with the assertion that his father intended to oust him in favour of John, effectively ended the peace conference, but there was more to come. Richard knelt before Philip and did homage for all the Plantagenet possessions except England, and Philip in return promised him the castles he had taken from Henry during their endless skirmishes. Then they rode off together, leaving an embittered King of England to reflect on filial impiety and gird up his defences.

On Friday evening, just before the Festival of the Nativity, the globe of fire men call the King Star blazed across the vault of heaven. The astrologers read the signs, and foretold the death of princes.

★ ★ ★

While King Henry kept Christmas in cold comfort and increasingly ill health at nearby Saumur, the propers of the season and the liturgy of the hours were

127

sung in triumph and joy at Fontevrault. Pine boughs and mistletoe mingled their scents with spiced wine and almond cakes.

From the womb before the day star I have begotten thee.

On the day after Christmas, Cecily was received into the community as a novice nun.

No one outside certain sisters and her confessor had seen her — at least not to talk to — since the day of her capture. She had kept to her cell praying and seeking God's will, Sister Beatrice told us. From the look of her at Divine Office, she must have been fasting as well. The habit, when they pulled it over her shoulders, hung on her like a sack.

'I renounce' is the vow on which the novice's petition for admission to the religious life is based. Mother, father, friendship, possessions, sensual pleasure — all are abandoned in favour of submission to the Rule, the yoke that cannot be lifted until death.

Receive me O Lord, according to Thy Word. Gloria Patri et Filio.

I did not think Cecily looked particularly

happy, but I hoped it would bring her peace. I ignored the pricking voice inside me which said it was certainly too soon; "Lady Abbess says she is ready," Sister Beatrice had said firmly and finally, in response to my timid questioning. The Abbess's face, as she raised and kissed her newest daughter, was worn like a mask and told me nothing. I asked myself what I had expected to see revealed there.

A few weeks later, on St Agnes's Eve, Cecily began having visions. You could say there is nothing wonderful in this; the Eve is the time of dreams and sendings, particularly for those granted the Holy Gift. Still, at Fontevrault it was a commonplace that the holiest nuns went quietly and unremarkably about their duties instead of chafing their knees in spiritual rapture, and in consequence perhaps, supernatural visitations were rare.

Hildegarde, buttressed by Lucy, brought me the news. I was startled. "Cecily? When? What did she say?" I lifted my hands from a pail of water, sleeves dripping. I had been scrubbing down the kitchen floor with a brush, a job the servants would finish after the students and novices did their stint of manual labour. It was not a completely unpleasant task, if one didn't examine the refuse too closely. The kitchen, with its huge spits and blackened bricks, was a place we were not encouraged to spend time in, so as not to harass the cooks or steal food from the larders. We were always hungry in those days.

"Last night in her cell, or so I heard," Hildegarde said, tapping a large cauldron experimentally. The echo proved it empty.

"Lady Abbess was summoned to her bed. She watched with her all night." Lucy's lips trembled.

"But what did she say?"

"As to that," Hildegarde said, rolling her eyes, "I gather it was more whom she said it to, if you understand me. As if *He* were right there in the dark with her. By the time she was finished, the nuns who had awakened were kneeling beside Lady Abbess, listening for more."

"Is she all right? What's happened to her?"

"Oh, she's fine," Lucy said pettishly. "Lady Abbess has seen to that. She's excused from duty and the Offices, so she can sleep."

"I hope she will be fine," I said, looking at Hildegarde. "Do you think it could happen again?"

She shrugged. "How would I know? *I* don't have visions."

Lucy sniffed.

As Lucy had indicated, that day Cecily did not appear in her place in the choir or in the refectory for meals. The Silences were observed with greater strictness than usual and the pealing bells, which should have broken the tension, acted as a prod instead.

Night brought little relief. Although I was too far away from where Cecily now slept to hear anything, I lay sleepless and expectant, listening in the dark. I was a little ashamed of my curiosity, which was not in any way spiritual. In fact I almost dreaded that I really might hear something, but I couldn't leave it alone. At length I slept.

Hildegarde had to shake me hard to wake me up. I struggled out of a dream

131

like a drowning swimmer surfacing for air.

"She's doing it again," Hildegarde hissed in my ear. "Do you want to come?" In response I threw back my blanket. The cold shocked me into wakefulness, and I shivered in my night shift.

Cecily's cell was the same in which she had spent her spiritual convalescence in the aftermath of Bertrand de Born. It lay close to the Abbess's quarters and had often been used for novices who were homesick or suffered other crises; Lady Abbess was a conscientious Mother to her flock. She knelt now beside the cot, sponging Cecily's forehead as if she had a fever. Perhaps she had. Her arms lay slack and open, like those of the old man in the infirmary who had been struck by paralysis. I had never thought to see Cecily in such a pose. Her face was very pale, but it was a brilliant pallor. Her eyes were focused on the crucifix hung on the wall. The Abbess continued to sponge her, from time to time leaning over to whisper endearments or encouragement in her ear.

Cecily paid no attention to her or

to anyone else in the room. Suddenly her eyes rolled upward alarmingly. I felt myself beginning to sweat, despite the chill.

"The light! The light!" she muttered, putting a hand over her eyes as if it hurt her. Lady Abbess made a small, economical hand motion and the lamp was moved to a holder farther off. In the moment that followed I became aware of the stillness and silence, as if every person present was holding her breath, spellbound.

Cecily tossed and moaned then cried out "O Glorious Sun!" She twisted on the bed. "My body is in torment but my soul is in delight. I embrace my Beloved. He draws me to Him. I am engulfed in His love."

She extended her arms rigidly overhead. "I feel the heat in my breast. I am burning in the Holy Flame." Her voice had risen in pitch. Lady Abbess pulled her hands down to her sides and held them. A shuddering sigh went round the room, followed by the murmur of a gathering storm. The air seemed to shake with feeling.

I stood motionless in the charged stillness, my throat knotted and swollen with tension. Panic rose within me, but I was so stricken I could not even raise my hands to my ears. *I don't want to hear this.* A number of sisters had gathered at the bedside, but only Cecily broke the silence. The shudders ran over her body in little waves like wind over water. Her breathing was shallow and fast. "He has come to me. He is here in my chamber. He draws me to Him." The Abbess hung on every word with agonized eyes, as if she were assisting at a birth. The flame guttered and crackled in the lamp. Cecily sat up, staring. "Take me in the arms of Your soul, Lord. Kiss my mouth, my head, my feet . . . as sweetly as you will . . . "

The cry, when it came, was filled with pain, and was my own. I ran unheeded from the cell to my cold cot and wept as I had not since childhood. That night I dreamed of a white road which led to the sea. In the morning I went to see Sister Beatrice.

8

THE scriptorium was comfortingly normal, arid and cool, filled with the rustle of parchment and the scraping of stylus on wax. Water dripped from the eaves into a cistern below: *plop, plop.* I slipped into a carrel by the window and waited until Sister Beatrice was free. She took her time, all the while watching me bird-like out of the side of her eye. The wood of the table's surface was stained with gilt and paint. I flicked some of it off with my fingernail. So many layers, so many years of quiet nuns, labouring in the scriptorium. My carefully chosen words, with which I planned to tell her about Cecily's vision and the guilt and revulsion I had felt, slipped from me completely. When I did speak, I surprised even myself. "I want to leave here."

"Ah." Sister Beatrice closed the partition and settled herself beside me, infuriatingly unimpressed. "I understand you were at

Sister Cecily's bedside last night."

I nodded.

"Well?"

"Well what?"

"I presume that your presence there has some bearing on this sudden decision to leave Fontevrault?"

"It isn't a 'sudden' decision," I corrected her stubbornly, realizing it was true. I had been coming to it for months, and just admitting it aloud caused me enormous relief.

"That does not answer my question."

"Then, yes," I admitted. "Last night was . . . horrible."

She nodded, still unperturbed. "Visions frequently are."

"I think she's mad," I said bluntly.

Sister Beatrice looked at me with interest. "Do you really? It could be."

"Stop trying to provoke me! You know she is. And Lady Abbess and all of you — of us — drove her to it." I was on the verge of tears.

Her eyes narrowed. "And who are you, Marian Fitz Walter," she said coldly, "to judge your Abbess and your Lord? Why should you assume the visions are false even if — and mind you, I don't admit it is so — your friend *is* mad? I don't need to remind you that some of the greatest prophets were called 'mad' in their day. So don't be so quick in your condemnation."

A sense of guilt made me persist when reason urged a retreat. "You weren't there, Sister. You didn't hear her. You make madness sound like some sort of Divine Accolade! It was embarrassing. It was . . ."

"Intimate?" One grey eyebrow shot up. "Child, I have lived in a convent more than forty years, and there is very little I have not seen or heard. The love of God can express itself in all kinds of ways, and some of them are physical. We are only human in the end." She looked at me with compassion. "Now listen carefully: if a religious vocation is to be fruitful it must cost something, it must be a real sacrifice as painful as the Cross. In that fire we are annealed and begin our new life. Cecily is paying the price now, that's all. You must trust to God and the love of the community, and let her go."

"But you don't know what she's been

through, what led her to this." I lowered my voice. "And Lady Abbess wouldn't have let her leave in any case. She wants her to stay."

"I expect I know a great deal more than you seem to give me credit for," she said drily. "I know there is something about that dreadful family of Cecily's that drove her here, and I know that Mother is very fond of her, so much so that she bent over backward to accommodate her after the poor child's problem with that man." Her tone told me she had consigned Bertrand to a particularly nasty sort of perdition. "My dear Marian, why is it so hard for you to see the hand of God in all of this? Surely this one great good can come out of Cecily's sorrow and pain. Why can't you believe that God speaks to her, either in visions, or through an accumulation of circumstance that finally brings her to His service?"

I shook my head. I wanted to believe it but I could not, which more than anything showed me I was right in deciding to leave Fontevrault. "And what if she is simply mad?"

Sister Beatrice shrugged. "Her soul can

be saved. And there are far worse things than such madness."

"That seems very hard."

"Nevertheless it is true." She sighed. "Now, will you tell me what's really troubling you? We've been talking about Cecily's life, not yours."

"I failed her," I said, looking at my hands as I tried to put the matter into words. "She needed my help, and I just didn't *see*." I told her what I could, keeping Cecily's confidence about her uncle and omitting the Abbess's injunction against special friendship. "In a way, that's why I need to leave here. I don't want to learn everything from books! I don't want to live by the Rule and ignore everything else I think and feel. I feel like my body and my soul are fighting each other." I raised my eyes to her face, which was calm and solemn beneath the dark veil. "I want to live in the real world," I said simply.

"I see," she said, in a manner which always indicated she saw more than one had related. "First of all, I'm sure I don't have to tell you how severely you failed your friend when you didn't come to one of us for help. That's what we would have done, you know — help, not punish."

I bowed my head.

"As for the other . . . " she drummed her fingers thoughtfully on the table-top. "I've been your teacher. I've tried to show you what books can do and what they can't. I would have thought, from what you've told me, that you would have seen how much more there is to be learned here than that, but if you won't see it you won't. Fontevrault may be a refuge, but it is not a hiding place. When you find something in your life you love enough to fight for you won't have to torment yourself with these questions." Her eyes held mine. "You will have to marry if you leave here. Are you prepared for that?"

"I don't know," I said honestly. "How *do* you prepare?"

"Are you asking *me*? Sweet Jesu. Not by reading books, I can tell you. Well, I should be sorry to see you wasted on some ignorant lout, lord or no. But that's in God's hands, or the King's, not mine. Now here is what you must do. First, beg my pardon for being rude and irreverent with me earlier."

I did so wholeheartedly.

"Second, wait six months, and pray. I mean it. You can do nothing in any case until you are out of mourning, and you must keep an open heart and ear. Don't try to direct God's will. Then, if you are still of a mind to go, we will arrange with King Henry for you to be sent back to England and whatever lies ahead of you there."

"Thank you, Sister," I said, profoundly grateful.

"There is more." She closed her mouth with an audible snap, biting off the words. "If you want to live 'in the real world', as you call it, there is something you must face. At the end of the six months, you are to go to the Sacristan and ask her to show you the chalice that accompanied you here. I know Lady Abbess mentioned it to you and said you might see it after you made your decision. But not before six months and the prayers, is that clear? *Now* you are dismissed."

She called me back before I reached

the door. "Marian?"

"Yes, Sister?"

"I have tried to show you how to find knowledge. But I never promised you that if you find it it will make you happy. Remember that."

9

LOOKING back, I see that I have rearranged the pattern of the past many times in memory, like one of those floor pictures the Romans made when they were masters of the world. Certain details, once added, give an entirely different cast to the mosaic. So it was with the death of the King.

Le Mans burned. Henry's life had begun there, and it ended there too, though he lived on a little longer. The city caught fire accidentally, in a futile last stand against Richard and Philip, but it might as well have been the deliberate pyre of his mortal hopes and affections. Better for him if he had thrown himself on it and died too. Instead, in misery and failing health, he turned to look back and curse God for taking the thing he loved most in the world.

He was wrong, certainly; he loved his son John more than any city men ever built. Soon after, as he lay dying at

Chinon, even this last illusion was taken from him: he discovered that John had defected to Richard and the French. And so he passed bitterly from this life on the sixth day of July, in the year of Our Lord 1189. The immense Plantagenet holdings — England, Normandy, Anjou, Maine, and the Aquitaine — went, after all, to Richard, to whom the King's last words had been "God grant I may not die before I have had my revenge on you!"

News of the King's death brought stonemasons and artisans to Fontevrault to begin preparations for the tomb. The effigy, prepared from the death mask, would not be ready for some time, but the grave had to be suitable for the ceremonies after the body lay in state. The pounding went on day and night, like a dirge. Meanwhile, the King's servants at Chinon had rifled everything in sight while the body lay exposed in the courtyard, so that his friends had to cover his nakedness with a borrowed cloak before he was sewn into the shroud. Then they began the slow procession on foot across the Vienne bridge and over the low hills to the Abbey church.

When the world breaks up, there is nothing left to do but gather the pieces. With everyone else, I began to think how they would fall for me. I was the King's ward; now the wardship would pass to Richard, or if he chose to confer it, to John. My property and my future would be administered with the indifference usual in such arrangements, but I was still determined to leave the abbey. I went to see the Sacristan about the chalice that formed part of my dowry.

She was expecting me, though the six months had a fortnight yet to run. "Sister Beatrice said you'd be coming," she said, smiling sweetly. Sister Sacristan had charge of the sacred vessels, altar cloths, vestments and treasures of the abbey; a brother supervised the collection of its feudal rents and other more worldly concerns. The sacristy of Fontevrault was thus untouched by commerce and gave evidence that the Sister's custodianship bordered on zealotry. There were rows and rows of chests, the wood burnished to a high gloss. These were of all shapes and sizes, and unmarked, though some principle of organization must have existed, since she went to a far shelf, pulled down a casket, and said with confidence, "This will be yours."

She didn't hand it to me, but carried it out of the sacristy and triple-locked the door. Then she led me to a curtained alcove where she laid a cloth on the table and placed the chest on it. "You'll want to be alone," she said, drawing to the curtain. A bee was buzzing around the window, trying to get out. In the heat and stillness of full summer I could smell the cedar and the wax, mixed with the sweet, lingering odour of old incense and the dried herbs the sisters used to keep the moths from the cloth.

I remember wondering, as I lifted the lid, whether I would recognize the chalice in the end. Certainly it was no family treasure, or I would have heard of it at home. The bee droned. The cloth was scarcely mouldy, owing no less to its quality than to the care taken in its preservation. I was glad I had seized the chalice firmly, when the covering fell away. My hand was shaking.

Even after the riches I had just seen in the sacristy, I had seldom beheld a

146

work of such magnificence. The enamel was translucent and fragile-looking, over the design. A man with a falcon on his wrist seemed ready to step off the surface onto the field. A woman held up the edge of her skirt in a dance. The top and foot glittered with precious stones, though the silver was tarnished. In all, it seemed that only royalty could have commanded such workmanship. Gently, I turned the chalice upside down. Someone had scratched at the bottom with sharp metal, but the faintest outline of the initials remained; *H.R.*

In the bottom of the chest was a scroll weighted down with a seal as big as my palm. I held it in my hand like a stone. The crown was there, and the orb and sceptre. *Something you must face*, Sister Beatrice had said. I opened the document, and read, in some clerkly script; *Presented to the Lady Marian (known as Fitz Walter) on the occasion of her birth by His Grace Henry King of England, Duke of Normandy, Count of Anjou and Maine.*

How long I sat there in the sunlit chamber I cannot recall. As Sister

Beatrice had told me, there were many things I had not seen, though the signs were there to be read. Now that my eyes were opened, I still could not take it in. Just then, above my head, the Passing Bell began to toll. Stupidly, I wondered who had died, until I remembered. The King had arrived at his last resting place.

Carefully, as if it could feel, I put the chalice back in its wrapping and closed the casket. I left it in the care of the Sister who did not meet my eyes. Then I went into the chapel, to say a prayer for the repose of my father's soul.

★ ★ ★

For the first time, Sister Beatrice seemed at a loss for words and even a little shy of me. "So you've seen it?" Her hands were busy but her eyes looked at me inquiringly. "You know?"

"It's true, then." Neither of us, apparently, felt comfortable putting the issue into words.

She did not answer, but then I had not really asked a question.

"What should I do?"

She seemed surprised. "Why, nothing. We are all in mourning now and will do what is proper."

I said nothing, but she peered at me with suspicion, as if her eyes were failing. "You aren't thinking of making some claim now that he's gone? You have no proof, after all. Only a few of us heard the story when you came, and the chalice seemed to confirm it. So did the contributions, regular as rent over the years. But notice I said *seemed*. How do you think Queen Eleanor would take to the news, so soon after the King's death? Or Prince Richard?"

I stood stubbornly, with my arms folded in defiance, not submission. I would not give in so easily, though I knew she talked sense. It seemed she wanted to take something from me before I had a chance to savour the gift.

She shook her head. "We never thought you'd find out like this, after the King had died. My advice is to sell the chalice or give it to the Church, and then forget all about it."

"Why did you let me find out then, if there's nothing to be done?" I knew this sounded childish, but I was hurt by her attitude.

"Why did *I*? Why did *he*, you mean. Whatever he might have intended for you, if there was ever anything at all, is over now. Listen," she said, with an urgency that commanded my attention, "are you still of a mind to leave here?"

I nodded. There was nothing now to keep me.

"Then you must continue with your plan. Prince Richard will return to England to be crowned, so there will be travelling parties aplenty. After that, no doubt he will leave for the Holy Land at once — the whole world knows he's been impatient to set out for months. Now, if you conduct yourself properly, you will inherit your father's" — she stressed the word slightly — "estates in England and Normandy, and as the King's ward a suitable husband will be found for you. You can probably even get a place at the Queen's court in the interim, assuming the King's Grace lets her out of Sarum prison. If, on the other hand, you . . . use the chalice, you declare yourself illegitimate and of course you will get no property from your mother's husband or from the King either. You would embarrass Fontevrault, who took you in." She paused, to let this sink in. "Henry, who might have protected you, is dead, and his successor will be absent from his kingdom, doubtless for a year or two at least. That would leave you at the sufferance of the Queen and . . . Prince John." She gave his name the curious pronunciation, a mixture of familiarity and dread, common to all the nuns of Fontevrault, where John had spent some years of his childhood. I had no sense of foreboding then, but later of course I would wish I had pursued it.

Sister Beatrice kept battering at my ill-considered dreams with her practicality. She gripped my arm. "You know the Plantagenet history," she whispered. "Each member of the family is suspicious of the others, usually for good reasons. How do you think they would regard a claim like yours, at such a time, from a stranger? They would think you are making a bid for power, even such as women have. Do you think they would leave you alone after that?" The fingers on my arm pressed into the flesh with the strength of talons, but I didn't wince. I was too horrified by what she seemed to be suggesting. "Well, thickhead, do you begin to see? You must say *nothing*. Do you want to put yourself in danger?"

She would not let me go until I had promised prudence, which I was glad enough to do now that she had shown me the world. For the present, I would remain silent. As Sister Beatrice reminded me, I had no proof of any connection with the late King, but when I searched my memory I became steadily more sure. It explained much of my mother's behaviour and — I still thought of him so — my father's too. I remembered my mother's hints and secrets, and her death in childbirth after the King's visit. And his face, looking into mine, promising that I would learn to read . . . Well, what was, was, and could not be changed. I had asked for knowledge, and knowledge is what I had.

I thought of my past and future, and of how much of my life God and Fate had made for me, and how much I could make for myself. Sister Beatrice had advised me to dispose of the chalice, but I would not. Now I could leave Fontevrault and the closed garden, and stretch out my hand to take what Fate had offered me. I had the blood of kings and emperors in my veins! True, I had to keep it hidden beneath the trappings of prudence and respectability, but it was there nonetheless, a secret flame to warm my heart.

Book Three

Locksley

1

I AM sorry, but I could not quite like Queen Eleanor. I should have; everyone else did, it was all the fashion. And why not? She was the Queen, she had just spent most of the last sixteen years in confinement, and she had, upon hearing of her son's elevation to the throne, opened up the prisons of England in his name. She was in charge of all the preparations for Richard's coronation, and in the course of arranging the revels and pageantry she was as mindful of the pleasure of the mob as of the nobility.

People always said she should have been a man, but that was foolish. Her character was shaped by her womanhood: by her beauty, by her years of flirting with the Romance of Love, and by her unhappy marriages. And she had many feminine gifts — knowing how to please without giving too much, an aversion to excess, subtlety, and a consciousness of her own charms (she was past beauty now) that she used to advantage. I don't include maternal tenderness as one of her virtues. 'Tender' is too soft a word for the fierce, possessive passion she had for Richard, whom she raised as her chief ally against his father, nor does it describe the varying emotions — from indifference to affection to loathing — she felt for her other children. Queen Eleanor was always original, and much besides.

In preparing for the coronation, she indulged the taste for the sumptuous which was her birthright as well as her inclination. This was more than flash and glitter; Eleanor was all silk to the skin. If Richard didn't quite go to his crowning drenched in attar of roses and radiant with rubies, it was owing more to his crusader's status than to sober taste. In fact, both Richard and his mother used paint, and I noticed that the Queen did not shrink from wearing what St Bernard had once termed the 'hair of lost souls now burning in Purgatory' to fill out her own thinning braids. Small wonder that the coronation was the most splendid and elaborate ceremony Londoners had ever seen. People said it would set the pattern for all that followed.

Richard's was the first uncontested, hereditary succession since his great-grandfather, the first Henry, was anointed with the Holy Oil, and I suppose that alone made it worthy of pomp. I couldn't help thinking, however, that the audience this show was really intended for lay mouldering beneath a stone slab at Fontevrault. Eleanor had forgiven her first husband for boring her, but she could never forget Henry's rejection. The intensity of her loathing, combined with the years of brooding while she was shut away in Salisbury, had grafted the object of her hatred onto her soul and heart. It would take more than his death to root it out.

It was strange to find myself a part of her household. Naturally, after so many years, few members of the old one were left, and in any case I doubt she would have had them back. Mirrors may lie, but sixteen years on the face of a contemporary do not. Certainly there was no one even close to her age (which must have been at this time closer to seventy than sixty) among us to reflect that truth. My own status as an heiress-in-transition (no longer a daughter and not yet a wife), the King's ward, and a product of a Fontevrault upbringing provided the perfect entrée to court life.

Nevertheless, I had to submit to an interview with the Queen before I began in her service. She received me in a small room off the Great Hall of Westminster Palace, which was being fitted out for the coming ceremony. The chamber was shabby, dusty, and full of brushes and pails. An ancient hanging, faded to grey, gave off a fine white cloud of dirt every time it moved. There was only one chair, and Eleanor occupied it. Her painted face was set like a statue of St Foy I had once seen in the abbey treasury, her eyes glittering jewel-like within the mask of her face. The hands which she spread before her in her lap were blue-veined, and the skin looked as thin as parchment. "You see what it's come to?" she said, when I came before her. She waved her fingers round the room with a look of disgust. "*He* let it get into this state through years of neglect.

Years when I . . . Well, the whole place is practically falling down. God knows what it will cost to fix it all up." She smiled, not at me, but at her own pleasurable thought. "Oh, I do love having money to spend again!" She narrowed her eyes and seemed to focus on me for the first time. "Which is not to say that any amount of money could turn Westminster into even a middling palace in France. It lacks the style. You liked France, didn't you?"

I told her that I had seen little of it beyond the Abbey of Fontevrault but that I had been very happy there.

"Well not *too* happy apparently. My daughter Marie writes me that she instructed a group of girls about the Rules of Love while she was visiting the abbey one year. Were you among them?"

"I had that honour, Your Grace."

"Ha! I thought so! I hope she didn't fill your head so full of stories your blood burned too hot for Fontevrault. *He whom the thought of love vexes, eats and sleeps very little.* I don't want any of that nonsense here — there's too much work to do. I may find you a husband in time, but if I catch you mooning and pining over somebody in this court I'll pack you off to your estates before you get a chance to see the Great World. I presume that *is* what you are here for?"

"I *suppose* so," I said, without thinking.

"You suppose so?"

"I'm sorry, Your Grace. I just meant that I couldn't stay in Fontevrault any longer. I was afraid that if I stayed there, nothing would ever happen to me!"

She looked up at me from her chair, her eyes amused but not kind. "How strange. More has happened in my life than I can even keep track of — I married two kings, one for policy and one for love, I tramped half way around the world on the last Crusade, I've survived prison, childbirth, and disappointments you can't even imagine — and after all that Fontevrault is the place I can't wait to return to. Some day I'll move back there, and then I'll never leave it till I die. God, I'm tired," she sighed. "Don't waste your time, Marian — old age creeps up on you before you know it. So, then," she said, looking suddenly brighter, "what do you think of London?"

This was less easy to answer than her other questions. Like most cities, London was much more admirable and a great deal more enjoyable from a distance. From the low rise of hills overlooking the walls, the city really did resemble the dream-like collection of towers and churches I had once named the centre of the world to King Henry. The sweep of view from Great William's brooding white tower to the abbey church of Westminster on the curve of the glinting silver 'S' of the Thames would have seemed magical to hearts more weathered than mine. The crenellations nipped at the very clouds.

I did not long indulge such fancies. Within the walls, the city's teeth had more bite. The wooden merchant houses, crammed to overlapping and jagged with ornament, threatened to devour older, more majestic structures. A motley collection of the maimed, the afflicted, and the 'ribauz' — the idle hangers-on who frequently erupted into violence — importuned one's every step. The streets were full of surprises, most of them unpleasant. In the butchers' quarters the blood of the slaughtered sheep and pigs pooled under the September sun amid piles of offal and swarms of flies. Natural functions, of humans as well as animals, were much in evidence. The Thames carried the odour of bilge, green-slimed timber, and other nameless stinks.

"It smells dreadful, and it's so noisy I can barely sleep at night," I told her honestly. "But it's . . . well, invigorating."

She pursed her lips. "Invigorating . . . The late King used to say that too." She gave me a hard look, as if I had deliberately chosen the reminder. I had mentally debated whether I would even tell her I had met the late King once, but now I would as soon brand myself with a hot iron. I hoped I was not making a terrible mistake in attempting to enter her service. "Well," she said, stirring restlessly in her chair, "you seem quick enough, and the abbey sends you a good recommendation. I will accept you at court. However, you must promise two things: first, that you will never repeat anything you might hear or overhear. I will not have gossips attend me. Second" — she sat up straighter and gripped the side of the chair — "you will not throw yourself at my son the King or attempt to be intimate with him, unless he himself commands it."

I promised her. I could not have 'thrown myself' at the man I presumed was my half-brother, though of course (I hoped!) she knew nothing of that. In any case, the injunction was wishful thinking on her part, or wilful blindness. The other promise I am breaking by writing this, but no matter. She is dead now and past caring what men say of her.

In many ways, living at court was not unlike Fontevrault, except that we lived by the Queen's precepts rather than St Benedict's. These were no less demanding. Obedience was exacted with the zeal of a Mistress of Novices. We rose early and retired late; Eleanor had much business. One of the tasks she pursued most furiously was her attempt to get Richard married and bedded before he left for Jerusalem. She must have examined the pedigrees of half the marriageable heiresses of England and the Continent, sometimes closeting herself with as many as three ambassadors in a single day. She threw dances and entertainments, thinking, I expect, to test the waters. If so, she found them chilly; Richard stayed away. Already the court was abuzz with whispers as to the reason why.

I had a number of opportunities to observe my half-brother when I waited on the Queen, for they frequently dined alone in her chambers. From what I heard there, I think what distracted King Richard was not the depraved pleasure he was rumoured to prefer but his obsession with financing his expedition to the Holy Land as quickly as possible. Incredibly, Bertrand de Born had resurfaced to taunt Richard (whom he had turned against, as he did everyone in the end) in some well-circulated verses he had formulated from the safety of the other side of the sea. The gist, for those who never heard them, was that Richard was deceiving God since he had taken the cross but had no real plans to set out. It made the King furious, but his dilemma was real: the Saladin tithe had been spent and the treasury at Winchester was as low as the Walbrook in a drought. At length his desperate cunning showed him a cow he could milk to fulfil his dreams and his duty — England, uberous with rich estates and ambitious office-seekers. Shortly after the coronation feasts were over, he put up for sale virtually everything the crown commanded — castles, manors, towns, public offices, titles, and all kinds of favours. Every significant public position in the country had to be repurchased, sometimes at exorbitant prices. Naturally enough, the King's popularity began to wear a bit thin, and his dismissal of experienced officials, replacing them with the highest bidders, gave rise to the rumour that he never intended to return to England at all.

To be fair to Queen Eleanor, she did try to talk him out of it. They were quite open about these conversations in front of their attendants (as I can witness). "England," the King said, "is full of little men who like only what they know. One step beyond, and they feel the dark reaching out for them. I can't live like that." "No one doubts, Richard, that you are larger than life," his mother replied tartly. Sometimes it would be long before the night fell back into silence. Their love for each other was the kind that tears its object to pieces, and did not lend itself easily to reasonable disagreement. Besides, it was apparent to everyone but Eleanor that Richard would not stand contradiction. When you raise a god instead of a child, it is no surprise if you end up serving him. She came back from these encounters as weary as if he had struck her.

Still, she preened for their meetings like a maiden. At first she fretted because most of her clothes had been made in the styles and colours popular when she entered the close confinement of Salisbury and now looked out-of-date. Of course, once she wore these lovely embroidered chainses or fur-lined pelisses in public, the style was revived and copied. It was important to tell her, in ways not too obvious, how young she looked. She had long since reached the age when preservation is the best to be hoped for, and she had chests filled with unguents and salves from as far away as Constantinople to help her coach her face and skin into a semblance her son would find pleasing. Just when one was tempted into sympathy by this unexpected vulnerability, she would rout such softening with one of the witty, spiteful, unanswerable attacks by which she amused herself at her inferiors' expense. She was always most popular with those who knew her least.

I waited often upon her toilet and on her suppers with the King. There was something at work between us. I had, in spite of all warnings, indulged certain fantasies concerning my parentage and gave myself consequence as a result. I was very young, and I'm sure my eyes said to her, 'I could tell you something, if I wanted to.' Luckily for me, she was far too busy and not interested enough to pursue it. But without a doubt, such hints and my own reserve intrigued her, and once or twice I caught her studying me with one of her cool, assessing looks. At those times I remembered fear and hoped she did not see any resemblance to my father.

However, it was her own appearance which concerned her most, and I was only an acolyte at that shrine. Night after night

169

we made the offerings: chests and coffers of the finest silks and linens and wools were pulled out, inspected, evaluated, and accepted or rejected with all the seriousness of the Eucharist. A great deal of time was devoted to preparing each evening's version of Eleanor. After the clothing came the jewels in enamelled coffers from Limoges. She must have kept every bauble given her from the time she left the nursery to have amassed such a collection. There were torques in the Viking style from the north of England, fillets of silver and a stone the colour of the sky which she had 'picked up' on the first Crusade, jet beads from Constantinople, and belts and pins and earrings and bracelets in all combinations of gems and gold. She had a true eye for taste, born of being a long time rich and royal, and never wore too much. Sometimes she affected modesty, and would put a piece aside as no longer appropriate to her age and condition. Woe betide you if you took her at her word.

Only once, while I attended her, did I hear her speak without undue deference to this persona she had created. The lamps were lit early; the days were growing shorter and the mists curled up like lace around the setting sun. Eleanor sat in the soft light before her glass, her wimple and the plaits of false hair set aside. Despite her perfume and the sprinkling of herbs and flower petals in the rushes, she smelled old. The room smelled of it too. Any child will know what I mean. One ceases to notice, as one gets older. "Bring me," she said, in the polite tone of command which was more effective than a shout, "the chest of jewels my husband gave me."

"King Henry?"

I had guessed wrong. The look was frosty, beneath brows and lashes that needed tinting again. "King Louis." Now that her first husband was dead the Queen regarded him with much more fondness. That he had reputedly never stopped loving her did much to sweeten his memory. I took out the chest, one of the largest, that contained his gifts to her.

She handled the contents tenderly, like pressed flowers which might fall to pieces. "This," she said, balancing a gold circlet on the tips of curved fingers, "was one of his earliest presents. I think I will wear it tonight." She lifted it slightly so that I could see. It was graceful work, with delicate tendrils and tiny flowers wrought in beaten gold, fresh and lovely looking. I thought she would sign for me to put on her veil and wimple so she could set it on her head, but she continued to turn it round in her hands.

"The last time I wore this I was fifteen years old," she said, on half a sigh. "We had quarrelled at our wedding feast; Marcabru had performed one of his famous songs about women hot with lust — 'Lady Goodandexcited' if I remember right — and my husband was shocked. He called it profane and frivolous and wanted me to send Marcabru away. I told him not to be such a pious prig. We made it up in bed, and he had this made for me in the Aquitaine. See," she said holding it up, "you can tell it comes from the South; you won't find work like this anywhere else."

"Would you like me to put it on for you, Madam?"

She seemed not to hear. I had seen the mood take some of the old nuns at Fontevrault; a pitcher's ear would serve for an audience. "I was right," she said, "he *was* a pious prig, but I'd already married him. In any case it hardly mattered then. I was in love with the idea of being the next Queen of France. And whatever else I was, I could move men with my beauty. When I walked into a room, I could hear the murmurs and the stirring, just quiet enough for respect. Now the women do that for my son." She looked down at the circlet in her hand as if she had just noticed it. "I am too old for this — put it away."

I opened the chest again and dragged it round. I caught her looking at my face behind her in the mirror. I don't know what she read there, but she said, "Well, aren't you going to protest? Tell me how beautiful I am still? I've fed on flattery for almost seventy years. Would you have me go hungry now?"

I answered her with the high humourlessness to which I was often led at such moments by youth and bad instincts. "There was a saying at Fontevrault, Your

Grace, that the fruit is sweetest when the season is ending."

Her mouth fell open. Then she drew a breath, and I knew I was in for one of those excruciatingly personal harangues by which she revenged herself on those who had displeased her. I braced myself. She burst out laughing. "I see they did not school you overmuch in tact."

I reddened, mostly in relief.

"It doesn't matter; I'm drowning in diplomacy as it is. Well, we must all live with our seasons or the world will laugh. But it is hard."

"Would it be easier," I asked, emboldened by her tone, "if you had not been a great beauty?"

Her eyes in the mirror glinted with malice. "So the plain like to tell themselves."

I said nothing.

"You see?" she continued. "Age doesn't improve our natures, it merely intensifies them. I used to be clever, and now I am cruel. Pay no attention. It comes from living long enough to see the results of all the things you've started. That's enough to give anyone a bad disposition."

She was still holding the circlet in her hands. She looked down at it, then at me. "I am not usually so frank with anyone but my son." She had, in fact, two, but 'my son' referred only to Richard. "You must be quite intelligent."

I bobbed warily. I did not fool myself. It was really a backhanded compliment to herself.

She held up the filigreed gold. "Would you like to have this?"

On that I could be firm. I did not want anything from her beyond a place at court. "No, madam, I couldn't possibly accept it, considering who gave it to you. You must keep it yourself."

"Oh, I quite agree with you. I didn't mean *this*, I meant *this*." She held up a small wooden crucifix she had resting in her palm. She looked as gleeful as a child who has just outwitted its friends in peas under the cup. "Abbot Bernard gave it to me before Louis and I set out for the Holy Land. It didn't bring us any luck, but I thought it might suit you."

I reached out for it; it was all I could do. Like everything made to Bernard's taste it was plain almost to ugliness, lest it give sinful pleasure to the eye. "Your Grace is too generous."

"I knew you would like it."

I picked up her wimple, to fasten it with some simpler band that had no history. She said to me, "What did you say your name was?"

I knew she knew it, because she had already called me by it when I helped her dress. Pretending to forget was a trick she used to put you in your place, to remind you of your unimportance in the World of Eleanor. "Marian Fitz Walter, Your Grace," I told her, suppressing a sigh.

"Ah." I saw a flicker in her eyes I couldn't quite like. "I think I shall have a talk to my son about finding you an interesting husband."

2

I WORRIED a great deal about that word 'interesting'. I need not have bothered; I had made only the slightest breach in the wall of Queen Eleanor's self-absorption and it soon closed round again. In the end it was the King's economic policies which resulted in my betrothal.

It is not quite fair to say that, like the English public offices, I was put up for sale to the highest bidder. The crown had the income from my property in any case until I married, and I'm sure that as far as Richard was concerned that arrangement would be satisfactory until I was at least as old as his mother. However, his departure was imminent, with the Queen to follow suit soon after, and as I had no family to fall back on I must be disposed of honourably and rapidly. Normally, with my estates, I could expect a match with a knight of middling wealth who wanted to enlarge his holdings, or with some older lord, perhaps a widower, who did not require an important heiress for a wife. Unfortunately, the market for husbands in England or Normandy, where I would expect to make my alliance, had been much diminished by the impending Crusade. Many had rushed to marry and beget an heir before setting out on such a long and dangerous adventure. I don't mean to suggest that all that was left were the halt and the lame (or those who loathed women altogether) but that there were difficulties in attempting to settle down at a time when the whole world was packing its bags.

I can't remember, with the emotion-flattening burden of years I drag along with me now, how I felt when I first learned that they had arranged a betrothal with the Earl of Huntingdon. I know that I was ready to leave London and the Queen's service; court life revolved around preparations for the Crusade, from which women were effectively excluded. Marriage was the next step, the direction I had inevitably taken by leaving Fontevrault, but now that it came down to it, I found myself in no great hurry. Nevertheless, here was an earl, offering to make me a countess. It was too exalted a match, and I felt suspicious; he must be in his dotage, or stricken with some dreadful disease. I made inquiries: what he *was* was poor.

It was easy enough to find out; his case had lately come up at court. One Robert Fitz Ooth had brought an action against his uncle, who had falsely claimed both the title and lands of the Huntingdon estates. These included the rich manor of Locksley Hall, not far from Nottingham, where Fitz Ooth had grown up the foster son of a forester and his wife. Some papers or some other indicator, long hidden, had at length confirmed his true position. Everyone had apparently been convinced of the justice of his case, but in accordance with the King's policy, it had cost him dear to regain his inheritance. There was only just enough left to permit a small settlement on a wife, preferably one whose marriage bed would be gilded with continental possessions. In view of the riches the Pursuit of Justice had poured into the royal coffers, the King and Queen were willing to part with my wardship income and my person. I was offered as a probable contender for Countess of Huntingdon. Betrothal would be contingent upon a satisfactory, face-to-face encounter; even in the dark ages of my youth a man wanted to know what he would be getting.

So at first it seemed that everything would go smoothly. The man himself was setting his affairs in order at Huntingdon; I wouldn't have to face him until he came down to London for the betrothal. As soon as Queen Eleanor left for the Continent, I would return to Blidworth to make preparations for the wedding and put the ghosts of the past to rest. It seemed the best I could hope for, provided that the Earl was amiable enough. Since no one knew him in London, rumour was no help at all. I remembered Chrétien de Troyes and his stories of Love and had to laugh at myself. I also reminded myself that Queen Eleanor and Countess Marie, who ought to know, had ruled that the Great Love the bards sang about could only exist outside of marriage. Still, what had I left Fontevrault for if I didn't want more than this bloodless conjugal transaction? I found I had been waiting for Passion to strike with the same rapt anticipation with which I had once hoped for the Calling, and to as little avail. The Queen was no longer the lusty Duchess of Aquitaine whose beauty had inflamed half the nobles of the Continent, and could not be blamed if her comforts were more important to her than the memory of joy. But I was young, and I mourned what I thought I was missing.

It was a cold day sometime after St Clement's Day (or the Festival of Smiths, as the Saxons have it) when King Richard left England on the first step of his journey. The year was waning, and the breath in the throat smoked the air. In point of fact the fleet — built to carry eight thousand men and appropriate cargo — would not sail from Dartmouth until after Easter, for Normandy and the rest of Richard's possessions had to be set in order too. Once the land was empty of him the troubles began. Richard sowed the seeds himself, like dragon's teeth, by appointing William Longchamp Justiciar, Chancellor, and

Papal Legate, and thus de facto ruler in his absence. This misshapen, ambitious toad was liked by no one and hated by not a few. He had been Richard's Chancellor in the Aquitaine, but he despised England. At the same time the King further complicated matters by naming as heir his three-year-old nephew Arthur of Britanny, the son of his dead brother Geoffrey, thereby giving his brother John every reason to go behind his back in usurping power and attracting support. I was glad to be leaving London for what I thought would be the relative safety and isolation of Nottinghamshire, where the Sheriff, as the King's chief agent, would be my guardian until I married.

Meanwhile, I waited in Westminster Palace for the arrival of the Earl of Huntingdon.

Christmas was grim. It is always a bleak season, but the candles at Fontevrault had brought light and warmth to pierce the darkness. In the far north, one of the ladies told me, they bring in a tree and deck it with tiny tapers; I liked the sound of that. In London it was all feasting and mummer's capering, but there was little joy behind the antics. The Queen and Longchamp had a row over the celebrations. He thought them too expensive and unnecessary besides. She won in the end, but his sour, grudging presence and her son's absence sapped the pleasure for her. I don't think she particularly enjoyed the mock battles between the Evil One and the Lord of Light. She had her own quite business-like list of real villains to deplore. As for Longchamp, he was like a bat in daylight at the revelries.

The first two weeks of January raged spitefully, storms coming one after another. The ways were flooded, or choked with churned up mud. Tempers were as short as the daylight. No one came.

Despite her age and the certain discomforts of travel, Queen Eleanor was eager to be off on her trip, and was restless and edgy as the day grew closer. Idleness was almost as hateful to her as it had been to King Henry, and her years penned in the sheepfold of Salisbury gave an added lustre to movement. Besides, it is always better to be leaving than to be left. Everything she cared about was now on the other side of the Channel.

Towards the end of the month, when the rains slackened a little, a messenger announced Prince John. On the third day after his arrival, the Queen sent for me.

I had not expected to attend her and had just washed my hair, which dampened my collar and dripped continually down my back. In winter it could take a whole day to dry. I waited for her to comment on my dismal appearance. She liked those who waited upon her to be as careful of attire as she was herself.

Instead she said nothing, and beckoned me to the hearth, which I was glad of. "Marian." She remembered my name. Her voice was kind. The betrothal was off.

Those who always expect the worst are seldom disappointed. Everyone knows that marriages are often cancelled, sometimes for the best of reasons, right up to the meeting on the church porch. But in this case, the circumstances were disreputable. Baldly stated (with even less tact than Queen Eleanor), the man had got himself outlawed.

The Queen shook her head over the incomprehensibility of it. It was one thing, she said, for a peasant, but quite another for an earl of England, however newly made.

I asked her what offence he had committed.

She frowned. "He tried to murder an agent of the King, who had come to punish one of his household for an offence against the forest laws. It was a clear-cut case, John says. I can't think what he was about. That's what comes of his sudden elevation, I suppose — it must have addled his wits. In any case, the man he attacked lived, or they would have hanged him." She looked at me speculatively. "Well, we can only be glad you were not betrothed or, God forbid, married." She sighed and shifted restlessly, a sure sign her patience was wearing thin. "It does present some problems. There will be talk — there always is in matters like this. Some of it may reflect on you. It may not be fair," she added, seeing me start, "but it won't increase your chances the next time around. The best thing would be

185

to get you betrothed to someone else quite soon. John says he knows someone who might be suitable, but I just do *not* have the time to worry about it now." She glared at me, as if daring me to protest. Naturally I said nothing, but I did wonder what I would do. The Queen would leave for France in three days and would not return for a long time.

"I'll leave it to John, then," she said, "and if he makes the arrangements, well and good. If not, I'm afraid it will have to wait till I have time for it. Meanwhile, I advise you to go back to your manor house as you planned. It doesn't do to leave your property too long without inspection. I daresay you'll be happy enough there."

It was not a question, but a dismissal.

And that is how I came to return to Blidworth not as a triumphant countess-to-be but alone and almost without prospects. However glad I was not to be marrying a murderous madman, I could cheerfully have wrung the Earl's neck for getting me into such a fix.

3

MY temper was not improved by my meeting with Prince John. I had never seen my half-brother. Since then, unfortunately, my life has offered me far too many opportunities for contemplating the Prince's character, so that now, as in the case of my betrothal, it is difficult to remember my first impression. I think he was then, as he remained throughout whatever befell him, dainty, meticulous, overdressed and fussily bejewelled.

Certainly I never understood him; one could not follow to its heart the twisting labyrinth of his character. If I had to guess I would say it had formed itself around rejection, but even that is far too simple. Hatred, resentment, trying to prove himself in the face of open ridicule of his capability — all this I could have understood.

Instead he behaved with silken solicitude towards his mother (who in some obscure way blamed him for his father's affair with Rosamund Clifford during her pregnancy and could scarcely bear the sight of him for years), and maintained a strong sentimental attachment to her until she died. At the same time he acted as if he cared for no one's good opinion, even that he could have gained through the simplest kindness. He hated power of any sort in others and could not keep from further abusing those he had already humbled.

He did, in a perverse stroke of fate which must have galled his mother, have an eye for women; there was no question of *his* dying without an heir. In truth almost everything about him seemed to irritate the Queen; no doubt she could not forget that Henry had favoured him and wanted to give him lands that were rightfully Richard's. Yet she championed his cause, and persuaded the King to lift, against his better judgement, the ban that would have kept John out of England until the Crusade was over. (He had come now to thank her for it, and to see her off.) Perhaps she felt guilty for loving him so little; there was no unravelling either one of them.

As the Queen had suggested, Prince John did indeed have someone in mind for me. After our talk, I wondered if this would be much better than the outlaw. My half-brother had personally signed the articles of outlawry and now proposed to divide the Huntingdon estates and possessions — including, apparently, myself — among his own supporters. One of these, a man from West Yorkshire, had been given Locksley Hall. His Grace thought my own estates would be a nice addition to Guy of Gisborne's.

By way of compensation he offered to bed me.

I later discovered that this placed me among a large company, both common and well-born. At the time, the suggestion merely terrified me and caused my flesh to shrink on my bones. Stupidly, I let him see it.

Whatever his other failings, Prince John was not one to miss a slight. The lapis lazuli ring, as big as a quail's egg, traced a blue arc in the air as he stroked the hair from his forehead. His nails were chewed to the quick. His eyes seemed to burn through me. "The idea does not please you?" he asked softly.

I stared at him in wordless horror. I could not force any sound out of my mouth.

He stepped very near to me, so that I could smell the scent he used. When he spoke, his voice was as silken as his mantle. "I can do it, you know, whether it pleases you or not."

It was then I saw my danger. What he had begun out of habit or boredom, he would finish, if he could, out of spite. Resistance would only excite his determination. He was, as I have said, the sort of man who had to keep besting his enemies even after they were defeated. If I went much further, I would place myself in that category and he would stop at nothing until he had me.

I cast about for something tactful to say. I could hardly tell him we were related, and I couldn't afford to offend him; he held all of Nottinghamshire as his own, and next to the absent King and the Archbishop of York he was my overlord. And he could marry me off to an impoverished, pox-ridden lecher if he really wanted to. I wondered what Guy of

Gisborne would think of his benefactor's claiming 'first night' privileges. Probably he would smile and submit, and blame me afterward. That would be the sort of man John would have around him.

"Well?" said the Prince. It was scarcely more than a whisper and might have been gentle but for the menace underneath. There was no doubt the man was dangerous. I sensed, like the rabbit before the snake, that he was about to strike.

I remembered, between one breath and the next, that he was fastidious to the point of daintiness, and saw a way out. I invoked the oldest prohibition. I turned away from him with what I hoped sounded like a maidenly simper. "Oh, Your Grace, I'm so surprised, I'm honoured, I really am." No doubt my blushes, which were real enough, reassured him, because he seemed to relax a little. I took a deep breath and said to the wall, "It's my woman's time, that's all — I'm sure Your Grace understands what I mean? The Church forbids it."

The Church also forbade sexual congress

out of wedlock, but for John that was beside the point. I scarcely dared look at him for a moment, but when I finally did I knew I had succeeded. He looked as if he would like to send me off to be purified at once, preferably by fire. Instead he repeated the essence of his mother's speech: that in the matter of my husband, he would deal with it if there was time enough; if not, I was well enough as I was. I could only agree, with relief. As I say, the interview did not make me rejoice in my prospects.

I didn't like myself very much afterwards, though I liked him still less. I had, by seeming pleased by his attentions, bent to flattery and abased myself. The court was full of people who lived that way, and I was no longer quite as naive as I had been about what royalty requires. Still, it disgusted me. I remembered Cecily and her uncle and felt ashamed at my lack of understanding. I made ready for my journey home with a troubled mind.

4

BLIDWORTH was familiar and uncharted, the same and not the same. Anyone who has come home after a long absence will know what I mean. The furnishings, the rooms, even the great hearth seemed smaller than I remembered, but other chambers, particularly the ones my parents had occupied, were as strange to me as if I had come on them for the first time. My mother's clothes were still entombed in the chests, preserved with herbs. I could not wear them, for all they had been made in France and of the finest material, too; I ordered them distributed to the poor in the village. The effects of her husband, the man I had known as my father, were completely absent; he must have taken them to Normandy, where he had lived out the rest of his life.

Sometimes I thought I would burst with memories. A late snowfall blocked the ways, smothering life and sound with white pillows beneath a pewter sky. Only the fire crackled and hissed. The north-bred wind screamed in the boughs and sang of my childhood. These thoughts were sweet and stinging, as such things are, but they showed me nothing of the truth. Those who could have uncovered it were gone.

Strangest of all was that I was now mistress of the household in my mother's place. I bore myself, I know, as if I expected scolding and discipline from Cook and Geron and the other authorities of my past; I couldn't help it. Instead they asked me everything, checking on the household accounts, the animals and produce to be sold at market, the material to be bought for the hangings and linen. I had some knowledge of such things from Fontevrault, but no grasp of practical details, such as market prices, and I was appalled at how much there was to learn.

I missed my studies and the mental rigours of Fontevrault. I also missed the companionship of girls my own age. I had hoped that Janet might still be in Blidworth, but Cook told me she had become a lay sister in an order in Yorkshire, in a place called Kirklees. It needed all of Cook's property, a tiny parcel of land given her by my father, to make up the dowry even for so poor a priory. She seemed quite unhappy about it. Janet was her only child, and much loved. I asked whether she had had the Calling, and when.

She squinted at me with something like hostility. "Why, after *you* left, of course, to go to that abbey in France. I wouldn't hear of it till she was older, and then I thought she'd forgotten. It started up again when we tried to fix up a marriage for her with one of the village boys. She wouldn't have him. She was on me night and day until I found a place for her. It wasn't easy, fixed as we are, but Janet's quick and the Prioress thought she'd be useful." She gave me a long look. "I wonder what she'll say when she hears you've come back, Lady Marian."

I heard the sadness in her voice with helplessness. I hardly knew what to say to her. I thought Janet an unlikely nun at best; the idea that she might enter the religious life because I had been sent to an abbey, as her mother implied, would never have occurred to me. I could understand Cook's frustration, but there was nothing I could do about it. I offered some conventional crumbs of comfort out of my experience at Fontevrault. I am very poor at being an example to others.

In March, as soon as the storms let up, Blidworth was visited by an agent of Prince John. He went through the manor's stores and directed Geron to send a portion to Nottingham before the next feast day. We had already paid our tax for the year, and under the wardship the remaining income should have gone to the King, but I warned Geron not to protest. I had heard enough at court to guess that John would try to build a power base in the counties his brother had granted him, and Nottingham was one of these. To do that he needed money, and if he didn't get it by collection he found a pretext to seize the source itself.

If I could see the danger, I'm not sure why Richard ignored it. For all their prowess on the field, the Plantagenets were often human-blind. He referred to his brother with open contempt, naming him John Softsword. In fact, John had a positive genius for exciting underestimation, and it served him well. Much might have been prevented if his family had taken him seriously.

The Prince's agent, in addition to directing the revenue collection, ordered two peasants in the village to be hanged for violating the Forest Laws. This caused some talk, because it usurped the verderer's prerogatives, and a great deal of trouble, because the usual penalty for a serious offence was maiming by cutting off the fingers and thumb. There were never any eager volunteers for the cutting, much less for a hanging. While a hangman was sent for, someone carelessly left unguarded the shed in which the culprits were being held, and they escaped into the forest. Luckily, the agent had gone back to Nottingham by then, and the corpses were not required as proof that the Prince's justice had been done. It was just the sort of situation that had got the Earl of Huntingdon outlawed.

The Forest Laws were trouble to everyone who lived in the woodlands and had been since the time of Great William. There was a royal hunting lodge at Clipstone, not far from Blidworth, so in our part of the country they were quite strictly enforced. No one but verderers and foresters, the crown's officials, could kill any beast the King might hunt for sport. It was forbidden as well to cut branches off a living tree or even to carry an unslung bow. Dogs had to be 'lawed' by having three claws cut from the forepaws. Naturally all this was a dreadful nuisance. The restrictions were generally honoured in fat years, but in lean ones, during a hard winter, say, or a bad harvest, it did not sit well with the hungry to deny them game, or firewood to cook it over. All in all the system worked best if the offenders weren't pursued too vigorously. What had happened lately, between Richard's quest for funds and John's for power, was that the pursuit was tightening up.

I was glad that the men who had escaped were not my bondsmen, for then I would have been responsible for them before the law and the taxman. Still, it was to no one's advantage to have outlaws in the forest. At best they lived off illicit game and got us all into trouble; at worst they took to robbing travellers. The greater roads were kept cleared back to discourage banditry, but the smaller ways, like those to Blidworth, were all overgrown. People grew more cautious and began to travel in larger parties, as they had done in the Bad Days before King Henry. Lent began, and passed, and on Good Friday the cross was unveiled on the steps of the altar, where we crept to it on our knees and kissed it. On Saturday all fires were extinguished except for the great Paschal candle, which kept an all-night vigil in the church. In the days before my parents' death Blidworth had its own full-time priest; since I had gone abroad to live and the manor house was closed, the village had shared with its neighbours. I intended to rectify this but had so far found no one suitable. Meanwhile, it was our turn for Easter.

I wasn't expecting much, after Fontevrault. Itinerant priests are the lowest and poorest of the sacerdotal hierarchy, and I learned from the villagers that this one was a Saxon to boot. That would mean we would hear Mass in Latin roughened by the harsh English tongue and perhaps by illiteracy as well. I was comfortable enough in English — my parents having thought it a harmless acquisition, provided it was not used in polite conversation — but I never liked it. All the words sound as if they are bitten off or coughed up at the end, and, as I have said, the accent can ruin graceful Latin or French.

However deficient he might be, it was partly my family's fault Blidworth had no better, so by way of compensation I ordered the finest feast we could afford for both the priest and our people, who dined at the house by tradition after Easter Mass. On Saturday the tenants bring eggs, so there would be plenty of puddings and custards, and since the Lenten restrictions were lifted on Easter Day we would have meat again for the first time in weeks. Geron had our fattest porker slaughtered, a great brute who had tormented him for months by attacking him every time he entered the sty. He took a quite personal satisfaction in his revenge.

The priest arrived in time for Mass, just when we had begun to despair of his coming. At first glance he seemed to exceed even my expectations. He had looks I particularly dislike: he was fat and fair, with features as oversized as his body. He was sweating heavily from exertion, so that moist hair clung to his forehead and water puddled on his upper lip. I stepped forward from the church porch to greet him as he slid off his horse, an arthritic piebald, like a sack of meal.

Unexpectedly, his eyes were dark, and fringed with thick short lashes. There was no reading his thoughts. His voice, for such a body, was curiously light and youthful. "Lady Marian Fitz Walter?"

"Father — ?" I had forgotten to ask his name.

"Father Tuck. God's greetings." He nodded to the crowd. "Shall we begin?"

"I thought," I began tentatively, "that you might want to wash and refresh yourself first . . ."

He waved dismissal, and I saw that

his hand was large, strong, and dirty, like the Saxon ploughman he looked. "It is the hour for Mass, and I must still hear Confession. We must not keep the people waiting." He said it curtly, and somehow managed to turn his lateness into a rebuke to me. I flushed, but I was in the habit of giving obedience to priests and followed him meekly into the church. When I confessed to a sin against charity, I'm sure he knew what I meant. He absolved me anyway.

The feast was no more comfortable.

Cook's creations surpassed the plain fare of the last weeks the way the moon dims the stars. I suppose it was having an occasion, and someone outside the household, that inspired her. Geron's pig was done to perfection, down to the crisp skin tinted slightly with saffron and masking the rich succulent flesh. The juices made a fine brown gravy which soaked the trencher, and the front of the Father's tunic.

He ate, not with the haste of deprivation or distraction (like King Henry), but with pure animal enjoyment. He tried some of every dish, and there were many.

I had to remind myself that I was far from Fontevrault and its monastic restrictions.

Later, when he had eaten his fill of cakes and gilly-flower pudding, he questioned me about the servants and the village people, some of whom were seated at the lower table. What I could tell him was apparently unsatisfactory.

"But what about the smith's baby that was born too soon? It should have had top milk from the manor, as soon as it was able. And young Molly, who went to Nottingham last year? Her parents still have heard nothing of her . . . " He went on and on cataloguing all the lives of Blidworth, and with them, my omissions. The worst sin I was guilty of, which he let me see quite clearly, was that I had not cared enough to find out.

He puzzled me. He spoke of these things irritably, as if they were a burden he bore but had no affection for, yet in the stewardship of souls I have never known anyone more scrupulous. He rubbed against me like a hair shirt, but I found myself wanting his good opinion. In fact, as Sister Beatrice might have told me, that is one of the functions of a hair shirt. To divert his line of questioning, I asked whether he had always been an itinerant priest.

"No, before this I was a hermit."

I asked him where. He certainly did not seem much suited to the contemplative life.

"In the forest, Lady Marian. Not far from here."

"Really? How long were you there? Why did you leave?"

"Yes. Quite a while. I left," he said, giving me an impenetrable stare, "because the forest was no longer a place I could be alone. Besides, I am needed in the world. Obviously," he added, making me blush.

"Did you ever think of becoming a monk?"

"Too easy."

I shook my head. I remembered Fontevrault and the Rule, and could not agree with that.

He seemed to take offence. "Perhaps you think the work of a poor priest isn't grand enough, my lady? Maybe you think I should have been a bishop or a Templar or a canon? Well, I am a poor Saxon by birth and not all doors were open to me. I would have liked to have been one of those things. Why not?" His voice rose. "If bishops can win salvation from God by eating and keeping women, and Templars by pride and killing, and canons by lending money at usury, St Peter and St Matthew must have been fools to suffer such grievous torments for God."

He certainly didn't look as if he had suffered any grievous torments, except perhaps at the hands of his fuller. I asked him, "You think it's more virtuous to live like the poor, then?" I could not help looking down at his empty trencher.

He caught my meaning at once, and laughed. It transformed him. "I don't think that at all. Hunger and rags don't mean virtue any more than they do disgrace. The poor don't want others to fall in with their lot, they want it changed." He lowered his voice. "I do it for the same reason you must take responsibility for your people: there is no one else."

And so on. There was certainly nothing

in him of the saints or martyrs, with their physical primness and long-suffering ways. He was of the world and the body, and his appetites, at least the ones he allowed himself to indulge, were strong. I discovered, over the course of the next week — which he spent baptizing and burying and performing other rites of passage — that he had an affection for ale as well.

Drunkenness only intensified his virtues and vices. He grew more irascible and impatient; his glittering eye was keener for the injustices he hoped to correct. Not, I'm sure, in the hope of good opinion: he never threatened and blustered when he could not perform, and if there was nothing to be done he kept silent. The village people did not love him, he made them too uncomfortable. But they trusted him, and they brought him their problems.

It did not take him long to take up the cudgel for the condemned poachers. I know how the Israelites felt when Moses came down from Sinai and interrupted their revels. The Father did not find me sporting with a golden calf, but when he came to the manor his wrath was just as hot. Beneath his tunic, rolls of flesh quivered with ire. I advanced to him shuffling, like a dog expecting a beating.

"But what could I do?" I asked, when he had finished berating me for letting matters get to such a pass. "They were not my bondsmen, they *had* broken the Forest Laws, and the Prince's agent took over everything. We were lucky they escaped before the hanging."

He fumed and sputtered, as if I had given him so many things to protest he hardly knew where to begin. Finally, he said between clenched teeth "You do agree that the penalty was unjust?"

"Of course."

"Then why didn't you lodge an official protest?"

I answered him honestly, with some shame. "Because I am afraid of Prince John."

He shrugged. "We are all afraid of Prince John, if we have any sense. Is your fear general or personal?"

"Both." I told him a little of what had passed.

He softened somewhat. I confess I knew my revelation would have this effect. "Still," he said, sticking out his lower lip in concentration and resting his hands on his formidable hips, "still, you should try to do what you can. You are obliged to. You have some power and they have none. You are French and rich, they are Saxon and poor . . ."

I almost sighed. I have yet to meet a poor Saxon who does not blame his plight on the Conquest of England well over a hundred years ago. The rich ones will tell you it makes no difference. It always seemed to me a ridiculous contention. "The law applies to everyone alike," I reminded him.

"Does it now?" Father Tuck was starting to kindle again. "A law is only as good as the man who enforces it. And when you have someone like the Prince . . ." He shrugged, as if the matter were completely hopeless.

Whatever else he was, he wasn't timid. If I had wanted to, I could have harmed him considerably by reporting the conversation.

He went on to depict the perils of

outlawry. "A man can lose his soul in the forest," he said, in a tone that made me shiver. "It's not the crime, not just that. It's the cold, and the dark, and the loneliness. Think of that when you're snug in your bed at Blidworth."

I concluded that Sherwood had cast its shadow on his own soul as well. I wondered if that was where his weakness for ale had begun.

He frowned suddenly, as if he had read my thought. He traced a line on the floor with the toe of his shoe, which gaped at the seam and showed bare flesh. He went on the attack. He looked up, and his eyes were malicious. "Why aren't you married, by the way? You certainly aren't *that* young."

I sketched for him the pitiful story of my betrothal to the Earl of Huntingdon, before he could pick up who-knows-what tale in the village.

He seemed to find this very funny. I didn't think it in the least amusing and waited for him to stop laughing. "I'm sorry," he said at last, "but it's just so . . . well, never mind. Seriously, though, you should get yourself married soon."

209

"It's not exactly in my hands, is it?"

"Then give a prod to whoever's hands it is in. Bad times are coming, and you'll be unprotected here without a husband."

"What sort of bad times?" I had my own ideas about what he was hinting at, but I wanted to see what he thought.

"I'm not a prophet," he snapped. "But I do hear things. It's plain as a pikestaff that when the King is gone his lieutenants will be fighting over the leavings in England like a pack of hungry curs. And the biggest and hungriest are this fellow Longchamp and His Royal Highness the Prince. I think you can imagine what I mean by 'trouble'."

"I can, but I don't really see what I can do about it," I told him.

"Just keep your ear to the ground. His Grace may dig himself into the places he already holds, like Nottingham. Try to stay out of his way if you can. Anybody who gets drawn into these troubles is likely to get kicked around. Particularly young ladies without husbands. If you need me, send a message to the church at Edwinstowe. Can you manage that?"

"I can manage," I said.

For the first time he gave me a smile of genuine friendliness. "I believe you," he said. Then the unreadable expression settled on his face again. "One more thing . . ."

"Yes?"

"My dear, if I were you I would stay out of the forest."

5

THE castle at Nottingham perches sharp and watchful as an eagle on top of a great rock. From the walls, you can look over the countryside, beyond the flat river valley to the high hills in the north. Below the rock, along the water meadows, the tents of the Goose Fair flapped and billowed in the autumn wind. If you got closer you could see the puffs of down from the poulterers' sheds, like pillows of soft dry snow. Often real snow fell on the Goose Fair, but this year the castle was lapped in the last fair weather warmth, and the air was as strong-scented with bracken as if it had been summer. From this vantage point, Sherwood seemed greenly peaceful.

Like many old and famous fairs, the Goose Fair had exceeded its original bounds and now encompassed much besides geese. The drinking booths were especially busy so the bailiffs spent most of their time separating brawlers and hauling off the indecently drunk. Most of the offenders were let out when they had slept it off. Suspected thieves and layabouts were held for the fortnight of the fair, to protect both buyers and sellers.

I had come with Geron to the Goose Fair to pay my respects to my guardian, the Sheriff of Nottingham. I had met him once, before I went to Fontevrault, just after King Henry had appointed him. I remembered him as stern and unfriendly, but I had been grieving for my mother then and could not trust my memory. I knew no ill of him; Geron told me he was known for his efficiency and had caused no scandals.

He was somewhat out of patience at being bothered by the King's ward (from whom he would get only a small administrative compensation) when he had so much else to attend to, and hid it badly. His face was as creased as if he had bitten a sour fig. Nevertheless, he rose to receive us, and told Geron politely he could go.

Like most ageing warriors, he dressed to look younger than he was; his tunic and mantle were too rich and bright, when plainness would have served him better. Still, one would not be tempted to laugh. Beneath his twitching eyebrows, his eyes fixed you with the stare of a master bowman picking his target. His neck and arms were thick, but his body carried no spare flesh. He was not a man to take lightly, on the field or off.

I made a deep curtsey and said I was sorry to disturb him when he must be so busy. He flapped a hand dismissively at the tents and stalls outside, as if he disapproved of their sloppiness, and of human nature in general for contriving such an affair.

"So," he said, gesturing me to a seat, "have you found everything in order at Blidworth?"

I said I had and commended Geron's stewardship, glad of the chance to offer the praise he deserved.

The Sheriff cut me off. "Our agents agree," he said, "except for the business of the escaped poachers, for which I do not hold you responsible. The foresters were slack. They will be replaced."

"Sir, the trouble resulted from

condemning the men to hang. The penalty was too harsh." It came out too soft and squeaky, and not at all the courageous rejoinder I had imagined ever since the priest had pricked my conscience.

The Sheriff scarcely attended me, and no wonder. "Sir," I began again.

He sighed impatiently. "Your womanly compassion does you credit," he said, reducing my protest to a fancy of the weaker sex. "But Prince John does not agree." He did not look at me. I don't think he was a bad man, just a realist. He was the King's reeve, but the chances were not insubstantial that the King would never come back. The Emperor had already drowned in the course of the Crusade, and the fighting hadn't even started yet. Meanwhile, John was not a man to let another hedge his bets. One would have to choose, and choose early. I decided to act on the assumption that the Sheriff had already made his choice.

"I think that if the enforcement is tightened up and the foresters more vigilant we can persuade him that such strict penalties will only be necessary as an example, once," he went on, "provided we get co-operation in the towns and villages." He didn't even look my way; he was preparing his speech for a more important audience. I thought, from the little I had heard and seen of him, that for him it was the order and enforcement that mattered. The idea of outlaws living in the forest killing game and harassing travellers must work in him like a thorn in the cloak. Whether the Prince, who collected fines and property from the offenders, would be satisfied with simply stopping the offences was highly doubtful.

We sat for a moment, in a silence I hoped signalled the end of the interview. I had paid my respects and had got off lightly. I rose to take my leave.

"I was almost forgetting," he said, with a smile that came out twisted from lack of use, "the matter of your betrothal."

I sat down again. My hands, which were shaking a little, I packed into my lap.

"Everything has been arranged," he said briskly and with satisfaction. "The Prince is quite pleased."

It was on my tongue to ask him if I would be pleased as well, but there was no advantage to giving offence. Besides, I don't think he meant to be unkind; it was clear the matter did not enjoy his full attention.

"Might I he permitted to know who ... ?" The ironic tone pleased only myself; he missed it entirely. In fact, he looked surprised.

"Guy of Gisborne, Lady Marian. Of course."

Prince John's crony. Well, perhaps that was unfair, but the name was associated with that unpleasantness in London, and I wanted to be cautious. "I see. His Grace did mention someone of that name the last time we spoke. Do you know him?"

He regarded me more attentively. "We've met. Sir Guy's estate is in the West Riding of Yorkshire, but he's been given lands in Sherwood. Not a day's ride from the royal hunting lodge, as a matter of fact. The Prince goes there often."

I would have bitten my nails if my hands had not been anchored under the folds of my mantle, in my lap.

"Could you tell me please, sir, what he is like?"

"The Prince? I thought you said you'd met him."

"I have. I meant Sir Guy."

"Oh, yes, I see." He smiled again. "Brave, very competent on the field, good with his hands, too, I think — oh, and handsome — all the things you young ladies like."

I began to perceive the disadvantage of having no father or male relative to handle this for me. I was clearly supposed to affect a maidenly delicacy about the betrothal, but there was no one else to safeguard my rights. I raised the only shield I had, albeit a small one. "My lord, has the King approved the match?"

He looked startled. "The King, as I understand it, is occupied with driving the Infidel out of the Holy Land."

"I am the King's ward. I can't marry without his approval."

I must have sounded mulish, for his face hardened. "The betrothal has the approval of the King's brother, Prince John. There is no reason for His Grace to be displeased by the arrangements; I guarantee he's much more likely to be glad it's been taken off his hands. He does have more important things to worry about, you know." He didn't add 'and so do I', but his tone said it all. "Now see here, Lady Marian, you don't want to make trouble about this. You haven't even met the fellow, after all."

I bent my head. "That's it, exactly. We haven't met. I know only what you've told me, and that is to his credit. But I am an orphan, sir, raised in a convent. And if this man is, well, unsuitable in some way, there is no one to stand as father or brother for my protection. I have to be sure of him, don't you see?"

He picked up his seal of office, which was resting on its stand on the table in front of him, and turned it over in his hands, flicking off bits of wax with his fingernail. The room had grown quite stuffy and warm in the fall sunshine, and the wax came off easily. The Sheriff sighed.

"You've said you have no father to look out for you, Lady Marian. Well, I am your guardian until you marry, so now I'll speak to you as a father would: you'd best make up your mind to take the man and not put on any missish airs. You can have no objections to him — I've told you so. And there is this — the Prince gave Sir Guy the Locksley lands and means to control Blidworth, too." He could not very well say that the Prince would have no opposition in Nottinghamshire, but it amounted to the same thing. I wondered what Sir Guy had done or promised in exchange for royal favour. With John one could never tell; it might only have been to spite someone else.

"You can't force a betrothal without consent," I told him.

He answered me with the confidence which had made him Henry's man before John's and, moreover, no one to be trifled with. "True enough. But a very heavy fine could be levied on Blidworth, and your property confiscated to pay it. I'm not saying you couldn't appeal to the King, provided you could get his attention on such a matter, and provided that he does come home. If he does not . . . " There was no need to elaborate. I began to see why Queen Eleanor was less than pleased about Richard's passion for crusading.

He stood up, impatient now to conclude a discussion he obviously found annoying and trivial. "You will be pleased to learn that Sir Guy himself is expected shortly, so we can proceed with the betrothal while you are here. If you stay near your quarters, I'll send someone there to let you know."

He seemed to take my assent for granted, as well he might. My choices were limited: (1) Accept Sir Guy or (2) Lose Blidworth. I did not fool myself over the Prince's ability to do this, and I thought the Sheriff was right about the efficacy of appealing to Richard. What was becoming clear was that, in this part of England at least, John was appropriating the perquisites of the crown to himself.

I could not even enter a convent without a dowry. I resolved to look very hard at Guy of Gisborne.

★ ★ ★

It was the horse, on top of everything else, that did it. At the Goose Fair there is a field for horses, like the market at Smithfield, but smaller. The rest of the year it is used for tilting at quintains or tournaments, so the ground is flat and well trodden for trying out your animal. This year there was a shortage of good horses all over England, since so many journeyed south to the Holy Land. Poor beasts; only a few would make it back again.

The shortage drove the price of destriers to a celestial level, of palfreys to the exalted, and even the work ponies we got by on at Blidworth to the high. The penalties for horse stealing were upped with the incidence. In all, it did not make for a promising showing on the field.

They led the destriers out first, the fighting horses a lord will give a new-made knight, or a rich man will buy for himself. The best are bred from Arab stock, huge and strong to support their armour and the buffeting of tournaments and battles. A good horse is intelligent, too; the stupid ones, like their masters, are just brutes and don't last long in combat. In London or Paris they can give you the bloodlines stretching back for generations; this year in Nottingham you would not be surprised to find that some enterprising merchant had crossed a plough horse with an ox and called it a charger. Geron said the present lot were mostly too old for further service anyway; their masters hoped to get something for them before they keeled over into their oat bags.

Next came the palfreys, the grooms leading them in as stately a procession as they could manage in the trodden yard, which was beginning to smell of horse piss and provide pitfalls for the incautious walker. One or two looked skittish and were taken out of the line; no one will buy a nervous palfrey, which is most suitable for ladies and ceremonious occasions. There seemed to be a shortage of both at the Goose Fair, but Geron said the Sheriff's lady had already bought the best of the lot, a big white with a soft mouth and gentle ways. I didn't pay much attention to the rest; I was getting bored with watching the horses and the crowd. They would be bringing out the rounci es next, horses of no particular breeding which are sometimes used for travelling or fighting, and then it would be the plain work animals. I turned to Geron to tell him I wanted to leave but he missed my look. Someone was calling out down the field, "a jennet, a jennet," and then the crowd laughed.

The crier was leading out a small, grey-brown horse which switched its tail and side-stepped warily in reaction to the laughter. The man tugged angrily at the rein, as if he blamed the beast. "It's a jennet, I tell you," he insisted, and the laughter increased.

The horse was no beauty but I couldn't see what was comical about him. "What's a jennet?" I asked Geron.

He opened his mouth but someone at my side spoke first. "A small horse, my lady, bred in Spain off the horses Roland left behind when he fell at Roncevalles. Mostly they are too small for English knights, so the ladies use them." I looked up into the speaker's face and nearly shied like the horse. He was almost excessively good-looking. His hair was quite black but his skin was fair and he had the blue eyes of a Celt. He smiled charmingly, showing white teeth. For all that he was a stranger, I could not help addressing him. "But why are they laughing?"

He folded his arms across his chest. "Because that is no jennet." His voice was amused and hard and self-confident. He seemed relaxed enough, but his stance had an edge to it, like a sword.

Geron touched my arm. "The gentleman is right," he said, nodding toward our neighbour. "It's only a plain hackney like all the rest. I expect the fool heard about a jennet somewhere and thought he'd get a better price. He should have known better than to try to pull it off at the Goose Fair. He'll be lucky if the Sheriff doesn't hear about it and fine him."

The man and horse were coming our way, more slowly now. The man looked sullen and out of sorts, resentment looking for an object. I knew, when he had got away from the crowd's jeering, that he was the type who would make the animal pay for it.

He must have sensed my interest. He

raised his eyes and looked right at me. A flicker of speculation lit them and he hauled the horse over to where we stood. Geron looked alarmed and disgusted at the same time. "My lady," said the man, sweeping off his trader's cap to reveal a greasy, hairless scalp, "I'm sure *you* will appreciate this fine animal. Gentle as a lamb he is, and of good bloodstock too, whatever these louts might say about it. I'm prepared to give you a good price." I noticed that, under Geron's sceptical gaze, no mention was made of a 'jennet'.

He put his hand up to the horse's neck as if to pat him but the animal rolled a white-rimmed eye and jerked aside, ears flattened. That at least showed good taste, I thought.

"The lady's not interested in your stock, nor in you either," Geron said. "Like as not you've beaten the sense out of it anyway." A small group had gathered round to watch the transaction, so the man sputtered in protest, gesturing at the listeners to demonstrate the blatant unfairness of such an accusation. At Geron's reply they had begun to tease him again. I liked them no better than the trader and wished they would be quiet. I doubted if half of them had heard of a jennet in the first place; like a dog pack, they had taken up the cry when the first one scented blood.

The horse, feeling his lead slacken, stepped over to where I stood and pushed at me with his head. His nostrils were blown wide, puffing sweet breath down the front of my chainse. He mouthed my sleeve softly, then took it in his teeth and tugged it.

It was as direct an appeal as I had ever seen, and I wondered for a moment if he had been trained for it. Looking at the trader, I doubted somehow that he had it in him to think it up.

Geron had told me once that there were two kinds of people in the world, identifiable, of all things, by the way they picked a puppy out of the litter. The first sort chose the puppy who was lively, bright, and aggressive — all the qualities of a good hunter. The second — whom he clearly held in scorn — chose the runt or the one who cried or whose mother had rejected it, out of pity. He invited me to guess who got the better dog, or even a serviceable one.

As an object lesson, it had been, apparently, a failure. "Geron," I began apprehensively, knowing what he would say. He had not known me from childhood for nothing. He groaned. "Oh, no, my lady, you don't even want to consider it."

"Why not?"

The trader, his practised instincts sensing a change in the wind, silenced his hecklers and sidled over. "I could give you a very good price," he repeated.

Geron went over the horse, feeling the leg joints and looking at the teeth. He clucked a few times and said, finally, "He seems sound enough, though he's nothing special." He shook his head doubtfully.

The knight who had told me about the jennet was still standing next to us. I'd forgotten all about him in my interest in the horse, until he said, "Forgive me for intruding, Lady Marian, but you don't want to allow your man to buy that horse, at least not if you plan to ride it yourself. The animal is below your station. You should get something better."

My 'man' looked sour at the intrusion into our affairs but said nothing. The stranger's speech and assurance bespoke money and position, even without the trappings of knighthood. I wondered fleetingly how he knew who I was and how he had come by his exaggerated notions of my 'station', but I didn't dwell on it. Gossip was the common coin of a fair like this one, and you could find out just about anything you wanted.

I don't know why I was becoming so determined to have this plain horse of doubtful suitability. Perhaps it was a stubborn reaction to the well-meant attempts to dissuade me. Perhaps it was the patient way the horse bore all the handling and discussing, after he had made his appeal. Most likely I just wanted to get my way about something, for once. I rewarded my helpful neighbour with a smile — no difficulty, given his astonishing good looks — and said to the trader, "How much do you want for him?"

The man named his price. He must have dropped it already, in response to all the opposition. I had no idea whether it was a bargain or not. I looked at Geron. He sucked his teeth.

He took my arm and turned away slightly speaking quietly. "It's too much," he said.

"Can't we get him to lower it?"

"A little, probably, but the price is fair as it stands."

"Well then?"

Geron sighed. "You can't afford it, Lady Marian, not even if you were getting Veillantif himself for the price, which I guarantee you are not. We can't come up with the amount, unless your guardian could advance you some of your income."

I thought of the Sheriff behind his table, administering my estate on behalf of the crown. "No." I shook my head.

"Then I'm afraid it's out of the question."

I would have to accept this, having no knowledge to contradict it. I had given Geron control over my finances, and so far I had no cause to regret it. Besides, he was undoubtedly right about the wisdom of the purchase. But wisdom is a cold comfort.

We turned back to the trader, whose face, which had been schooled into patience, curdled in defeat.

"I'm sorry," Geron said civilly. "Her ladyship has decided against the horse."

I put my arm around the horse's neck in a kind of apology. I shouldn't have, because it let the seller and everyone else know where matters stood, but I was near tears and I didn't want to stand there while that greasy-headed ruffian glared at me. The horse's rough, clipped mane was a welcome distraction.

The trader grunted and jerked at the headstall. "I'm sorry," I repeated miserably, as much to the horse as to the man. "Please don't take it out on the animal."

He gave me a look just short of disrespect that said clearly, "What's it to you, then?" and stalked off the field.

Geron and I followed suit in silence. My steward, who had a more mature perspective on life's necessities than I did, let me sulk in peace.

An hour later I was applying myself to the disagreeable task of paying court to the Sheriff's wife in her fine, fashionable solar in the castle. Like her husband, she had consequence and dignity; unlike him, she exacted the deference owed her with the thoroughness and zeal of the keeper of a toll gate. As she was also intelligent, one had to be careful. She would not miss so much as a raised eyebrow, or overlook the barb in a compliment however deep it might be buried. In that respect she was like Queen Eleanor, but she lacked the malicious sparkle which made Eleanor's exhausting presence worth it.

After a time, we were interrupted by a servant, asking for me. My relief lasted only until I remembered the Sheriff would send word when Guy of Gisborne arrived, and then I decided I would gladly have played courtier to Black Annis, the blue-faced hag who haunted the forest, if it would have postponed that ordeal for the moment.

However, it seemed I was wrong. The servant had been looking for Geron, couldn't find him, and sought me instead. He was most apologetic, but the man had insisted on knowing what to do with the horse, and had sent him to find me at once.

"Horse? What horse?"

He shrugged. "It's a horse, my lady, and the gentleman says it belongs to you. That's all I know." He closed his face stubbornly in determined ignorance.

I stifled the protest I was about to make, curtsied to the Sheriff's lady, and asked permission to withdraw.

She nodded, and the circle of attention closed round her again. I followed the servant down the outer stairs and into the stable yard.

The grey-brown horse was cropping hay with a tearing sound which fell heavily into the afternoon silence. It might have been his first meal in a long time, but I doubted it. His gusto seemed practised, and something about it reminded me of Father Tuck. I laughed, and the man who was holding him turned around.

Some knowledge touched me then. My voice was full of it when I spoke.

"You sent for me?" I asked him.

"I've done this badly," he replied,

but his voice held no apology. In fact, his assumption of my pleasure, of my acceptance in the end, could be read in every arrogant line of his body. "I meant to give it to your man, not to trouble you with it, but I couldn't find him. Will you," he asked, flashing white teeth, "do me the honour of accepting this horse as my gift?"

"Thank you, but I couldn't possibly."

His mouth fell open, then he flushed. "I'd forgotten. Of course you can't know who I am. I'm — "

"Guy of Gisborne. Yes."

He looked disappointed. "I wanted to surprise you. Who told you, the Sheriff?"

I shook my head. "I guessed. Why else would you want to give me a horse?"

He had let the reins slip from his hands. Half turning, he took them up again with a lazy grace which seemed to come as naturally to him as breathing. "You'll take it then, won't you?"

I drew a breath, trying to think how to put it. "It's very kind of you. I admit I wanted to buy him myself. But you must see that I can't accept such a gift."

"Whyever not? We're betrothed."

"We are *not* betrothed. That's the whole point." I said it much too loudly and definitely.

"What do you mean?" Something clouded and altered his face, a touch of uncertainty moving behind the smooth façade of assurance his looks and position had given him. A rebuff, once he accepted it, was clearly something he would find hard to forgive. "The Sheriff said it was all arranged."

"So it was, but not with me. There is no one else to speak for me, so I have to arrange it for myself. And I wasn't consulted."

He smiled at my tone, the confidence back on his face as closely fitting as armour. He said, not unpleasantly, "I understand you have recently returned from a convent in France. Is it possible you wish to go back there?"

For a moment I thought I could discern, beneath the gentle tones, the hint of a threat. I dismissed the idea almost at once; he had neither the motive nor the power.

I smiled in return. "I don't have

the Calling. And I have not said I won't agree to the betrothal. Couldn't I have just a little time? Since you know I lived with the nuns until last year, you can imagine this is all quite new to me."

He laughed. "I'd forgotten you have reason to be suspicious. Last time they promised you to an outlaw."

"And Prince John rewarded you with his lands and his betrothal," I reminded him gently.

He dropped the horse's rein and reached for my hand, raising it to his lips. "I'm well content with both," he said softly, making me feel his power — and, admittedly, his considerable attraction — as a man.

This was not the right moment to ask him about his connection with the Prince, nor, in the normal course of things, would it have been my place to do so. I reminded myself I might be yoked to this man for life; one had to step carefully at the beginning of the path. The caveats clanged like bells in my mind, along with all the prudent reasons for caution. "Why did Prince John give you the land?" I asked him. "Are you his friend?"

He looked surprised, then wary, and then, frankly annoyed. His expression said clearly 'What business is it of yours?' though he managed to frame his answer with more civility: "Why do you ask?"

I lowered my eyes, clasping my hands in front of my waist like the nun I had almost become. "Why, it's an honour, isn't it?"

He shrugged. "I suppose it would be, but I do not *have* the honour of his Grace's friendship. In fact, we have scarcely met. He's come over from the hunting lodge once or twice, that's all."

"You performed some service for him then? Or your family did?" I hoped I sounded innocently curious.

"Not at all. I don't really know why he gave me the land in preference to others, except that my father was loyal to King Henry and died in his service in France. Possibly the Sheriff recommended us. I really couldn't say."

He sounded straightforward enough, and I found myself relaxing.

"I have an idea," he said, grinning

suddenly. "I think you might like it. The hall at Locksley is quite run down — dust in the arras and all that — so I've installed my mother there to see to fixing it up. Why don't you join her there for a visit? I've business in Nottingham for a few days, but then I could ride up and escort you back to Blidworth whenever you're ready. I take it your steward is free to accompany you?"

"He's awfully busy now, getting the estates ready for winter . . . "

He frowned but said nothing.

It really was a most considerate suggestion. "But it might be a good idea," I ventured.

His mouth curved. The beautiful lineaments of his face could rearrange themselves rather quickly. "I knew you'd think so. You can ride my horse."

"Your horse?" I was flustered into forgetting the original purpose of our meeting. He saw it quickly, as one does who is used to summing up his advantage on the field. He looked pleased. "Oh, well . . . "

He shrugged. "I only bought it for you. I haven't the least interest in owning the animal myself. You might as well borrow it for as long as you like."

"Will she mind?"

He looked at me as if I were one of the lunatics tied to the rood screen at Mass. "It's a he, but I doubt it."

I laughed. "I meant your mother."

His eyes widened. "Of course not," he snapped. Evidently he was not a man who could laugh at himself easily. So far I had met very few who could. It was time to put an end to this before the strain of the conversation made one of us say something regrettable. "I'd like to visit Locksley," I told him. "I appreciate your asking me, and I'll accept your loan of Dun Crump."

"Dun Crump?"

I gestured at the horse, who had amiably returned to cropping grass. "I had already decided to call him that if I bought him."

Sir Guy reached for the reins again to pull the horse away from its meal. He would never be fit to ride at this rate. Dun Crump rolled a baleful eye at his new master and side-stepped away, edging closer to me. He tossed his headstall in an attempt at defiance, before the man's stronger grip reined him in. Where I had once seen supplication in the liquid brown eyes, now I imagined a question.

"Well, we'll have to see, won't we?" I answered him.

★ ★ ★

The Sheriff was not pleased with what he perceived as my unmaidenly truculence. "I told you," he said, leaning his great arms on the trestle so that his face was very close to mine, "to get it over and settled, here, in Nottingham. And now Sir Guy tells me you are not only not betrothed, but you have even refused his gifts."

I said nothing. It was apparent he was just winding up. "Good God, Lady Marian, what do you want? The man's rich, handsome, and he'll be powerful too, take my word for it. I shouldn't have to tell you you're a very lucky young lady. If you let him see how headstrong you are it's likely he won't want to marry you at all, and then where will you be?"

Though he was clearly annoyed, he

spoke as he might have to one of his own daughters. "Sir," I told him, "I have refused nothing except to take a gift until we are officially betrothed. I have agreed to visit his mother at Locksley. If all goes well, we will proceed with the betrothal when I return."

His casual dismissal told me more about the reality of my position than all of his previous speeches. His mind had clenched like a fist around his plan and that was that. "It's of no consequence," he said, not even angry now. "Whatever the outcome of the visit, you will be married, and married soon, to Sir Guy. I promise you that."

6

A DAY or two later Geron, Dun Crump, and I set off for Locksley Hall, accompanied by a groom and a huntsman Sir Guy had hired in Nottingham for duty on the new estate. The baggage carts and pack animals followed along, carrying the possessions I had brought to Nottingham and the pots and cloth and skins purchased for the Locksley household at the Goose Fair.

The day looked to be fine and warm, and only the mists and blue-tinted air betrayed the autumn. We clanked and rattled along in style, scaring up late butterflies and woodland creatures, who rustled off in the sheltered undergrowth. The shadows of the trees fell long and thin across the path, a reminder that comfort out-of-doors could change quickly. The sun came out beaten and burnished bronze rather than the heavy gold of a summer afternoon.

The way we were taking — not,

properly speaking, a road but a faint track through the greenwood — seemed to lead straight into the heart of Sherwood, if you could say that such a place had a heart. I had lived by then a number of years in Blidworth, counting my childhood, and I had never seen anything to justify the tales told about the forest. Still, it pulsed with a secret life of its own, and I could not quite shake off the feeling that if you penetrated far enough, you might discover things you would rather not know.

By midday we had lapsed into the silence of the road. Not a leaf or woodlark stirred except at our passing, and I could hear the cool noise of the water in the stream we followed broken by a sudden animal plop. A way off, something larger — a hind perhaps — clattered through the thicket of birches. I began to feel sleepy, lulled by the warmth of the sun on my clothes and the swaying, clop-clop cadence of Dun Crump's feet on the path . . .

Half dreaming, I watched the forest roll along, blurring and reforming itself as I struggled to keep my eyes open. Amid the dark and drying ferns and bracken something wavered among the green. A face. For a moment it was so much a part of my dream that I scarcely noticed, till some buzzing of reality in my head stung me awake. I looked again, stiffening, and in that one startling moment something hissed past my ear, ruffling my hair as gently as a bird's wing.

The sudden din, after the quiet, frayed the senses. Shouts seemed to bounce back and forth off the tree trunks. Behind me, a horse screamed. The wood was suddenly alive with what looked like moving bundles of old rags. One of them ran up and threw an arm over Dun Crump's mane, reaching for the reins. There was something odd, I thought, about the arm. The horse reared and neighed anxiously. If I had been a better rider, or if I had had him long enough for him to know my mind, I might have controlled him. As it was, I clung to his neck and mane trying to stay on, and let him do what he wanted.

I could feel his fear through the bunched up muscles in his shoulders. He snorted, then sprang forward off the path and lunged into the forest. The ground was rutted and uneven, and broken by patches of box and goat-willow and wood grasses. The whitened trunks of birch and hornbeams flashed by like lances in a tournament. I dug my fingers into Dun Crump's mane, trying to slow him down before he stepped in a rabbit burrow and broke a leg, but he ignored me. Ahead I could see the faint glimmer of a stream catching the sun that filtered through the branches. I thought the horse would stop when we reached it — the bank shelved fairly steeply, and the boulders made dark, thrusting shadows at the edges. Doubtless it would be swollen with the autumn rains as well.

Instead, we took it at a treacherous speed. At the last second the animal hesitated and swerved, his hooves slipping and ringing on the wet stones. The water splashed around my legs, and then he stumbled, sending one hoof jamming down into a swirling pool. His fall threw me clear of the water, but my head struck a stone. The world turned black and painless for an unknown piece of time.

★ ★ ★

At some remote, submerged level, I knew
I had to get out of the darkness, off the
ground, back into awareness and light.
The jolt had been enough to make
me wonder where I was and what had
happened when I did open my eyes; the
events unrolled themselves backward in
my memory with frustrating slowness,
beginning with my fall from Dun Crump.
I sat up too quickly and stumbled back
dizzily, bracing myself against a boulder.
The horse was nowhere to be seen. At
least he could not be badly injured if he
had taken himself off. The nuisance was
that I had no idea where to look for him,
and it would be a long, hot walk back to
the road . . .

I came then to the farthest edge of
recent events, and with the return of
memory came fear. Something terrible
had happened on the forest path that
the confusion and my sudden flight had
obscured from me. We had undoubtedly
been attacked by robbers, though there
was something about the shapeless,
ragged forms my mind still could not

touch. Geron would be frantic with worry; I would have to get back as soon as I could find my way. I do not think even then I imagined there would be anything seriously amiss, despite the screaming and the arrows. Geron would have taken care of things, Geron and the men Sir Guy had hired. I would have to be cautious, but the trail would not be hard to follow. Dun Crump had blazed through the wood with the furore of the Wild Huntsman and his demon dogs.

I was just nerving myself to start back when I heard the sound. From the rocks beside the spring came the rattle of pebbles, the scrape of a foot. I pushed myself hastily to my feet, gasping, just as the shadow dropped across my path like a black cloth. I thought, for the second time that day, *this in danger*. My body was slower. I stood as rooted to the ground as the sapling beside me. The forest seemed vast, empty, and silent.

"Who are you? What — what do you want?" I said. My voice came out in a sort of thin whisper. I doubt if he heard me at all. I stepped back from the tree to take the sun out of my eyes so I could see him better. I cleared my throat to try to speak again. It was the last sound I made before I choked in horror.

Sometimes, at the edge of nightmares, there is a face which, if you behold it, will bring down the final lurking calamity. I saw it now. The lesions and ulcers of leprosy had rearranged the features into something that mocked Genesis and all of man's pretensions. Conceivably, if I had seen such a thing in the leprosarium at Fontevrault I would have been moved to a desperate pity; alone in the forest it caused quite another reaction. Showing my obvious, shrinking horror was the worst thing I could have done because it cut off the last possibility of civilized conduct, but I couldn't help myself. He lurched suddenly towards me with unmistakable menace, a horrible laugh coming out as twisted as his ghastly features. I screamed, pushed off from the tree, and ran heedless over the uneven ground, much as Dun Crump had done.

My feet crunched dry leaves beneath the leather of my riding shoes. The sleeves of my surcoat caught on the thorns and twigs of bushes as I passed, and I had to rip the linen with a jerk. The sun beat down on my layers of clothing without pity, so that I was panting and sweating, but the implications of removing any of my clothes, even to run faster, filled me with a shivering horror. My wimple snagged on a tree branch and was pulled off; I did not stoop for it. I heard him coming doggedly behind me.

If I was slowed by my clothing and condition, he was even more hampered by his disease. Leprosy numbs the extremities like cold, so that the leper has to bind them to prevent further mutilations. This gave him a hobbling, shuffling gait, but it did not stop him. He came steadily on; even when I had to stop and pant for breath I could hear him crashing through the leaves and bushes as I had done.

I had not seen him with a bow, like the others at the road, but perhaps his hands were too far gone for that. In any case he had not spitted me with an arrow when he had the chance. Possibly he carried only a knife. Either way I had no weapon, not even a lady's dagger, and I was tiring fast. I ran on blindly, not knowing the terrain or where I was going or could go. There were great oaks here and there now, but the undergrowth was sparser. I could hide in the outcroppings of rocks or even behind one of the great trees, but of course I had left a trail. He could simply run me till I dropped like a fox or a wounded stag.

I began to think how I could kill him.

Fearful creatures haunt the lonely places, they say. Black Annis roams the forests and the wasteland hills, or waits in her clawed-out cave for disobedient children to stray by. Their dried skins flap from the oak bows; their scattered bones stick up from the ground, little knobs pressing into the feet. Once, it had been a sweet terror, a shiver from the safety of the hearth, like watching a shipwreck from the shore.

The branches that scratched and tore at my legs and clothes seemed to have invaded my chest as well. Every breath was a sobbing agony. I stopped, ducking behind a tree, and struggled to regain my strength. The pain eased a little but each time I rested and started up again I had less to give. I held myself quiet, stilling panic, and strained to listen. There was no sound.

Hope and fear gave wings to thought. Ahead of me was a dell, slanting up the side of a rocky slope. One side was covered in a thick, steep tangle; I shoved the boughs aside and pushed my way through. Now, for the moment at least, I could not be seen, and I had the briefest chance to search for what I wanted.

At length I found two possibilities. One was a jagged chunk of rock broken off from a boulder; its heft was good and its size was big enough, if I was lucky, to knock out my pursuer. I didn't care if it killed or maimed him if it would end the nightmare. The other less likely object was a piece of a stout tree branch, dried but not too rotted, that I had some idea of using as a club, if it came to that. There was no time for anything else.

I scrambled up through the thicket until I found a cleft in the boulders where I could lie up and watch. Above me there was an overhang of rock which looked to be popular with a large number of birds. A prickly juniper bush grew half across the cleft, hiding me, I hoped, from below. Anyone who entered the dell in search of me would have to pass just below, within reach of my outstretched hand and its rock. Again with luck, I could crack him right on the skull.

The sun was slanting low now, in the way of autumn. The cleft lay in shadow, but I could still feel the warmth of the rock beneath my palms. I narrowed my eyes against the sun and stretched flat against the rock to wait for my pursuer.

I heard the movement long before I saw him. I was clenching and unclenching my hands around my weapon so hard that they began to cramp with the effort and I was afraid I would not be able to wield it when it was time. My body was as still and stiff as a tree root; my clothes were damp with sweat by turns hot and cold. I could hear him pause occasionally, probably to look for my trail, and then come on. Squinting and straining through the tangled branches, I could just pick out the figure stooping, as I had thought, to examine the ground. Some trick of the light turned his clothing, which I knew to be a filthy brown, as green as the surrounding forest itself. My heart gave a painful kick of fear then settled down to an erratic thumping.

The figure, dwarfed by distance, moved nearer to the dell. Even the shambling stride had straightened with confidence, or excitement. He looked, from this perspective, more dangerous and less horrifying. I watched and waited, as one would watch a slithering adder. Then, in a swift movement both puzzling and disturbing, he veered into a stand of trees and disappeared from view. I slid forward on my perch, trying not to rustle the bushes, and craned my neck to see. I saw nothing, heard nothing, except the soft stirring of the breeze through the dry brush. Then, as gently and impersonally as a child, something tugged once at the hem of my clothing.

I wrenched my body around in one jerking movement, but before I could scream he was on me, one hand clasped over my mouth. Mercifully, it was wrapped in cloth so that what it covered was hidden and not next to my skin. Even so the stench of the rotten sacking and of the sickness itself was overpowering, so that I gagged on my intaken breath. He must have been afraid he would kill me right off because he shifted a little and I could breathe easier. I could also see his face.

The sight made me squirm and struggle, resisting his touch from somewhere deep in my body that lay beyond thought or purpose. His other hand, which was already fumbling under my clothes, came up to strike me, hard, across the face. He muttered something under his foul breath, curses or threats, but I didn't listen. My ears rang. He raised his hand to hit me again, and his palm slipped against my mouth. I got it free for just a moment and screamed. It was little more than a shrill gasp, but enough, apparently, to panic him. I couldn't imagine why, when there was so clearly no one to hear. Instead of hitting me, he pulled out a knife — old and rusty looking, but doubtless sharp enough to cut a throat. He stuck the point into the base of my neck. I lay still, tensed, unable even to pray. He stayed just as still on top of me, a dead, stinking weight whose breath came in rattling warmth next to my ear. The moment seemed to go on forever.

Satisfied at last that I could not resist, he left the knife resting next to my head and slid his hand up along my leg, jerking the layers of my clothes up to my thighs. At the same time, he started thrusting himself against me with little moaning noises. He fumbled with his own rags, by God's kindness out of my field of vision.

In an instant more he would rape me, and after that he would probably slit my throat. My hands groped desperately for one of my weapons and closed at length on my stick of wood. Awkwardly, it was in my left, but I clutched it as if it were a remnant of the Holy Rood. Then I brought it down as hard as I could on the side of his head.

The blow struck his ear and he howled with pain. He reared back on his knees and flailed at me with the stumpy remains of his hands. I tried to beat him off with my stick but he knocked it out of my grasp. I closed my eyes as he hit me again and again. There was no help, no salvation, no relief, only black despair and a terrible animal fear . . .

Against all impossibility, help came. I felt rather than saw or heard it, because my attacker froze, the rage and lust exchanged suddenly for alarm.

I had heard no one approach, but that is hardly surprising. Now a voice, whose origin was obscured by the leper's bulk, said sharply, "Get up." The weight shifted on top of me and rolled off. He got to his feet stiffly, staggering a little. Then he spun swiftly and reached for the knife beside my head, leaping with surprising speed and thrusting it in the direction of the voice. In that instant I could see who had spoken and much else besides: the man was short, fair, and clearly startled by resistance, since he held a bow fitted with an arrow aimed directly at the heart. Moreover, he was wearing a homespun tunic of Lincoln Green, and I saw at once that he was the man I had confused earlier with my pursuer. All this fell into place in the space of a few heartbeats, between the leper's futile lunge with the knife, my shouting "look out!", and the thrum of the bow string at it launched the arrow into its target.

A man does not die from an arrow wound all at once unless he is lucky. From where I lay propped up on my hands I could see the stumps of his fingers clutching the ground beside him, digging down into the earth, and his lips drawn backward over clenched teeth. He twitched like a pinned moth, jerking in a horrible parody of his earlier lust, until his last breath left him in a great cough and a bubble of blood. The archer was looking down at the body in astonishment and what seemed to be regret. His feet were still planted in battle stance, but the bow had slipped unnoticed to his side. "Why did he do it?" he asked, of no one in particular. He used Saxon speech, made harsher by emotion. "He could see it was no use. I had him covered."

The throng of feelings pressing down on my soul and senses left no room for pity for the dead. I had pulled myself up to where I knelt, shivering violently, with my arms wrapped around me. I could not speak, even when he asked me, "Are you all right?" as kindly as if he were my father. For all that he was clean and whole, I could not answer him, but could only hug myself and rock and shake wretchedly, like a demented being. Which, in a way, I suppose I was.

Leprosy is a bitter affliction; I know that. *The Lord shall make the pestilence cleave unto thee, until He have consumed thee from off the land* . . . Much later, Father Tuck tried to make me see that it is not merely the disease itself, horrible as that is, which can shrivel a man's soul as it numbs and corrupts his flesh. To be a leper is a sorrow that cannot be lessened by sharing. He invited me to imagine how it would be to excite terror and revulsion in every sentient being one met, to be forced to warn off longed-for society with a bell, to live under the constant suspicion — one's own, as well as the world's — of meriting such ghastly punishment through some grievous sin. He himself would not speculate as to whether the sickness was the consequence of wrongdoing, saying only that, Job-like, one must bear it and thereby find a portal to eternal salvation.

I heard this and honoured it in my

mind, but it could not touch that part of me, buried deep, that the experience had transformed forever. In Fontevrault, the nuns used to say that Evil had a smiling countenance, a bland, enticing exterior, the apple that masks the worm. I was ready enough to believe it, after Bertrand de Born, but since that day in the forest, Evil, or whatever it is that dwells in the darkness and feeds on the misery of man, has had that leper's face. Tuck has said I am guilty of confusing ugliness with sin and virtue with beauty, like most of humanity, but it goes deeper than that. I know it took a long time for my body to feel clean of it. I'm not sure my spirit ever has.

All this came afterwards. Then I was numb with physical exhaustion and shock, and the great weariness which follows extremes of emotion. My rescuer was eyeing me speculatively. "Are you all right?" he asked again, this time in rough French.

I nodded. Even this was a great effort.

"Poor child," he said, though he was not that much older than I. "It's over now. No one will hurt you." He said

259

it soothingly, rather as one talks to a frightened horse. Then he bent over and put his hand under my arm to lift me to my feet.

I jerked away. I couldn't help myself; I couldn't bear anyone's touch, not for the moment at least. To make up for this rudeness I pulled myself together a little and spoke to him. "I'm sorry." My whisper cracked shamefully, half aloud, and I drew a breath to speak again. "I haven't thanked you. How did you know — how did you find me?"

"I found a horse." His plain, matter-of-fact tone was somehow immensely comforting. "It's lame, and I thought the rider might be injured. I followed your trail, and when I was below, in the thicket, I heard you cry out. Can you stand now, do you think?" He held out his hand as if it were an olive branch, and this time I took it. I was still shaking a little.

He looked at me a moment and seemed to hesitate before he spoke. "I have — friends — near here," he said slowly. "You should have rest and some healing herbs, I think, and then we can see you on your way to wherever you are going."

I thought I must have misunderstood him. We were in the deep forest, far from paths or the dwellings of any but wolves or other wood animals. Even the Forest Law might not extend so far. All about us was a tangle of undergrowth and grasses; the most solitary hermit would not choose such a place. However, I did not want to offend him, after his kindness. And besides, I could not find my way out by myself.

"I'm surprised to hear there is a house so far in Sherwood," I said carefully, "but if your lord and lady will help me — "

He laughed then, not cruelly, but with genuine amusement. "Never mind," he said at last. "It's not your fault if you know nothing. There is no house, but we can offer you shelter, and I give you my word there is nothing to fear. Will you come with me?"

My wits, which had virtually deserted me throughout this entire ordeal, began slowly to revive. I had not previously asked myself what a man would be doing in the middle of the forest armed against custom and the law with a bow, and obviously familiar with its ways. If he had been a verderer or bailiff's man he would have said so. That he was not nobly born was demonstrable in his French as well as in his appearance, yet he did not trouble himself with deference or any of the conventional courtesies which smooth the meetings of the high and the low. No doubt he was a hunter, and probably as outside the law as the man he had saved me from. I did not, in my exhausted state, find this particularly alarming, though I retained just enough presence of mind to resolve not to give him my real name and destination, in case he was more than a simple poacher. I did not want to be held for ransom; what I really needed was to get back to Geron and the others at the road. I said I would go with him but that first I needed to wash off the pollution in some pool no one drank from. "I'll burn my clothes afterwards, but in the meantime I must at least find water."

He looked down quickly at his hand, the one he had helped me up with. To his credit, he tried to hide the action when he saw me notice it. I didn't blame him. Lepers may touch nothing in a market place except with a long staff or rod, and are forbidden to wash even their possessions in a common stream. My attacker had rubbed himself and his clothing all over me, enough to infect me many times over, if God so willed. The thought made my flesh crawl on my bones.

The pool, when we reached it, was shallow and a little brackish in spots, but I submerged myself clothes and all, from my scalp to my feet. I did not care that I now smelled damp and a little brackish myself, or think what I must look like. I felt better. The ineffable worst had already occurred, and I felt more cheerful about what was to come. While I sat beside the water in a patch of sunlight, I sketched for my rescuer — who said his name was John — the details of the ambush as I had seen it. I told him we had set out with a small party from Nottingham with some goods for Newstead Priory, where we were to lie over on our way to visit my sister and her husband at Blyth. I also said my name

263

was Marie, which was similar enough to Marian so that I would remember to respond. As a lie it was not bad, being both hard to refute and calculated not to excite much interest in myself or my party. I added that the best thing would undoubtedly be to find Geron and get back to Nottingham as quickly as possible.

"Yes, you're right," he said abstractedly, not meeting my eyes. "I'll see someone goes to the road, don't worry. But come with me now. You're not in fit shape to cope with what's happened there, not till you've rested and eaten a bit and finished drying off." He gestured toward the distant trees, from which we had come. "I'll have to see he's buried too, before the animals get him. It's all we can do right now. Later, maybe, some holy man will say a prayer for his soul."

As before, I thought his voice was tinged with pity and regret. I had not thought of burial and had walked away from the stiffening body with no desire other than to put it behind me forever. So much for my training at Fontevrault, for years of kneeling for divine offices, for the lessons of the saints and the exhortations to charity and virtue. I was ashamed to note how little of it had actually grafted itself onto my character.

* * *

"Wait here," he said at last, when we had walked what felt like the entire length of Sherwood. My damp clothes dragged at my progress, as did the dry brush, however much it crumbled to the touch. I was too tired to go much farther in any case, and sat on the ground without ceremony, my back against an oak. The roots pressed up under my thighs but I was too weary to shift position. I was also hopelessly befuddled as to my whereabouts, a fact not lost, I'm sure, on my guide. I watched him disappear into a coppice with a contentment born of resignation and John's own comfortable ways. He made no more demands than an old shoe, and he was plain and straightforward by nature rather than design. He used none of the short man's exaggerated gestures of bravado, though he was no more than a hair's breadth taller than I. In all, it did not seem unreasonable to leave my immediate future safely in his hands. I moved against the knots and boles pressing insistently into my body and tried to get comfortable. In a few moments I was nearly asleep.

After a while, I heard him coming back. Heard, rather than saw; he was speaking in the native tongue with someone else, and I was the subject of the conversation.

"Good God, John," the strange voice said. "She looks terrible. I thought you said she was nobly born."

"The horse had a rich saddle, I tell you, and her clothes were good, before all this. Remember, she's had a hard time of it. He beat her too. Besides, she doesn't speak a word of Saxon. I tried already."

I had forgotten that my face would be swollen and bruising from the blows. How bedraggled my clothing and hair must look defied imagination. It was all I could do not to put a hand to my head in dismay, but I remained motionless, eyes shut. I had no scruples

266

about continuing to pretend ignorance of English. I needed to learn whatever I could, to protect myself.

I heard their footsteps stop a few feet away from me. I knew how a sheep must feel when the dog approaches. I said, "Oh, I must have fallen asleep," and opened my eyes. I was looking up directly into the eyes of the stranger. They were grey, very clear, and very much alive.

I suppose he was handsome. He was not especially tall, except by comparison with John, but he was broad-shouldered and fit looking in the way of knights rather than of peasants. His hair was brown and straight, and his face, not surprisingly, was darkened by the sun. He frowned slightly, and when he became aware of my notice, his expression became closed and wary.

"What's your name?" he asked peremptorily. It was not the French of France but of England, but it was very good.

I told him the same fiction I had given John. His expression changed not one bit, and I had the disquieting notion he realized full well I had lied to him.

267

His disbelief stung me, as if I had been truthful with him in the first place.

"What's yours?" I asked, a trifle rudely.

I was not prepared for his answer.

"Robin Hood."

"Don't be ridiculous."

The eyes widened just a fraction.

"That's not a real name," I insisted.

"You've heard of me then?" The voice was smooth enough, but I knew he was laughing at me.

I must explain.

Whatever men say now, and they say much more than they know, at that time 'Robin Hood' was a name for hearth tales and twilight, a faery — or 'wood-wose,' to use the old word — who lived in the heart of the wood guarding the shrines of the Old Gods. Once these were banished by Christianity he had lost his power to do ill or good and faded to no more than a sigh in the tree boughs or a riffle of wind at the water's edge. He was said to go about in a green cloak and hood, and to be an expert at hiding. As I have said, Sherwood was full of such stories. Every village could boast a grandfather who claimed to have met him in some lonely way, though it was bad luck to go seeking or to spy. Most often he was described as withered and brown as carved oak, and he could change his shape at will, as all the First People are said to do.

Nevertheless I could not quite believe this was the being who had just introduced himself. "I'd imagined you as older, somehow," I told him.

As before, I had the sense that he saw through my words to my thought. There was an unmistakable flash of amusement beneath the mask as well. "You're right, of course. But if the wood-wose minds my borrowing his identity he hasn't let me know." He looked at me intently. "The outside world seldom comes visiting, to remind us of our old lives. Here in Sherwood, everything can be made new, even names. I'm sure you know that."

So he did know. And he had something to hide himself. It was no more than I had expected, and I was suddenly very tired of banter. I made an effort, hampered by exhaustion and stiff legs, to stand up. The tree supported me obligingly. "John said you would help me find my way back to my travelling party. If someone could bring my horse, I think we should be going. My stew — my friends will be very worried."

A look — whose meaning I could not decipher — passed between them. It was John who answered me. "Your horse is lame, miss. We'll have to lead him back. Your friends will have gone back to Nottingham, so we'd best be heading in that direction to meet up with them. I promise you," he added, in response to my look of dismay, "there is no one left on the road who needs you. We sent someone out to check."

It would take far too long to walk the horse back; Geron would be frantic by now. "Couldn't you lend me a horse?" I asked him. "Then perhaps you could lead my own back later? I'd pay you for your trouble, of course."

The man who called himself Robin Hood laughed. "We don't keep a stable here, Myrtille."

"Marie."

"Ah yes. And we will conduct you and your horse back out of kindness and charity. We do not want your money."

"I'm sorry," I said, and blushed, annoyed that he had made me feel defensive and apologetic.

"Gently, Robin," John said in the Saxon tongue. "She meant no harm. Remember what she's been through."

"I know." The man sighed and closed his eyes, as if he were withdrawing into some private world of pain and shutting out the visible one at the same time. It made me wonder, again, what had brought him to Sherwood. I would sooner have bitten off my tongue than ask him. "She's harmless enough," he said to John. "Now where in God's name is that betony brew?"

An old woman appeared with the mixture, which had been heated over some fire I could not see or smell. I was startled to see a woman there, a part of what was obviously some larger camp. She pressed the crude drinking vessel into my hands without a word. The odour of betony curled up with the steam, pungent and healing. In Fontevrault we used it in poultices on wounds; dried and steeped in wine or water it was the sovereign remedy for everything from headaches to hysteria. The infirmarian said it would even cure fear, if one could manage to take it 'when the fear came'. The smell of it now was homey and comforting; the old woman watched me drink deep then nodded, content. I thanked her, which she appeared not to notice, but when Robin spoke to her she preened herself like an ancient cat, stiff in her dignity, but enjoying the attention. I was reminded of the way some of the very old nuns turned girlish in the presence of a young priest in the confessional. I shook my head to clear it; the comparison was ridiculous. Some memory touched me then, prickly and insistent, but so faint I lost it.

"Well," said John, when I had drained the cup, "if you are rested enough, it's time to be moving on."

★ ★ ★

Dun Crump was clearly sulking. His expression, if that term can be used for a horse, suggested that he had endured quite enough; first the attack on the road, the wild ride and his fall, and then his laming and rough handling by strangers with hard hands. His own groom, some hay, and a warm stable would soon set him to rights, but like me, he would have to wait a while for his comforts.

John and I parted with Robin on the edge of the forest clearing. They had, after all, found me an animal, a broken-down pack horse which even the wolves might have scorned to make a meal of. The trip would take as long as walking, but at least my feet would be spared. Dun Crump simply twitched his tail and lowered his head as if overcome by the shame of having to limp along behind such company. Perhaps he really did think he was a jennet.

"You can be there by nightfall," Robin said, "or a little after. It's not so far if you know the forest."

"Thank you for helping me," I told him, since he seemed to be in command. "If there is anything at all I can do . . . "

The wary, distancing mask settled itself on his face again. Then his eyes met John's in that now-familiar excluding look. "There is nothing, but it would be best if you don't tell anyone what you've seen here."

I was about to say that I had seen precious little and was not likely to boast of meeting someone who called himself 'Robin Hood' in the woods.

"And please don't try to come back here." It was as abrupt and effective a dismissal as any of the Queen's. He began to walk away.

"Why on earth should I want to?" I flung back at him, stung.

But after all, he was serious. "Make sure she doesn't know the way," he added to John, in English, and then he returned into the forest.

John looked at me in dismay. The other man's meaning, even without translation, had been distressingly clear. "Why is it so important to him?" I asked. "I'm hardly likely to come back to some outlaw camp. That's what it is, isn't it? An outlaw camp?"

"Yes," he said quietly, helping me to mount my horse, "that's what it is."

"So you live by taking illegal game and robbing innocent travellers." I regretted this at once, after all he had done for me, especially when the barb was not really meant for him at all.

He gave me a steady, level look which shamed me further. "We live as we can. And not always by our own choice."

"I'm sorry," I said, and meant it. "I wonder" — I floated the words out gently like a fishing line — "what *he* did to get himself outlawed."

This was not the manor fish pond. John said nothing.

"Did he kill someone?"

He glanced back with reproach. "I'll not tell you that."

"It must have been serious," I persisted.

He turned full around to look at me. "Of course it was serious. What do you think it means, to be cut off from everything that meant anything in your old life? Do you think that happens for nothing?"

There was nothing to say to this, so we rode along in silence for a while. After a time I ventured, "Are you — were you — from around here?"

"From Hathersage," he answered shortly.

"Then how did you — " I stopped before I asked it. His whole manner

275

clearly discouraged such prying.

Surprisingly, he finished the unspoken question. "How did I get here, you mean?" The path had narrowed so that the horses could only travel single file; I couldn't see his face. His voice floated back to me, disembodied but hoarse with emotion. "I chose it, that's what I did. I brought it on myself."

I waited like a child who has been promised a bedtime story. "I never took much to ploughing and planting and the rest of the life I was born to. And then . . . well, you'll have noticed that I am short for a man? My mother's husband was very tall."

"Oh."

"There was nothing proved, mind you, but they took against me just the same. Anyway, I was — am — handy with the bow. I practised until I was good enough to enter service. By this and by that I found work with a forester, but he was as rotten as an oak before it falls, may the maggots eat him. He tried to use me to cheat an innocent man of his land and estate, but the fool almost got himself killed instead. That was when I met Robin and pledged myself to him, as his man."

"'Robin?'"

"Oh yes. It's not his Christian name of course, but he went by it when he was a little boy. That gave him the idea in the first place."

"But why would you join up with an outlaw, or stay with him if you don't have to?" I asked him. "The Sheriff of Nottingham will always take archers. He's an honest man and would not hold whatever the forester did against you. Besides, it's not as if this Robin Hood can offer you anything like protection or an honourable future. Why cast away the world for someone who's done God-knows-what terrible thing?"

His voice, when he finally answered, sounded amused, though I found myself incensed on his behalf. For some reason it irritated me that the man in the wood could give so little and command so much. There was no mistaking the intensity of John's feeling, though it was of the woman-excluding, you-wouldn't-understand variety. He said: "A man like me needs a good lord, Marie, just the way a woman needs a good husband. The trick for both is in finding one."

"And did you?"

"Oh yes. I'd not leave him lightly, not even to get out of here."

"I don't understand."

"I didn't think you would," he said, with satisfaction.

"But," I persisted, "he's hardly a 'lord' in any sense, and even if you don't leave him, what service can you do him? Apart from the odd illegal deer, that is."

I heard rather than saw his smile. "I've already told you you don't know everything. But I will tell you this: he has been injured unfairly, and I want to help him get his rights. And now we are entering a part of the forest where it is far safer to listen than to talk."

That put an effective end to conversation, as it was no doubt meant to do. In fact I was so exhausted it was less trouble to ride in silence. Towards the end of the journey I had to struggle just to stay on the horse, which bumped and plodded along in the near darkness. It seemed impossible that the sun had not yet set on the day on which I had started out from Nottingham full of anticipation and high spirits. Enough had happened to fill a lifetime of nightmares, and I felt the soreness of it in every part of my body and mind.

The castle perched above us like a beacon, still tipped in sunlight.

"I have to leave you here," he said, dismounting in the deep shadows of the last stand of trees before the town. I had a glimpse, for a moment, of what it really meant to live outside the law, beyond the pale in the most literal sense. "It's not full dark yet. They'll still let you in the gates. Just follow the path. You'll be all right."

I took Dun Crump's reins from his grip and turned to thank him. I thought his fingers trembled a little when our hands touched and his eyes looked away from me. For the first time in that very long day, he behaved as if he took some notice of the social distinction between us. "Tell the Sheriff where the ambush took place," he said wearily. "He should send men out right away, if he hasn't had the news already."

"Won't he find your camp then?"

"No," he said with grim certainty. "He won't find us. But don't pin your hopes on catching that renegade band of lepers, either. They'll be miles off by now, and the forest is a big place to hide in."

He sounded as if he spoke from bitter experience.

"If there's anything I can do," I began, wanting to touch him in the warmth of my gratitude but not daring to. A moment before I would have done it, but not now. "Money, or anything you need. I know *he* said you didn't want any, but I'd like to make things more comfortable for you, if I can. My steward could arrange something, since you don't want any talk. He'll be grateful too. He must be dreadfully worried — he hasn't seen me since I bolted from him on the road."

"Your steward? Your steward was with you on the road?" His look was hot and troubled and made my muscles tense, just when I was so near to safety. I realized I had inadvertently revealed that my rank was higher than I'd let on, but I hadn't imagined he would react with such surprise. I wondered if I had misjudged him.

"He is dear to you, this man?"

His gentleness set my teeth on edge with premonition. When I answered him I seemed to be shaping the words out of cold clay. "He is all that is left of my family."

His strong hand slid under my elbow to steady me. "My poor child." He cleared his throat. "They were all killed in the ambush."

I stared at him, stricken.

"We didn't want to tell you, because you had already been through so much." His grip on my arm tightened. "Do you . . . is there someone? Some guardian or friend to look out for your safety? I would not have you go into Nottingham unprotected."

My mind seemed to take a very long time to consider his question. Then the answer emerged slowly, like a shape in the mists. I nodded, finally. "Yes, there is . . . someone . . . I can turn to."

He peered into my face. It was now nearly dark and I would have to go at once or spend the night in the forest, a prospect which filled me with such horror that I almost ran from him then and there.

"You're sure?" he asked me.

"Yes," I told him, and he released his hold on my arm. I left him and led Dun Crump by the path to the Nottingham gate.

* * *

Much later, after hours of partial explanations and outright lies, and of dodging a battery of pointed questions, I bundled all my clothing from gloves to the skin into a pile and burned it in secret. I am sure I do not need to explain why I did not reveal my intimate contact with one of the lepers, nor why I stole from the ladies' dorter to the hearth in the still hours between Matins and Lauds to accomplish the purification. I had cut my hair and scalded my flesh with near boiling water as well. The burning was ashy and incomplete and made a quantity of fibrous refuse. I had to poke and prod for quite a while to finish the process. The flames held all the images I was trying so hard to banish from my thoughts. Leisure is the enemy of forgetfulness. Geron's face floated before me in the darkness. John had been wrong; not everyone had been killed in the ambush. One of Guy's huntsmen had escaped and returned to Nottingham, so the Sheriff had sent his men out while I was taking the roundabout route back from the outlaw camp. All they had found was the bodies, picked clean even of their clothes. They tracked the lepers a little way into the forest, and then they lost the trail. Tomorrow, or as soon as I was mended, I would have to go back to Blidworth to give the news to Geron's wife and daughters.

I had never felt so alone. Now that Geron was gone, there was no one left in my life — excepting a handful of servants — whom I had known no more than a few months, and no one I could trust with certainty. I had severed my ties with Fontevrault in favour of moving into a greater world, in which I was now visibly floundering without friends or family or purpose, and my social position (though only I realized it) was founded on a blatant fraud. I had not come to terms with the ambivalent distinction of bastardy and royal parentage, and my inclination to defy other people's wishes for me had not brought me happiness or success. Besides, I had come to the point in my life when I wanted permanent bonds and alliances. I was tired of depending on the gifts and directions of others.

I remembered in time that it is easiest to fall into the sin of *accidie*, a kind of despairing sickness of the soul, in the bleak hours between night and morning, and went at last to bed.

Not long after this, after Geron and the others were buried, I plighted my troth on the porch of St Mary's Church, Nottingham, to Guy of Gisborne. The Sheriff looked on beaming, and had the good grace not to gloat.

7

MARRIAGE, unlike love, is a serious business. By the time the couple crushes the strewn flowers beneath their feet and dodges the handfuls of grain on the way home from the church, as much haggling has taken place as at a lifetime of Goose Fairs. The union of propertied principals is like a treaty between hostile kingdoms, except that the terms are more lasting. Every possibility must be provided for in the disposition of the estates, and if a man wants to recover his liberty between the betrothal and the marriage, he has to forfeit four times his initial deposit in penalty. Women are not supposed to succeed in extricating themselves from the arrangements unless they are very rich. The entire matrimonial process is ponderous, legalistic, and discouraging of passion, a fact long ago noted and codified by Andreas the Chaplain and Countess Marie in their treatise on Love.

Tell all this over twice on the fingers of your hands and you will have some idea of what is involved when one or both of the parties is royal. The negotiations lurch and lumber along with all the speed of a cart on a muddy track, and a lot can happen — death, war, or, as in the case of Alais Capet, loss of that spotless condition so desirable in queens — before the union is actually sealed.

That is why the King of England's marriage was so remarkable, even more because he had so little to do with the arrangements. In a space of time more suitable for opening the discussions, Queen Eleanor had overturned the Capet betrothal of years standing, found her son a reasonably suitable bride, and seen the marriage performed and consummated. By May, England had a new Queen, Berengaria of Navarre.

Scarcely anyone is so naive as to wonder how Eleanor managed to get news sooner than other people. But news, early or late, trickles down eventually and explained much of her haste in getting her son married. The Crusade was not going well. The English contingent in advance of the King had settled down before the walls of Acre to suffer epidemics and a slaughter so terrible the local river ran for a week with blood and lumps of flesh. Meanwhile the travelling monarchs, Richard and Philip, had begun to quarrel bitterly. The threats grew ugly and dangerous.

And then, soon after he arrived in Sicily, Richard began acting strangely. With the Plantagenet penchant for gestures worthy of a miracle play, he proceeded to indulge himself in an orgy of repentance. He appeared before the bishops and archbishops assembled for the feast of Christmas and regaled them with lurid and (reputedly) specific details of his unholy lusts. Moreover, he was kneeling and dressed only in a piece of sackcloth around his loins. It is not difficult to imagine the sensation this created among his variously shocked and titillated audience; however short-lived his contrition, rumour of it must have reached England and Eleanor with the first sailing. There is no news so dreadful that someone doesn't want to be first with it.

After Richard's 'confession', Eleanor made her move. Whether or not he would now be more receptive to taking a wife, she could not go wrong in chancing her arm. Prince John and Longchamp were splitting England into two administrative camps, each briskly accruing power. The King needed a son, a firm, uncontested heir. Then too, the alliance between Navarre and Toulouse was very good for the Aquitaine. Eleanor's vision was wide as an eagle's, and just as sharp.

The wedding took place in a small chapel in Limassol, Cyprus, after so many delays that there were already whispers about the bride's compromised virginity, at least among those to whom the groom was a stranger. I never heard much about the ceremony — whether Richard dressed with his usual splendour, or if the bride looked radiant behind her veil. No matter; the bells pealed throughout England in honour of our new Queen, while the old one savoured her triumph and settled back to wait for her labours to bear fruit. Like most meddlers, she was not prepared for disappointment, and no one could have been more amazed when her son went back to war without getting his wife with child. No doubt if she could, she would have climbed into his bed and accomplished that for him too.

My own path to matrimony was smoother than the King's, with just one bump along the way. I wanted Father Tuck to say Mass and bless our marriage, but Guy wouldn't hear of it. The Abbot of St Mary's, York, had already consented to take part. I disliked him on sight when he came down to Nottingham to see the Sheriff on business. He was unctuous as chrism and worldly, his hands weighted down with ruby rings and one gigantic beryl. Worst of all, he was condescending. He had a reputation for a sharp eye for the abbey finances and a hard hand with his tenants. I could well believe it. I told Guy I understood why we could not spurn his blessing or his participation, but that I wanted Father Tuck as well. He refused, insisting that the Abbot would be insulted. I had not yet learned to avoid battles I couldn't hope to win; still, it was our first argument, and I lost it.

Guy was not much at Nottingham

during the period of our betrothal, as he had left his Yorkshire properties a long time unattended. There is no bailiff or steward so conscientious or honest, he said, that he won't take advantage of his master's absence. When he was in Nottinghamshire, he was all civility and attentiveness. He brought me gloves stitched of the softest deerskin from a doe he had killed himself. He gave me a mirror, cunningly wrought in the shape of a water hyacinth so that one seemed to be looking in the depths of a tiny pool. It had come from Constantinople by way of France. These favours, his face, and his fortune made me the envy of the other ladies lodged at Nottingham, and this went a long way towards making me content with my lot.

Anyone — that is, anyone but the highest and the lowest, who often know their life's partners from the age of swaddling bands and knuckle-bones — will understand what I mean when I say that I scarcely knew my husband when I married him. We went through the days of feasting like two carvings on the cathedral tympanum, forever turned outward in greeting. The celebration is an ordeal of exposure and a torment to the stomach: the Sheriff, in his last act as my guardian, spared no expense from my estate to provide the most exquisite foodstuffs available. We had stewed lampreys, a real delicacy little to my liking, and a roast of pork basted on the spit and served with garlic sauce. This was followed by chicken in cardamom and a custard tart with dried figs, imported dates, and marrow meat. For the sweet course, there was a concoction of crushed rose petals and ground almonds, and simpler, lighter honey cakes.

The henap, an expensive wine cup with a cover, passed from hand to hand. I scarcely looked at Guy when he served me, so I could not tell what he was thinking. Drink, even in the form of spiced wine, took its toll along with the food, and by the late afternoon there were few without headaches and drooping eyelids. In addition the room was stuffy and stale, and so were the jokes about the wedding night to come. We left singly to change or wash on occasion, so as not to leave our guests unattended. I very early abandoned my wedding finery for more practical clothes, and as the rushes grew ranker and the tables greasier my hems and elbows suffered accordingly.

All this gave as little clue to Guy's feelings and character as my own conduct did to mine. Perhaps all the rituals are meant to pacify and soothe, so that one is lulled into confidence about life as a couple. Or possible it is only numbness and exhaustion that make the prospect of a return to normality so desirable. I only know that when the friends of the groom led him to our borrowed bedchamber — where my deputed attendants had undressed me and arranged me in the great bed like the prized sweetmeat of the end of the feast — and when they withdrew laughing over the coarsest and oldest of jokes, the door closed me in with a near-total stranger.

★ ★ ★

I was almost too tired to care. Guy, it seemed, was drunk.

292

Far from dulling him, it gave him a glittering edge like a sword, and made him look more than a little dangerous. He slipped out of his surcoat with feline grace and cast it, on the tip of his finger, across the room. It landed with eerie accuracy upon the clothes peg. He grinned, lurching a little, hands on hips.

I pulled the covers up around my chin.

No woman who grows up in a knight's household is innocent of the sight of naked manhood, even aroused manhood. But it is quite different when the lance is pointed at your virginity, ready to press a lifetime seal on the marital union. In the face of that, I defy anyone to debate the virtues of the sweet solaces of the upper parts (*superior to that of the brute beast*) versus the delights of the lower parts (*at which all lovers chiefly aim*), as the knight and lady do in Andreas the Chaplain's little book. In fact, at that moment, wit and banter were the farthest thing from my mind.

Guy wasn't laughing either. He pulled the covers away and raised up my shift with a speed that left me breathless with nerves. His fingers pressed into the flesh of my upper arms and his knee forced an opening between my thighs. "Are you ready now?" he asked, shifting his weight to his elbows.

I closed my eyes. I knew what he was going to do, but I had no idea what it would be like. How did I feel? Mostly curious, and a little afraid. This would be a part of my life from now on, so there was no point in shrinking from it. I think I knew even then that while Guy would accept my shyness he would not tolerate a reluctance stemming from anything more than that. I would not risk a blow to his considerable pride and vanity. I tried to smile. The heat of Passion, the carnal frenzy that Tristan and Iseult or Lancelot and Guinevere had wrecked kingdoms for, was totally beyond my imagination.

"Cheer up," his voice said in my ear. "You'll get used to it."

I don't know what I expected, but it wasn't this relentless jousting. He battered me hard and fast, despite my body's lack of co-operation. I couldn't help it; the target was too small. I tried not to go rigid as a board and bit down on my lip to keep from crying out. He bit me too, about the neck and breasts. Finally he groaned and stopped thrusting, still half inside my body. The linen chafed against my back and the bed hangings closed in all our scents: of stale wine, of sweat, of blood and the nether fluids. I didn't move until he got up to use the nightjar.

He came back presently and looked into my face. I don't know what he saw there in the dim light. "All right, then?" he asked.

I nodded, unable to speak. Guy patted my shoulder and then turned matter-of-factly on his side, pulling the linen over his head with a sigh. In a little while he seemed to be asleep.

It hurt, but I had expected that. Probably he was rougher than he had intended. I had discovered that Guy was an aggressive man, coiled tight inside with his desires and ambitions. His ardour was quick and combative, as if he wore armour even for this trysting. His passion, if you could call it that, had spent itself briskly; my own had not even begun to mount. I minded most that there had been no amorous wooing; I felt mastered and overcome. Worse, I had not even a shred of privacy left. And then, at the bottom of everything, lay the nagging question, persistent but unwelcome: *is that all?*

The sounds of the feasting continued to rise up from below, threaded by the sweet notes of the harp and vielle. It seemed impossible that the world could go on, unchanged and incurious, when my life had so altered. I got up and blew out the bed candle, and ended my first day as a wife.

★ ★ ★

The tree branches were dark and grasping, tearing at my clothes like beggars pursuing a coin. It grew dimmer and hotter, though the boughs groaned and shrieked in an invisible wind. I ran on until my feet were leaden and heavy as the air, sinking into a ground thick with old leaves which smelled like death. His breath was hot on my shoulders, his spittle burned where it touched my skin.

The eyes were yellow and lambent with unholy flame.

The wolf growled, his teeth bared, his tail wrapping his belly. I turned. I could see his fur, matted with dirt, and his mouth open to take my life. He leapt . . .

★ ★ ★

Guy was shaking my shoulder. I woke up oak-headed and confused, with a vile taste in my mouth. The linen felt moist and salty. I had a hard time remembering where I was.

"Are you all right?" Guy asked me. "You were shrieking like the screaming skull."

I remembered now. I pulled the coverlet over my breasts, which were exposed. My husband pulled it down again. "You're sweating, too. Are you sick?" His concern sounded overlaid with mild distaste. I could not blame him too much. Our first morning together had not begun auspiciously, and one never knows what one is getting.

"No," I told him. "I just had a bad dream."

His finger circled my breast absent-mindedly. I looked away in embarrassment, but the nipple swelled and grew warm of its own accord.

"What was it?" he asked.

I shrugged, which was difficult under the circumstances. "I was running through the forest. I couldn't get away. It caught me, just at the end."

The stroking was becoming more insistent. I arched my back in spite of myself.

"What caught you?" he asked languidly.

My breath was shortening. "A wolf. Ouch!" His hand came down and slapped my thigh playfully, but it stung. "Why are you laughing?"

He propped himself up on an elbow and looked at me as if I'd told a very good joke, which I found annoying. He wouldn't explain, so I asked him, "What's a screaming skull, then?"

His hand stilled. "Not 'a', 'the'. There's only one that I know of, please God." He laughed again, a little maliciously. "You'll meet it soon enough, when you come to Gisborne. It's one of the family, *your* family now." He poked me in a tender place. "Whoever it was was buried in the root cellar at Gisborne, and when they tried to dig up the body in my grandfather's day the skull shrieked bloody murder every night till they put it back. I imagine it feels at home there."

I felt a chill and shivered a little.

"Oh, did you like that?" His hands had grown busy again. It was some time before we descended to breakfast and our waiting guests.

★ ★ ★

Far from making me a rich woman, my marriage made me dependent and powerless. I had already lost some of my continental holdings as a fee to the crown for inheriting any land at all, and now Guy would take over Blidworth in my name. My dower lands, which I received after the consummation, were meagre; it seems the Sheriff had not bargained particularly well on my behalf. Widowed, I would also get Locksley Hall, if the King or someone else didn't get it first. The royal need for revenue made future calculations impossible. William Longchamp was now exercising taxation and confiscation functions on behalf of the crown, but it was widely believed that most of what was taken went into his own coffers. The shrieks of protest could be heard from one end of the country to the other.

After the wedding feast, we set out for Locksley again, with a large party of our retainers to escort us on the road. The forest was said to be more dangerous than ever. The Sheriff, Guy said, had been disturbed by reports of an organized outlaw band, an actual community sprung up within Sherwood. I held my tongue, pinned by an unwilling loyalty to my rescuers.

We assembled within the walls of Nottingham before we left by the postern gate. I was seated on Dun Crump, having paid my respects to the Sheriff and his lady, and the women who had befriended my marriage. It felt like I was leaving my last refuge, but of course I had quit that long ago. Possibly I was dazed with excitement and the usual fatigue which plagues a newly wedded wife, or I might have noticed sooner. Guy's retinue was tricked out in his livery. I had seen it before, I must have, but I hadn't remembered. The device of the house of Gisborne was a rampant wolf.

8

LOCKSLEY HALL, half castle and half manor house, lay so deep in the forest the woods looked blue, even in the morning light. The stone had been carried from the north in hide slings in Great William's day and now it was blurred and mellowed with age. Wild honeysuckle grew with unkempt vigour around the outer walls, descendant of some decades-old escape from the garden. The wooden towers of the inner house, the living quarters, peeped over the pale. The handful of wattle and daub cottages, where the villeins lived, looked clean and rather better than the dismal ones in Nottingham. It is strange that they should now be all that is left. Some lizards live there, dragging their bellies over the ruined walls, and barn owls hoot from the foundations, scaring up mice and sparrows from the ivy. For a long time, that was all. The malice that destroyed Locksley fired the cottages too, but the rain came before they burned. So they stand, still.

Memory paints a sweet picture for me, layered by time: my bees buzzing in the hawthorn bushes, the orchards ripening in the richness of summer, the herb garden of plants grown from seeds I had brought from the monastery garden in Fontevrault. I never think of it rimed with frost. The fire warms the hearth beneath the blackened rafters, the incense burns sweet in the chapel, the sun shines still into the solar at the very tops of the trees. It is hard now to see it as it must have been on that very first day, when I came as the bride of Guy of Gisborne.

Much clearer, sharp and edged with brightness, is the memory of my first meeting with Guy's mother, Lady Iseult. She was standing alone at the end of the hall as we entered, with her back to the arras. Her mouth was smiling but her eyes were not. "I prayed for your safe journey," she said over my head to Guy. "You should have sent someone ahead to warn me, so all would have been prepared. Cook had planned your favourite dishes . . . " Her eyes found me then, as if for the first time, though I had felt them piercing me when my feet had crossed — too loudly — the empty hall. "Welcome, my dear, to your new home."

I knelt and made obeisance to her, though I was not obliged to. I saw surprise flicker over her face, then calculation. I'm sure she hoped to find me biddable, just as I hoped to find her kindly and unmeddlesome. We were both destined to disappointment.

The blue silk of her surcoat rustled softly as she extended her arms toward her son. He extended his as well, taking her by the elbows and leaning forward to peck her cheek, thereby avoiding her full embrace. A lifetime in a small gesture. I thought I saw anxiety in her eyes, and the dregs of bitterness. Guy hurried on, saying that the servants would make a mess of the unpacking if he left them unsupervised. I wanted to remind him to have a care with my books, but I knew that everything I said was being judged to a feather's weight and I couldn't make even that small assertion.

Lady Iseult's attention returned to me.

"You'll want to wash and to rest after your journey. Guy says you're to have the best solar. Follow me, and I'll show you where it is." Her tone told me she had occupied it before me.

"If that's inconvenient for you, I'm sure we'll be happy in another room," I told her.

"Oh no. Guy was very particular about what he wanted. Besides, *I* don't mind where I sleep." She looked at me with satisfaction. She had managed, quite subtly, to put me in the wrong.

The solar was lovely, with more windows than usual, opening into the trees almost at the level of the birds. It gave light and privacy at the same time, at least in the months it was not shuttered against the cold. The hangings were from France — a hunting scene, masculine but attractive. In the corner was a perch for hawks and falcons, a common practice where the mews would be cold and expensive. Still, it was no longer the fashion in France and I didn't like birds making messes in the bedroom.

Lady Iseult noticed the direction of my interest. "You'll be wanting to change things, I suppose. It's all right if the perch goes. It was here before we came."

Changing things, clearly, was a dangerous topic. I asked her, smiling, "What shall I call you?"

She smiled back. "Why, whatever you like. It doesn't matter to *me*. Why don't you ask Guy?"

Guy's mother was handsome enough, though the beauty that marked him was clearly not her doing. She dressed, as I have noted, richly, but not with confidence. Her finery was worn like armour against life's uncertainties. Guy's father died before she could conceive again but after he had performed the unnamed service for the Empress Maud that had elevated him to knighthood and the Gisborne estate. His widow, left with too much affection and too little imagination, had bestowed everything on their son, who spurned the gifts with an insistence just this side of rudeness.

It was not, on the whole, a promising situation for a daughter-in-law. I felt she watched me jealously for signs of her son's favourable attention and that she would only approach amity and contentment when my position with him deteriorated towards her own. In time she would become very happy indeed, but that was still in the future. Meanwhile, I waited in vain for hints that she would be leaving Locksley to return to her dower house at Gisborne. In her circumstances I would have much preferred my independence, but then I did not have a seemingly bottomless well of unrequited affection for Guy, nor did my happiness require his physical presence.

★ ★ ★

Within a short time of our arrival at Locksley, Guy disappeared 'on business'. He was vague and a little furtive about it, so I didn't question him. Though it left me to bear the full brunt of Lady Iseult's company, I was grateful for his absence. I couldn't say why, exactly, except for the bruising bouts of love-making which had become neither more tender nor more satisfying. We got along well enough, but we were still relative strangers and we needed a rest from each other's company. Besides, there was a tension, an expectancy, about my husband which infected the household while he was present, and I'm sure I was not the only one relieved by his departure.

I began to put my new life together. Next to my solar, in a curtained alcove above and behind the hall, I decided to create a work room and library, where I could do my needlework or copy from my books undisturbed. The light was good, and the room was dusty with disuse. A yew bow, slender and strong, and a pile of hauberks of varying ages were the only occupants. I set the newer ones aside and wondered fleetingly what had become of the outlawed earl who had lived here from boyhood. There was little clue to his character remaining. It seemed likely, under the circumstances, that he had crossed the seas and hired himself out for knight's service to some landed lord. That was common enough, with so many dislocations from the Crusades and revenue raising. A hard fate, but not a cruel one.

As soon as the alcove was swept bare,

I sent for my maid servant to help me arrange my possessions. Agnes always came promptly, but her reluctance to serve me seemed rooted in her bones. That puzzled me, since the position should have been prized within the household. I don't know why I liked her; the impulse was perverse. She belonged to the Hall before Guy had acquired it and maintained, I suspected, a sturdy if discreet loyalty to its lost lord. Lady Iseult, for some reason, was determined to get rid of her, which of course fuelled my sympathy. Moreover, she was the estate's responsibility, being orphaned and unmarried. A sickly childhood had left her saffron-skinned and dreadfully thin, and she had grown quite tall. She was unlikely now ever to be husbanded, and I thought she bore this quite well. Perhaps that's why she appealed to me. It certainly wasn't because of any attachment on her part. In my presence she seemed closed up and suppressed, and I felt guilty.

My 'books' were mostly middling parchment copies from the Fontevrault library I had made myself. I hadn't been allowed access to all the works, and some were off limits even to the nuns. I always brooded over those locked treasures; I still do. My own fragments were mostly from the church fathers, though I had managed to sneak in some Aristotle and Abelard, and, most precious of all, a little Ovid. So far from any centre of learning it would be very difficult to get anything more. For that matter, I couldn't envision what I would do with my little library once I had set it up. Guy could read, just; he seemed to regard having a literate wife as a creditable asset, like hair of pale gold or skill with the harp. What I feared was that in time my fragments of learning would grow soiled and spiritless as an overworked weaving, a dusty reminder of youthful zeal.

Agnes handled the parchment with care but without the undue reverence of the unlettered, which pleased me. In fact she revered little and feared less, as if life had already shown her its worst. Certainly she didn't hesitate to speak her mind. She picked up a parchment from the chest and squinted down the roll, peering at some invisible world. "Where did you get all these, my lady?"

I explained to her about Fontevrault, the abbey library, and the scriptorium. "What use are they?"

It was a question requiring the wisdom of ages, or no answer at all. I shrugged, a gesture I had learned in France. "You read them, and it gives you instruction and pleasure."

Her expression showed me how that sounded. "I don't know how to read."

"Would you like to learn? I could teach you."

"No thank you, my lady."

We worked then in silence for a while, storing the pumices and quills in compartments of the chests where they would not be damaged. When the writing things were finished I sorted out my other treasures, the family mementoes, my rosary and even one scruffy old scrap doll I had played with at Blidworth. Everything that meant anything from my old life I put in this room, except for the one object I had not yet come to terms with and which I did not dare to reveal. The chalice was secreted at Blidworth, in a hiding hole secure even from the eyes of Guy's appointed bailiff.

Agnes straightened at length with a finality which asked for, but did not demand, dismissal. It was like being waited upon by someone to whom one owes money. Her eyes fell on the yew bow in the corner, where I had placed it out of the way. She reached out a hand to touch it, a gesture which seemed both involuntary and compulsive.

I thought this might be a good moment to loosen her tongue. "Agnes," I asked her, "have you always lived at Locksley Hall?"

She jerked her hand back and looked grimmer than usual. "No, my lady. I was born on the estates at Huntingdon."

Of course. The Fitz Ooth heir to the Huntingdon earldom had grown up here. But how had it all come about? Having more than a casual interest in the story, I was determined to pry information from her. Her reaction suggested this might be difficult. "Oh yes," I responded, with devious intentions, "did you come with the outlawed Earl?"

She looked down at her feet, the equivalent in another of gazing at the horizon. She gave a barely perceptible shake of the head.

I wouldn't let her off so easily. "When then?"

"In the time of the forester."

"What forester?"

Her tone scorched the floor rushes. "Him that was master here before the Earl."

That did intrigue me. It was too grand a house — just — for the crown's administrator of the Forest Laws, and how did the Huntingdon heir fit in? "But how?" I began, but she gave me no more chances.

"My lady, if you do not need me for the books, I promised Hilda I would help her in the kitchen. She's ailing today and can't manage by herself."

"Of course, go ahead. We'll talk some other time."

She turned and drew back the hangings, to disclose my mother-in-law just outside. Lady Iseult's expression did not reveal how long she had been standing there. "I thought I'd see if you needed any help, *chérie*," she said smoothly. Agnes she dismissed with a wave of the hand but scarcely waited till she had turned the corner before she said, "Such a pity about that girl, don't you think?" in a voice loud enough to reach the outer walls.

I said nothing.

She changed course. "And it's past time to do something about her. She's insolent and a trouble-maker as well. I've told Guy so a hundred times."

I reflected that that had probably been Agnes's salvation. His mother told him everything a hundred times, and he was unlikely to start paying attention now. I said I had found her close-mouthed but not particularly insolent, and that she worked hard enough. Besides, I reminded her, Agnes had no place else to go.

"Oh," she said, looking at her hands as if she could barely keep them under control, "I daresay you wouldn't notice her familiarity. In fact, you encourage it with the sort of conversation you were having when I came in." She had the good grace to look a bit embarrassed. Her eyes flew to my face. "Guy wouldn't like it."

I couldn't decide whether this was a

threat or just the absolute criterion she lived by, like the Benedictine Rule. I guessed it was something of both. "This is my home now," I replied, as gently as I could through gritted teeth. "It's only natural to be curious. However, if Agnes has been insolent to you, I'll certainly see to it that she's corrected."

It was just the slightest reminder of our respective circumstances and responsibilities, but the effect it had on her was remarkable. She grasped my sleeve with her hand, then fastened on my arm. "You don't understand," she said, with obvious sincerity. "It's best not to go poking and prying too much. You don't want to stir things up. If you want to know something, ask me."

Her feelings were obviously intense, but what were they? I tried to get her to tell me what she was hinting at, but she grew as reticent as Agnes had been. I had no idea what it was I wasn't supposed to 'stir up'. I began to think it was time I made discreet inquiries into the recent history of Locksley Hall.

★ ★ ★

315

Guy came back briefly, full of excitement and mystery. He seemed quite pleased with himself. He announced that he would be off again almost at once, with about half of the men who owed knight's service to Locksley, Blidworth, and Gisborne. I asked him to tell me what his plans were.

He chucked me under the chin, smiling. "I can't tell you that, not yet. I may be gone some time, so you'll have to run the estates yourself. Stephen knows what to do — he was bailiff at Gisborne before this. If there's anything you need to know about the household, just ask Mother. I'm sure the two of you can work things out. Try not to worry. I'll be back as soon as I can, and if I'm right, our fortune will be made." He leaned toward me conspiratorially. "I can tell you this: I'm going away on very high business. The highest, in fact."

"The King's business?" I asked him.

He laughed gaily. "You might say that. King's business! Remember, I'm sworn to secrecy, and so are you."

"But I don't know anything."

"Ah, well."

When he had gone again, the household settled into a routine. My *belle-mère* — I could not say 'Mother' and usually addressed her without any title at all, contriving to look at her directly so there would be no mistaking whom I meant — and I set up separate spheres of influence, and rubbed along like opponents across a chess board. There were some squabbles, naturally, too tedious to recount here. I began to discover that small instances of spite and rivalry, more than life's great and terrible events, could wear down your soul, drip by drip, until there was nothing left.

Because Guy was not at home, we missed the tournament given at Blyth in honour of the Crusaders' victory at Acre, though a few of our younger knights went to try their luck. I doubt if many festivities were held in Philip's France; the triumph was all Richard's. The King may have had a minstrel's gift, but war was the music he made best. Acre was a harbour citadel, heavily defended; now it could not be long before the Holy City must fall before the greatest warrior of the age. We didn't hear till later, when the adventurers came trickling·back, of the slaughter of the Infidel prisoners. Some three thousand hostages — including children — were butchered in chains as a result of Richard's inability to conclude a mutually satisfactory agreement with Saladin for the exchange of prisoners. It was at Acre, too, that the King sowed the seeds of so much that followed. In fairness, it had been a murderous siege, and perhaps his judgement was weakened by illness and short temper. At least a thousand soldiers saw him tear down the banner Leopold of Austria had planted on one of the towers and fling it into the latrines. The venture had thus become, publicly, Richard's enterprise, and his will and opinions would be carried to the point of insult. How Leopold avenged himself would shortly become the talk of Europe; King Philip, in poor health and doubtless sick of losing every skirmish with Richard, sailed home to France.

Meanwhile, though the wooden quintains in the tilting yard were fashioned as Saracens and the Plantagenet leopards flew over the tournament field, Richard was becoming a distant and remote figure in his own kingdom. You could hear it in the knights' talk after Blyth. Clearly he had all the qualities from which great legends were made, a sort of modern-day Roland. Unfortunately, no one really expected him to come back. Even if he had the valour of Hector, the generosity (not to mention the temper) of Achilles, and the brilliance of Alexander, he was a stranger to England and likely to remain so for so long anything might happen.

That left a void only another royal presence could fill.

When I was a child, my father had been held out to me as the guardian of my virtue, the arbiter of my actions, and the castigator of my faults, despite his frequent and lengthy absences. However, it was my mother, with her soothing, her exhortations, her pieties, and her judicious applications of the oak-switch, who mattered most. In England, we were discovering that it was little different with the King.

9

THE long lovely autumn turned cool at last. The breath smoked the air in the mornings, and the stars made a bright necklace around the treetops. Lady Iseult and I ordered the Samain fires lit, the beacons that would ensure the sun's return after the sleep of winter. If any ghosts walked abroad that year, I didn't see them, though we offered prayers for the dead in our chapel. As for demons, there were enough of those within.

In the blood month we slaughtered the extra animals, salted down the meat for winter, and made the blood into pudding. The pigs were turned into the forest to forage. Fires crackled in the grates and the rowans roared in the wind. It was the last invigorating time of year, before life settled into the confinement and simmering bad tempers of an English winter.

The feast of Christmas came and went.

Soon the roads would be barely passable and we began to watch anxiously for Guy's return. We had had no word since he set out, so when a lone rider asked admittance at the gate we assumed that Guy had sent a message or a herald for his imminent arrival. In a sense he had, though our visitor was no messenger but a travelling minstrel.

Normally Guy and I would have greeted him first, in private, to get the news; there is no host so tone deaf he won't receive a bard. Such courtesies — not to mention lavish hospitality and a generous fee — go a long way toward preventing the airing of one's own family business in front of the neighbours, though of course nothing can stop it entirely. Gossip is a minstrel's stock in trade. So, presenting a harmonious front which would do credit to a Saxon shield wall, Lady Iseult and I received this one together. He called himself Alan of the Dales.

He was altogether an oddity. The best troubadours were off making tales of the Crusade, of course, and in any case nobody would expect to find Blondel in the depths of Sherwood forest. Alan had the look of some wood creature, small and dark with quick movements and watchful eyes. His mouth turned up at the corners in secret amusement, like so many of his calling. His French gave way at times to Saxon harshness, and a Welsh lilt at others. I was glad to see he did not affect the clownishness of some minstrels in this part of the country — the half-shaved moustache, the painted face, the simian capering rightly scorned by those who regarded their calling as an art. In fact, he was possessed of an elfin charm, and, if I'm not mistaken, a very sound bit of self-respect. He even managed Lady Iseult.

"Ah, madam," he said, bending over her proffered hand — its swollen knuckles imperfectly disguised by a livre of rings and bracelets — "rumour does not do justice to your beauty. I had hoped to find your husband at home. Has he not yet returned from London?"

It was worth enduring just to see Lady Iseult deprived of speech. "M-my husband?" she stammered.

"Are you not the young wife of Guy

of Gisborne, but recently wed?" he asked. They were the words of a pander, but he saved himself by uttering them in a tone of amused banter, as if they could not possibly be believed. Except, of course, that they were.

My mother-in-law blushed to the edge of her head-dress. "You are mistaken. Here is my son's wife," she said, in a tone more suitable for having produced a piece of mouldy cheese. "*I* am Lady Iseult, Guy's mother."

"My mistake, my lady," he said, sliding his eyes over at me in a way that suggested he knew I would understand. Still, I wouldn't help him. I waited while he bent over my hand, then asked formally:

"You've had some news of Sir Guy? Did you meet along the road perhaps?" London, he had said. I didn't know what Guy could be doing there. I preferred, in front of this Alan, not to seem ignorant of my husband's business, though I doubt if that would be news to him. As a matter of fact, he looked as if very few things could surprise him.

He glanced meaningfully at the wine jar. I took the hint and served him myself, in the guest's cup. Lady Iseult and I seated ourselves beside him, one on each side, holding our filled cups while he drank. "I had assumed, my lady, that your husband was at home," he nodded at me this time, "because most of those who rode south with the Prince have already returned. I've met a few stragglers on the road myself."

"The Prince?" I gasped, destroying all my pretensions. "Prince John?" Lady Iseult said nothing but registered no surprise, a fact I noted and stored for later interpretation.

"You haven't heard then," Alan said, with some satisfaction. Big news meant a fat fee. "His Grace and an assembly of bishops and barons — among whom, I understand, was my lord of Gisborne — deposed William Longchamp and sent him into exile."

"But how is this possible?" I exclaimed. "Longchamp is the King's Chancellor as well as Bishop of Ely and the Papal Legate. There is no man more powerful in England outside the King himself." Or more hated, either.

Alan spread his hands. "You ladies

know I am only a simple singer of songs," he said, not modestly at all. "But I've heard that the trouble began when the Chancellor had His Grace Geoffrey, Archbishop of York, arrested when he tried to take possession of his see. His Grace was abused rather shamefully, and the move wasn't popular."

This Geoffrey, for those who don't remember him, was, like me, the bastard offspring of King Henry. He had been banned from England with John, but when Richard relented in the matter of his far more dangerous legitimate brother, Geoffrey assumed that permission likewise extended to himself. Moreover, Queen Eleanor's intervention had secured him his ecclesiastical office in Rome, and until he took up the administration of his see at York, all of its revenue flowed into the Chancellor's coffers. He had a legitimate grievance with Longchamp, and it became a focus for more widespread discontent.

In extremis, the King's regency council was authorized to check the Chancellor, and they now met to discuss the issue in London, backed by Prince John and his barons. Longchamp faced the gathering with the warning that the Prince was beyond doubt attempting to usurp his brother's crown and that they had more to fear from him than from anyone else. Nonetheless, Longchamp was banished from Britain. The council named the Archbishop of Rouen head of the government and Prince John de facto heir of Britain. The deposed Chancellor feared for his life and fled England disguised as a woman. "He had long golden braids wound under his headpiece," laughed Alan, his troubadour's eye savouring the details, "and a surcoat of the best embroidered silk — in blue, I heard. Nothing but the best for William Longchamp, even as a woman!"

Lady Iseult was all aflutter at the news, and with her own secret knowledge, whatever it was. I guessed she could not be trusted with much. She tossed her head fretfully, asking, "What can it mean? What can it mean?" over and over till Alan had to answer her.

"Dear lady, I am not the one to ask. Your son can tell you better. I expect it will mean that if — God forbid — something should happen to Coeur-de-Lion in the Holy Land anytime soon, his brother's Grace will be King, and those who helped him in his ascendancy" (he said this lightly, no emphasis being needed) "will be rewarded accordingly. However, it would not be wise to dismiss the Lord Chancellor too quickly. He is a powerful man, and cunning, and he has the King's trust. At least that is what I hear."

I thought it might be prudent to determine what Alan's own sentiments were. "And I hear," I told him, "that Longchamp hired troubadours of his own to sing his praises in the market-place. They, of course, will be out of work now."

I couldn't tell whether what flashed in his eyes was anger or amusement. "Do you perhaps suspect me, my lady?"

I raised my fingers non-committally. "Even His Grace the King has his bards."

He smiled. "King Richard has no need to pay for songs of *his* deeds. If need be, he can always sing them himself."

He had. I had heard him. I said nothing.

Alan was watching me. "I don't know how it seems to you, Lady Marian, but every calling has its honour. We may serve a master, but we don't sell lies. A song is like love: you do it from the heart or you're a bawd."

Lady Iseult was annoyed at any conversation that so long excluded her and thrust herself into it. "My dear, don't go pestering our guest when he'll be wanting his dinner." She beamed at Alan. "Afterwards, maybe we can get him to sing us something about Guy."

* * *

After dinner came the songs. The quinces and pears were simmering over the fire, and the hall was filled with anyone who wanted to hear the minstrel sing. There were not many absent. Winter is long for everyone, especially if one is soured and fretful from lack of diversion. The flat wooden bottom of the vielle shone like a polished mirror in the firelight, and the notes were true. We settled back with a sigh of expectation and contentment.

Like a tinker, Alan had something for everyone, much of it borrowed but repolished to a pretty state. For my mother-in-law there were some appropriate verses to The Lady — mysterious and no longer young. My own dedication was a reworked paean to Diana. For the servants there were some delightful little fables of Renard, a clever fox who had studied the magical arts in Toledo and constantly outsmarted his foes Isengrim the wolf and Tybert the cat.

Then, after he had refreshed himself at the wine jar, he sang a tale of Robin Hood. It took me some time to recognize it, lulled by the wine and the sweetness of the music and the comfort of the hearth. Then the story began threading its way through my memory, and the pattern emerged clear. I have lost most of the words now; Alan wouldn't write them, and much was added and changed later on. That evening was the beginning.

The hero of the story used only the wood elf's name, but his own had been blackened by evil relatives and he had been outlawed unjustly to a life of questionable pursuits within an unnamed forest. With his friend the giant Little John, he appeared mysteriously to help those in need, in this tale a knight who had mortgaged his estate and was about to forfeit it to a greedy (also unnamed) abbot who coveted his land. The outlaw lent the knight the money to pay the debt on the security of Our Lady, who promptly discharged it by sending a monk from the offending abbey straying into the forest with twice the sum in his saddle bags.

It was a good tale. Everyone laughed, even Agnes. I hoped I was the only one in the room who knew it was true as well. I was sure that the 'greedy abbot' was our overlord for Gisborne, the Abbot of St Mary's. Guy had told me not long before that his lordship had been quite put out when an impoverished knight who had pledged a very desirable piece of land to the abbey as security for a loan had unexpectedly come up with the money to redeem it. Guy had laughed without sympathy when he told me; St Mary's was one of the richest landholders in the north of England. He said he had also heard in passing that the abbey cellarer had been robbed of a great sum in tenant's quit rents while journeying through the forest.

I wondered what the truth of it was, and whether Alan himself had met my outlaws, or if he was just passing on another man's song. I didn't think so; it had the passion of originality. I wanted to question him after he retired for the night, but if I went unescorted to his bedchamber it would spark gossip that would not burn out all winter. After so many revelations in one day, I wondered what else he could tell me to trouble my peace. I felt as if I were standing on the edge of some dark, deep valley, unable to see the other side.

★ ★ ★

I went looking for him next day in the stables, where the servants said he had gone to look after his horse. This was a fine animal, doubtless the gift of some happy patron, and I commended his concern.

The day was dark and dull, with a

mist that lay on the cloak like frost. I had to lift my skirt to avoid trailing it in the mud of the yard, and my shoes sucked a little when I pulled them out of the ground.

Dun Crump gave a whinny of pleasure when he heard me coming. In the quiet it startled me a little, but not as much as the two figures in the shadowy stable, who jumped apart hastily.

"Agnes," I said, as gently as possible to spare her dignity, "please go back to the house now." I thought she would have spoken but the man motioned to her and she went.

I turned my anger on its proper object. "Sir," I said, letting him see I knew where the fault lay, "you have abused the hospitality of our house."

"How so?" Alan asked me.

It made me angry that he would ask, as if a servant could be dallied with and then abandoned when his calling took him on. I thought of Agnes's plainness, and solitude, and how defiantly she bore it. And, I must admit, I was remembering Cecily and Bertrand de Born.

I said, more crudely than I had

intended, "I don't know what she has done or consented to, but Agnes deserves better than to be used for your selfish pleasure. It would be bad enough if you gave her money, but you buy her with hope and flattery, and some solace from her loneliness. It is worse than cruel, and I will not have it in my house."

He stared at me with incredulity, then his face changed and, surprisingly, he raised my hand to his lips. I jerked it away. "You are mistaken in my character, Lady Marian, as I believe Agnes is mistaken in yours," he said. "I was a guest in this house before the Gisbornes came here, and Agnes is an old and cherished friend. I would never do anything to hurt her. She knows that."

"There is no one so honey-tongued as a bard. You realize that I will have to question her about it?"

He smiled. "I think you will be satisfied." I relaxed a little and leaned back against a hay-rick.

Alan too seemed more at ease. "Agnes tells me you've been asking her questions about her past," he said.

"I was curious," I admitted. "About

333

Locksley too. Besides, I'd like to help her if I can. Since you say you're her friend you might as well know that Lady Iseult's taken against her for some reason and wants her off the estate. If she insists, my husband may go along with it."

His dark eyes regarded me intently. "And you've no idea why your mother-in-law has 'taken against her', as you say?"

I shook my head. "Not really. Well, she's not as tactful as she might be about the days before Locksley came to the Gisbornes. And she doesn't go out of her way to flatter my *belle-mère*, which can be dangerous. But there's more to it than that, I'd swear it."

Alan pulled a piece of hay from the rick, studied it with as much care as if it were a reliquary, and then threw it down on the ground. He seemed to have come to some decision about honouring me with his revelations and looked as if I ought to be grateful. Never mind that he had shown himself the companion or worse of outlaws, or just been caught dandling my maid. As a display of self-confidence it was impressive.

"Did you know that Agnes had a brother?"

"She never mentioned it."

"She would not. The forest court ordered him blinded and gelded. The job was botched and he didn't survive. Agnes won't talk about it, but I've heard the rack is nothing to what he suffered before he died."

"What did he do?" I asked in a whisper.

"Cut some wood, dug a ditch, and killed a red deer, I believe, at the order of Robert Fitz Ooth, whose man he was. I wasn't here when it happened, I only heard about it later."

"But surely," I said, reasonably certain of my ground after a long acquaintance with the Forest Law, "those offences would be finable to the estate, and killing a deer isn't punished by such mutilation until the third time."

"I can't say. I don't know the Forest Law. But one man who did was Fitz Ooth. He was raised here as the foster son of a forester. He swore before the court that the estate had been granted some exemptions on land use and certain

335

hunting rights in the time of the forester and that those rights had been reaffirmed during all the troubles with the late King Henry."

The 'troubles' during King Henry's reign were one of his bitterest legacies: in the late, losing days of his wars with his sons, he had seized on the idea of using the Forest Laws to squeeze more money out of his barons. It wasn't a new idea, but its application was severe and most damaging both to the King's reputation and the credibility of forest justice. If the privileges granted to Locksley had withstood this tempest, it seemed that Fitz Ooth and Agnes's brother should have had a good case. I said as much to Alan.

"You would have thought so." He folded his arms.

"Well?"

"You'll have heard that Fitz Ooth was named Earl of Huntingdon for a short while?" Alan asked.

I nodded. I hoped he didn't know about my near betrothal to the man.

"When he took that title there was a change in the privileges attached to his forest holdings. Or at least that is what the local forester swore before the court. He said he warned Fitz Ooth time and again that Locksley had been reafforested and that he was violating the laws in cutting trees or permitting his men to take deer."

Something pricked at my mind but I couldn't reach it. "How did he respond to that?" I asked.

"He denied that the forester had said anything to him, or that he had been notified of any change in the status of his holdings."

"Ah. And the fines would have been awful, of course. Whose coffers did they go into, do you know?"

"There were rumours, my lady, but it will serve no one, least of all you, to repeat them."

"And the forester who gave false evidence? What do you know of him?"

"Very little. He succeeded Fitz Ooth's foster father, but of course he didn't get Locksley Hall."

"And perhaps he didn't feel adequately compensated?"

"Perhaps." He was being very cautious.

"But I still don't understand about Agnes's brother." We had been speaking just above a whisper. A passer-by, seeing us huddled together, would have leapt to one conclusion. I recollected this just in time and moved apart from him a little. I also resumed speaking in a normal voice. There is nothing more likely to attract notice than the appearance of secrecy.

He shrugged, but not with indifference. "I don't think it was intended. But the forester was so insistent that Fitz Ooth and his men had been warned that the court wanted to make an example of someone. Her brother had undeniably taken a number of deer, so he was condemned to mutilation. Fitz Ooth attacked the forester when he came to see it done and nearly killed him. That's how he got himself outlawed. Afterwards, they made the penalty harsher and took the poor boy's sight — and gelded him as well."

"Sweet Jesus," I said.

"Exactly."

After a while, I said, "Still, what's done is done, and Agnes has to go on with her own life. Her brother will not come back."

"Very true. But she dreams that Fitz Ooth might."

I was shocked. I said sternly, "Alan, you forget yourself. You must not say such things to me."

He gazed at me imperturbably. "Your pardon, my lady. I had thought we were speaking frankly."

"Nevertheless, there are some things I may not hear."

"As you wish."

"In any case, it's ridiculous. Tell me, you knew this Earl of Huntingdon — what was he like?"

He said tonelessly, "He was my friend."

"I'm sorry. I only meant . . . I only wanted to know what happened to him."

He shook his head. "I've said I wasn't here when it happened, and I never saw the Earl again after that."

"I think if he's still alive he'll have gone to France or somewhere to fight for some lord. What other choice would he have?"

"It seems likely enough," he said

gravely. "It would certainly be the intelligent thing to do."

"As for Agnes," I told him, "I'll do what I can. But if you could get her to hide her feelings a bit it would help."

"I'm sure she can do it. Women are natural deceivers."

That made me dislike him again. "If they are, it's because men have made it necessary." He looked amused at my annoyance. "Why don't you make a song about it?" I added.

He straightened, brushing the flecks of fodder from his clothing. "Perhaps I will."

And so we left it. It wasn't until later that I remembered that I had forgotten to ask him how he had come by his tale of the outlaws and the Abbot of St Mary's. I decided to put it by for the moment. Alan had a secretive nature, and if he wanted to walk the darker paths of the forest and sing about it afterwards that was his business. I was sure he needed no warning from me about the dangers of tweaking His Lordship's nose in public. He looked to be the type who could land on his feet.

It was just as well I didn't pursue it. Some rumour of our meeting must have reached Lady Iseult, because she fixed me with a basilisk's unwinking stare and scarcely let me out of its perimeters until he left. Besides, he had given me enough to think about already. There was one thing I had not asked him, when he had told me the story of Agnes's brother. It would have shamed me as much to ask as it did not to, but I felt myself a coward. The thing was this: whether or not my husband had had any part or foreknowledge of it. I didn't think he could have, but so much was left unsaid that I couldn't be sure. I could have asked. I didn't. I had my reasons: I already knew myself to be pregnant with Guy's child.

10

THE winter seemed to last forever, casting even full day in blue tones and nights silver as the moon. It was so cold even the stars must have sputtered in the sky. I saw them every morning when I crept shaking and miserable from my bed, to purge my stomach into a pail. Often I couldn't make it to the garderobe. I tried to, but the sickness came on me in a bilious bubble, rising and bursting with inconvenient speed. Sometimes even the pail wasn't near enough. It was sufficient to make anyone live chaste as an elephant.

Throughout all of this ordeal, surprisingly, it was Agnes who supported me. I don't know what had passed between her and Alan, but without ever speaking of it she let me know hostilities were suspended. It seemed a sort of probationary period. She took to sleeping on a pallet in my bedchamber and woke immediately when I pitched back the covers. It is impossible to exaggerate the gratitude you feel for someone who is willing to hold your forehead while you vomit. An intimacy of sorts, a small solace during those wretched months, developed between us, and bit by bit she confided scraps of her past life and began to share her thoughts with me.

She often conveyed much more than she realized. She was full of pent-up devotions and fantasies. I suppose it would have been unusual if she had not had feelings for Alan, but I foresaw much pain that way and little joy. Once, I tried to talk to her about the lost lord of Locksley, around whom she had also fastened impossible hopes. It was a touchy subject to say the least, but she would be ill-served if she did not put away such thoughts. Fitz Ooth had been canonized for her by his defence of her brother, and her feelings for him were as intense as if he had been a saint in fact. That Guy held Locksley as tight as a fist with the blessing of the law, the Sheriff, and a Plantagenet prince did not matter to her at all. She stopped just short of saying its erstwhile master would return at need, like King Arthur from Avalon.

"But Agnes," I reasoned, "where would he come from, and with what? A man needs money and men to take land by force, and do you think the King would let him keep it even if he succeeded? Besides, King Richard has named the brother of the King of Scotland to be Earl of Huntingdon. It's part of his plan for keeping peace in the north. You'd not expect him to go back on something like that, would you?"

Her silence suggested not that she did not know the answer so much as that she could hardly trust me with the information. In that she would have been right, if the whole idea had not been so preposterous.

"You're right," she said at last, "we'd best not talk about it. But don't worry — if aught happens at Locksley I'll make sure no harm comes to you. I think the Earl would have wanted it that way."

I suppressed a sigh. I was getting a bit tired of stories of the noble lord of Huntingdon. "I imagine the Earl would like nothing better than to see all the

Gisbornes at the bottom of Locksley's well," I muttered.

"That's as may be," she said, looking down at her hands, which were large and calloused, "but in spite of everything I don't think he'd want anything to happen to you."

"Me?" I asked, surprised. "Why not to me, particularly?"

It was her turn to look startled. "Why, because he knew you, my lady. He told us all so, when he was fixed to marry you."

I felt . . . what was it? Fear, I think. And confusion. "I have never met the Earl of Huntingdon in my life," I told her. "I am sure of it."

She shook her head stubbornly. The Earl had said so, and my denial was nothing to that. "Perhaps you don't remember then. It was a long time ago, he said, when you were children. He said you stood up to some bully at a watering hole, and that was the kind of wife he wanted."

I don't remember what I said to her, with what words I thanked her and excused her to her duties. I don't know whether I admitted then that the memory had come back. I sat at my work table arranging and rearranging the scrolls and writing tools and remembered. His face and form were gone now, hard as I tried to recall them; it was too long ago. But not his presence, which had parted and stilled that rowdy group of boys. Nor his approval of my small defiance of the bully who was plaguing a sullen, defenceless child. A forester's son, the guard had said. Despite the difference in our ages and circumstances, we had been, for that one brief moment, friends.

I had been right to feel afraid. On top of Alan's revelations, this was news to trouble my peace. It wasn't only that Fitz Ooth had remembered me favourably and, when the change in his fortune made it possible, wanted to marry me. But the man whose house I now lived in, whose belongings I had helped clear away, the man my husband had dispossessed, now had a character to go with his name. While I sat rich and comfortable in the very room he had occupied, he was doubtless living the life of a mercenary on the fields of France or the Holy Land. Try as I might, I could not reconcile the boy of my memory with the man Prince John claimed had tried to murder the King's agent in cold blood.

★ ★ ★

My husband came home at last, pleased and sleek as a cat that has bagged a particularly tasty bird. The feathers were all but sticking out of his mouth. He looked very handsome, hard and windburned, and, for once, relaxed. He seemed happy enough to hear my news, which in fact his mother had been first with. He offered to sleep in the hall with his retainers to ensure my comfort. I accepted with relief. Of course we would not lie together now, but I had not realized how much his presence would burden me until the prospect arose.

Guy was ripe with news. Some of it was rotten fruit by now, but still tasty for us. The Longchamp affair echoed on and on. From France the deposed Chancellor excommunicated the English regency council (he did not go so far as to name Prince John). The council retaliated by confiscating his property and putting his see of Ely under interdict. The poor people of Ely had thus spent Christmas unable to buy or sell, eat, or drink with the communicant world, denied both marriage and burial in the year's harshest season.

And King Philip was in France, back from the Holy Land. Stories were circulating of attempted poisoning and treachery so great he had been forced to depart for fear of his life. The principal villain appeared to be King Richard. Philip had given thanks publicly to God at St Denis for delivering him safely out of Richard's hands. Then he proceeded to demand the surrender of his sister Alais, still in confinement in Normandy, and the return of Gisors to France.

I asked Guy whether he had heard what Richard had to say about all this.

He smiled. "News travels, but not that fast. Not that I can't imagine."

"But does he mean to stay on? How can he, now that the French King is at his back and hostile as well? The regency must be in shreds . . ."

Guy shrugged. "You would do better to ask whether he means to come back at all. The man's obsessed with being the hero of Christendom, the Saviour of Jerusalem. He's already been stricken with tertian fever, and if he doesn't die of disease, I doubt he'll be stopped by anything less than an Infidel sword before he takes the city. And from what I heard from Philip's men, that could take years."

"'Philip's men'? Where did you talk to Philip's men?"

"In Portsmouth." It was late, we had filled up the evening talking of Longchamp, and Guy was relaxed by wine and success. "I was there with the Prince," he said. "One or two of the returning crusaders were there on some business of their own."

"What were you doing in Portsmouth?" I ventured.

He shifted a little on the stool. The flickering firelight kept rearranging the planes of his face. His eyes were dark and impossible to read. "There was a force assembled in Portsmouth, making ready to sail for Normandy. We were going," he added, anticipating my next question, "to garrison Gisors or the Vexin."

"But you didn't go?"

"The Queen prevented it."

"Queen Eleanor? I thought she was in France."

"She was, until she found out Prince John was coming over. They say she beat the tide out of the harbour getting back to England."

"I don't understand, Guy. If the Prince was gathering forces to garrison Normandy against whatever Philip might do, why would the Queen prevent it?"

The charming lift of his eyebrow was as eloquent as a shrug and a little too practised. "Who knows? Maybe she fears she's lost one son and won't risk another. Has anyone ever understood the dragon Queen?"

I reflected that if the Queen was little understood, her capacity for understanding others had always been excellent. If she had so excited herself to prevent John's expedition, she must have mistrusted his motives.

Before I had leisure to digest this, my husband broke the biggest news of all — that the Prince himself was on his way to pay a private visit to Locksley.

★ ★ ★

I suppose it was an honour. Guy and Lady Iseult seemed to think so, and John certainly acted as if it was. I was less enthusiastic, since it confirmed what I had feared, that Guy had become the Prince's man. Fortunately, most of the party remained at Clipstone Lodge to hunt, so we did not have to entertain a royal entourage. God be thanked, the winter larder was adequate.

I had to keep reminding myself that this was my half-brother, as if only the blood tie could explain the intense mixture of interest and loathing I felt for him. I was not so foolish as to fear that he would renew his attentions; my pregnancy and Guy's favoured status spared me that. But I felt tense and anxious in his presence and kept wondering what he was up to.

For one thing, he set himself to charm me. He brought me a talisman against the pain of childbirth. He looked over my library and promised to send me some copies of works from his own. He taught me a Latin song, brought over from the court at Paris.

He played it on the harp himself, with great skill, and evoked, in the darkness of the hall, the Huntress kindling her pale lamp from her brother's flame and stirring, with the breath of night, hardened hearts to love again. It was a lovely song, silvery and chaste as the moonlight it described, and quite remarkable from such a singer.

"Bravo, Your Grace!" Guy said smiling when he had finished. "That was most excellent."

The Prince bent over the harp. "I don't have Richard's skill at composing," he said, with perfect ease, "but I do like to play a little. Though lately I've had very little time to practise." He smiled at Guy.

I asked him, when he had put it by, how his mother did, recalling for him that I had once been in her service.

He showed me his teeth. "I remember that very well, Lady Marian. I suppose the old — Her Grace is well enough. She keeps much busier than I would like."

He slithered around on his cushion as if he had an itch that wouldn't scratch. "I see that *your* mother is content to stay at home," he said to Guy. "Why does mine have to parade all over England and France getting up to God knows what?"

Lady Iseult, who had been dozing a little, stirred and puffed herself up at what she perceived was a compliment. I almost smiled too when I thought what Eleanor's reaction would be.

Guy said lazily, "It's true my mother is content to let me manage her affairs. But then, she has only one son."

The Prince leaned back against the wall and stretched his legs out in front of him. "So has mine," he said on a long sigh.

Lady Iseult sputtered into action. "Oh, no, Your Grace," she told him. "I'm sure your mother rates you very highly."

John shrugged diffidently, as befits a man of modesty, and looked down at his feet. "How kind of you to think of my feelings, madam."

Something crept along my spine like a cold-footed insect. Nothing much had been said that could not be John's recognition of his mother's acknowledged partiality to Richard. But Guy was looking amused, and the air was full of complicity and double meanings.

I thought that if I were the King, Jerusalem or no I would catch the first sailing ship to leave the port of Acre and head for home. And I began to feel afraid in earnest.

After this, I tried to open my ears and eyes. The Prince came and went between Clipstone, Locksley, and the houses of his supporters. Once he brought Geoffrey the Archbishop of York and the Abbot of St Mary's to our home. I did no more than kiss the ring, and then they retired to a private chamber. Even Guy was not privy to their discussion. If I had been naive before, only wilful blindness could have kept me from noticing that something strange and furtive was going on. There were rumours that the Prince wanted to divorce his wife and marry Alais Capet, cementing an alliance with France that would make him king if anything happened to Richard. There was no proof of anything other than that he had made himself powerful in his brother's absence. But I was almost sure that the Prince was perilously close to some sort of treason, and if he fell, my husband would go down with him.

Not that Guy was necessarily convinced of that. I did try to talk to him, despite the knowledge that if I pushed him too hard he would cease to tell me even the little he let fall. I also knew he would hate my interference every bit as much as the Prince hated his mother's. But I had to try. I had our child to think of.

"Why are you worrying?" he asked me smoothly, when I had broached the topic. "I've become the friend of a powerful prince, that's all. He has honoured our house with his company. He brings you presents and sings verses to you after supper. You should be pleased, not suspicious."

"Do you trust him?"

"Should I not? He has been generous, and he keeps his promises to those who serve him well."

"And to his brother the King?"

He smiled then, which was a measure of his confidence. "What would you have him do? The King is charging at the gates of the Holy City like some maddened bull, and with about as much success. You won't find me, or the Prince either, the only one to suggest that the King's heir should prepare himself to take up the kingdom in case, well, if something unfortunate should happen. No one wants to go back to the days of Stephen and Maud, and the fights over the succession."

I heard him in frustration. The speech was too glib; he had used it already, or got it from someone who had. "Then why doesn't he prepare himself in honour, instead of conspiring with King Philip against Richard, behind the backs of the regency council and his own mother? You know this is just what Richard feared, when he wanted to ban the Prince from England. I'm worried, Guy, about what he might do next. And so, I think, is his mother the Queen."

I shouldn't have mentioned mothers; it always set him off. "Queen Eleanor is only a woman, and a meddlesome one at that. What she wants or doesn't want need not concern us."

"His mother," I said, through clenched teeth, "knows more about statecraft than your Prince does about pricks, which is saying a lot."

He looked as if he could scarcely contain his exasperation at my wilful stupidity. I took in another breath to speak, and he drew back his hand warningly. "You'll have to hit me then," I told him, "because I will say this, for the child's sake if not your own. I apologize if I have offended you. But I am afraid of what Prince John will do out of lust for the crown, and what you will be forced to if you serve him. I don't doubt he can move like a serpent in a reed bed when he has to, coil and coil again. In the end he may be able to wriggle out of the nets he has woven. But what about you, Guy? Are you willing to put your life in danger? And what about this child?"

He dropped his hand, the enthusiasm rekindled in his face. "The child! The boy is what I'm thinking of. You must see that! He could be an earl. He could be anything! My son. If I have the friendship of the King . . . Look, the Prince will land on his feet, you've seen that yourself. It's no more than betting on the champion in a tournament — less, really, because it's more of a sure thing." He put a hand on my belly, where the baby was growing. "For the child's sake, I will promise you I'll not be led into treason. Will that content you? Now you're not to worry," he added, in a tone that was far from solicitous. "Mother tells me you've been sick enough already. I've asked her to make sure you get more rest. If you won't take care of yourself, someone else will have to see to it."

He left me feeling discouraged and penned by the child I bore in my body. Locksley, under the supervision of Lady Iseult, would be as close a confinement as a sheepfold, and afterwards the baby would anchor me to the Gisbornes forever. Whatever his protestations, Guy was drifting unresisting toward treason, and he had made it clear he would not allow me to get in his way.

I no longer feared to ask by what means he had acquired Locksley Hall and all it contained. Besides the greater issue it did not matter, and in my heart I knew, had always known, the answer already.

11

OF the time that followed it is hard for me to write. Not just because of the pain, though there was enough of that, but because I remember it only dimly, as if it were all shadows and smoke. There is a mercy to pain; it eats up the hours or days with the appetite of a wolf, and when it is lifted only a trace remains in the mind, a pale image in a misty glass.

The first thing that happened was that our priest, Father Robert, took ill in the chest and died· of too·much fluid there. He suffered horribly, gasping for breath that wouldn't come and rattling in his throes. He went blue, too. I had not cared much one way or the other for Father Robert — he was too ineffectual to excite any strong feelings — but his lonely suffering made me sad.

The Abbot of St Mary's promised to find a replacement 'suitable to a noble household', which meant that it would cost a lot in money or in grants and gifts. I resigned myself to the Abbot's choice, who would doubtless be much worse than merely ineffectual. In the interim I suggested Father Tuck.

There were a number of reasons for this, most of them selfish. It's true he was free and could benefit from the fee even temporary service at Locksley would bring in. But what I really wanted was someone to talk to, someone whose loyalty was, if not to me, at least not to the Gisbornes or the Prince. I wanted to confide my worries about my husband and Prince John to someone who would keep my confidence and give me straight-speaking in return. It would hardly be appropriate to burden Agnes and fan the coals of resentment, and there wasn't anybody else. So I asked that Father Tuck be sent for, but Guy wouldn't hear of it, until I lost the child.

That is the haze I cannot penetrate, the months I drifted deep in misery and pain when I purged the baby. The boy was born dead, may his soul rest with God, and afterwards I sickened with childbed fever. At first it seemed that my whole body was pushing from the inside out, and then that my insides were rotting away. Perhaps they were. After that I lived in a twilight world of half-heard words, fevered imaginings, and the comfort of oblivion. Lady Iseult told me afterward that I cried out again and again for Father Tuck, and in the end, fearing the illness was mortal, they sent for him.

And so I lay in darkness, and time passed. In the world outside, the King of England, heeding at last his ruling council's urgent pleas to come home, concluded a truce with Saladin and turned his face from the Holy City without ever setting foot in it. The world settled down by the watchfires to wait for the return of the King. His absence lengthened; the fires burned down to embers. Richard Plantagenet had vanished without a trace from the sight of men.

Book Four

Sherwood

Book Four

1

SOMEWHERE outside a jackdaw croaked, warning off intruders. Sensation came back piece by piece: the shrill, tuneless notes, the rustle of cloth on the floor grass, the whisper of far-off voices, like a breeze. The room was warm and close, the coverlet heavy and smelling of sweet woodruff. My limbs felt bloated and boneless, and immeasurably heavy. I moved one leg cautiously.

"She's coming round again," said a voice above my head.

Gaps in memory can be merciful. Even as my senses struggled for this gentle consciousness, the mists of pain and fatigue in which I'd wandered for so long were already beginning to dissolve. The tiny grave at Gisborne and the anguished aftermath of grief and illness had been muffled by the sleep I drew round me like a blanket. Now the healing had begun. I opened my eyes then.

Light sliced my skull with a sword's

thrust. I squeezed my lids shut on a face illuminated by memory, one I thought I had dreamed in my delirium.

"Marian. Lady Marian."

Too late now to retreat into the darkness. "Janet?" I still could not believe it.

She smiled. "You do remember me, then. I was afraid you would not. Deo Gratias, the worst of your illness has passed."

"Wha — what are you doing here?" My voice creaked with disuse, like a rusty portcullis. So must Lazarus have felt, recalled to life. "You were in my dream. You and Blidworth and my mother . . . " My mind was as numb as my mouth and I could not explain, but she understood me.

"I'm real enough. Your husband brought me." She patted my arm reassuringly and put a jar of potion to my lips. "Drink this now, and rest. When you're stronger, we can talk."

The liquid was warm and herbal, and my mouth was dry. Even so small an effort tired me. The bed hangings seemed to swing and sway, and then to close around me like cerements. I should not have conjured Lazarus, I chided myself, as I slid once more into sleep.

When I opened my eyes again it was to darkness, lit by the gentle glow of the bedside candle. The hour marks showed it was very late; someone had been generous with the tallow, lest I wake to blackness.

Agnes was watching me from her cot against the wall. When she saw me stir she got up and came to the bedside. "Can I get you anything?"

"In a moment." In the dim light, she looked tired and dishevelled by sleep, and much softer. I gestured toward the foot of the bed. "Will you sit down and talk a little? I'd like to thank you for your care all this time, and there are things I want to know."

Agnes looked as if she had her doubts. She sat down gingerly, withdrawing into the smallest possible space on the coverlet.

"I remember when I was . . . sick," I began, "that I asked for Father Tuck, and that he came. Is that right?"

I thought she hesitated.

"I didn't dream that, surely?"

"No."

"And did he say Masses for . . . for . . . ?"

"For the little one's soul. Oh yes, my lady."

I relaxed a little. "When did he leave, then?"

She pursed her lips and frowned. "He hasn't gone, Lady Marian. Since you started coming round, they wouldn't let him near you."

"'They?' What do you mean?"

"Sir Guy and Lady Iseult, and . . . that sister from Kirklees. *She* wouldn't let anyone come to you, not even me."

"I'm sure she meant well," I said absently. "I've known her since I was a child. I'll send for the Father tomorrow. But now — "

She bent toward me and lowered her voice. "Have a care, my lady. A lot happened while you were sick."

I could scarcely attend her. "But now," I continued, "you will have to help me to the garderobe. The jar is full, and I need to stand anyway. I hope I never have to do it lying down again."

This business haltingly completed, we

lurched back toward the bedchamber. Janet stood waiting, cradling a steaming cup and smiling. "I'm glad you're better," she said, "but you really shouldn't be up. I heard you stirring, so I brought this to help you sleep." She set it down and took my other arm, so that the two of them bore me along so firmly my feet scarcely touched the floor. Agnes kept silent, her muscles tense beneath my wrist. Janet's grip was strong too, under the rough cloth of her tunic. She hoisted my feet up to join my body on the bed. "I'll just get the potion."

Agnes stayed by the bedside, arms folded. Her expression was grim. "What is it?" I asked her.

She shook her head. Janet came back with the cup and thrust it under my nose. "This is scabiosa, and some poppy. It will strengthen your blood and liver, and help you sleep. Drink it down."

I began to balk at so much cosseting, like a child who refuses to drink its milk. I set the jar aside, smiled sweetly, and said, "Thank you, I'll just sip it. We'll talk tomorrow, shall we? I've disturbed your rest enough." She looked as if she would like to stay and watch me swallow it. "Good night," I added firmly.

When she had gone, I handed the brimming cup to Agnes. "Take this out with you, will you?"

For the first time, she smiled. "Aren't you going to drink it?"

"After what we just went through to get to the garderobe? This is the only time in hours I haven't bulged like a leaky wineskin."

She took the potion out of the room with such evident satisfaction that I wondered, before I fell asleep, what Janet could possibly have done to have so offended her.

★ ★ ★

In the morning I felt much improved, my head clearer and my body less like a straw-stuffed mattress. I was already impatient of my weakness, an indulgence only a healthy body can afford. Agnes helped me into a seat by the window overlooking the courtyard. I could not get enough of the light, or the life below.

Lady Iseult came in quietly and sent

370

Agnes out. I remembered, when I had lost the child, that I kept apologizing to her. We were past that now. She smiled at me, tentatively, and brought her sewing to the windowseat. "You really do look much better," she said.

"Thank you. I think I will recover after all. I wasn't sure for a time."

She nodded. "And you will bear more children." This was my mother-in-law's version of encouragement, so I said nothing.

She misunderstood my silence. "You will. You are young." Her voice lacked conviction, as well it might, since childbed fever often leaves a woman barren.

"I pray God it may be so," I said.

"It's in His hands."

"Yes."

Silence.

"How is Guy?" I asked her, feeling awkward.

"Well enough, I suppose."

I looked up at this. She had spoken almost tartly.

She bent over her stitches. "He'll be in to see you this morning. Before he does,

371

I have something to tell you, something he wouldn't like." She shook her head, as if in wonder at her own audacity. "You have to get rid of her," she hissed. "Sister Janet. Send her away."

"Why?"

She still refused to look at me. "Don't ask me that. I tried to make him, but he won't, so you'll have to if you can. That's all I want to say."

"I haven't even heard how she came to be here in the first place," I told her. "She says Guy brought her. How is that possible?"

"I can answer that." The arras shifted for my husband. Behind him came Janet.

Guy's kiss felt cool on my forehead. "You had us all frightened," he said. "You were off your head, like a lunatic. You kept raving about lepers, and outlaws in the wood. When I went to Gisborne I called in at Kirklees Priory to see if the sisters could offer any help. They are famous in our part of Yorkshire for their healing and their herb lore. Then when I found that one of the lay sisters had known you as a child, was willing to come back with me . . . " He gestured broadly at Janet, who came forward.

"It seems I owe you a lot," I told her. "It was kind of you to come, and of course I'm glad to see you again, after so long."

She said quietly, "I have been happy to do it, Lady Marian. It's what we are trained for, at the priory." She seemed very detached, and far from the bullying personality I remembered from my youth, or even from the authoritative nurse of the night before. I couldn't think why I hadn't noticed earlier how beautiful she had grown as well.

Lady Iseult, who had remained at her sewing as at a battlefield, said briskly, "I'm sure we're all very grateful to the sister. But of course she'll be wanting to get back to Kirklees now that Marian is so much better."

This was fairly bald, even for my mother-in-law. Guy said angrily, "She'll do no such thing, not until Marian is much stronger. I'm surprised at you, Mother."

I sat still as a piece on a chess-board, while moves I didn't entirely comprehend were made around me. I had leisure, then, to notice the swift, upraised look that passed from Janet to Guy, and the answer in his eyes. It lasted a moment, no more, but that was enough.

Janet turned a modest countenance to my mother-in-law. "It is kind of you, my lady, but I will be happy to stay as long as I'm needed. I promise you it's no hardship."

As soon as I thought I had chewed all this over enough, and felt a little stronger, I sent for Father Tuck.

The Father looked as if he had been ill himself. He was still fat, but his face was puffy and the skin taut and mottled. His eyes were blue-shadowed from lack of sleep. He took my hand. "I'm glad you're better, my child. It's a hard thing you've suffered, but with God's help you will endure it. Be thankful you have been spared to take up your life again."

"Without children?" I asked him, my eyes stinging.

"If need be. You will not be sent more than you can bear, I promise you," he said gruffly. "Besides, it's too early for despair."

I swallowed and smiled at him. "You've

softened a little, but you still scold me. I've missed you. Thank you for coming here. I'm sorry they — the Gisbornes — have been hard on you."

He shrugged as if it were of little consequence. "I'm not a suitable chaplain for a noble household, Lady Marian. I am coarse. I get drunk. I speak the common tongue. You can't blame them too much. Now that you are getting well, I can get back to my real work, among humbler folk."

"There is something you could help me with, before you go," I began hesitantly. "Something I need to tell someone."

He adjusted his tunic as if arranging the confession stole and then moved closer to where I sat. "Well?"

"I've had little to do but lie still and think these past few months," I told him, "that is, when I wasn't off my head or in pain." I pulled out, then, from the confusion of the past, some facts he could place in a pattern of sense. I laid them out like tiles in a mosaic: how Locksley had been taken from its rightful owner with the collusion of the Prince and then given to Guy, how Guy had ridden with John to try to win King Philip's support, how the Prince and his followers gave every appearance of plotting treason against the King.

If I expected shock, or some very grave reaction, I was disappointed. "Is that all?" he asked.

"Are you suggesting there should be more? Or that it's not important?"

He said, more gently, "My dear, I'm sorry for your unwilling involvement in this. I'm not sure how to advise you. But it's hardly a surprise to anyone in England that Prince John covets his brother's crown. With the King in prison — "

"*What?*"

His mouth fell open like a beached fish. "You haven't heard? Nothing? He's in the hands of the Emperor. No one's sure where, or how, exactly. People say Leopold of Austria caught him in a peasant's hut travelling overland near Vienna, and turned him over to the Emperor. For a price, I don't doubt."

I couldn't believe it. "What will happen to him?"

Tuck lowered his voice till it was

scarcely louder than the hiss of steam from the pot on the fire. "If King Philip and Prince John have their way . . ." He made a despairing gesture. "The Prince has been to Normandy already. He called himself Duke and paid homage to Philip, or so they say. I heard he even promised to marry the Lady Alais, King Henry's whore . . . There's no telling what may happen. One thing's sure, though: Richard's worth a pile of ransom, alive."

He told me more then, about Richard's settlement with Saladin on the threshold of the Holy City, the return of the crusaders, first in a trickle and then in a full tidal swell, and the prolonged and unexplained absence of the King. No one was sure what he had been doing afoot in Austria, attended by only a few knights, when he certainly knew of Leopold's enmity. The only undisputed fact was that he was being detained by the Emperor, while the serpents were free to bite where they would.

I was still weakened by illness, or I might not have given way to the tears that pricked my lids and spilled over onto my lap. It was all so sad: the inglorious end of the pageant of arms that would take back Jerusalem, and the chaos and cruelty that would descend on England with her king not dead, but immobilized. In the face of that, it needed more strength than I could muster to face the future with hope.

"If you have any tears to spare," Tuck went on relentlessly, "save some for this poor country. If there is a ransom, we won't get off lightly, you can be sure of that. If not, like as not there'll be civil war between the Prince and the Chancellor, or a war with Britanny over the succession. And wars cost money."

"You think Prince John would dispute the lawful succession if the choice goes against him?"

"If Richard's heir's a child in the nursery? Don't be simple." His eyes sank deeper in their pouches of flesh. "What I began to say when we started all this is that this isn't the time to make waves about your husband's dealings with Prince John. Sir Guy — and you — could be very well placed now," he added bitterly.

I sat up straighter in my chair, the better to face the ordeal to come. "It's odd you should say that," I said, not looking at him. "I was going to ask you if you, thought there was any possible way I could get out of my marriage."

His hand came forward and covered my wrist. The gesture was friendly and comforting, but firm. "That is illness talking, and grief as well. You have not thought."

I shook my head. "I have, I told you. If I stay with Guy, I will be drawn into plots against the King. I don't care a pig's whisper for Richard personally, but it is against my honour to continue in this." I would not tell him it was against the grudging bit I owed to Henry and Eleanor too. "Besides," I continued, "the Earl — Fitz Ooth — was *innocent*, I'm sure of it. I have to live with that every day I eat the bread from his fields and sleep under a roof that is rightfully his. I . . . I have reason to believe he was a good man who deserved better than that. I don't want to add any more to my account. I loathe the Prince. I *loathe* him. I will not help him *or his friends* cheat his family and the kingdom, the way he cheated the Earl of Huntingdon. Let him wait for the crown to come to him lawfully, if it comes at all."

Tuck's grip tightened until his nails scratched my wrist. "Carefully," he said quietly. "We are not Cosmas and Damian, to come back from the flames. Have you thought that most people would counsel that you need do nothing but obey your husband, which is your duty in any case?"

I didn't know whether he was advising or tempting me, but I had gone too far now to turn back. There is an intoxicating quality to such speech, and an illusion of freedom, however costly and foolish. "As to that," I told him, "if I go on unresisting, I'm sure I could come in time to believe it *is* my duty, and that I am innocent. But that wouldn't make it true."

He folded his arms across his chest and looked me in the eye. "Are you quite sure that it's your honour that's involved, and not just your wounded pride?"

I stared down at my hands. "I don't know what you mean."

"I think you do."

I raised my head then. "Have you heard something?"

He shrugged. "There is talk in the kitchen. And I have eyes."

"And I have only a suspicion. There is nothing confirmed. What would you advise me to do?"

He frowned. "If that were your only grievance against your husband, I would advise you to forget it. It is a wife's lot to bear a man's infidelities. Even the Queen was not exempt from it."

"And if there is more to it than that?"

"You seem to think that change itself will mean improvement. How do you think to undo this marriage, if you do not prove to be barren?"

I winced, and said hurriedly, "There are certain misrepresentations that were made to me about Locksley, and Guy, and the Prince. And since I am — was — the King's ward, it could be argued he would not have given his permission for me to marry, if he had known."

"And if the King doesn't come back? There are ways of making sure he does not, if his enemies are evil· enough."

"I'll face that if I have to. No, don't shake your head like that. I'm not so stupid I don't know what I'm risking. Don't spoil it for me. I want to, I don't know, do something, decide things for myself for once. That's all."

"That's *all*? So what would you do?"

"I hadn't thought beyond getting out of the marriage. I can apply to the Queen, or the Archbishop of York . . . "

"Who have nothing to do but consider your petition, I suppose. So you would run away, and save yourself. But will that stop your husband or the Prince, or help the King?"

In spite of the excitement of making plans, I was beginning to get tired again. "How am I supposed to prevent my husband from doing anything, much less the Prince? I have less influence over Guy than his mother does, and he wouldn't listen to her even about the weather."

Father Tuck's voice was scarcely more than a breath in my ear. Up close, I could smell the sour tang of mildew and old ale on his tunic. "There is another way. You could stay as you are, and keep your eyes open. I can put you in touch with someone who could use any information you give."

I shrank away from him. "You mean spy on my own household?"

"Yes, exactly that," he hissed at me. I had discovered that Tuck rarely flinched from the sort of brutal honesty that calls things by their right names. As a technique, it was curiously persuasive; reality might prove better than his articulated worst, and no one could ever say afterwards he hadn't been warned. "I should add," he said, piling on his building blocks of misery, "that it's not only dangerous, but could also end in your husband's losing Locksley if you're successful. You would have to be prepared for that."

"What would I have to do?"

"Get stronger. Watch and wait, and see what the times bring. Can you do that?"

"Yes," I said, more relieved than I cared to admit that, after my burst of passion, I would still have time to recover before I must act.

"Good. And you will do nothing for

the moment about an annulment."

"For the moment, no."

He ran a ragged, stained thumbnail around the edge of his neckline, and then chewed on it. "Touching Sister Janet and your husband . . . " — he seemed to wait but I said nothing — "you must purify your heart and be sure of your motives. Meanwhile, be careful when you drink her possets."

"*What*?" I seemed to be saying this often.

He glared at me. "Don't give too much weight to it. Just have a care, that's all. She's young and inexperienced, and I found dried nightshade among the herbs she brought with her preparations. When I spoke to her, she said it was forbidden at Kirklees, and it must have come there by accident or someone's carelessness. There is no reason not to believe her." He continued to look at me from beneath his brows, as if he dared me to say otherwise. He sighed, heaving his shoulders. "Since then I've supervised the preparations myself, and she may think I don't trust her. She's touchy, that one is. So she might slip off to brew them in secret to prove she knows how. It is even possible," he said carefully, "that her potions delayed your . . . ah. . . recovery."

I shivered. Nightshade is the devil's tool, and will open Hell's portals if you take it in small amounts. In large doses, you will not only look in, but stay there.

Tuck shifted his gaze. "Even if there is something between her and Sir Guy, she would have little to gain by harming you. You said you knew her as a child. Were you friends then?"

I searched my memory and found mostly happy times. "As much as we could be. Janet was quicker, braver, and more talented than I was, so if our roles were reversed I would have been her second-in-command. As it was, we were pretty much equals."

Tuck smiled. "There at least is a motive of sorts, though I doubt it's a strong one. No, we must assume she means no deliberate harm to your body, in any case. But I should send her back to Kirklees as soon as you can contrive it. For her sake more than yours. And in the meantime, don't show her, or anyone, your mind on . . . what we've discussed. Don't trust anyone except Agnes."

He bent over me and made the sign of the cross in the air above my head. "If I guess right, we won't be having many private talks after this. When I am sent away, you can reach me at Edwinstowe if you have need. I'll be able to get messages to you, never fear. Now rest, and think on what I've asked. *Benedicite.*"

2

IT was Ransom rather than Death. It was set at 100,000 silver marks, a sum to humble Plantagenet arrogance and maim the royal finances. As Tuck had said, it was the people who paid, who were as much the powerless victims of Richard's enterprise as the vanished souls of Acre, now no more than a shriek of memory. A nation of Jobs sprang up over night. The churches gave gold and silver from their altars, the richer monasteries their finest reliquaries, the Cistercians a year's crop of wool. Barons and land holders were taxed at one quarter of a year's income, which had to be wrung from each level of the estate's production down to the lowest villein. The words of Joel — *That which the palmerworm hath left hath the locust eaten; and that which the locust hath left hath the cankerworm eaten; and that which the cankerworm hath left hath the caterpillar eaten (I:4)* — were popular in the pulpits.

387

I worried that we could not raise our portion without some household hardship. The management was back in Lady Iseult's hands, and I was surprised to notice that she practised little economy: the tallow was used as lavishly as before, the rushes changed no less often, and there was still meat at our table. Our steward, who would scowl over the waste of a penny's worth of fodder, continued about his duties with a smooth countenance.

It was less easy than I had imagined to watch and wait and do nothing. My stomach began to churn with the anxiety uncertainty can produce, and I grew restless and tense. Guy did not come back to my bed. He visited me in my solar in the mornings, where we exchanged brief, polite words on household matters, strangers straining for civility. During one of these conversations I broached part of a plan I had for whatever might remain of our yearly income.

"I know we can't have much left after we pay the ransom tax," I told him, watching his face for a reaction, "but do you think we might make a money gift to Kirklees Priory?"

He stared at me suspiciously. "Why?"

"Because of Janet, of course. She tells me they aren't well endowed, and times will be harder now. She's been very generous, and I'd like to repay her in some way. Of course, *she* can't accept money; it wouldn't be permitted. So I thought . . . if we had enough . . ."

He looked at me as if he couldn't credit my stupidity, and then I knew that what I had suspected was in fact true. Worst of all he adopted the tone of voice he had previously used only with his mother. "Don't worry," he said soothingly. "We'll have the money to make any gifts you like." And then he laughed.

★ ★ ★

I'm not sure whether it was more annoying to be thought naive and stupid, or to be pleased for suggesting a kindness I in no way intended. The first bothered me more but the second pricked my conscience. This is how I had formed my plan . . .

I had been spending my convalescent afternoons in the solar talking with Janet, or rereading my library while she worked precise, beautiful stitches into a cloth. I even tried to compose a few love lyrics in the Provençal style, but they made me wince and rub them out immediately. I no longer had the knack, if in fact I had ever had it, even at Fontevrault, where haste and hiding always made the audience more appreciative. Nor did I know what was in fashion. Janet never asked to hear what I had written, but the difference between our products, her fine needlework and my messy parchments and scratched-out wax, put me in mind of Blidworth and my mother's reproaches.

Our meetings were cordial, but there was a reserve on Janet's part and a suspicion on mine which made it impossible to guess we had once been close childhood companions. "You've changed," I told her.

"I should hope so." She sewed on placidly. "Kirklees should have something to show for itself."

"Are you happy, then, as a nun?" I

hoped she was. I still felt I had an interest in her destiny.

"Not as a nun," she reminded me, "but as a lay sister. We didn't have the dowry to enter, though they'll take very little these days." She raised her eyes to look into mine. "But yes, happy enough. I have all I need."

"You know that your mother . . . that she suggested . . . " I wasn't sure how to put it, but I wanted to know the truth.

"That it was your doing, because you went to the abbey in Anjou," she finished for me. "Yes, I know. It gets worse with every telling. You needn't let it trouble you, if it does. She won't accept the fact that I would have clutched at any straw to get out of Blidworth and away from her."

"I liked your mother," I interrupted, shocked.

"She wasn't your mother. Besides, you liked everyone then. Even me."

As there was no possible answer to that I said nothing.

"And Kirklees was a good opportunity," she continued. "I admit I got the idea when your father sent you to Fontevrault.

391

But anything was better than staying at Blidworth and marrying Will Scarlet, which is how mother had it arranged. I had to get out. I suppose you don't understand that," she added mildly.

"I think I do," I said, with equal blandness.

"But you came back," she said, misunderstanding. "You married."

"Yes." In the silence, I could hear something rustling along the wall, or inside it. Mice, probably, or an owl stirring in his sleep. "You regret it? Not marrying, I mean?"

Her lids dropped to form full, pale moons over her eyes. She shook her head. "Why should I? I have independence, position. I am valued. And for myself, not for my land or fortune. I regret nothing."

I turned my pen round and round in my fingers. "I'm glad to hear it. Do you think you would enter the order as a nun instead of a lay sister if the dowry was provided? Take vows of poverty and chastity forever?"

She smiled a little to herself and sewed busily for a moment. Then she said briskly, slipping out of intimacy, "Certainly, Lady Marian. I'd regard it as the greatest and highest privilege. How could it be otherwise?"

And that is how I conceived and later justified my not-entirely-noble plan to make Janet a full-fledged nun. The gift to Kirklees would form her dowry and would set her among the well-born society of the vowed community, the served instead of the servant. I did not doubt that ambition and talent would one day make her a prioress, at the very least.

★ ★ ★

Sometimes, when the walls of my cell seem too close, the blankets rough and the bathing jar full of ice, I think of what I cast away, and of how I came, step by step, to be the Marian who did it. The results can be judged, but the causes are another matter. They spread like the roots of an oak tree, twisted and tangled beneath the ground: who can tell which provides the most nourishment? I had lost a child, sickened, been duped by — at the very least — a greedy and devious man, and I had been shamed in my own house. You could tell it outraged honour or a fine sense of duty, just as it is possible to call sulking in one's tent the Wrath of Achilles. As a matter of comfort, I would rather not have to unearth all the subterranean structure. It is enough that what happened, happened, and that I have paid dearly for what I might have set in motion out of spite.

Janet went back to Kirklees, with all the pomp and escort of a beloved relative. I added the money chest and a private letter to the Prioress as to how the contents should be used. The message went privily, with one of the guards. As soon as she left, Guy came back to my bed.

I was expecting it, of course. I could have delayed for a bit, pleading fatigue or a return of the fever, but I could not put him off forever. It was an unspoken condition of my agreement with Father Tuck. What I was not prepared for was my own reaction.

He was standing in a pool of light cast by the torch in the corridor. He pulled the hanging to, and the pool dwindled to a red, flickering ribbon. His feet were wide apart, and he had his hands on his hips.

"What do you want?" My voice came out in a sort of croaking whisper. I tried again. I saw him smile.

"What do you think?"

At this, or at the smile, some tiny burr of anger stirred within me. "Get out of here!" I told him. "Leave me alone."

He made a sharp movement of impatience, a small gesture, but one containing so much suppressed violence that I felt myself flinch back against the pillows. "What are you talking about?" he said, advancing on the bed.

"What I said," I told him, clutching the covers up under my chin. "Do you think you can come straight from *her* bed to mine, after deceiving me in my own house?" My blood had begun to race and my breath came short in my throat. If I wasn't careful I would reveal too much.

"You're raving. That's the illness talking." He took my arm and held my wrist back against the pillow, one leg half up on the bed. He smelled of horses, leather, and drink.

"I mean it, Guy."

He swung his knee over between my legs and at the same time grabbed my other wrist, so that I was pinioned beneath him on the bed. His face was very close to mine. He looked genuinely puzzled, but there was anger there as well. "What did you expect?" he asked me. "You're my wife." As if that explained everything.

"I don't want to," I said slowly, in his ear. "Don't I have anything to say about it?"

"No," he said, and proceeded to yank at the coverlet. I heard it rip. He pinned the top of my body to the bed with his chest and tore at his own clothing.

"Stop, Guy," I told him, trying to jerk my head away. "I'm warning you," I added, pointlessly.

I had forgotten how resistance excited him. "Shut up, you bitch," he said, thrusting his left hand over my mouth. I couldn't breathe. I wondered if I would smother, tossing and squirming on the mattress. He forced his way inside my body, gasping and thrusting. He climaxed with a wild cry, like a beast.

I lay there able to breathe at last, humiliated by my own weakness. *That which a lover takes against the will of his beloved has no relish.* I almost laughed. Why had Andreas's Rule come into my mind? The Countess and her chaplain had been right: Love exerts no power between husband and wife. Guy did not love me, so I had not even that small mastery over his life. On the other hand, he could take my body, my property, and my children and do with them whatever he wanted, and I was helpless to stop him. Helpless. The word burned like bile in my mind. For the first time, I really understood what was behind the Courts of Love. (The Countess had told us, but I had heard her too young to understand.) It was not romance, but power.

Bitterest of all was the thought that I had once had the power of choice, and I had chosen wrong. Oh, I had been deceived in the particulars, but I had still made a mistake in assessing Guy's character. Now I would have to undo the wrong I had made.

After this, there was a time of quiet, but things had changed. Outwardly I was compliant enough — there was little use in anything else — but I was gathering my strength for the final break. Meanwhile, I watched and waited, as Tuck had advised me to do. I watched my body, too, in case it might betray me. Agnes helped me with the potions that would keep me from getting with child, and for good measure I used herbal rinse as well. It is a grievous sin, but I was desperate not to be pinned to Locksley and to Guy. I paid for that too, in the years when, with equal desperation, I wanted to have a baby and could not. But that was after.

One night, in the hours between (by Fontevrault reckoning) Matins and Lauds, I awoke to the sound of movement in the courtyard and the neighing and whinnying of horses. I was alone; Guy's side of the bed had cooled. It was full dark, only the guards' torches flickered, but nothing showed among the great lightless pools. Whatever had disturbed me moved furtively, contriving at silence.

I had taken the blanket off the bed to cover my nakedness, but I could not descend into the courtyard or be seen by our men and servants wrapped only in bedclothes. I pulled a fur gown off a peg and hunted unsuccessfully in the dark for some shoes. The floor was very cold. I passed to the top of the staircase that descended to the ground. Somewhere, below me, a voice called "What are you doing up?"

Guy came bounding up the stairs two at a time, causing them to rattle and shake. He threw an arm around me, all protectiveness. "Look, you're cold," he said, "and your feet are bare. Come back inside." At the same time he tried to swing me away from the stairs and turn me around toward the bedchamber.

I resisted. "Wait. I heard something down below. Was it you? Look!" Before he could answer, I pointed at an upraised face which had been caught, fleetingly, in the light of a torch. "There's Stephen." Stephen was our steward. "What's he doing?"

"If you'll come back to bed, I'll tell you," Guy said quietly, and with unusual patience. "I don't want you getting sick again."

As he would doubtless prevent my finding out anything on my own, there was no point in resisting. "All right," I said, when we were back inside, "what's going on? It's the middle of the night."

"What are you worried about?" he countered. "The men are on duty. No one can get in." His eyes were cool. "Or was it someone on the inside you were worried about? You're jumpy these days, aren't you?"

I shrugged, struggling for nonchalance. "I haven't been sleeping well," I said pointedly. "Anyway, it was caution, nothing more. I heard the sounds. What would you have me do? Someone might have been sick, or in danger."

He smiled. "If they had, you are scarcely fit to help. It's nothing for you to worry about. Stephen and I were laying in what we've collected for the Kings ransom, and the Blidworth portion just came in. We'll store it here and then send it on to Nottingham when we have enough. I thought it best to put it by secretly, and that's why we're doing it at night. The local people are bleeding as it is, so why tempt them unnecessarily? There's a great deal of money in there already."

I nodded. It might even be true. "Where did you hide it?"

He waved vaguely in the direction of the bailey below. "It's in a hut down there. Don't worry, it's quite safe." He gave me a swift look before blowing out the candle. "I've posted guards. No one can get in."

Guy was as good as his word. The storehouses were guarded day and night. I couldn't think of any plausible reason for trying to see into them, once I was turned away. I wasn't sure myself what I was expecting to see; we owed the ransom sure enough, and it did have to be stored somewhere. It was just too smooth, too compliant on the part of one of Prince John's supporters. I thought of sending word to Father Tuck, but I had nothing definite to tell him. Only a vague sense of uneasiness, and he would not thank me for troubling him with that. So

I said nothing. It was the swollen stream, before the floodgate breaks. But I have never been good at reading signs.

I expected, from day to day, that the treasure would be sent to Nottingham, under the Sheriff's escort or our own. It was not safe to send large sums of valuables anywhere without sufficient guards; there were too many ways things could disappear. There were even stories of robbers attacking armed men by daylight along the forest ways. The rewards, I suppose, were enough to justify such incredible risks. But as far as I could tell, nothing was sent out, though more than once I awakened at night to find Guy gone and the torches flickering in the bailey. By now, if I guessed rightly, there must be a pile of riches in our storeroom, a disturbing thought. I did not believe the local villagers were the only ones susceptible to temptation.

I had enlisted Agnes as an ally, and she did not fail me. In fact, now that Janet was gone she affected a much better humour and scowled less. She said she would keep a discreet watch on anyone or anything I asked her to, but neither one of us knew what to watch. On an afternoon when I was in the mews with my hawk Lucinda (a bird with the soul of a ribauz and my fiercest hunter, though since she always tried to slash me with her talons I never really liked her) Agnes brought the news that Alan was back in the neighbourhood, and would like to see me in private.

I raised my brows at this. "In private? At Locksley? This isn't France, you know."

Agnes looked unimpressed. "He says it's important."

"All the more reason to be careful, and discreet." I chewed my lip, thinking.

She cleared her throat. "Could you ask him to compose something for Lady Iseult? As a surprise? That would be an excuse for privacy."

I looked at her suspiciously, but her face was grave. "No one would credit it," I told her. "Guy has his saint's day soon — that might be reason enough. You'll attend me, of course."

Lucinda, neglected on my wrist, turned a baleful eye towards us and jumped suddenly on my arm, cutting through

403

the sleeves and shredding the exposed skin. It might have been worse; her talons had just been trimmed. Nevertheless it burned and bled, and the fact that it was my own fault was no consolation. "Merde," I said, shortening the creance and restoring, the hawk to her perch. "May your next sparrow stick in your throat."

In the darkened mews, Agnes laughed. The sound was remarkable.

★ ★ ★

Alan looked every inch the gaudy minstrel, turned out in crimson hose and tassels on his tunic. His clothing made him conspicuous, but his calling gave him protection and entry everywhere, and encouraged eccentricity. Bards, always in favour with everyone but clerics, were enjoying wild popularity owing to the rumour that King Richard's secret prison in Austria had been unearthed by his friend and favourite, the troubadour Blondel. "You look successful," I told him, somewhat sourly. My bandaged arm was throbbing.

He bowed over my hand and murmured something flattering, and said he had made some songs he knew I'd be interested in. However, he put off servility like an unwanted cloak when we were alone. "Father Tuck sent me," he said curtly. "He's had word of something you'll want to know."

His tone was even enough, but my blood was chilled nevertheless.

"Prince John has had a duplicate made of the Chancellor's seal, and he's using it." He looked at me meaningfully, as if I should understand more by this.

Our eyes met, and I looked away first. "I don't understand," I told him.

"Well, think what the chief business of the chancellery is these days," he said, a trifle impatiently. "The Prince is collecting the ransom intended for the King's release by using his own agents with duplicate seals. Then whatever he gets goes into his own coffers rather than the Chancellor's." He paused but still I said nothing. He dropped his voice, though we were alone except for Agnes, who stood waiting just outside the chamber. It was hard to resist the temptation to lean forward conspiratorially. "It is believed that to do this he is using the houses of his friends to collect and store what he has stolen from the treasury. The chests come and go in secret, but if they are discovered — well, they are sealed with the royal seal. It's nearly foolproof."

I sat back in my chair and put a hand over my eyes.

"You'll have guessed what I'm going to say next," he said quietly.

I nodded. "That Locksley is one of those houses."

He did not reply, having no need.

"You have proof?" I asked him. "I have to know beyond doubt."

Alan sounded sympathetic for the first time. "The house has been watched. The riders who bring the chests belong to the Prince's household. The treasure is being kept in the shed next to the cheese cave, as far as we can tell. If you have to set eyes on it yourself, you'll have to find a way past the guards. It would be too dangerous for anyone else to try."

I thought a moment. The place was the same I had seen from the top of the stairs, and of course it all fitted. "That won't be necessary," I told him, striving for firmness. "What should I — what does the Father want me to do?"

He shook his head. "Not here. Somewhere safer. Can you find an excuse to get to Edwinstowe?"

"It won't be easy, but I'll think of something. I will have to be attended, and with guards."

"That doesn't matter. You'll be meeting a man in the church there. He'll be dressed as a monk. If you're careful, no one will suspect you."

"I don't like it," I said, feeling panicky. "Who is this man? Why can't I meet with Father Tuck?"

Alan shrugged. "I didn't say you wouldn't see the Father. He asks that you first see this man and then decide if you are willing to help, to do what he asks. I promise you will understand everything when you come to Edwinstowe . . . "

3

THE church at Edwinstowe sits in the middle of a small clearing with the other village buildings, in the deepest part of Sherwood. The saplings were hacked back every year, but the low growth was still thick and tangled. Not far off, the villagers claimed, there were oaks so massive each could shelter a hundred men beneath its branches' pavilion. The old tracks still led that way, but they were overgrown. People were afraid of thieves and evil spirits and unnatural beasts, and stayed close to their own hearths.

The little church was old too, with some of the original stones from the days before Great William. I could pass under its lintel without bending, but a man would need to stoop. The interior was dark and quiet, and I could smell the fat from the candles. The cool stone leached damp into the still air.

A single figure waited at the altar,

head bowed and hidden within the plain monk's cowl. By prearrangement, I came up behind him, went down on my knees, and said quietly, "Brother, I am in need of your help."

You must not believe that I had given no thought to whom I would meet in the darkened church. I had a theory, and every reason to think it correct. Still, when he turned, his face shadowed by the hood, I was startled and confused. I knew his eyes, which were regarding me steadily with an expression of cool dislike.

He moved back beside me, half turning in the pose of one counselling a penitent. I scarcely felt the floor beneath my knees. His mouth turned up slightly, and he said, "So you do recognize me, after all."

I barely nodded. He continued to scrutinize my face. "You're disappointed."

I roused myself at that. After all, he had been kind to me once, after a fashion, and his friend John had saved my life. "Oh no," I said quickly. "Just surprised. I had thought . . . that is, I expected it would be someone else."

He raised an eyebrow in a gesture I remembered. "Oh really? Who?" He sounded mildly curious and a bit bored.

"It doesn't matter," I said, suddenly fearing I might jeopardize the person I had in fact expected.

"Your secret is safe with me," he said, still sounding indifferent. "You know what I am, and my neck is in the noose as it is for coming out of hiding. If you have — or had — any reason to think someone else is involved in this business, it would be safer for you and all of us if you just spit it out."

I lowered my eyes. "I'm not sure. I don't even know him. Or at least . . . Well, I thought the outlawed . . . the man who was the Earl of Huntingdon would be mixed up in it somehow. He held Locksley before my husband. He has a better motive than anyone I can think of." I shrugged. "Perhaps he's dead."

The half-smile widened, and twisted. "He's not dead."

"How do you — " I began, then nearly choked on the words. What stopped me was his face. I half rose from my knees, but he put out a hand to pull me down again. There was no need for him to speak. I knew. I think I had begun to know when I said 'the outlawed Earl of Huntingdon', but I can't imagine how it had taken me so long to put it all together. Then, like a second wave, came the memory of that first, earlier meeting, a long time ago in Nottingham.

"You're blushing," he pointed out. "I really did surprise you then? You had no idea?" He sounded incredulous.

"How could I? That time in the forest you called yourself by some ridiculous name . . . "

"Robin Hood."

"Yes. And you let me think you were just an outlaw. You never said you were an earl."

"Keep your voice down, will you? What did you expect?" I drew a breath to speak, but he overrode me. "As a matter of fact, I wasn't an earl then and I'm not one now. King Richard gave Huntingdon to the brother of William of Scotland, and I somehow doubt he'd relinquish it to me. Moreover, 'that time in the forest' as you put it, I seem to recall that you were somewhat less than honest yourself."

Worse and worse. I felt myself growing hot and had to will myself not to hide my face in my hands. "You knew who I was, even then?"

"Not then, no. But afterwards," he said calmly. "I promise you it's of little consequence."

"But that *was* you, wasn't it, that time by the waterhole when I was a little girl?"

His voice lost its bantering tone. "Yes," he said coldly, "but that time need not concern us now."

I shifted on the floor, taking this in. "Then why did you bring me here? What do you want from me?"

He kept his head turned from me, eyes on the altar, the very picture of piety. "That's the question, isn't it? Father Tuck says you have a conscience. I think you owe me something."

I waited, scarcely daring to breathe, for what he would say next. I looked at the sun-browned face that had become a mask, the brows drawn down in a grimace of what might have been concentration, or pain, and decided that, whatever he thought of me, his words would not come lightly. That only served to make me more apprehensive.

"I promised Tuck I would be honest with you," he said, keeping his eyes on the cross. There was an infinitesimal pause. "I want Locksley back."

I swallowed, and thought how to answer him. "I — I expected that. But I can't give it to you."

"Of course not. But King Richard can. And might, if I can see that the ransom money Prince John has so cunningly misappropriated finds its way to London after all. It's a long shot, but it's all I have."

I sat silent, thinking. The return of the ransom would not be enough, of course, to get him Locksley. He would first have to discredit its present lord. "You'd implicate Guy?"

His eyes left the altar and slid sideways to look into mine. "Yes."

"Even though the King might never return and it could all be for nothing."

"Yes."

I felt, vaguely and inexplicably, something like shame. "I understand," I told him.

"Do you? I doubt it. I grew up in the Hall, did you know? They sent me there, far from Huntingdon, to live with a forester they had let it to. It was supposed to be mine, if I stayed out of the way and did as I was told. They told me I was a bastard," he said matter-of-factly. "My parents were dead. My uncle was the Earl of Huntingdon. And Locksley would come to me. It was all I had. It might have been easier, if the forester had been kind . . . It was all I had."

"But I heard in London you had taken your family to court with some proof you were the rightful earl. How did that happen, then?"

He shook his head slowly. "There *was* proof — a hidden parish record which had escaped destruction and an old clerk who would take an oath — that my parents were married after all. My mother was Saxon, and my uncle had blackened her name for years so he could inherit, even though he'd known

414

the truth. I had to stop him."

A small curve in his lips made it seem as if he were smiling, but I couldn't imagine anything amusing in such a story. "So much trouble for so little. I was Earl of Huntingdon just long enough for the Prince to try to buy me, as he has . . . so many others. When I refused, he made a deal with my uncle instead. John would help him get rid of me, in exchange for Locksley, and, I suspect, a hefty contribution to the Prince's purse. Locksley was to be used to reward a particularly loyal friend, or so we heard. Nothing can be proved, of course. Alan said he told you what happened to Agnes's brother. In the end the King upset the plan by naming the King of Scotland's brother as my successor to Huntingdon, and my uncle was left out in the cold. The last I heard he had left for France."

"Serves him right," I muttered, without thinking.

"What? Oh, I suppose it does. But I suspect he would have lost in the end anyway. You really can't trust Prince John, you know," he said. Now he did smile, but the effect was chilling.

"You still haven't told me what you want me to do," I said. He made me feel inadequate and somehow to blame. Whatever sympathy I felt for him was mixed with the feeling that he was very well able to look after himself and not a little dangerous. He continued to watch me dispassionately, with eyes the colour of a winter sky. "It's not my fault," I insisted.

"You married him."

I heard what he really meant to say: *I chose you, and you chose Guy.* "You owe me something," he had said. At the moment, I felt I owed him an explanation.

"Do you think I would have, if I had known? He swore to me he owed nothing to the Prince, had no reason to expect special favours. Do you think he would tell me he was in league with John? That Locksley came to him stained with blood? For all I'd heard you tried to kill the King's agent in cold calculation and deserved to be outlawed."

"And now you've turned against him," he went on, just as if I'd said nothing.

416

I felt the colour coming hot into my cheeks. "Yes, but not just for that. He's betraying the King with the Prince, and that is against my honour. I'd like to save myself, if I can."

"You make it sound like one of Alan's ballads," he said rudely.

"That's fine — you can sneer if you want to. You know I wouldn't be here if I didn't agree that you should have Locksley back. Whatever motives I might have for helping you are none of your business. Guy has Gisborne, and I have Blidworth, and we can get by nicely on that." (I meant after we had annulled our marriage, but I would not give this arrogant outlaw a window into my private unhappiness.) "There is one thing: don't ask me to help you put my husband's neck in a noose. He may put it there by himself, but I won't help *you* ruin him. As you say, I married him."

"I — "

The door to the church stood open to the afternoon light, which meant that anyone passing or entering cast a shadow across the threshold. Someone's bulk blocked the doorway, and I turned slowly, and, I hoped, casually. "Just a little longer, Roland. Does Agnes have the herbs we need?"

"Not yet, my lady. But when I asked her, she said to tell you she was almost ready. In case you were ready yourself, that is."

He sounded hopeful. Edwinstowe offered few distractions for my husband's retainers. "Good," I told him. "I'll be with you soon. Lord Robert," I began, when the man had gone.

He grimaced. "No. I told you: just Robin."

"Whatever," I said, to pay him back. "I have to leave soon. Do you want my help or don't you?"

"I want your help."

"Well then?"

"I'm fairly sure the Prince will want his treasure soon. He's not the type to let it lie long under someone else's roof. My guess is that he'll collect it at the hunting lodge in Clipstone, or else send it directly to Nottingham."

"To *Nottingham*?"

"You are an innocent, aren't you?" His voice held a touch of malice. "You

418

must have known the Sheriff was for the Prince."

I shook my head. "I doubt it's that simple." I gave him the assessment of the Sheriff's character I had formed during my stay in Nottingham, that he was a decent man in a bad situation who had thrown in his lot with the probable winner. "But I don't think he would do anything so base as to subvert the King's ransom money," I told him.

"Perhaps not, if the Prince were to leave him alone to act on his honour." He gave the last word a mocking emphasis which I decided to ignore. "But he won't. He'll bribe or bully or blackmail him into doing what he wants. Whatever his private reservations, the Sheriff has gone too far now to be considered anything but John's tool."

"So, Nottingham then."

"Right, and your job is to find out where and when the treasure is going, or failing that, to let me and my men into Locksley to steal it."

"Sweet Jesu. You don't want much."

He closed his eyes wearily. "I would hardly take these risks if all I wanted

419

was a small favour." He gave me some hurried instructions about what I was to look for and how, but nothing that lessened the apparent difficulties.

"All right, I'll try," I told him. "But how will I get word to you?"

"Tell Agnes. She'll know whom to contact."

"You don't trust me," I realized, with indignation.

He sighed deeply. "Not entirely. And besides, I'm trying to protect you. You can't be too careful."

"Then I'll pass along a warning of my own. You're probably right about the Sheriff, but I do know this much about him: if you steal the treasure out from under his nose, he'll come after you. And I think he will be a very bad enemy."

"I know that," he said quite gaily, "but I don't have much to lose except my life, and if I have to go on like this forever that's worth very little to me. You, however, are still in possession of a home, a name, a reputation, and a small fortune, if I remember correctly from the proposed marriage contract. That's a lot to throw away, even if you think now that it doesn't matter. I'm here to tell you that it does. So be careful, won't you?"

"I will," I promised him, as I rose to leave the church. "I can take care of myself."

I never heard how he responded to that.

★ ★ ★

It was a lovely afternoon. From the window of my solar I could see that the distant larches had already taken on the fullness of their brilliant green, and the birds outside had come home to mate and sing. The water ran high in the stream beds and the earth glistened and swelled. I sat daydreaming, inhaling the dry tang of scrub grass in the sun. It made me want to stretch out, catlike, on some meadow lawn. In the corner, Agnes hummed snatches of Alan's latest tune, which she claimed was a love song.

I wondered how far away the cloud was that was puffing and stretching itself across the expanse of sky visible through the window frame. Was it a mile? What would it feel like to take it in your hands like dandelion seeds or the softest goose down, to lie upon it and go drifting around the cool blue dome of heaven . . . ?

"I have good news for you," my husband said, in a tone that made me doubt whether I would agree. "I know how worried you've been about the safety of the King's ransom in the storehouse, so I —"

I looked up quickly. "Worried? I haven't been worried, particularly. Why would you say that?" I knew the answer already, of course. He had had the treasure watched, and I had not been careful enough.

He shrugged. "As you like. The Sheriff will dispatch a party soon to see it gets to Nottingham safely, and from there on to London. I don't deny I'll be relieved myself. It's a big responsibility." He sounded quite sincere, as he no doubt was. He took out his little ornamental dagger, a fine, polished one with a bone handle, and began flicking absently at his nails. I watched the parings fall to the floor and waited for what he would say next. "And by the way," he added casually, "Prince John has sent word he'll be up from London about the same time. There's a hunting party at Clipstone."

"Hunting? Now?" I asked incautiously.

"Why not? The deer aren't at their fattest yet, but it should be good enough sport."

"I was thinking," I said, more acidly than I intended, "that with his brother the King a captive, the King of France attempting to invade Normandy, not to mention all the administrative troubles we seem to be having here, the Prince might be far too busy to go hunting with his friends, in season or out."

In the corner, Agnes coughed.

"You have leave to go out," Guy told her. "That girl gives me the creeps," he said, when she had gone. "Always skulking around, and so *ugly*." He almost shuddered.

"She's not that bad. She's just unhappy, so she doesn't try. Will he be coming here?"

"Who?"

"Prince John."

"Oh. Maybe. I don't know."

"Well, when would it be? Soon?"

"I told you I'm not sure."

"Well, if he did come, would it be within a month, or a week, or a few days? I have to know, Guy," I insisted, to forestall his rising irritation. "If we are to entertain him and his party properly, I have to be prepared."

"Oh, within a fortnight then. But I've told you he may not come himself. And anyway, you don't need to worry about it. You can safely leave that sort of thing to Mother. She always handles it right."

"Naturally," I said, and didn't even bat an eyelash.

* * *

Agnes was waiting for me in the mews. It was the perfect meeting place; there were few hawks now that the austringer had been turned off for stealing. Everybody stole nowadays; it was the only way some people could deal with the cutbacks the King's ransom necessitated. You could turn a blind eye to it up to a point, but the austringer had made himself obvious, and under the circumstances Guy could hardly tolerate a thief around the manor. So far he had not found anyone else he could trust to fill the position. I tended to Lucinda myself, half hoping when I flew her she would be carried off by a sudden wind or her own savage instinct for freedom. Her training deteriorated, but she returned to the fist with the stubborn consistency of a homing pigeon. She was hooded now, but made soft, irritated noises from her perch.

Agnes watched me in composed silence. Her years in service had conditioned her not to initiate conversation, but she made it a virtue, seeming wise and calm. "Do you know how to get a message to them?" I asked her. It was safest not to name names.

She nodded.

"Can you be sure it won't find its way into the wrong hands?"

She nodded again, serenely.

"*How* can you be sure?" I asked her, irritated.

"I'm sorry, Lady Marian. You know I can't tell you how the messages are passed, not unless — you know I can't tell you. Please don't ask me."

"All right. But *I* have to trust everything — even my life — to them, and they don't trust me at all."

She shook her head rigidly, so that her whole body swivelled. "It's safer this way. That's all I know. I have to stick to that."

"Of course you do," I told her, feeling defeated. "Look, here's what I've found out." I told her what Guy had told me, and what I had guessed, that Prince John's 'hunting party' was hardly coincidental with the collection of the treasure. "I can't be sure whether it's destined for Nottingham or Clipstone, but I'm sure it will go out within two weeks. Tell them they will have to watch the roads. I would bet on Clipstone since the Prince will be there; after that it can be moved on with the Sheriff's connivance and no one the wiser. Can you remember all that?"

"Yes. But," she cleared her throat, "they will need to know more."

"Well, if I find out anything else, I'll let you know. It won't do anyone any good if I make Guy suspicious."

She opened her mouth as if she would

say something, but in the end she changed her mind. After this, I felt much better. I had done what I could. The fate of the ransom money was out of my hands. I had satisfied my honour. I had not been discovered. On the whole, I was quite pleased with myself.

If only it had been that easy.

4

THE days slipped by like sand in a sieve. Guy still could not confirm any plans, but Lady Iseult was busy with the cooks and at her most insufferable, which was something. The 'Gangdays' were coming up, for the beating of the bounds, the procession reaffirming Locksley's boundaries. The feasting was small-scale and subdued, but everyone turned out for the column marching behind the cross and the village banner. The bells and shouting made a commotion to wake the dead, and by the time the small boys were ducked in the boundary brooks or had their bottoms bumped against the traditional trees, the procession had become a near riot. It happened every year, but this time the winter's deprivations and uncertainties brought forth a spring of wildness that was anything but gay. A grazing sheep was hacked up with hunting knives, a cat was stoned, and some people in the procession were trampled when the rioters broke loose. One of the injured was Agnes.

Fortunately, she had only sprained her ankle — though badly — when she was shoved into a ditch, or she might have added lameness to her other misfortunes. She lay on a cot in the hall, her eyes dark and her face shadowed with pain. "I'm so glad you've come," she whispered to me with a desperation that made me wonder if she was dreadfully hurt after all. "Come closer."

I bent over her. "What is it?"

"You've got to go out there. Right now. It's already late."

"Out where? Late for what?" I felt her forehead, to see if she had a fever.

She grimaced. "There's a message. I'm supposed to meet — our friends, and then report to you. You'll have to go in my place. My lady," she added as an afterthought.

"Why show up at all?" I asked her. "If no one comes, they'll just know you couldn't make it and try again later. Wouldn't that be safer?"

She shook her head fiercely. "If I

don't come they'll think I've been caught. Someone will come for me. Alan promised."

I thought it highly unlikely he would try to keep that promise, but the look she gave me made me give in. If I were careful I could minimize the risks. After all, there was still enough confusion from the procession to provide a cover. "All right," I told her, "what do I have to do?"

"Take the south track," she whispered. "The fifth oak tree you come to on the right, turn in thirty paces. You'll see an arrow in the top of a tree. If it's white, wait there. If it's a dark one, come back at once."

"Heaven help us, have you been doing this all this time? It's near nightfall now, and I might miss the arrow altogether."

"Best get going then," she said, unmoved.

The fifth oak was easy enough to find; it was surprising how many oaks were in the forest round Locksley when you began to count. I discounted the seedlings getting started from acorns as impossible to keep track of (did the ones behind or beside the big trees count as well?), much less enumerate. In this philosophical and somewhat muddled fashion I came to the tree I was satisfied was the oak in question; it was not too far down the track to be dangerously distant from the house, but you could not be seen or heard from here either. I pulled my mantle up around my ears and my headpiece down, so that a casual watcher could not have seen my face. Then I turned right, and began to count out thirty paces. The light was growing very dim, and the roots were twisted, so I kept my eyes on the ground. The woods were still and silent.

Twenty-five . . . twenty-six . . . I lifted my eyes. I had emerged into an open space. Across it, in a tree top, something white stood out against the dusky trunk. I crossed the clearing quietly, and leaned up against a young oak that stood where the track plunged back again into the black tunnel of woods. The bushes rustled just behind me. I whirled, and I think, in spite of everything, a shriek worthy of the screaming skull was on my lips. Someone grabbed me, and pulled me up to him brutally, and his hand came down hard over my mouth.

He was very strong, and it hurt me. I scratched at his hand and struggled. "Keep quiet, will you?" he hissed, and I recognized the voice. I stopped fighting and went slack in his arms. His hold relaxed. "You're not Agnes," he said, and turned me around.

"How perceptive of you," I said furiously. "Is that your excuse for mauling me like that?"

"You were going to scream," said Robin "Do you deny it?"

"How do you know what I was going to do? You were behind me, creeping along and scaring me half to death."

"You had your shoulders hunched," he insisted. "You were going to yell. And anyway, don't get all lady-of-the-manorish with me. You know the need for caution as well as I do. Where's Agnes?"

"She sprained her ankle. She can't walk. She sent me."

We glared at each other in the near

darkness. "So?" I asked him. "What is the message?"

"Look," he said tartly, "are you sure you want to go through with this?"

"Quite frankly, no, especially if you're going to behave like some Visigoth taking Rome."

He laughed, which was even more maddening than his strongarm tactics. "Fair enough," he said. "Why don't you sit down there," he gestured grandly at a tree root, "and we'll talk."

"I have to get back," I warned him, "before I'm missed."

He leaned back against the trunk and reached above him, pulling out the arrow. "Well," he said with studied calm, "I just didn't want you to be surprised when I turn up at Locksley."

I gaped at him. "What do you mean, 'turn up at Locksley?' You couldn't possibly do a thing like that!"

He smiled. "Oh, you won't have to worry; I'll be in disguise."

"You're mad," I told him with conviction. "You can't seriously believe you can walk into Locksley, where you grew up and everyone knows you, disguised as the merry monk of Edwinstowe, or whatever, and not be recognized. There's no reason — "

"There's every reason," he said, suddenly quite grave. "I've got to get the treasure out."

"*By yourself?*"

"John will be with me, and some of the others. Besides, there'll be you and Agnes, on the inside."

"Oh no, absolutely not. Have you been sleeping in a bean field or what? I told Agnes to tell you to watch the roads and take the treasure when they move it out. Didn't she give you the message?"

"Yes, she told me. You expect me to attack an armed caravan of the Prince's men with a handful of underfed outlaws and some bows and arrows . . . ?"

"From what I hear, it's been done," I said quietly.

"Perhaps, but for a prize like this the guard will be full strength and watchful. Don't you see that what *we* lack in might can be made up in guile and secrecy. I have it all worked out: I'll come dressed as a potter, and you'll be interested in buying my wares. Then . . . "

434

I couldn't believe I'd heard him say that. "Dressed as a *what*?"

"A potter," he said cheerfully. "You don't have to look like that. It's a disguise I've used before with great success. As a matter of fact, I used it at Nottingham when John was, ah, forced to accept the Sheriff's hospitality for a while. The Sheriff's lady was so taken with my pots that I had to give her the last five of them before she'd let me go."

"I suppose you throw them yourself at your kiln in the woods?"

He flashed me an annoying, cocksure grin. "Not exactly. I have a friendly arrangement with a real potter."

"Well, you can make other arrangements for this adventure. I can't permit you to come into my — into Locksley and do something like that. It's too dangerous for all of us. The penalty would be worse than outlawry, you know."

He folded his arms and looked at me. The light had faded into blue twilight, so that I could not see him well, but his whole body sent out an intensity which was almost palpable. "I'm trying to be patient," he said, in a tone which sounded anything but, "because you are risking a lot, and also" — I heard rather than saw the smile — "because just now you stopped yourself from saying 'my house'. However, the plan is not open to discussion, unless you have something more positive in mind than your refusal. You can co-operate or not, as you see fit. But it would be very much safer, for you and everyone else, if you went along."

"Are you threatening me?"

"Not at all. Well, yes, I suppose I am. It's more like blackmail, but I'm just stating facts. If you betray me, I will take you down with me, I promise you that. Now listen — there isn't much time. Here's what I plan . . . " He outlined it for me in some detail. I felt as if I was in the middle of a bad dream and could not make myself wake up.

"One thing," I asked him.

"What's that?"

"You haven't told me when."

He looked surprised. "Why, tomorrow, of course."

★ ★ ★

436

Naturally, I didn't sleep a wink all night. I lay without moving in the big, closed-off bed, seeing nothing and thinking of everything. I went over every detail of the proposed scheme for getting the treasure out, and conjured up a hundred ways it could go wrong. I wondered what the outlaw would do and say if he were caught. Guy would kill him outright, I was sure of that, without waiting for the Sheriff's justice, or the Prince's. I tried not to think of what would happen if he implicated me, of what Guy would do then. My husband was some distant, merciless figure whose revenge would be terrible and swift. The naked, momentarily vulnerable body lying next to me in sleep didn't enter into it at all. Last, but scarcely least, I reflected on what I would be setting in motion if the plan succeeded, on what I would eventually lose. I had come to love Locksley, and I would lose it, it was as simple as that. I worried in the darkness, trying to see another way, but for all my struggles I couldn't think of anything else to do. Eventually, the sun came up.

My ears had strained for the sound so

long I scarcely believed it when I heard the wagon wheels bumping and scraping along the rutted road. It was all I could do not to run to the gatehouse and look out, but instead I stayed where I was, hanging spices in gourds from the east window. Now that warm weather was here, there were smells that needed masking. Besides, I would know everything soon enough.

The wagon was old, with a carefully mended cover and straw packing for the jars and pots. It certainly looked authentic, and so did the driver, when he dismounted in the courtyard. He was all brown, from the tips of his heavy shoes and leg coverings up to the cap fastening under his chin, brown as earth and just as dusty. He was right; it was a good disguise. I was beginning to perceive how easily he could put off one identity and take on another. Even the knightly bearing I had first noticed in Sherwood had been replaced with the stoop of a man used to toil, the demeanour of deference.

The cloth over the back of the wagon lifted, and someone else climbed out. He was a youngish man, dressed in the same nondescript fashion, and not one I recognized. That was to be expected; he could not introduce anyone else who might be known here. The others would be waiting, hidden outside our gates. The two of them shuffled amiably about, bowing to Stephen, and keeping their faces averted from his scrutiny in apparent awkward modesty. They asked, as we had planned, to see the lady of the manor. What none of us had foreseen was that in response Stephen produced Lady Iseult. I had lingered by the window, waiting to be summoned, so I got to see her coming through the stableyard on the steward's arm, smoothing her skirts and scattering wary chickens in her path. Unfortunately, she looked up just at that moment and saw me too. She straightened visibly, head up and eyes forward, and stepped directly into the stable midden.

I withdrew quickly from the window. I couldn't hear what she was saying, but her gestures at Stephen were eloquent enough. In that temper, with her dignity wounded, she was hardly likely to be receptive to solicitations from itinerant craftsmen. I set the spice gourds down, and ran as fast as I could to find Agnes.

When I came out into the yard some time later, I saw that I had guessed right. Robin and his unnamed assistant were standing dejectedly by the wagon, Stephen was waving toward the gate, and Lady Iseult was striding purposefully in my direction. I came up beside her and took her arm, smiling. She looked slightly taken aback. Don't overdo it, I reminded myself. "No good?" I asked mildly.

She shook her head. "Not as far as I'm concerned," she said, with a hint of challenge. "Of course, *you* can take a look if you want, but they aren't up to the quality I've tried to insist on for the house." Her tone told me that I was insufficiently conscious of my disadvantages.

"Then there's no need for me to look, as long as you don't want them," I said. "It's a pity though — that potter's coming now seemed like a real stroke of good fortune."

"What do you mean?"

"Oh, didn't you hear?" I asked innocently. "There's been an accident.

One of the girls dropped the wine jars, and broke quite a few of them. She'd hurt her ankle yesterday, and I suppose she got up too soon and it gave way on her. I'd thought that if any of these were acceptable, we might replace them. After all, with the Prince coming . . . "

"Sweet Jesu," she said. "Why didn't I hear about this?"

I lowered my eyes. "I believe it has just happened, *Belle-mère*." I hoped she would not ask who had done it.

"Well, if you *will* keep idiot servants, these things will keep happening. I suppose we'll have to buy some of the man's wares now. You there!" she shouted at Robin, "Wait a moment. Don't go away," she added, though he had so far shown no inclination toward leaving. I could not help flashing him a triumphant look as we approached.

I must say he handled it beautifully. His whole being seemed reanimated, just as if he couldn't get over his good luck in snatching a sale from the jaws of defeat. He pointed out the virtues and characteristics of at least ten different jars, though to my eye they all looked

441

the same with their dark green glaze and uniform shape. "And," he said, by way of summation, "they are guaranteed not to leak."

"That's what you say now," I told him, "but you and your apprentice will be far away when the wine drips out all over our table and guests."

He drew himself up, as if offended. "Seeing you don't believe me, my lady, I'll prove to you that I'm offering quality goods. We'll fill up all these jars with water and let them stand overnight. In the morning you can pick out the ones you want to buy. Isn't that fair enough? With this good lady's permission" — he bowed grandly toward Lady Iseult; he had seen how the land lay there quickly enough — "my man and I will pull up in a corner of your courtyard. We'll not trouble you for lodgings. We can sleep in the wagon."

"That's all right then," said my mother-in-law, much more warmly. "There'll be a nice supper for you too. Just ask in the kitchen."

I began to reconsider the story of the Sheriff's lady and the pots. I also began to think that just possibly the preposterous plan might work after all.

★ ★ ★

It was full dark when I pushed back the covers and the hangings and slipped from the bed. Guy groaned once, and stirred, but while I stood motionless his breathing slowed and became deep and regular. I shivered, but I could not risk pulling on more than my shift. The night was very still, and I could hear the guard coughing on the steps below. I scuttled across the rushes to Guy's clothes chest, where he kept the key to the treasure room. Of course he had not entrusted it to me or even to his mother along with the other keys. The lid creaked slightly when I opened the chest, but I soon felt the outline and held the weight of it in my hands. I held my breath, listening, but there was still silence. I tied the key with a leather thong I had taken from the mews. Then I wrapped it in my shift and went out of the chamber.

When I was sick so long I had developed an aversion to using the night jar and always got up to go to the garderobe when I could. The guards were supposed to look the other way when I passed, and most of them did. In any case the eccentricity served me well, because it meant I could wander about at night unremarked. I went into the garderobe chamber, tied one end of the line to the peg securing the window covering, and threw the key out of the window, so that it hung down the wall. I heard it clunk as it hit, not a large sound but magnified to a thunderclap by my apprehension. When it died away I expected something dire to happen, but nothing did. I let out my breath, which I had not even realized I'd been holding. My part in this was over, at least for the moment. The rest of it — the wine laced with poppy, the key in its dangling place, the small diversion — was not my responsibility. Be natural, Robin had said. I used the pit for its traditional purpose, then went back to my bedchamber, where, by now, Guy was snoring.

Much later, I was startled from sleep by a shout. Guy was pulling on his tunic and a cloak. "What is it?" I asked, not needing to feign grogginess. "What's wrong?"

"Something's burning," Guy said briefly, and in fact the tang of smoke had entered the room. I reached for my own shift and mantle on the peg.

It was a measure of Locksley's readiness that the yard was already full of men. "What's on fire?" asked my husband.

Stephen was on the steps, completely dressed. "I'm sorry you were disturbed, my lord. One of the wagons caught fire, but we've got it out now. It spread to that potter's wagon too, so we pushed them both outside the gates, in case there are any sparks or smouldering embers. But I think it's all out."

"And the treasure room?" Guy said quietly, between clenched teeth.

"Still locked, sir." He looked at me for a moment and then seemed to shrug. "I regret to say," he began in a tone that indicated he was not sorry at all, "that the guard on duty evidently had too much to drink and fell asleep. Luckily some of the others were more watchful or the fire might have got out of hand before it was noticed. No harm to anything important, if you take my meaning. But I'll see the man is punished."

"By God, you'd better. I want him flogged for this. I'd better get the key and make sure everything's all right."

My blood turned cold in my body. The key, if all had gone according to plan, was even now dangling from the garderobe window ready for me to collect and replace it in its chest. I should not have gone back to sleep. I thrust myself up against Guy's body in a manner there was no mistaking and said, "Can't it wait? It's late now, and you need your rest." It was all I could think of to do.

My husband looked at me in surprise, as well he might. Stephen smiled patronizingly and said, "Everything appears to be in order, my lord. I see no reason for you to disturb yourself before morning. Good night then, my lord, my lady." And he left me to finish what I had started.

"My God," Guy said wonderingly, "you do blow hot and cold, don't you?"

I thought he was too vain to hold out for long. "No woman likes a cold bed forever, Guy."

He peered at me in the dark. "There's more to it than that, isn't there? Something more you want?"

I knew how to answer that. "Yes," I told him, "I want a child."

"Well, in that case . . ."

Afterwards, of course, all I could think about was getting the key from its hiding place and putting it back into the chest. It was more dangerous now; more of the household were about after the disturbance, and in any case it would soon be daylight. I rehearsed the return so many times in my head that I felt the key's image burned on my mind, its heft a permanent weight in my hands. The thought possessed me like a song.

It was back on its thong, still dangling from the window peg. There was nothing to suggest it had ever been removed, except that the fire had been set. By now they should all be far away, the treasure stowed safely beneath water-soaked linen in the back of the potter's wagon, which had been pushed outside the gates, obligingly, by Locksley's own men. And no one the wiser . . . I tried not to think about what would happen to the guard on duty at the treasure room, the one who had drunk Robin's doctored wine and fallen asleep. When he discovered the loss, Guy would be out of his mind with rage and fear, and he would vent it on this hapless man, among others. I think I believed, then, that if the worst came to the worst I might be able to intercede on his behalf.

But first I had to get the key back into the chest. As before I hid it in the material of my shift and made my way quietly back to our chamber. The bed curtains were drawn, and there was no sound. I knelt by the chest and lifted the lid with painful slowness to prevent its creaking. At the end, it groaned, just slightly, and I froze. A swirl of air from the corridor stirred the rushes outside the door, but still I didn't move. Finally, hearing nothing, I withdrew the key and put it back where it had lain. The lid slid down soundlessly.

It was over. I had not been caught. I took my first relaxed breath in countless hours and settled back to wait for daylight and the discoveries of the morning.

5

THE hours of darkness were the longest, in the shadow of the axe about to fall. In the light, the day's rituals made a better hiding place in which to wait. The morning was surprisingly far along when the stroke fell at last.

"Have you seen that potter?" Lady Iseult asked, when she had cornered me in the library. "The pots are there, but I can't find him or the wagon."

"The wagon started to burn last night, and Stephen had it pushed outside," I said casually. "I haven't seen him today. Did they leak?"

"What? Oh no, he was right about the quality, so I suppose we'll make them do for the Prince's visit. Curse the man's impudence, now I'll have to hunt him down. Stephen!" she called, and went off on the search that would eventually and inevitably lead to the discovery of the missing ransom.

No prisoner can tell his honest
  thought
Unless he speaks as one who suffers
  wrong;
But for his comfort he may make
  a song.
My friends are many, but their gifts
  are naught.
Shame will be theirs, if for my
  ransom, here
I lie another year.

Richard's song, composed in captivity,
was all over literate England and doubtless
the continent as well. There were various
versions, according to the singer, but the
gist was always the same. I was writing
them down. *After my death they wilt
have grievous wrong If I am prisoner
long . . .*

"Marian!" Guy's sudden entrance and
grip on my wrist, which whirled me from
my seat and scattered the parchment, was
less frightening than the look on his face.
He was alternately red and white with
anger and fear, and his eyes were those
of a man pushed to the very edge of
violence. But not toward me, I reminded

myself. He couldn't know . . . Lady Iseult, who had followed in his wake, looked sick and spent, but when she came to the doorway her eyes focused on me with speculation. "The treasure's gone," he said in a strangled voice. "All the money and goods we'd collected for the P — , we'd collected. It's gone. Do you know anything about it?"

"Do you mean the King's ransom? You mean it's been *stolen*?"

He flashed a look at Lady Iseult. "Yes. Answer my question."

I did not have to fake a reaction. "No. I don't — didn't — know anything about it. What happened?"

He ignored my question. "Mother thought you might." He had not let go of my wrist.

I looked at her. "Why?"

In spite of her fear, her voice held a note of triumph. "I saw you, early this morning. Kneeling by the chest."

"Where I keep the key to the treasure room," Guy said in a flat voice.

I turned back to him. "Is it missing?"

"No," he said, still watching me.

"Then what are you talking about?"

"Someone took all of the ransom treasure out of its hiding place last night, someone who knew where it was hidden. Whoever did it used the key, because the lock wasn't broken."

"And you think *I* took it? I was with you last night," I reminded him. "Perhaps there's another key."

His look told me he had already thought of this. He loosened his grip. "And the chest?"

I shrugged. "I don't know. I had one of my walking dreams last night, after the fire, and I woke up away from the bed. I'm sure I didn't take the key, and I'm quite sure I didn't steal the King's ransom in my sleep. This is serious, Guy. What are we going to do? What are we going to tell the Queen, or the Chancellor?" It was true about the walking dreams, and Guy knew it. Whenever I was anxious, and that had been often enough since my marriage, I would wander in my sleep about the bedchamber, usually intent on some earnest purpose I could not quite remember when I woke. It was a plausible excuse, as far as it went.

Guy looked, if possible, even grimmer. "We won't tell them anything yet. First we'll move heaven and earth to get it back. I'll stop at nothing," he said, looking at me.

"I agree," I assured him. "We've got to think of every possibility. Have you questioned all the men? Are any of them missing?"

"Yes and no. The only people unaccounted for are that potter and his assistant. They disappeared during the night. Now that I've been asking, some of the servants thought one of them looked familiar. It seems likely they were here before and got wind of something. There's a party out after them, and I intend to go myself now that I've talked to you. Meanwhile, the gates are sealed. No one is to go in or out." He looked at me with cold eyes, so that I knew I had not entirely convinced him of my innocence. "If it was the potter, it is still possible he had inside help. If I find out you had anything to do with it, I will kill you myself. That is a promise." He did not touch me, but his tone was so matter-of-fact I had no reason to doubt he meant it. He strode from the room before I could compose myself to answer, but Lady Iseult lingered behind.

"You weren't asleep," she said accusingly. "You were kneeling. I saw you."

"Look, we are all worried. Let's not make it worse. I've explained about the sleepwalking. Guy knows it's true."

"You were dressed," she persisted.

I shrugged. "What can I say? There was a fire, and Stephen came up. Later I went out to the privy. Of course I had put on my night shift, and kept it on. Why were you outside our room looking to see if we were dressed or not?"

If I hoped to embarrass her, I did not succeed. She ignored my jibe, intent as she was on trapping me, on exposing my betrayal of her son. Well, I had done it, so I suppose I couldn't blame her too much, but her zeal was unnerving. "Oh, I'm sure you're right," she said. "I'm sure you have a reasonable explanation for everything that's happened. But that doesn't change things. I know you're lying."

"*Belle-mère*, why would I betray my husband, not to mention the King? What would I do with the ransom money? My honour is at stake in this too," I said truthfully.

Her voice cracked suddenly with temper. "Do you think I don't know you've been asking questions, poking and prying into things that don't concern you? I warned you not to! You've found out something, haven't you? You've taken it upon yourself to ruin my son. Don't think I'll just stand by and let you do it. I'll get to the bottom of this somehow, and then I'll have proof of what you've done. Guy will have to listen to me then. You'll be sorry you ever came here!"

"I am going," I said, with what I hoped was an air of outraged innocence, "to lie down. If there is any news, please send it to me." I left her rudely, even considering the circumstances, but I needed to put an end to the conversation and get away to think. Other than the incontrovertible evidence of my having been at the chest, there was nothing definite Guy or Lady Iseult could impute to me at the moment. Though some need of my mother-in-law's could clearly be satisfied by my involvement, I doubted

Guy would be pleased to discover his wife's treachery. He would not overturn every stone to find evidence to implicate me. On the other hand, sooner or later the two of them might wonder whether all the questionable circumstances — my interest in the treasure, Agnes's breaking the pots, my enthusiasm for love-making just as Guy was about to check on the treasure room, and the problem of the key — might not add up to a certainty after all. I had to decide what to do before that could happen, because in that event, if Guy and his mother did not avenge themselves on me, Prince John certainly would, and that was a prospect that made me stutter with fear.

When I got to our bedchamber, Agnes was waiting for me. "I've saddled Dun Crump," she said.

Sometimes, when you are thinking about what the monks and chroniclers are pleased to call history, it is good to remember that the pattern of great events is made up of tiny, independent moments woven together, as the warp and weft make up, in the end, a tapestry. Occasionally, one thread can change the whole picture. This was one of those moments in the lesser pattern of my life.

I stared at her in amazement.

"You'll have to go," she said, almost sternly. "I heard the ruckus when they found the treasure missing. Lady Iseult is convinced you had a hand in it, and it won't be long before Sir Guy comes to see it that way too. She's down in the kitchen now, asking how all the pots got broken. Do you want to stay long enough for her to put everything together? She's like a hound after the scent."

This was no more than I had thought myself, but the speed with which she had concluded I must leave startled me. I had not been ready for that. "But where?" I asked her, sounding, even to my own ears, like a little child. "Where would I go?"

She looked at me with exasperation. "To him. To Robin, of course."

"To the *outlaws*?"

"Quiet, please, my lady. What choice do you have? You have no family to protect you."

I thought. "Yes, I could do that. I

could hide out in the forest until the stolen ransom is sent to London. Then there would be proof, and I could place myself under the Queen's protection. But . . . Agnes!"

She jumped. "What is it?"

"What about you? You can barely stand on that ankle. Is there another horse?"

She shook her head. "The search parties took them all. They would have taken Dun Crump, but I told the groom Sir Guy wanted him saved for you especially, and that he was to tell anyone who asked that the horse was lame."

I let out a breath. "Sweet Jesu, you do take chances. What if he had checked with Guy? Well, what does it matter now? My horse can carry us both. Can you get back to the stable on your own? We mustn't be seen together."

She stuck the offending ankle out in front of her and smiled. "I can do what I have to do."

"Amen to that. We must do it quickly then. There is still the sentry to get by. You've given me an idea about that.

And I suppose I ought to change into something darker, and more suitable for travel." I went to the chest and pulled out a dark green overdress, or *bliaut*, and mantle which would serve admirably for riding less conspicuously in the forest. If I had thought about it I would have chosen more carefully, but abundance was a habit not easily put aside, and I had not yet come to terms with the consequences of what I was about to do. I looked about the room quickly for something I might want to take away with me, but the only objects I treasured were my library, which I could not carry in a saddle bag, and the chalice, which was buried at Blidworth. I put some coins, a belt, a necklace, and the minimum of writing tools in a leather pouch and then went back to my writing table. I wrote a few lines on a parchment, dried the ink, and sealed the document. Then I went out to meet Agnes.

In the end, it was easier slipping out than I had expected, mostly because Guy had not given specific instructions regarding me. The sentry protested only slightly that his orders were to permit no one to leave, but I won him over by waving the document I had prepared under his nose and intimating that it was a message for an important personage at Clipstone.

He paled and looked knowing, so that I knew our involvement with the Prince was common knowledge among our retainers. "But you can't mean to go unguarded, my lady?"

"Of course not," I told him. "My maid accompanies me, as is fitting, and we will be met on the road." I lowered my voice. "You understand, I am travelling privily. There are good reasons why the person I am meeting cannot be seen here yet. My husband trusts you with this information, but you must not tell anyone else." Thus flattered by his inclusion in the affairs of the great and powerful, he wished me Godspeed and waved us through. I hoped Guy would not deal too harshly with him, but that, like so much else, was out of my power.

For a while, we followed the track to Clipstone, in case we were being watched. When I was sure no one was following us, I pulled off into a clearing, out of sight, and dismounted. After we had taken a drink and stretched our legs, I asked Agnes, "Now where to?"

She looked at her feet. "I don't exactly know where the camp is."

"*What?*"

"They tell no one, and Alan says people are led in and out blindfolded. It's safest that way. I haven't been there myself."

"Agnes, we can hardly criss-cross Sherwood forest, hoping to run into them. There are animals and men, too. It's too dangerous to wander about in."

She shrugged. "I thought we should go to Edwinstowe, first. I'll ask around there. Somebody will know how to get a message to them. You'll have to hide of course, my lady. Someone might recognize you."

I felt my confidence, and the courage I had summoned for the break with Locksley, ebbing away. The leaves were whispering in the trees, and the road seemed to stretch on and on until it melted into a shimmering haze on the very edge of sight. I felt very weary. "In default of any other plan, I suppose that will have to do," I told her. "Father

Tuck may be able to help us. But if I'm not to be recognized, you'd better stop calling me 'my lady'. It doesn't really fit any more, anyway." We stood still and listened but heard nothing. The sun was beginning to get low. "We should go then, but I think it would be better to leave this track. We are fugitives now, and the wild places are safest."

A small lane branched off in the direction of Edwinstowe, winding through a wood of ancient oak trees. I turned Dun Crump into it, and we rode slowly into the day's green shadows, till Sherwood closed behind us like a door.

6

I SPENT three days hiding in a shepherd's hut, being chased by ravenous fleas. Their enthusiastic banqueting rendered me nearly sleepless for three nights as well. Tuck was not in Edwinstowe and would not be back until the following Sunday. It was not safe to wait in the village; fortunately, the hut was nearby and deserted. We had nothing to eat but the provisions Agnes had thought to put in the saddlebags, and these were meagre enough. Market day came and went, but I thought it better to go hungry than appear in such a public place. By the end of the third day, I was wondering if imprudence might not have been preferable to starvation.

Father Tuck, when he came at last, confirmed my worst fears. His comforting bulk filled the small doorway, and as I turned and saw him I was just about to throw myself into his arms and cry on his shoulder when he said, "Thank God you had the sense to hide! Sir Guy and his men are combing the forest for you."

That distracted me. "I would have thought they'd be looking for the stolen ransom instead of Agnes and me."

He crammed his large body into the tiny hut and peered at me in the dim light. "My dear child . . . " He cleared his throat. "You haven't told me what happened. But your husband must know you had something to do with the treasure's disappearance or you wouldn't be here. It's clear he hopes you will lead him to wherever it's been taken."

My mouth fell open. The last thing I'd thought of, when it should have been the first. "Sir Guy," he went on, "has even called on me at my lodgings in the village." He settled himself on a musty blanket facing the entrance.

"What did he say?"

"Not the truth, you can believe that! He told me you had had a . . . . misunderstanding, and that he was worried about your health and safety. He thought you might have come to me. I told him I'd been gone, but that I hadn't seen you." He sighed. "I'm sure he's having me watched."

I was glad I'd taken precautions to get a message to him secretly. I looked worriedly outside the hut. He seemed to catch my meaning. "Oh, don't worry about this place," he said. "I've given it out that there might be plague here, so everyone will keep well away."

I shivered.

"Suppose you tell me what happened," he suggested.

I sketched briefly the events of the last few days. When I had finished, he gave me a long look and said seriously, "I should not have let him involve you."

I didn't answer.

He said, "You're afraid, aren't you?"

I said, as directly as if we were in the confessional, "Yes." I met his eyes then and added, "I asked to be involved, so I had to take what came, didn't I? You warned me, and so did he. It's not your fault it's worked out this way."

"Brave words, my dear. Thank you. But have you really given any thought to what you're going to do now?"

"Didn't Agnes tell you?" I asked, surprised. "We'll take refuge in the outlaw

465

camp until the treasure's sent to London, and then I'll apply to Queen Eleanor."

He frowned. "She told me, yes, but I hoped you might have come up with some other plan by now. Is there no one else who would shelter you?"

"Who would take me in, when the Prince may be after me? I can't go to Blidworth, Guy controls that, and the house in Normandy is out of the question since Philip's pact with John. Believe me, if there was *any* alternative I would take it. You don't think," I asked him, struck by a sudden terrible suspicion, "that *he* might refuse to shelter us?" I was realizing, rather belatedly, the implications of what Tuck had said. "I'll be bringing danger on them, won't I? If the Sheriff finds out I fled to the outlaws he'll know who's behind the recovery of the ransom money."

"No, no, it isn't that. Robin can take care of himself. And if you disappear into Sherwood, it's as if you slipped off the face of the earth." He looked at his feet. "I don't think he'll refuse to shelter you. But I still wish you wouldn't go."

"But Agnes says you told her to come

here if she was in trouble."

"I don't deny it. But Agnes is Agnes, and you are someone else. You're an innocent, Marian. Oh, I know you've been married and lost a child, but you don't know much about life. I'm afraid you'll be hurt, and I'm afraid you'll be in danger. I'm — I'm fond of you, and I'd protect you if I could."

"Thank you. I'm not sure what you're hinting at, but if you can think of another place I can go I wish you'd tell me."

"I can't, more's the pity." He sighed, and rose to his feet, scratching. "So be it then. I'll be back to get you when it's dark, and I'm sure I'm not being followed. I'll have to blindfold you and lead you in on my old mount, so it'll be slow going. Bring only what you can carry, and bury the rest. Remember, you're going to *disappear.*"

★ ★ ★

Deprived of sight, the other senses become exaggerated, tenser, and less reliable as guides to action or understanding. The night sounds — of crickets,

467

a fox barking, the leaves shaking on the branches, a rustle in the undergrowth — seemed louder and closer, and more alarming. I could smell, too, beneath the overlay of Dun Crump and the more pleasant scent of trodden grass and new leaves, the dampness of the forest floor. We rode steadily, without speech, and I could feel the darkness growing, as if we were penetrating deeper and deeper into a cave. I had lived a great portion of my life in some part of Sherwood, but here, in its most ancient heart, I felt like an intruder.

"You can take off the blindfolds now," Tuck said at last. "We're almost there. I'll have to leave you here for a bit while I ride on ahead and let them know we're coming. Just stay with the horse, and I'll come back for you."

After the black emptiness of no sight at all, the dazzling profusion of the night sky stabbed me with its brightness. Even the Queen had never worn such a mantle. The oaks loomed large and pearly in the light, their branches forming great dark nets to catch the swimming stars. The air seemed to shimmer and grow warmer, and I lost my sense of unease. When, at length, Father Tuck rejoined us and we rode toward the camp, the only sensation I was conscious of was a great weariness. On the edge of sight a fire crackled and flickered, and distant voices rose and fell in the clear air. I approached it half in a dream, suspended between waking and sleep, like one of my night walks. At length Dun Crump halted, and Agnes and I slid to the ground. I hardly noticed that someone's arms were there to catch me, until I saw who it was. He kept his hands under my wrists and looked into my eyes.

"My lord," I said softly, "I must beg you to shelter us. We have nowhere else to go."

"I'm sorry," he whispered, not taking his eyes off mine.

"It doesn't matter," I told him.

"Tuck said you were caught," he said, still keeping hold of my hands. "What went wrong? Did he . . . did anyone hurt you?"

"Oh no . . . He . . . they didn't catch us exactly," I mumbled. I was near to falling down with exhaustion, and Agnes had dozed astride the horse the last few miles of the trip. I didn't think I could face telling him the whole story before I got some sleep.

He dropped my hands. "What then?" he asked, in a different tone from the one he had used before.

Something of my distress must have shown on my face. John, who had appeared out of the darkness to stand beside his friend, said quietly, "The girl's half dead on her feet, Robin. Can't it wait till tomorrow?"

"Oh, yes, please," I said gratefully. "Could we sleep now? We're very tired."

"I suppose," he said levelly, "that it's safe to let it rest until morning. John, can you find them somewhere to sleep? I think there's some extra bedding in one of the shelters."

John found us a blanket each and led us to a patch of long grass beneath a great oak. "This should do all right," he said. "you'll be safe here. God be with you."

I did not stay awake to reflect on the stroke of Fate that found me homeless and bedding down among foxes and weasels and other forest creatures. I threw myself down on the hard ground, rolled in the blanket, and fell fast asleep.

★ ★ ★

I awoke to find the sun shining down through fluttering leaves and my body as stiff and sore as if a horse had walked over me in the night. My skin was uncomfortably damp, and my clothes scratched. Agnes was nowhere in sight. I could hear dim voices all around me, but I saw no one. For the first time, I understood how people could live undetected in Sherwood and the other great forests, provided, of course, that one did not succumb to the discomforts. I pulled myself to my feet, hung the blanket over my arm, and went in search of the water I could hear rushing by in the distance. A wash was the first order of the day.

I came out into a clearing and found the water making dark pools swirling among the tree roots. The stream was cold but its touch was clean, and the sound of its passing was sweet and peaceful. There was no one about. I took off my garments one by one and washed them in the pools, and when I had spread them to dry on the branches and rocks I got in myself and let the water flow over my whole body, up to my chin. The morning was cool, but I climbed out reluctantly. The water was healing, and as tonic as a tisane. I wrapped myself round in my night blanket and sat on the bank waiting for my clothes to dry.

"Holy Mother!" someone said, with evident exasperation, right behind me. "What do you think you're doing out here?"

The tone told me who it was, even if I had not recognized his voice. Last night's softening, even sympathy, might never have been. I didn't turn around but said coolly, "Having a wash. I didn't leave the shepherd's hut for three days. And there were beastly fleas the whole time."

He moved around so that he faced me, but I noticed he left his bow unslung and kept glancing around the dell, a fact as easily attributable to my state of dress as to any imminent danger. "So that's where you were, while your husband was turning Edwinstowe and Blidworth upside down for you," he said casually. "I wondered about it, last night."

"Look, would you mind if we had this conversation later? You can find out anything you want to know from Father Tuck. I'd like to be alone now, so I can get dressed."

"I ought to do just that, and leave you to get what you deserve," he said in a dry voice. "But you — "

"Pray don't trouble yourself on my behalf," I interrupted him coolly. "I'll be perfectly all right."

He drew in a breath, let it out again, and said, "I seem to remember your saying something of the sort in Edwinstowe. And here you are." He paused, maddeningly, to let his reminder sink in. "If you will stop bristling at everything I say and listen for a moment, I have to tell you that it isn't safe for you to be alone out here. The forest is a wild and dangerous place. Have you forgotten what happened to you the last time?" Then, seeing my look, he added, "I'm sorry to be cruel. But worse than that can happen to you if you wander around by yourself. Besides that, the Sheriff's men will be after us soon enough, once he puts two and two together. No one, without exception, is to go off alone. When you want to bathe, let one of the women know. Several of you will go out together, guarded. If you want something, ask me or John or Alan, if he's with us, but don't do anything on your own. Do you understand what I'm telling you?"

The blanket I was wrapped in covered me completely, but I was suddenly conscious of my nakedness beneath it. "Yes, certainly I do," I told him, stung by his tone. "You're telling me I'm virtually your prisoner, though I hardly see by what right."

He sat down beside me, crossing his legs peasant-style upon the ground. "You give yourself too much importance, as usual," he said calmly. "I have no claims on you, and I certainly don't want any. Don't think I'm not grateful for your helping me get into Locksley, but let's face it, I'm in a lot more trouble because of your presence. Whatever I personally might owe you, I can't let you endanger the safety of anyone in this camp because you are headstrong or reckless, or whatever it is that motivates you. You have to do as I say because the rules must be followed for the protection of everyone. If you don't agree to this I will have you escorted back to Edwinstowe at once, and you can fend for yourself. Not because I want to, but because I have an obligation to take care of my people. *Now* do you understand me?"

Well, that was clear enough at any rate. I nodded. "What choice do I have?"

"None whatsoever. Now I'd like to ask you some questions about what happened at Locksley, and then I'll take you back to camp and introduce you. There's a schedule of chores, too, cooking and cleaning up and looking after the animals, anything that needs doing. You'll have to take your turn with the rest." He looked at me with a glimmer of amusement, as if he relished the idea. "While we're at it, I think it better if we just keep calling you 'Marian', or 'Mary' if you prefer. It's for your own safety — no need to publish your whereabouts."

"Marian will do," I told him. "It's plain enough."

"I know it's hard for you to put these things aside, but it's necessary." He was not smiling now. I knew that he referred to more than my name and titles. I had forfeited, possibly for a long time, my home, position, security, and, as the world would see it, my honour. I was just beginning to perceive how painful that loss would be. He continued to watch me. I thought he meant to warn me as well that I would have to set aside the expectation of deference that would have come as naturally as breathing from the forest people to 'Lady Marian'. It sounds easy enough, but the habits of authority are as hard to shed as skin. Still, I remembered what he himself had lost because of my husband and the Prince, and I bit back my complaints and said only: "I understand you. I won't cause any problems."

"Why do I find that hard to believe? Well, it's a beginning at least. Do you want to get dressed first, or tell me what happened at Locksley?"

I looked him straight in the eye. "If the chivalry of the forest includes your turning your back, I'd prefer to get dressed."

It did, apparently. I began the story breathlessly, even before I had finished pulling on my still-moist garments, so that he had to stop me and ask some questions before he understood. After that he sat immobile and almost without expression, asking for clarification once or twice but otherwise saying very little. When I had come to the end, to the point where Agnes and I had decided to take flight, he said only, "You seem to have made a peculiarly large number of people suspicious of you at Locksley. If you had been more . . . careful, you might not have had to leave."

I flushed then, flooded with anger and embarrassment, but mostly anger. "Perhaps it's because I don't have your practice at deception. What ails you, anyway? Look what I risked to help you get hold of the King's ransom! You should be grateful to me, and instead you sound as if you suspect me of something."

"Really? I wonder. It's all a little too easy, don't you think? Your concern over the injustice at Locksley, your willingness to help, even if it meant betraying your husband and his family. And now here you are in my camp, because you let yourself be seen, just when I've got possession of the ransom."

I felt too shocked for speech. The injustice of what he implied almost choked me, after what I had done for him. No, not for him, I reminded myself; for my own honour, for what I thought was right. The notion calmed me a little, so that I could speak. "You can't mean to suggest you think I'm here under false pretences, as some sort of spy for Guy or the Sheriff? Ask Agnes how it came about, if you don't believe me. This is . . . this is . . . unbearable."

His grey eyes looked bleak and wintry, as they had when I first saw him at Edwinstowe. "I'm sorry," he said simply. "I've had to learn that I can be certain of nothing. By your own admission there was little more than a shadow of suspicion on you, yet you fled. I can't help remembering that it was your husband who stole Locksley from me. Even if you are all you say, I still find it hard to trust your too-easy complicity. I keep asking myself why you would do it. Are you really honest? You even lied to John about speaking English, when he saved you from the leper."

"I didn't lie," I said wearily. "He assumed it, and you'd already made rude remarks I wasn't supposed to understand, so it just seemed easier to go on pretending." I felt thoroughly dispirited by his assessment of my character and wanted the conversation to be over. I was certain I had made a terrible mistake in coming to Sherwood, but it was too late to go back now. "Look," I told him, "you've made your doubts clear enough, but there isn't much I can do about it. I'm not sure it matters anyway. I don't think I can really explain to you why I tried to help you if you don't accept what I've told you so far. Tuck understands, and if that's not enough for you I don't see what else I can do. I'll try to stay out of your way and not be a burden. I've said so already. Why don't we just leave it so for the time being?"

"It appears we'll have to," he said, getting to his feet.

The glade was still cool with shadows. I had leisure to think, as I followed him from the waterside, of his openings and closings. He was no fool; he knew what I had risked and lost, and if he trusted me as little as he suggested he would never have let me come to the camp. Yet whenever he treated me with any kindness or sympathy so that I began to relax, he hastened to remind me how precarious my position really was. It was almost as if he wanted to hurt me, to pay me back for some wrong I had done him. My relationship with Guy seemed to bother him particularly, like an itchy cloth that rubbed him into irritation. His lack of regard was wounding, and it made me feel, not for the first time in my life, quite lonely. Of my own free will, I had put myself in his power; whatever we might have been in the outside world, in Sherwood he was a great lord, and I was only an initiate into its mysteries.

7

IT was a life out of life in the forest, strong and fierce in its discomforts and loyalties. Even in summer, the sweetest of seasons, it was as hard and unyielding as the oaks themselves. Beneath and sometimes within the trees, we lived only from one hour to the next, so that even the meanest shepherd's hut offered more luxury. The camp, such as it was, had to keep moving, lest the cookfires be seen or the tracks leading in and out become too well-trodden. During the day, we ate together in the open or under portable shelters of leaves and woven branches like tents, before the men went off to hunt or watch the roads or gather information. Women washed and repaired the meagre supply of garments, gathered nuts and acorns and edible plants, and cooked. Most of the women had come to be with their husbands or sons or fathers when they had parted company with the Law, so they were free to go to the market towns and buy food or cloth or other necessities. It was a life more suited to the days when people painted themselves blue and danced naked round the fires, but it had its rhythms and its rules. The cord that bound us tightly as a plait was our common danger, and the sense of living outside the world. In fact, this apartness was something like the community of Fontevrault, both a fact and a state of mind.

Even the food reinforced it. What we ate was stolen from the King. Half a lifetime spent within jurisdiction of the Forest Law made me choke on my first bit of venison; this was a crime, carrying dreadful, agonizing penalties. When hunger drove me to eat at last, I felt as if I had transcended some awesome barrier. If the others were troubled by such thoughts they didn't show it, but they had lived with their plight longer, and in any case it was not a thing one cared to share with others.

From sunset to dawn our lives were secret from one another. Whatever dreams we had, whether of home or freedom or riches or even comfort, we did not speak of them. Nor was it anyone's business if any two went off together into the darkness, so long as no one came creeping to your bed uninvited. Still, when I saw unmistakable signs that Agnes and Alan were sharing a bed, I was taken aback. I told myself it was concern for her feelings and her future, which was ridiculous under the circumstances. I tried to keep the edge off my comments when I remembered that at Locksley she had been scorned and servile; here, for better or worse, she had a measure of freedom and attention. I also discovered, to my chagrin, that I resented the fact that she was no longer my servant. Truly, it was hard to shed the habits of the past.

Alan came and went, practising his art in the outside world. Times were hard and he earned less than usual, but he was kind enough to bring most of it to Sherwood. I have never quite understood Alan. He was a boyhood friend of Robert Fitz Ooth, but I never saw the warmth between them that was so obvious between Robin and John.

He was both perceptive and cool, a natural observer who yielded little of himself. There was a sharpness to these observations which made it difficult to be entirely easy with him, as if you were always being weighed and found slightly wanting. However, this aloofness gave wit and freshness to his verses, and he entertained us whenever he came to camp. In fact, Robin and the outlaw life itself seemed to inspire his best work, even if his stories were, he admitted sheepishly, somewhat different from the facts. He was working on a long story about the first meeting of Robin Hood and a seven-foot giant named Little John, which involved their meeting on a narrow bridge and nearly clubbing each other to death with oaken staffs in an attempt to knock the other off. I listened with amazement while all of them, Alan and Robin and John, traded jokes and added details as the tale spun itself out over several nights. That not a word of it was based on reality didn't seem to diminish their pleasure in the least. The only comfort was that if you did end up in one of Alan's stories, the likelihood was you wouldn't recognize yourself.

If you had troubles, John was the one you took them to. It seemed to me that John asked very little of anyone except himself, yet he gave without stinting of his time, his ear, and a sort of sexless affection. I don't mean that he was unmanly, for he was certainly skilled in the masculine arts and was brave and aggressive enough when he needed to be, but he didn't let his manhood intrude on his feelings. Or perhaps it was only that he never made you conscious of your own sex, or his, as others did. His devotion to Robin was of this same detached sort, but no less intense for all that. He seemed to have no other particular friends, but everyone loved him.

There was one other in Sherwood who touched my life, though I didn't know it. One day, when I was pressing the whey from goat's milk in order to make cheese, someone said softly at my shoulder, "Lady Marian." I turned, surprised, because no one used my title any longer. The person at my elbow looked scarcely older than a boy, with black hair and a smile that would have melted tallow. He looked familiar, and I thought a moment before I placed him. "I remember you," I told him. "You came to Locksley with Robin."

He gave a mock bow. "The potter's apprentice," he acknowledged. The smile faded. "I just wanted to tell you that I'm sorry if we got you into trouble. It was my job to climb up the wall and replace your key. I fear it was too late."

He looked so apologetic I wanted to hug him, but of course I didn't. "It's not your fault. I overslept, and then someone saw me putting it back. Please don't worry about it."

"I'm glad you don't blame me, my lady, because . . . because I knew you once. At Blidworth."

I looked at him, amazed. He was not quite as young as he looked, then. "What is your name?"

"Will Scarlet. I was outlawed for poaching just after you came back from France."

"I'm sorry. I remember. Father Tuck helped you, didn't he?"

"Yes. A good man, the Father. None better, when he's sober. Anyway, you're not to feel sorry." He grinned suddenly. "I was guilty as charged, as a matter of fact."

"I won't then, if you'll remember not to call me Lady Marian."

"Sorry. The old life dies hard."

"I know that well enough."

"There is one thing, though . . . "

"Yes?"

"When I was at Blidworth, before I was . . . sent away, there was a girl. I was going to marry her."

"Yes?" I asked again, feeling chilled. I had remembered to whom he was betrothed.

"You knew her. Her mother was the cook in your father's house. She went away to study with the sisters at some priory in Yorkshire. I wondered what became of her."

I swallowed. "She joined the religious order. It's called Kirklees. She'll soon be a fully professed nun."

"A nun? *Janet*? Because of *me*?"

I suppressed a smile. "I believe she's quite happy there. I saw her recently, when she came to Locksley to nurse me through an illness." I decided to tell him nothing unpleasant about issues which were now, after all, totally irrelevant.

He beamed in her reflected glory. "That was Janet, sure enough. So generous, and so smart. Too clever for me by half. She had a lucky escape."

I nearly bit my tongue holding back what I wanted to say to this kind innocent. Then the moment passed, and after that it was too late to say anything at all. I let it rest there.

★ ★ ★

When I had been in Sherwood some weeks, and three shipments of ransom treasure had been 're-routed' on their way between several local manor houses and the Prince's hunting lodge at Clipstone, and then hidden within the great hollowed-out forest oaks, I wrote to Queen Eleanor. I used a stump for a writing desk and a crudely cut quill for a pen. Robin and John and Father Tuck argued over every sentence, made me read each one back at least three times after it was finally agreed upon, and expressed exasperation with the final product. I couldn't blame them; the matter called for a tact as delicate as gossamer, each word a potential blunder. I had only a small piece of parchment I had taken away from my library, and I had to save some of it, so I refused to copy it again. In the end we avoided openly blaming the Prince and just stated that the ransom had been misdirected through greed and treachery and was now being restored. Robert Fitz Ooth asked nothing more than to be of service to their Graces, and to prove his good faith and compliance with the law in so far as it was in his power. We awaited only the Queen's instructions on where and how to deliver the ransom.

Of course he hoped for more than that, even if he wouldn't admit it to himself or anyone else. While John ruled as a king in all but title in Nottinghamshire (and elsewhere) he could not get Locksley back, but the Queen might be able to lift the sentence of outlawry in Richard's name. As soon as Alan headed south with the letter, hope began to work like a leaven throughout the camp.

Fortunately, the Queen was in England,

and we received a speedy reply. I recognized her own brisk, business-like hand; she had not even trusted her scribe. Armed guards would be sent up the Ely road; she named a meeting place, and a date. "Ely?" I asked Alan in surprise. "Longchamp is back then?"

He nodded. "I heard the regency council allowed him back in England provided he concerns himself only with the ransom business. Not that that isn't enough to keep anyone occupied these days."

Robin asked: "Will the Queen see me?"

I looked at him in surprise. "Were you planning to go? It could be dangerous!"

He smiled. "So is staying here. How else can I plead my case?"

"Robin, for an outlaw to come into the Queen's presence could mean death. Send someone else. Send Tuck. Or me."

"*You*? Have you thought that your husband or the Prince might have poisoned her against you? You can't count on her protection any more than I can."

"Well, Tuck then."

"Robin," Alan said at last, "I don't know if she'll see you or Marian or anyone. I didn't see her myself. God knows I tried. But she was closeted with William Marshal and the likes of me couldn't interrupt them. I passed the letter to a . . . friend I have at court, and she slipped it to the Queen. The reply came the same way. My friend said the Queen had made inquiries about me and seemed to be satisfied. But that's all I can tell you."

"Tuck?" Robin asked, turning to see his reaction.

"Oh, I'll go, with you or alone, you know that," he said gruffly. "But queens are queer cattle, and you know I've no truck with court life. I'm not sure I'll do well by you. But I'm game."

"We'll go as monks," Robin said, lost in his imaginings of the adventure. "When we get to London — "

"Not London," Alan interrupted. "The treasure will go there. I've heard it's already stacked high as the chapel door inside St Paul's. But the Queen's at Canterbury."

"Canterbury, then. It's settled."

But shortly before they were due to set out for Ely and the rendezvous with the Queen's men, the Sheriff of Nottingham came at last, looking for blood and vengeance. He rode up the main road from his castle to Mansfield and into the turning to Clipstone with a great part of armed men, stopping at each village to take hostages. One messenger was dispatched from among them to our camp with the message that if the outlaws of Sherwood did not show themselves and return the stolen ransom at once all the hostages would be hanged. He reasoned, not incorrectly, that our existence and safety could not have been maintained without at least the tacit complicity of neighbouring villages. The idea was to make them hate us, and drive us out.

I note, even now, the 'us'. Like the sound of the sea on a clear night the dream comes back to me from afar. I could not tell you, then or now, what it was we lived for. Robin wanted Locksley back, but what was that to anyone else? Most of the forest people had faith in God's justice, but none at all in the King's. They were Saxons mostly, with that race's suspicion that their troubles lay at the feet of their Norman oppressors. (Robin's mother, the wronged Saxon lady of virtue, was no small part of his hold on them.) Yet there was hope, even if it was just to slip quietly back into what people on the outside called 'life', whatever its abuses and discomforts. And there was pride, too, in being the instrument which kept the danger away from oneself, and from each other. As for me, I felt a great wind blowing at my back, pushing me on toward an improbable purpose, which, when I began to perceive it, caused me to dig in with my heels and resist with all my might.

When we received the news that the Sheriff had ridden out with his challenge, I never expected to see what I had seen in my father's house and in my husband's, the preparation of armed, mounted men for combat. We lacked a great supply of hauberks and shields and destriers, but none of the men was of the knightly class (except Robin) and they would go as bowmen on foot. But it hadn't occurred to me that the summons would not be met openly, in the time-honoured terms of battle or tournaments. I must say in my own defence that the hopelessness of such an engagement did not really suggest itself to me either, or I might not have been so surprised when I found out what was actually intended.

Which was this: that at the moment the hostages were gathered to be hanged, when time had all but run out, Robin and John and some others would ambush the Sheriff's party and rescue as many of the unfortunate victims as possible. This seemed to me to be cutting it too close to the bone: if something went wrong the hostages would almost surely be killed. I said as much to Robin. "And if you do save them," I added, "all that will be left for them is to join us in Sherwood. They won't be able to go home again."

He gave me a straight, untroubled look. "You think I should give myself up?"

"Of course not," I said, annoyed. "But if you offered to meet the Sheriff in battle, he would set them free."

A sharpening silence. "For the Earl of Huntingdon, perhaps, but I doubt if an outlaw of Sherwood is entitled to the honours of the field. What would you have me do? Ride in with all my men under the banner of the Major Oak, against knights trained and armed for combat? Who do you think I am, William the Conqueror?"

"He's right, Marian," said John, who had been listening. "Our best weapons are stealth and surprise. The prisoners will be close-guarded. The only time they'll be out in the open will be for the hanging. There's little enough chance of rescuing them as it is. Besides, we'll be short of the men who go with the ransom. If we don't turn up for our meeting with the Queen's men, she'll never believe us a second time."

"You're right, of course you are, I see that. It's only . . . well, think of them waiting there to die . . . not knowing, and it's because of *us*."

"Which is why I plan to be there to save them and not meeting with the Queen in Canterbury," Robin said evenly.

He stood straight in front of me, his foot on a birch log, the light patterns shifting over his green mantle as the breeze ruffled the leaves above us. He looked, not young, but full of the richness and experience of life, a man in his prime, a leader who could summon the allegiance of other men, even here. The Lord of Sherwood, master of oaks and acorns. So much wasted. I saw in that moment what it had cost him, and how hard he had struggled against bitterness and despair.

"Then let me go in your place," I offered again. I couldn't bear his disappointment any longer. "Or at least with Tuck. I'd always planned to throw myself on the Queen's mercy anyway. I know her, Robin. She's difficult but she's fair. She won't refuse to hear your story."

"You would plead with the Queen for me?" I watched his face change, and his long assessing look. I saw him ask himself whether I would do.

"You can trust me," I added, seeing the doubt that remained in his eyes.

He frowned. "It's a great risk. She might believe you, but if she's turned against you, where will the rest of us be then? On the other hand, she does know you . . . I can't *ask* you to do it, Marian, but if you want to go . . . if you think you could help . . . Well, it's a chance to get out of here. Maybe you should take it."

I wish you would ask me. I didn't say it. I just waited.

"Well, if you're sure?" I nodded. "Thank you, then. I'll go and talk to Father Tuck."

I watched him go, but when I noticed John watching me I lowered my gaze.

"Don't worry, lass," he said quietly. "I won't give you away."

"I don't know what you're talking about."

"Right." He sighed. "Have you thought, then, about your future? About what you want to do?"

"I've decided," I told him miserably, "that when the ransom is sent to London, I'll ask the Queen to find me some out-of-the-way convent which will shelter me until . . . until this is over. Then I'll go home to Blidworth and never leave it again."

"I'm sure you know best," John said, inscrutably.

8

AS soon as I had definitely made up my mind to go to Canterbury, which, under the circumstances, seemed the only sensible course of action, I began to think of the thousand things that might go wrong. That the journey would be dangerous as well as tiring I discounted; there would be as much peril and chance of discovery if I stayed in Sherwood. But I could not ignore Robin's warning that I might not be believed, that Guy and the Prince might have poisoned the Queen's ear. They would have every advantage in doing so, and my flight would seem rather a confirmation of guilt than not. At best the Queen would be preoccupied with her struggle to free her son from captivity, so that I could depend but little on her attention or her protection. All this I saw, as clearly as I could see Eleanor before her mirror, trying on her jewels and dreaming of youth.

I saw, too, that I would have to risk it, for Robin's sake if not for my own. The ransom might get lost amid the clerical chaos of London, but if I could convince Eleanor of her obligation to the outlaws she would not forget. It was when I tried to imagine how I could confirm for her that her son the Prince was a traitor to his own brother that I saw the hopelessness of the whole project. Whatever doubts she might harbour about John, she would not thank anyone who made the facts so plain to her she could not turn a blind eye. In the Greek stories, it was the messenger bringing bad tidings who was slain.

There was one other thing, of course. Though I had never pretended to acute powers of discernment, I found that I had been indulging in some wilful blindness of my own. I was humbled, I was grieved; I repented, though I hardly knew of what. In short, I was courting (if that can be said to be the right word) the very disaster which had befallen Tristan and Iseult, Lancelot and Guinevere. It was hardly a tonic to my humiliation that

I was only saved from the sin itself by indifference if not dislike on the part of the object of this attachment. Even if he had returned my feelings, I saw little hope of anything beyond the misery and suffering Andreas the Chaplain defined as the very essence of Love.

The easy attainment of love makes it of little value; difficulty of attainment makes it prized, Andreas had written. I suppose it was natural enough that I would turn to him, my rescuer, when I had fled a bad man and a bad marriage and flown straight into his arms on a night when the stars sparked like crystals burning white in a black sky. It would have been natural, if I had found a welcome there. But in the daylight, I had met suspicion and reserve, and the coolness appropriate for Guy of Gisborne's wife. However much I tried to laugh at my own folly and conjure up the Rules of Love, the fact remained, no longer even remotely amusing, that I was in love with Robert Fitz Ooth.

The truth, Sister Beatrice had once warned me at Fontevrault, is not guaranteed to make you happy. Though I had no expectation of happiness, at least I didn't have to make things worse. I would go south with the treasure, and throw myself upon the mercy of the Queen.

On the eve of our departure, Father Tuck, who had taken a day to arrange his affairs in Edwinstowe, came back to the camp to say Mass and hear Confession. Since he was my Confessor, I told him everything. As I suspected, he enthusiastically approved my plan to stay in the south, even before I confessed to harbouring a thought whose very contemplation was a sin.

"I feared as much," he said sadly. "Remember, I warned you of it when we spoke at Edwinstowe."

"Well, you might have been more specific, then," I told him. "I didn't even suspect it myself, and I didn't know what you were talking about."

"Am I a pander, to put ideas in your head?" he huffed. "I might have been wrong."

"It's ironic, isn't it," I remarked with some bitterness, "that all my honour and loyalty are owed to Guy, who is dishonourable and weak, while I can give nothing to this man, who is so much better."

Tuck frowned. "That is God's law as well as man's. Don't ask me to excuse you from it."

"I'm not. Besides, there is still a chance I can unravel all this without compromising my 'faithfulness' such as it is. If I could get the Queen's ear, or the King's . . ."

"Even so, don't count on it. It will be much more difficult now that you've run away from Locksley." He lowered his voice. "Your coming here will cause gossip and speculation. How that will affect your case against your husband I leave you to guess."

I bowed my head. "Then it's just as well Robin has no suspicion of my feelings nor any interest in returning them. That's my last line of defence, even if it is small comfort."

"Hmmph," said Father Tuck, without much sympathy.

* * *

Then, too soon, it was time for farewells. I had asked Agnes, for form's sake, if she would like to accompany me to the Queen, but she said she had no wish to leave the forest where she had found so much happiness. That *her* happiness was much greater than Alan's one could not fail to see, and I don't doubt she knew it. It seemed to be enough for her. I did not worry her with fruitless nagging but just wished her well. When I came to the point of leaving, I found that I would miss her. I told her so, and she smiled, shaking her head and saying nothing. Praise slid from her like the snow. I could never tell what Agnes was thinking.

"And so," Robin said smoothly, both hands on hips and looking up at the sun, "it is time you were off. Father Tuck?"

"We are all ready. God willing, I should be with you again in a few weeks' time. God save you, Robert, and all who go with you against the Sheriff."

"And with you, Father. Take care you don't underestimate the danger." He looked at me. "Nor you either." He put on a smile that looked like something taken out to wear. "After this, I hope you'll be able to put everything behind you and get on with your life."

I regarded him. We were back to the wary manner, the closed-off excluding silence, the polite but firm invitation to disentangle myself from his affairs. Well, that was clear enough at least. I held Dun Crump's reins in my hands and realized I should have groomed him better while I was in the forest. At first I hadn't even thought of it, till John had reminded me in the kindest fashion that if I did not see to it, no one else would. They were short of stable hands in Sherwood. "I have to thank you," I told Robin, "for letting me stay here, and for giving me your protection ——"

"Such as it was," he said drily.

"Such as it was," I agreed. Why couldn't we get beyond this banter? In a few days the Sheriff's deadline would run out, and then he might be . . . I refused to let myself think about that. Or about the fact that this might be the last time I ever saw him, whatever happened. I took a breath. "I hope . . . I hope everything goes well with the Sheriff, and of course

I hope that you get what you want in the end."

"Thank you." A real smile this time. "If you get Blidworth back, we won't live that far apart. I hope you'll come see me."

"Delighted," I told him blandly. "And if *you* get Locksley back . . ."

He lifted my hand and kissed it. My heart twisted in my body. "Well, why not?" he said.

* * *

The cathedral garden at Canterbury was surrounded by a high wall. The day was cool but the daffodils were out, opening in the morning sunlight. Two nuns, black-clad and silent, sat on a bench in a warm spot next to the wall. The Queen sent them away courteously, and they disappeared into the shadows like wraiths.

Eleanor had aged since I'd last seen her, three years before. Her skin was stretched taut over her beautiful bones, and there were circles under her eyes, which looked feverishly bright in their sockets. Her hair, braided beneath her wimple, was yellowed white, the colour of old age. Her hands shook a little, in her lap. She seemed stripped down to essentials, with no energy to spare for vanity or games. The basic Eleanor at last.

Her lack of glamour touched me, till I saw the hard lines around her mouth. The Queen was still a formidable opponent. I remembered fear.

"Well?" she asked, in a voice of surprising strength. "What is this all about?"

I told her what I could, that I had come to plead the case of the outlaws of Sherwood Forest, who had returned the King's ransom money to her custody. I told her the ransom had been side-tracked before it reached the Chancellor's coffers and that the outlaws had stolen it back. I didn't mention the Prince by name. She nodded from time to time but made no comment. I thought she would ask me how the ransom had become 'side-tracked' in the first place, but then it came to me that she probably knew very well that the Prince had made a duplicate of the Chancellor's seal and was stealing the ransom for himself. After all his other activities, it could hardly come as a surprise.

What she did ask me was: "How is it that *you* are pleading the case for a bunch of cutthroats and thieves living in Sherwood? It's not that I don't appreciate their help, but wasn't Fitz Ooth outlawed for attempted murder? And what about the rest of them? Poachers and idlers at best, I imagine."

I was glad Tuck had not accompanied me into the Queen's presence. I was disconcerted, but I had rehearsed my answer. There was no point in telling her I had been living in Sherwood with the outlaws myself. "Oh, Your Grace, Father Tuck of Edwinstowe asked me to intercede for them because I was once in your service. Robert Fitz Ooth was cheated out of his title and his manor house by his uncle and . . . a wicked forester." I sketched the tale for her, again omitting the role of Prince John. It was like telling the story of Jack the Giant-Killer, and leaving out the giant. "And the others . . . the others were mostly driven to Sherwood by hard times. People are hungry, Your Grace. If they steal food for their tables by poaching, who can blame them? The ransom tithe hasn't left much — " I broke off sharply, realizing what I had said.

Her mouth twitched a little, in what might have been a smile. "You always were a tactless girl," she said, with a hint of malice. So the Old Eleanor was still there after all, beneath the skin. "Some of the churches have unscrewed the silver hinges off of saints' coffins to contribute to the ransom, and even Canterbury" — she gestured toward the great cathedral — "gave its altar plate. Times are hard for all of us. Country people have to contribute something too." Her hands started to shake again and she stilled them in the folds of her skirt. "But you still haven't told me the truth about your part in this. John told me he found you a husband, and that you cuckolded him and ran off with the family fortune. Is Fitz Ooth the one you left him for?"

My knees buckled under me, and I had to sit down on the hard ground. "Oh, madam," I said despairingly, "I was afraid my husband would blacken my name. I haven't done anything against my honour, I swear it. The money I 'ran off with' was the ransom. That's why I left."

She sighed and closed her eyes, fingering a big amethyst cross on her chest. "Be careful now, this matters. Your husband — what is his name?"

"Guy of Gisborne."

"Yes. He was party to stealing the ransom money?"

"Yes."

"And he follows Prince John?"

I bent my head.

"I didn't hear you."

"I . . . I'm sorry, Your Grace, it's just that I . . . Yes, he is the Prince's man."

She rocked back on her stone seat, twisting the amethyst on its chain. "Don't fret, child, he's hardly the only one. Richard has himself to blame as much as anyone — the barons didn't want an absentee king. Well, what do you want me to do about it?"

"I . . . do about it, Your Grace?"

"Yes. About Fitz Ooth. The outlaws. You."

"Robert Fitz Ooth would like his manor house at Locksley returned. And they . . . they would all like the articles of outlawry lifted."

She rose and turned her back on me, apparently gazing with fixed attention at a tree planted next to the garden wall. She turned back and looked at me, her eyes opened wide. "Impossible."

"But, Your Grace, you could order the Sheriff . . . "

"No, no. You don't understand. I can order nothing at all. The Prince has considerable strength in England, and Nottingham is his capital. He has an army ready to ride with him whenever he commands it. My job is to prevent civil war breaking out. I have to bring the King home as soon as I can, and the rest will take care of itself. When Richard returns, we can show our gratitude, but till then . . . "

Something of what I felt must have shown in my face. She said, impatiently but not unkindly, "It's no use tearing yourself up over what can't be helped,

Marian. I learned that a long time ago." She shrugged. "You might apply to Longchamp about the articles of outlawry. He has the power to revoke them if he's willing to hear the case. But it will take a snail's age, and I really don't think it will do any good. I'll write him a letter, if you like." She looked at me assessingly. "He's in St Albans. But don't go yourself. Send the priest. Better yet, send a boy, preferably a pretty one." She sounded quite matter-of-fact. I wondered if she would be so bloodless if it were Richard. "So, then," she added briskly, though her voice had begun to sound tired, "what about you? What do you want?"

I struggled to find the right words to tell her. What I wanted I couldn't have, so I would have to settle for undoing the tangled mess I had made of my life. "I want . . . I want to get out of my marriage."

"Aha! It is Fitz Ooth, then!"

"Yes, but not in the way you think." I told her what I had thought when I learned about Locksley, and about my unwillingness to go along with Guy's

511

schemes. Of my feelings for Robin I said nothing. They were no one's business but my own.

"Well, I daresay I can help you there. You haven't been as careful as you might be if you want to keep your reputation, but I'm sure we can find *some* grounds for getting the thing annulled." She smiled. "I got myself unwed from a king, after all, and this small marriage shouldn't present too many difficulties. It will cost you, though. These things take time and they're dreadfully expensive. Who is your overlord for your English property?"

"The Archbishop of York for Blidworth, Your Grace. But . . . "

"Well?"

"My husband controls all my property. I have no money of my own, not even for my keep."

"Yes, of course . . . " Her eyes had a faraway look, and I wondered if she was remembering her years in Salisbury, when she had depended on Henry's whim for even an hour's freedom. "You can pledge some of your property as surety against what I'll advance you," she said

512

at last. "I'll write to the Archbishop too. Geoffrey owes me a favour. Meanwhile, I think you'd better hide yourself in a convent for a while. There's a small one starting up near Boston in the fen country. I'm to be patroness, and two sisters from Fontevrault will be travelling there tomorrow. You can go with them — they were here before, weren't they?" She looked about her, as if she expected them to appear upon her thought. Then she rang a small bell, and a servant did appear with the magic, effortless speed royalty can summon. "Ask the sisters who were in the garden to please attend us," she directed him. She turned back to me. "It's a modest enough place for the moment, so your keep won't cost you much. But I have big plans for it when . . . Richard returns." She went on to tell me, pleasantly, about her plans for the convent, as if that were all she had on her mind.

I soon ceased to hear what she was saying. The nuns had come back into the garden, and one of them was Cecily Lusignan.

9

CECILY and I set out just after dawn the next morning on the journey that would take us west to London and then north through the fen country toward Boston. I can still recall the sights and sounds of it. The fields were green and the sun was warm, and in the trees the birds flashed and sang. We bathed in cold streams and feasted on fish and bread beside the roadside. Cecily's fellow nun, Sister Julian, was a sweet, silent girl who seemed content to ride on in silence while we talked ourselves into hoarseness behind her. I had said farewell to Tuck at Canterbury; he would follow Longchamp to St Albans with the Queen's letter, and then he would go back to Sherwood, and Robin.

I found Cecily much changed, and yet the same. Her youthful promise of beauty had been fulfilled; the admiring glances of the escort the Queen had provided were amply justified. She was still reserved, but her reserve was no longer a barrier she hid behind. Instead, it seemed as if her interior life engaged her whole being. At first I was shy of her because of what had happened at Fontevrault and because so much time could not have failed to change us both.

But by the time she had told me news of all the nuns at the abbey and piled memory upon memory (so that by the end we had got round to Hector, who had confounded monastic science and sophistication by producing a litter of kittens), I found courage to ask her if she was happy in her life.

She smiled. "Happiness is a heady wine, Marian. But I will tell you this: I feel like I'm standing in strong sunlight now, and all my ordinary life before this was a blur and a shadow."

I remembered her uncle and the desperation that had driven her to the church. "You found peace, then?"

She laughed with uncomplicated pleasure. "Yes, it is peace, but what a strange peace it is. You have to work at it all the time, and there are long hours and demands and disappointments and no time to rest . . . But it is peace all the same. And joy. And love, too," she added looking at me sidelong.

She reminded me of what Sister Beatrice used to tell us about Our Lady, that she is blessed in her gentleness and sweetness, but the source of these qualities was her strength of soul. That was what I sensed in Cecily — Sister Cecilia — now. Strength.

So I told her everything, without evasion or subterfuge, taking care only that no one else could overhear us. It was such a relief that it poured out of me in a torrent. When she had questioned me on the details, and made the soothing noises friendship demands under the circumstances, she asked me: "You think you found it then? That Love that Countess Marie told us about?"

"If it's Suffering, then I've found it aplenty," I told her. "And it does consume the mind, rather. Beyond that I don't know."

"You don't think it could be simple lust?"

"Cecily!"

"Well, complicated lust then. Seriously, remember what Sister Beatrice taught us: there is the flesh, and there is the spirit. What you're describing definitely belongs to the flesh. I don't think it's possible for a woman to love a man with that great, disinterested emotion that takes you outside your own self. That is the love of the soul, and it exists only between man and God."

"What is it then that makes you sacrifice your pride or your riches or even your life for the object of your love? What is it that makes you feel that your own life is worth less than the feeling that you have for this person?"

She raised her eyebrows and looked at me. "Sin."

"Oh, Cecily," I said, disappointed, "you can't have any idea what it's really like."

"Love? Listen, Marian, I'll tell you something. I'm not worthy even to speak of such things but I want you to know. What I saw at Fontevrault — the visions — that was just the beginning for me. Since then God has been an intimate presence in my life. I sense Him with every breath, within some part of me so deep I can never reach it. It's like being at the very centre of the fire, where the coals burn white-hot with His absolute and infinite power. What is your attachment to this man next to *that*?"

I scanned her for signs of the madness I thought I had seen at Fontevrault. I saw none, only excitement, and a kind of blazing sincerity. "How can I argue with you?" I asked her. "I've never experienced what you're talking about. But I've been thinking, and it seems to me that the flesh and the spirit don't have to be at war. If you really love somebody, even in the puny human way I've described, then it makes you more noble, not less, and it elevates your soul. It's what makes man man even if it is a pale shadow of divine love. I can't believe God disapproves."

"If you believe that," she said drily, "then why are you here?"

"Why did I leave him, you mean?"

"I meant, why aren't you going back?"

"Because he doesn't return my feelings.

I'd only make things worse for both of us by staying. But if he loved me, I would never leave him."

"Even though you took marriage vows before God and to go with this man is a mortal sin?"

"Yes," I said fiercely.

We agreed to disagree.

My dreams were troubled that night. I had tried not to think about what was happening in Sherwood, but the Sheriff and the outlaws had had their meeting, and for good or ill the outcome was already decided. I tossed and turned on my mattress in the house of a village priest who took us in, there being no finer accommodations nearby. With Eleanor's purse we could have bought an entire inn, but money is only as good as the opportunity to spend it. Tomorrow we would reach our destination.

In the morning I was cross with sleeplessness and something else that nagged at my peace. There was a tightness in my throat, and my heart beat faster. The slightest comment irritated me beyond reason, so that I had to bite my lip to keep from snapping at my companions.

Cecily looked at me wonderingly but said nothing.

The morning's slanting shadows fell long across the track as we plodded along, the damp ground sucking at the horses' hooves. I could smell the wet of the marshes and the tang of the distant sea, even so far inland. Dun Crump's hooves drummed slowly but with mounting insistence on the packed earth, like the tabor's beat. Closer and closer ...

The air was heavy and moist, pressing down until each breath was deep and full of effort. A midge buzzed and bit me; I flapped at it furiously. Each step, each swaying motion became a torment.

Well then, I asked myself, how long are you going to go on fooling yourself? Don't you know by now what you really want?

If I did, replied the part of me that was fond of libraries and learning about life second-hand from the words and mouths of other people, would I be here now, riding down the track towards the convent where I can wall myself away from the pain?

Hiding?

Yes. He doesn't love me.

I'm sure you know best, said that other self, in John's voice.

We had come to the fork in the road. To the right lay The Wash, and the rivers that drained into it, creating, in places, a boggy marshland of dangerous quicksand and uncertain footing. That way lay the track that led to Boston, and Eleanor's convent. To the left lay Nottingham, and Sherwood forest.

I pulled Dun Crump up to a halt. "Cecily," I called aloud, though quietly.

She pulled her pony in beside Dun Crump, looking solemn and defeated, but not angry. She sighed. "You're going back to them, aren't you?"

"I have to. I can't go on not knowing what's happened to them. To him. Besides that, I won't ever know if there's even a chance for us if I don't go back and face him. I don't know if I'll stay. But I can't go with you now, I just can't."

"I don't suppose there's any point in reminding you how dangerous it is for you to be riding into your forest all by

521

yourself? That's the Prince's territory, isn't it?"

"I'll stay off the main roads. I don't think anyone's looking for me by now, so all I'll have to contend with is robbers and wolves." I felt suddenly much better, almost light-hearted.

"I'm afraid I'm the one who put this idea into your head," she said ruefully. "All that talk about love . . . "

"I've wanted to go back since the day I left there," I said truthfully. "Tell Queen Eleanor . . . well, just tell her."

"Will I see you again?" she asked calmly, in a way that suggested she didn't think she would.

I reached over and took her arm. "I hope so. How long will you be in England?"

She shook her head. "Just a few months, until we get the convent going. If I don't see you . . . "

Sister Julian and the escort were fading into the shadow down the path. They would soon be out of sight. "God go with you, Marian," she said and wheeled her pony on the track. When she had gone a few paces she turned again. "Don't forget what Sister Beatrice always says," she called. "'There is nothing bad you can do that's so terrible some saint hasn't done it before you.'" Then she rode down the track, and Dun Crump and I were alone on the road to Sherwood.

★ ★ ★

At first, the ride went smoothly enough. I kept off the main road to Nottingham and took the lesser tracks whenever I could. Sometimes, when I thought I heard someone coming, I dismounted and led Dun Crump into shelter until he had passed. I met few travellers, and after a while I began to enjoy the adventure. Then I had leisure to worry about what I would find when I did get back. All sorts of terrible pictures passed through my mind. The camp burned to cinders. Bodies. Robin's corpse hanging from a gallows in Nottingham . . .

I shook my head to clear it. I would find out soon enough, and tormenting myself beforehand would not help me deal with whatever I did find. At least I had the satisfaction, if that is what it was, of knowing that this time I had decided for myself. *I* chose this. Not Guy or the Queen or even Robin. I kicked my heels into Dun Crump's flanks and we flew as fast as I dared toward the heart of the forest.

I didn't run into trouble until I reached the cut-off which would bypass Blidworth and Edwinstowe and the other forest villages, and sidle up to the area where the camp had been when I left. There was only one dangerous spot, and that was where it cut the road to Clipstone, King John's hunting lodge. I had not taken this way before, but Robin had told me about it, and Tuck used it when he wanted to travel unseen.

In a space of time uncomfortably short for sensible excuses, I found myself lost, or nearly so. The daylight had broadened; the path was clear through the break of trees. Occasionally the branches drew in and overshadowed it with their green boughs, but the going was quick enough, even among the tangled roots. The only problem was that the terrain no longer looked familiar, and without landmarks it is perilously easy to lose your sense of direction. I was not some foolish Londoner who could not go half a day's ride from its walls without finding himself befuddled; I knew wood-lore and how to find my way out-of-doors. Still, it had never been my best talent, and if I got really lost I could wander in the forest for days before finding the camp. That had been our safety in Sherwood, and now its protection was turned against me.

The afternoon was wearing away when I found a swift flowing stream and some ancient willows beside it. I got off Dun Crump and led him to drink, then I leaned up against the grey-green trunk and closed my eyes. The breeze was very warm and the boughs were creaking. I could have wept with frustration. I had made a mess of things. It would be a tremendous, exhausting effort to find my way, and Robin and the others might have moved camp by now. My muscles ached with strain and exertion and I had had little to eat. I knew, above all, that it would be folly to sleep, unprotected, before I was sure of my way out, but weariness beat down with the sun on my head and body, and weighted down my lids. If I can just rest for a short while, I told myself, then maybe I'll feel better, have more energy to continue on. So I gave myself up to the spell of the afternoon and dozed briefly at the foot of a great grey tree, with a bole for my pillow. It made me long even for the lumpy mattress of the priest's second-best guest bed.

I slept badly, half-dreaming and full of unease. When I awoke I felt thick-headed and without a sense of time's passage. It might have been hours or minutes. The sun was in my eyes. I shifted and turned my head to clear my vision. What I saw made me shake my head and look again, to be sure. But he was still there.

I was not afraid. He had come like part of the dream and seemed part of it still. I watched him in silence. In fact, we stared at each other across a small clearing.

"You are brave to come into the coppice alone. Not many do, now." He spoke the old language of the Saxons, but the words were stilted and the accent singular.

"I am lost," I said simply.

He smiled. "I thought so," he said

happily. "That is why I intruded on your dream. Can I come closer?"

I nodded and rubbed my eyes. He took a few steps toward me, and I saw he was not as small as I had first thought. He was dressed in coarse woven wool dyed the colour of the forest, in greenish-brown. His hair seemed to have picked up the tint as well. His skin was tanned and weathered to the colour of old bark. I could not even begin to guess at his age.

"I'm glad you're not afraid. I've seen you before. You were a little girl at Blidworth, and lately you've been living out, in the forest itself. Like me."

"That's right. Who are you?"

He stared at me with bright eyes and I wondered if it was forbidden to say. "Robin Hood," he said at last.

I took a breath to reply but held it in, keeping silence.

The eyes twinkled. "I know well enough the name's been bandied about lately, borrowed by some fellow with no good claim to it, but I don't really mind. Some people call me a wood-wose, or the Green Man. If you like, think of me as steward of the forest."

I swallowed. "Are there . . . others? Or are you alone?"

I could not read his face, but his voice sounded a little sad. "There were many once. There is a life in the forest eyes like yours cannot see, a life filled with things both good and evil, like the outside. And as they do in the greater world, things change, though more slowly. Where there were many, now there are few. The Forest People are dwindling, like the forest itself."

"I'm sorry," I said, feeling, not for the first time and certainly not for the last, the grief of time and change.

"Don't be. By the time we diminish into legend, you and your kind will be dust as well. Besides, it is not a sorrow for you. If I'm not mistaken you will have your own soon enough."

That woke me up. "Can you help me?"

He shook his head. "I can set you safely on your path, that is all. More than that is not in my power."

"I'll be grateful for that, then." I felt

close to tears. "Is there anything I can do for you?"

The lined, gnarled face split into a joyful smile. "Thank you. I've enjoyed . . . talking. And you and your friends could put out seed cakes or a rabbit once in awhile; that would be more than enough. Now I will show you the way to where you wish to go. You have chosen, and must step into the river of your fate."

"Will I see you again?" I asked him, just as Cecily, hours earlier, had asked me.

The wood-wose, if that is what he was, shrugged as if it were not important. "Perhaps, when you find the stars beneath your feet. Now look up at the branch of that great tree there. There is a cuckoo sitting on the limb."

I looked where he was pointing, and sure enough I saw the bird.

"In a moment, he will fly off," he said. "Keep your eye on him as he flits from tree to tree. If you follow him, he will lead you to the path you seek."

I watched the bird closely, fearing to miss its flight, till I recollected I would have to get Dun Crump first in any case. When I took my eyes from it at last and looked about me, there was no one there. I was sitting as before, in a stand of willows, leaning against the trunk of one of them, near a stream. The horse was eating grass contentedly in the clearing. The sun was full on my face. I pulled myself to my feet hurriedly and climbed onto Dun Crump's back, just as, in a neighbouring tree, the cuckoo ruffled its feathers, called once, and took wing.

10

THE camp was still there after all, but it was in chaos and did not have the feel of victory. I tethered Dun Crump hurriedly and went in search of news. I met John coming to get me. "I heard you were back," he said, without surprise. "You'd best come with me. He was wounded."

There was no need to ask who 'he' was. "Is it bad?" I whispered. It had been three, no, four days. If it had festered . . .

"Anything can be, here," he said grimly. "It was an arrow in the shoulder. I cut it out, but it was hard going and I'm not sure if I got it all. Agnes said you learned to dress wounds at an abbey in France. Will you have a look at it?"

"I'll do what I can, you know that. But I've no special skill with arrows. We can make a poultice, to draw the evil humours out." I told him what herbs I would need. "And garlic, too, if there's

531

any left. I know we bought some last market day."

"I'll get what you need," John told me. His tone said he would get it if the herbs were locked in the treasure room of Nottingham Castle. "He's here, under the shelter."

He was lying on a rough bed of vegetation, ferns, and dried shrubs, with an old cloak under his head. The coarse cloths on his shoulder were already stiff with blood. His skin was pale, and the hollows under his eyes looked bruised with pain and exhaustion. A circle of worried onlookers had gathered round while Agnes bathed his forehead with a damp rag. As John and I walked up he opened his eyes and said to them: "Now go on, all of you. I'll be all right, and it's safest if we move the camp. How can I possibly get any rest with an audience watching to see if my chest keeps moving?" The circle dispersed obediently, some grinning. Agnes's hand checked when she saw me, and he turned his head and looked at us for the first time. He frowned. "*You?*"

"How are you feeling?" I asked him.

He would not be deflected. "What are you doing here? I thought you'd be with the Queen." I saw a sudden fear leap into his eyes, and he tried to raise himself on his elbow. "What is it?" he gasped. "Nothing's happened to the ransom? Where is Father Tuck?"

"Now look, lie down and don't worry, please. I just . . . changed my mind and decided to come back. Nothing happened to the ransom. It's safely piled in the crypt of St Paul's with all the rest. Father Tuck has gone to St Albans. I promise I'll tell you all about it as soon as I've seen to your shoulder. Now do lie back so I can look at your bandages."

He settled into his rush bed and shut his eyes tightly. Even such a small exertion had him breathing rapidly. "I never thought I'd see you back here again," he mumbled, distantly. Over his head and mine as I bent over him, I felt rather than saw the look John exchanged with Agnes. Then John slipped off quietly to get the herbs I'd requested.

"Don't talk," I said, setting myself to undo the stiff and rather nasty wrappings. "This may pull a bit."

"Do you really know anything about dressing wounds?" he said, between clenched teeth.

"I admit we didn't treat too many arrow injuries at Fontevrault. Mostly cuts from tool or knives, things like that. Bedsores, too."

"Wonderful."

"Would you rather I left it to John? I — Oh!" The first sight of the exposed wound was sickening. The edges were jagged and raw-looking and the gaping hole oozed fresh blood. It looked inexpressibly painful, but relatively clean. I sponged it off with some fresh water while Robin stared with fierce concentration at some distant point in the forest.

"Will I live?" he said at last, with a faint echo of his joking tone.

"If I have anything to say about it," I said softly, in a voice he was not meant to hear. More loudly I told him, "Here comes John with the herbs and garlic so we can make you a poultice. You'll smell like a rabbit stew for a few days, but after that you should be fine. Hold on now, this is the last bit that should really hurt."

Fortunately, he fainted when I applied the warm poultice to his shoulder, so I could pack it on and bandage it up without hurting him any further. I said to John, who was helping me from the other side of the patient, "I haven't asked you yet how this happened. You don't have to go into details if you don't want to. I suppose it must have been awful. Did they hang the hostages, then?"

John looked at me oddly. "Why do you think that?"

"You mean you saved them?"

He nodded. "Every one."

"Then how?" I gestured at Robin.

"One of the hostages was scarcely more than a boy. He was so frightened he couldn't sit his horse and fell off. Robin stopped to pull him up behind him. That's when one of the Sheriff's bowmen got off the shot, when the rest of us were riding away."

"So, you succeeded after all," I said, still puzzled by his tone.

"Aye, you could call it that. But now the Sheriff has a face as well as a name to hunt and it will be something personal between them. He doesn't look like a man who'll give up easy. He's seen who we are and how we operate, and next time he won't be caught napping." He shook his head. "I tell you Marian, I'm worried. If returning the ransom doesn't work, or if King Richard doesn't come back soon, we are all done for. The Sheriff and Prince John will see to that."

"I told Robin as much a long time ago. I think he's known it all along, anyway. It's funny," I told John, tucking a blanket around the newly bandaged shoulder and smoothing down the rough bed as much as I could, "when I imagined all the disasters which might befall you — and I covered everything from the Sheriff's burning the camp to imagining you . . . swinging from the gallows in Nottingham — still, the one thing I never thought would happen was that he would be wounded."

Robin groaned and stirred on his makeshift mattress. "You've been listening to too many of Alan's stories," he said faintly.

★ ★ ★

Nobody seemed to think it strange that I had come back. I enjoyed a brief, minor celebrity because I had returned with the Queen's gold and the Queen's gratitude, such as it was. To me it seemed that I had accomplished precious little beyond extracting a vague promise of future consideration 'when Richard comes back'. The gold was much more valuable in the present, though I would have to mortgage some of my lands to pay it back. But I had done the best I could, and we had to take the future, and our deliverance, on faith. Meanwhile, I was relieved that no one asked me why I had not stayed in the south, as I had intended. It was bad enough to endure John's half-hidden sympathy and Agnes's knowing smiles without having the whole camp speculating besides.

Robin's wound seemed to be healing cleanly, though it still troubled him with stiffness and throbbing. His arm was weak, but the gaunt look was gone from his face and he was able to wash and dress himself with only a little help from John. He expressed his gratitude to me quite formally and said nothing further about my going or staying. Of course it was far too late for me to go anywhere, now. I was effectively marooned, as much an outlaw as all the rest.

The Sheriff kept us close-pressed, as we had feared he would. He sent small parties of men into the woods at various times by all the major tracks, but it was more harassment than a full scale attack. Fortunately, he had his own problems in Nottingham and could not commit all his men to finding a band of elusive outlaws. Still, we doubled our watches and changed camp often, and John set a few ambushes that had the effect of discouraging our attackers from a too-deep penetration of the forest. There were other intruders in Sherwood as well, mostly villagers sent farther and farther afield to trap the King's game in the face of the rapacious ransom collections. As the temptation to poach had grown, the penalties had become unbelievably harsh, but the threat of immediate starvation was even harsher. Our sentries observed a number of these desperate trappers, though they were rarely observed in turn. Sometimes, when the snares were empty, we left them what we could spare.

One day, when I was sitting in my linen shift, patching for the hundredth time a rent in the elbow of my sleeve and indulging in the as often repeated self-reproach of not having brought along more clothing, Robin came up to me carrying a big basket, which he set down on the ground beside me. It promptly wobbled and fell over, before he righted it again. I watched in fascination as the whole process was repeated. "What is it?" I asked him.

"A peace offering," he said. "I thought you might like something to nurse now that I'm no longer in need of your ministrations."

"You've brought me a snake, how nice."

He laughed. "Why don't you look and see?"

I reached gingerly for the basket, which spilled again almost in my lap. A ball of woolly brown fur pitched out onto my skirts, wobbled to its feet and began yapping angrily. "Oh, a fox cub," I cried, delighted.

"A dog fox," Robin informed me,

"with very sharp teeth. One of the men found a vixen in a snare, and near it was her earth, with this little fellow calling for his dinner. I'd say he's been weaned onto mice and things already, or he wouldn't stand a chance. I thought you might like to take care of him for a while."

"Thank you," I said, looking down at the orphaned creature who was poking around my lap with his squat nose. I had never seen a fox at such close quarters before, except a dead one, and I was surprised at how different a cub's features were from an adult's. A memory, as sudden and unwelcome as a rash, came to me of how I had originally acquired Dun Crump.

"What's the matter?" asked Robin.

"Nothing," I said, shaking my head to clear away the thought. "I was just remembering another time someone gave me an animal."

He frowned. "I only said 'take care of it for a while', and I meant just that. This may be your first fox cub but it isn't mine. They aren't like horses or dogs who stay with you as long as you let them serve you. You don't become a

540

fox's master. He'll run off in time. Some" — here he paused and smiled — "little vixen will come along, and then you'll have to let him go. He'll turn very mean if you don't."

"Fair enough," I told him. "Do we have enough food for it?"

"I don't think he'll eat much yet. And if you give him some bits of bone and feathers to play with he'll soon get the idea and start catching his own. They're very smart."

"Of course he is," I said, already feeling sure this would be the smartest fox who had ever graced Sherwood, though I was not quite fatuous enough to say so. "I'm going to call him Renard."

Robin rolled his eyes but made no comment. "John's making you some kind of cage so he can't run off." He paused. "You'll remember what I said, won't you? It's not forever, not even for very long."

"I'll remember," I told him. "And by the way, I accept your offer."

He looked alarmed. "What was that?"

"Peace."

"We'll see," he said, sounding amused.

11

I CAN'T say whether Renard was the smartest fox in Sherwood (having only limited acquaintance with others of his kind), but I am positive he was the most diverting. After so much worry and sadness, it was a tonic to have something to laugh at again. Unlike his famous namesake — the clever fox who was the hero of epic folk-tales peopled with regal lions, frustrated wolves, and wanton hens — he was not particularly good at outwitting anything, but then he never had to resort to trickery to get his dinner. His danger lay rather in becoming too lazy to hunt on his own, because he dined off whatever we ate ourselves. He did make high, pouncing leaps at imaginary prey, but I'm not sure he associated them with anything so violent as killing. I hoped he would learn to feed himself by winter; Robin promised me that he would, and I contented myself with that. Meanwhile, he would lie along a low tree branch, flicking his brush for balance and cocking his head beseechingly until I gave in and scratched his white chest so that he lowered his ears in pleasure. It was small wonder he didn't have to work for his supper. Robin said that since the rest of us were all poachers anyway one more could hardly make a difference.

The days of summer crawled by in watchfulness, and still Father Tuck and his party did not come back. Robin's shoulder mended slowly and he began to display the irritability of a lengthy convalescence. It's one thing to submit to the care of others when you are helpless and deathly ill, but something else when you start to feel better. His body could not possibly respond to the demands he made on it for adequate strength, and the results were frustrating. He paced the camp restlessly, asking for news or looking for occupation, flitting from task to task like an angry bee.

One day he asked me, "Can you shoot?"

"I'm sure I could," I told him.

"Well, neither can I, at the moment. Would you like to take turns with a target?" He grinned maliciously. "You should be just about my match, while I get my strength up."

"Besides which, I'll be available to chase your arrows. How could I refuse when you flatter me like that? As a matter of fact, I really would like to learn. I have a feeling it might be useful."

His smile faded and I realized that beneath the banter he had had the same idea. It was not reassuring. Of course I had practised archery as a child at Blidworth, but the skill was hardly in demand at Fontevrault and after that I had had little time to pursue it. I had not thought to need it more than needlework or herb lore.

Robin gestured inquiringly toward Renard, who was looking mournful shut up in his cage.

"Not on your life," I said, with some vehemence. "If anyone turns him into a fox collar for my winter mantle, I don't want it to be me. He's been out today already."

He shrugged and picked up his own bow, made of yew wood, and handed me a smaller one. He carried the quiver full of arrows and his dagger as well.

Archery, like balancing on a log, is a great deal harder than it looks. There are a thousand things to keep track of all at once, things an experienced archer's body, unfairly, remembers for him.

"No, no, no," Robin said, for what seemed like the fiftieth time. "You're letting the point fall too far to the left when you draw, and that's the second time you've struck your arm with the bowstring."

The target stood in the middle of a clearing not far from our latest camp. The sentry was within hailing distance in a nearby grove, so such exposure seemed safe enough. I squared my stance, sighted, and pulled back the bowstring feeling its tension beneath my fingers. The arrow sped wide, with an audible pluck I knew would exasperate my teacher. I went wordlessly to collect my spent arrows and set myself to shoot again.

He came and stood behind me, his hands empty. "Relax," he suggested.

"That's easy for you to say," I muttered, between clenched teeth.

He put his hands on my shoulders,

turning them. "Widen your stance a little."

I obeyed him.

His arms came round my back to where I was holding the bow. A pause. My breath quickened.

"You're pulling left," his voice said in my ear. "So aim to the right a little. There, that's right. Pull back the string with your fingers. Don't touch the arrow." His arms came away from me suddenly, leaving me frozen and singular, like a statue. "Now loose it evenly. Don't pluck."

I did, and got off a much better shot, though still a little wide of the target. The next and the next were better still, to my immense relief. "Your turn now," I told him.

He looked doubtful.

"Come on," I insisted. "My arm's tired, and at least you can show me how to stand and aim." I knew he did not relish an audience to his private war with his own weakness, but I was afraid that if I left him alone he would strain himself to the point of exhaustion or beyond.

"You won't get better if you quit as soon as your arm gets tired," he said, but he picked up his own bow, set the arrow's white cock feather outward, and placed his feet wide in the same line as the arrow's flight. He squared his shoulders, drew the bow to his chin, sighted on the target, and loosed his shot. It struck the target, but he was used to slitting the wand in the centre three times out of four. He grimaced. I could almost see the grim determination hardening his features. He shot again, wide of centre. The next one missed the target altogether. By then he was white and sweating, his muscles clenched in pain, one hand covering the injured shoulder. "It's too soon," I told him.

He shook his head desperately. "No time," he whispered.

"All right, but at least let me collect the spent arrows. Some of my shots are lying over near that hornbeam." I gestured towards the grove, where, now, some jackdaw was raising an awful racket.

He nodded and bent over, resting his hands on his knees. I wanted to say something so badly I had to bite my lips to keep from opening my mouth. I picked up the arrows nearest the target and then went farther afield to collect my own earlier efforts. One gave me a little trouble; it was tangled in some weeds next to the thick undergrowth at the grove's edge, and I had to disengage it carefully, so as not to disturb its balance. I was just lifting it from its bed, my back to the clearing, when I was flung heavily to the ground, one foot twisted under me. I was looking right into Robin's face as he lay on top of me, his hand covering my mouth. Even in his weakened state his grip was so strong I couldn't move, and he had come after me so swiftly I hadn't heard his step. I thought . . . I expected . . . well, a second look made me reconsider. He did not look like a man transported by animal passion. He had turned from pale to a ghastly grey, and I could feel his heart racing next to mine. He looked as if he might be sick. "All right?" His voice was scarcely more than a breath in my ear.

I nodded, ignoring the searing pain in my leg, and he removed his hand.

"There's someone close by, coming through the forest," he said, in the same disembodied voice. "Don't move."

"A rider?"

"Three, at least, by the sound of it." One rider he could have handled, his tone told me, even wounded and staggering from exhaustion. "Look, I don't think they've seen us yet. Can you wiggle back behind that tussocky stuff where you won't be seen?"

"We both can."

He shook his head, a fierce movement which jolted both our bodies. "If they saw me, they'll come looking here, and then they'd find us both. And anyway, I'll have to find some way to warn the camp."

"But you might get killed!"

He sucked in his breath in a sort of furious exasperation. "And how do you propose to stop that?"

I couldn't think of anything to say. He shifted his weight slightly. I straightened my bent leg, experimentally. It still hurt. "All you'll do," said Robin, with a kind of angry patience, "is get yourself killed as well. Do you think I want that on my conscience? I don't have the strength to make you crawl back there, but please, for once, will you just do as I ask without arguing?"

I gaped at him in astonishment for a moment and then turned to move. His hand shot out and pinned my wrist. "Wait."

It was hard to see lying down, but I didn't dare raise my head. Finally I got a glimpse, through the green on the far side of the clearing, of three riders. It was too far to tell, but it looked as if they were cloaked in the simple tunics and cowls of the monastery. It was so quiet I could hear the clop of the horses' hooves on the packed ground and the skittering of kicked-up pebbles. We lay still as stone ourselves. I could smell the bitter-dry tang of summer grasses and hear the blood beat in my ears. Suddenly there was a shout from the other side of the clearing, and over my head an arrow sped skyward, its white nock quickly disappearing from my line of sight. I never saw where it fell. Robin sat up, exclaiming, "Thank God! It's Father Tuck. The arrow's the signal."

I didn't realize I'd been holding my breath until I let it out in one relieved gust. "I couldn't see very well, but I didn't think they looked like Sheriff's men. Why are they all dressed as monks?" I asked him.

"That's what made me think they were Sheriff's men," he said, quite gaily. "That disguise has been used more than once, sometimes with horrible success. Ask Alan about it some time. He knows all the stories."

"Like 'Robin Hood and the Potter'?" I ventured.

"Not in the least," he said, still smiling. "I would never stoop to abusing people's trust for the clergy by impersonating a man of God's cloth, or not for base purposes anyway. You can ask Tuck about it yourself when we get back to camp." He stood up and offered me his hand. I took it and started to rise, but fell back when my leg gave way under me. In doing so I jerked on his injured shoulder, so that he dropped to his knees as well.

"Sorry to make such heavy weather of it," I told him, when the colour had come back into his face. "I'm afraid I twisted my leg a bit when I fell."

"When I knocked you down, you mean." He leaned over the member in question, poking and prodding while I tried not to wince. "This could give you trouble if you put too much weight on it. I'll have to carry you back to camp."

"You'll do no such thing," I retorted. "You'd set your shoulder back two weeks, if you didn't end up crippled for life."

"If I say I'll carry you, I'll carry you," he said, through gritted teeth.

"You wouldn't care to make a small wager, would you? Wait!" I cried, alarmed, when he showed every sign of taking me up on it. "I don't want to end up face down in the clearing."

"Would you prefer to lie here debating the issue till we die of starvation?"

"We could call for help," I suggested.

"I could leave you here on your own," he countered.

"I've thought of a compromise," I said at last. I have to admit I was enjoying myself immensely. "Why don't I back up to that tree, you can help me get to my feet, and then I'll put my arm around your good side and we can hobble back to camp that way?"

"You think this is funny, don't you?"

"Funnier than getting caught out by the Sheriff's men."

"I have to agree with you there." He sighed. "All right, let's get you up, and then we'll get back the best we can."

He let me drag myself to the agreed upon tree, so that I had to rest a moment with my back to it before I could muster the strength to try to stand. My leg really did hurt. I sat looking at it speculatively, wondering how much trouble it would be and how long it would take to heal, until he touched me on the shoulder and said, "Come." He reached down to take hold of me, and I slid my arm around his waist. He lifted me gently, and I supported myself on my good leg and by leaning against his shoulder. I could feel the heat of his body through his tunic, and the surge of blood in my ears. Neither of us moved. Encouraged by our stillness, a hart passed through the trees near at hand in a flash of white. I hardly saw it. I half stood, stricken, as if I had been pierced with a wound. All that was left to me was the longing to leap into the mindless dark, to be consumed there. I offered everything up to the pyre — pride, honour, independence, privacy. Unable to speak, I looked into his eyes and saw my own troubled desire mirrored there. His hand came round my head to grasp my unbound hair, and his mouth came down over mine. The kiss was as warm and fierce as the sun's blast on an August afternoon. My limbs were loose and trembling. Then, just as fiercely, he thrust me away. "I can't," he said, "or rather I will not."

I was too dazed for speech, and he seemed to take my silence for agreement. In fact, even afterwards I could not think of anything I might have said which would not sound stupid or importunate. "Ah well," he said briskly, "I think John has found us anyway." He beckoned to a distant figure who had appeared on the edge of our archery field. How long he had been there I had no way of knowing. "John can help you back to camp," Robin said, avoiding my eyes. "I must go and see Tuck. What will he think if I'm not there to greet him?" And he stooped to gather my arrows and bow and went off to collect his own, leaving me to his friend's attentions.

My eyes filled with tears of humiliation and embarrassment. The mouth may lie, but the body does not, and I could not have made my feelings plainer if I had written him a dozen love songs. John was all gentle kindness, which nearly undid me and made me bite my lip. He knelt beside me and felt my leg all over with his small, patient hands. "Does it hurt?"

I watched Robin crossing the clearing, his arms full of bows and the arrow quivers, his shoulder squared against whatever Tuck had to tell him. "Yes," I said.

He looked up sharply.

"It was all a mistake," I told him. Then hearing the bitterness in my own voice, I added, "We thought they were the Sheriff's men."

John bent over my foot again. "So that's the way of it, is it?" he asked softly. He seemed satisfied with the condition of my lower limbs, straightened, and lifted me up as easily as if he really were seven feet tall and a blacksmith besides. "You'll have to be patient," he said, in my ear. "I know it's not for me to interfere, but you haven't known him as long as I have."

"I don't know what you mean," I stammered unconvincingly.

He ignored me. "He's lived at a stretch for a longer time than a man should, and it's taken its toll. He's set his life toward one goal and lived for nothing but, if you understand me."

"He doesn't want any distractions, is that it?"

"By all the saints, Marian, it's much more than that. Even he can see he might fail, and then he'd be left with less than nothing. He has too much pride to tie anyone to him in that case. He'd want you to be free."

"It's too late for that," I said quietly.

"I know it." He grinned. "We all do, seemingly, except for Robin. So don't give up."

"John?"

"What?"

"Will he fail?"

He kept walking, treading lightly over

the woodland floor. "Almost there," he told me.

"You haven't told me what news the Father brings," I said. "You must have spoken with him."

He set me down gently on a log and broke off one of its upper branches, a limb about four feet long. Then he began to whittle and shape it with his knife. Knowing he would get around to telling me in his own good time, I said nothing and sat watching him. His hands moved smoothly over the wood, back and forth. When it was pared to a fine, glossy surface, so that not even a splinter of roughness remained, he handed it to me. "This is to lean on, till your leg heals," he said. "Go on, try it."

I stood, and let it bear the weight of my sore leg. "Thank you, it's just right. Come on John," I said, unable to stand it any longer. "Will Longchamp help us?"

He shook his head. "Tuck says the Queen's letter was the only reason the Chancellor saw him at all, and then he laughed when he heard his request. Longchamp said Richard himself, from his prison, had just confirmed Prince

John in all his lands in England and Normandy, and that if the King didn't want to seem to give offence to his brother, he, the Chancellor, certainly wasn't going to take him on either, especially about something as small as this."

It wasn't until he told me that I realized how little I had really been expecting any other outcome. I hoped Robin wasn't too disappointed. I sighed. "Well, then, it all comes down to waiting for the return of the King. Did Tuck hear anything about when that might be?"

He shrugged. "From what he can tell, nobody knows. The ransom's been raised again, by 50,000 marks. The Emperor asked for hostages from all the great families, against payment. Tuck heard London's in an uproar, and the Chancellor's up to his ears in people raising holy hell about sending their children to the Emperor. So nobody's worrying much about anything else."

"Oh Sweet Jesu, will that mean another levy? How will people pay it? We're down to the bare bones as it is. And where will it all stop? The Emperor can just keep raising the ransom, and John can keep stealing it." I added despairingly: "The King could be there till Domesday, and there's nothing anyone can do about it."

He smiled ruefully. "Don't go borrowing trouble — we've enough as it is without worrying about what might happen as well. Besides, don't underestimate the Queen. From what you told us she's a powerful ally. For the rest we'll have to trust to luck."

"I wish you'd picked something else to trust in," I told him. "We haven't had the best of it lately, have we? In any event, I should still question Father Tuck to find out more, if I can. Where is he now?"

He said, without pity or censure, "He's drunk."

"Oh." I felt quite tired suddenly, as if I had paddled my boat upstream for a very long time.

"Poor Marian," said John, not sounding terribly sympathetic. "I never thought to see you mixed up in all of this that day I took you back to Nottingham Castle."

"Well, neither did I! The ironic . . . the odd thing is that after that . . . that awful thing" — I still couldn't speak of my encounter with the band of lepers easily — "happened here in the forest, I married Guy for a kind of safety. And then I ended up running back here to be saved from Guy. What a liar he turned out to be!"

He looked taken aback at my vehemence. "Was he?"

"My God, yes he was. Do you know, he *promised* me that he had nothing to do with taking Locksley away from Robin, and that there was no reason at all for the Prince's favour. He kept insisting to the end that we were just collecting the ransom for the King. Then when Robin took it, he threatened to kill me if I had anything to do with it." I flushed, remembering. "How could I go on living with him? I wanted to get out of my marriage before I ever knew about the ransom, and even if I die here and never get Blidworth back, I would still prefer it to going back to Guy."

"Dear Marian, why haven't you ever told Robin you felt like that?"

I looked at him. "Robin?"

"It might have saved us all something. He's been cutting himself up for weeks at the thought that you might still have some affection for your husband, in spite of everything."

"How could he think that?" I asked, surprised. "Tuck knows. Oh, but that was in the nature of a confession," I remembered. "Anyway, even if there had still been fondness between us, it would have vanished when I left him, especially since he must be sure by now that I helped steal the treasure. Why else would he have maligned me to the Queen?"

John studied his knife, which he had been polishing on the edge of his tunic, with absorbed attention. "But you see," he said softly, without looking up, "Robin's worried that he might have to kill him if their paths cross at the wrong time."

I felt as stricken as if he had slapped me across the face. I sat back down on the log. "I hadn't thought . . . God knows he deserves disgrace for siding with the Prince instead of the King. And if he should meet death on the field, fighting against Richard . . . But at Robin's hand?" I shook my head, feeling sick. "John, he won't even touch me now

561

because of Guy," I said miserably. "How would it be between us if he kills him? It would tear him to bits."

A short time before he had been all gentleness. Now, seeing my look, he sounded almost angry. "I think that depends more on you than on Robin. What did you expect? I'm not saying it will happen. But they're enemies now, with much more than Locksley between them. If you can't face that, you'd better ask yourself if you really want this great love you seem to be pining for. This isn't one of your hearth stories, you know."

He did not say, though the unspoken thought hung like smoke in the still air, that if the life threads of Robin and my husband crossed, it might not only be Guy's that was cut.

"I shouldn't have come back, then."

"If I thought that, I'd have said so. Besides, it's too late, in all the ways that count. It's out of your hands."

"So what can I do?"

"What all of us must," he said. "Live life as it comes, and keep faith."

"That sounds too easy," I told him.

He smiled. "I've always found it

middling hard, myself."

"Do you suppose," I asked him, "that when we're all old and well fed, living in our manor houses and surrounded by saucy grandchildren, that someone will sing one of Alan's songs about Robin of Sherwood, and we'll smile and think, 'that was the happiest time of our lives', and wish we could live it all over again?"

"No," he said, and laughed.

12

THE rains came early that year, crowding out the brisk, glorious days of the English autumn, and I began to realize what spending the winter in Sherwood would really mean. Summer showers were uncomfortable enough without real shelter or warmth, but to endure the fierce cold of the forest soaked to the skin, underfed and underclothed, seemed scarcely possible. Yet most of the others had lived through not one but several winters, though some had sickened with chest ailments and fevers, and some had died. Like the damping rain borne on the autumn wind, there was a prickly sense of some change to come, not dreaded perhaps, but inevitable as the fall of leaves and the first drifting flakes of snow.

The Goose Fair came and went, and the Sheriff held an archery contest whose fame seemed curiously widespread and inappropriate until Alan commented that of course it was designed to lure the foremost archers in the neighbourhood into competing. It was like the Sheriff, I thought, to concoct such a plan: did he really think an appeal to vanity could so override the dictates of common sense?

Still, the invitation was shrewder than I first realized. The night was full of frustrated would-be archers stamping their feet against the cold and spinning tales of what they would have done, if only . . . with all the heat of men who know they can do nothing. Alan, whose wits were even nimbler than his fingers, made a game of it and invented a long ballad about the Sheriff's offering an arrow with a golden head and a silver shaft as the prize for an archery contest, hoping to induce Robin Hood and his men to compete. Of course the outlaws enter the contest disguised and slit all the wands and win the prizes, and the Sheriff says he's surprised Robin didn't have the nerve to appear, but that even he couldn't have shot any better than the winners. The poor Sheriff is left 'chafing in his grease' and raving mad when a letter informs him of the truth after the contest is over. Alan always made the Sheriff sound befuddled and slightly comical in his songs, but that was Alan's way with everything. It certainly made the camp feel better.

Robin said nothing, though he laughed with the others. Now that he might be getting closer to the resolution, for good or ill, of his problems, prudence weighed heavily upon him. Soon the Emperor would have to let Richard go or he would have to have him killed. He could not keep him locked up forever, once he took possession of the ransom and the hostages. What King Philip or John would try to do then remained to be seen. Having staked everything on this one throw — the return of the King — Robin could not afford to leave the game until he saw how the dice fell out, but it irked him. If he loses, I thought, watching his face, he will accept the Sheriff's challenge or something like it, rather than wait to see what game Fate dealt him next. He has reached the end of what he can take.

As it was, I had little enough chance to observe him, since he was away from camp a great deal and avoided my company when he was present. I confess I felt prickly and irritable myself, as if something uncomfortable had lodged under my skin. I had not felt so restless since I decided to come back to camp. I said as much to Agnes, when we were pounding clothes on the rocks at the stream's edge, shivering with cold whenever the water splashed our bodies. On such a day at Locksley, I would have called for a warm bath and a dry gown, and spent the morning in my solar instead of going out. I tried without much success to put that thought from my mind. Instead I warmed myself by beating vigorously on the faded and patched cloth, until Agnes had to remind me we could not afford to destroy it. Her presence was companionable, however, and I found my troubles flowing out of me like the water down the stream bed. When I had done she considered me in silence for a moment and then said, "Do you really mean it, Marian, when you say you don't understand why you feel this way?"

"Why yes," I told her. "Of course," I

said carefully, "it's natural to be worried about the future and going cold and hungry until the King comes back, and all that, but this is more. I can't sleep, and I feel so wretched all the time. And I . . . I can't control my thoughts."

She paused in her scrubbing and gave me a long, clear look. "Well, it's plain as a parsnip in a cabbage patch to me." She continued to look at me until I lowered my own gaze in embarrassment. "Why the two of you want to make it so complicated is what I *don't* understand."

"Well, it *is* complicated," I said.

"Has the Father been on at you by any chance? Ah, I see that he has. You can imagine how much worse it's been for me. I'll tell you what I told him, and you can listen or not, as you choose. Half of mankind comes together without the blessing of the Church or the Law, and not necessarily the worst half either. At least with Alan and me, no money changed hands, and no one got sold for a bit of land or a title. Can you say the same for yourself and Sir Guy? Is that what you want for your life?"

"No," I shivered, "but I'm not sure I

can get what I do want."

"Then settle for what you can get. That's what I've done." Agnes had become much more opinionated since she came to Sherwood, and she sometimes treated everyone like a bullying maiden aunt. Her tone suggested I should not question her further, that I had been effectively sorted out with the laundry, as I suppose I had. I wondered what would become of her, of any of us who survived, when we lived in the civilized world again. So many of the rules and buffeting and interactions of outside life that had shaped us in the greater world were missing in the forest. It made you feel very free sometimes, and at others simply loose around the edges.

★ ★ ★

With the passing of the season, Renard grew into young foxhood. All the fox stories I've ever heard malign his character, from the original Renard's method of pushing the wolf's wife out of a tight place (which so enraged Isengrim) to all the villainous duping of innocent

569

lambs and chickens recounted by Marie de France. I'm not sure what it is about the fox that inspires all these stories, though I suppose it might be taken as a compliment. Actually, though Renard would hardly be pleased by the comparison, he reminded me quite a bit of a cat. He would leap to catch the leaves between his teeth before they fell, and then look absurdly pleased with himself whether he caught one or not. He was keenest at night, when he could hear before anyone the sounds of the dark, of stealthy bellies drawn over the grass or the small cries of the hunter and the hunted. He brought mice and moles, and once a rabbit, to our 'den' to share his dinner, and looked offended when no one accepted his offering. Toward winter he developed the rank dog-fox smell that Robin said meant he was entering his maturity. With some reluctance I kept my part of our bargain and started letting him spend more and more time out of his cage, but most times he would just lie about on some perch above ground level, daydreaming of who knew what. He too seemed to be waiting.

We stole no more treasure, on the King's behalf or anyone else's. The Prince was undoubtedly more successful, having more freedom of movement, and the opportunity of a second and third levy of the ransom tax. Robin and John and some of the others made several lengthy forays into Barnsdale and Yorkshire, where they were known only by reputation and not by sight, but little came of it. The bare trees made hiding and ambush nearly impossible, though they favoured the Sheriff's men no more than us, and we were spared the harassment of the summer months.

Unbeknownst to us, the Prince and the Sheriff had more urgent business. In December, the first instalment of the ransom, aptly named the Lion's share, was dispatched to the Emperor, accompanied by Queen Eleanor herself. There could be no doubt she meant to bring her son back, and soon. Philip and John, meanwhile, were trying to implement their infamous plot to bribe the Emperor to keep Richard in captivity a little longer, a year or so, or perhaps indefinitely. The particulars of this plan, when they were finally published in England, remained hazy for obvious reasons. In any case the Prince sent word to all his strongholds, of which Nottingham Castle was the greatest, to fortify themselves against his brother's return.

There are details of that long winter in Sherwood I can recall even now with the sharp clarity of an icicle, though it is far away in time and the comforts of my convent cell soothe my body if not my mind. The cold, mostly. It beat on the skin and the chest like a bludgeon, driving you far down deep into yourself and consuming every effort except that needed to keep the flame of life kindled. We shared cloaks, beds, fire, and such shelter as we could contrive, and it was never enough. Love, learning, songs, everything that had existed for me only weeks before was stamped out brutally in the face of this animal need to endure. If it had gone on longer there would have been nothing left of me, whether we survived or not. By the end we hardly spoke, clamping our teeth shut to keep them from chattering.

In February, Richard was released from captivity and, in the company of his mother, made a triumphal progress down the Rhine river to the sea and liberty. The snows did not melt immediately nor the trees burst into bloom. In fact, Prince John and his supporters had given it out some time before that the King was dead, and the rumour had grown irresistibly strong. I half believed it myself, cut off as we were from the south and news. None of us knew it when, upon setting foot on English soil, the King made a gleeful and somewhat ironic pilgrimage of thanksgiving to the shrine of his father's old enemy at Canterbury. After that he hurried northward, to lay siege to Nottingham.

Meanwhile, we had our own problems. A sickness had visited the camp, a burning fever with swelling in the neck and evil humours in the lungs. In the midst of the winter's privations, it's no wonder so many caught it. The oldest and the weakest died, a village woman whose husband had been outlawed for setting traps two years before, and her son, an idiot, who was the man's only child. She'd had the baby late in life, after years of barrenness, and it had proved her undoing, and the boy's. We sent for Tuck, but in deep winter even Edwinstowe was far away, and he came too late. He was still in camp when Agnes fell ill with a terrible swiftness, shivering and burning by turns, and clutching my hand. On the second day, she began calling for Alan.

"You've got to send for him," I told Robin, after hours of it. "She'll get no peace otherwise."

"I can't." It seemed we still had enough energy to argue. "It might be dangerous."

"She might die, without seeing him again. Surely that's worth some risk."

He folded his arms tightly across his chest, a gesture I had come to know. It meant he would stick to his decision in spite of himself. "I hope she doesn't die, but if she does, at least it need not be unshriven. I don't have the right to risk anyone else's life just to bring Alan here. The last time he left he planned to spend some weeks with the lord of Mansfield, and do I need to remind you that the road there runs very close to Clipstone Palace?"

"But Robin, we watch the Clipstone road ourselves, and you know no one's been seen there in some time. The Prince is away, and his forces seem to be gathering at Nottingham. Robin," I beseeched him, "you don't know what he means to her."

"Don't I?" he asked, almost bitterly. "I think I do. Everyone here has others outside who are dear to them. Agnes has been luckier than most. Some have died without ever seeing their loved ones again. Believe me, I am sorry. All we can do for her now is try to help her get well. And incidentally, please try not to get sick yourself."

I went back to her bedside resolved to wait and see, but as the hours lengthened and she got no better I became determined to act on my half-formed plan, which was, in effect, that I would go to fetch Alan myself. As I look back on it dispassionately, I see how foolish that was, that the illness would probably have run its course in either direction before we could return. But I tormented · myself with thoughts of Agnes's kindness to me and of what she had already suffered, and I think the winter's despair had altered my judgement for the worse. That I might be in particular danger if I left the forest I discounted. Guy would have stopped looking for me by now, and unless I ran straight into him somewhere on the road I felt easy enough on that score. After all, I'd recently ridden miles through the forest by myself without mishap (if you didn't count getting lost, and meeting the wood-wose). Besides, the waiting was getting to me, too. I couldn't stay huddled by the fire in Sherwood, dreaming of spices and eggs, when there was something I could do. In the forest, you were what you did, and action — even a possibly futile one — was an antidote to the feeling of powerlessness that engulfed us all.

At least I was not so witless as to attempt to make the trip alone. I persuaded Will Scarlet to accompany me, in part because he had lately travelled with Tuck and knew the roads, and in part because he was young and light-hearted enough to consider the whole project as something of an adventure.

Fortunately there was a brief thaw so we could travel mired in mud rather than snowdrifts. It was a journey of no more than six miles as the birds fly, but there was no telling how long it would take if the road was difficult. We set out at once, telling no one except one of Will's closest friends, the boy Robin had saved from the hangman and been wounded for. He was to tell where we had gone only when our absence was noticed. In any case, an hour's start would be enough, and we hoped to be back before anyone could start worrying seriously.

The morning crackled with frost, and the grass snapped under Dun Crump's hooves. Slate grey clouds lowered against the frozen earth. I could feel the chill penetrate to my bones, but it could not stifle my sense of elation at leaving the confinement of camp and being out on the road again. We were half way down the Clipstone Road before I realized I had shaken off a great many of my former fears, just as if they were excess weight in the saddlebags. That it might have made sense to retain a few of them could not curb my feeling of release. Dun Crump caught the mood and wanted to run, but I dared not let him in such tricky footing. Will's mount pranced ahead of us, churning up slush. An owl, disturbed, hooted in some distant tree branch. Otherwise we saw and heard nothing, not even a hoof or foot print, to indicate we were not the first on the road in a long time. So we came without incident before the dwelling of the lord of Mansfield, and sent in to ask whether Alan was lodging there.

I might as well admit, since I am telling everything, that it was at first a surprise and then a grief to me that I was treated by the porter with condescension, as if I were a village tradeswoman with something to sell, and a poor product at that. I had certainly not forgotten that my clothes were over-worn and under-cleaned, with visible mending, nor that my hair was dressed without the benefit of a mirror or of ornaments. But vanities and illusions die hard, and I had thought that breeding and education would set me apart. I saw in the porter's eyes and manner that I had now become an outlaw in form as well as in fact.

Alan was not there. He had departed some days earlier, after a stay of several weeks. No one knew where he had gone, not even the kitchen maid, who was said to be inconsolable, or her father, who was merely irate. The porter gave Will an exaggerated wink when he delivered this news, and looked astonished when I glared at him.

There seemed nothing left to do but go back at once. We bought provisions with our meagre coin; in Mansfield we would not be recognized. I wished I had brought along more of the contents of Eleanor's purse. The provisions were both scarce and costly, as the ransom levies had skimmed not only the top milk but the bottom as well, and times were hard for everyone. Still, some winter vegetables were available at outrageous prices, and I bought what I could. The sick at camp could eat them in a broth. There was a blanket, too, but we couldn't afford it. I was all for stealing it, but the merchant was suspicious and watched us closely.

When we had done all we could, we started the journey back.

Disappointment made me silent, and Will, who had chattered to me all the trip out, was quiet as well. The thin bare branches made a brown net through which the late light of winter shone, clear and cold. The wind blowing out of the woods froze my nose and throat, making them burn. Once we heard the high sound of wolves calling, and then one of them loped past us near the road, intent on his own business. Otherwise, only my thoughts disturbed me, and I forgot to be cautious. We had ridden some way beyond the Clipstone turning before I realized our tracks were not the only sign of activity on the road. Someone else had passed that way recently, a rather large party, by the look of it. Will dismounted to look at the prints, and I led the horses into the wood beside the lane.

"The Sheriff?" I asked him.

He shrugged. "Could be. The men were armed, most of them, and the horses are big. The impressions are too heavy to mean anything else."

"The tracks are very fresh, though. I

wonder why we didn't meet anyone on the road."

Will made an eloquent gesture with his head in the direction of Clipstone Palace.

"Oh, lord, that must be it. It might even be the Prince. In that case there are sure to be more following."

Will straightened and stepped out of the road. "Unless I am mistaken, we're about to find out for sure. There are horsemen on the road now, coming fast."

I looked down it quickly, but a curve made it difficult to see very far. Will waved me back. "Let's get the horses out of sight," he whispered. "Back there, a slope and a hollow to hide them in. Quickly!"

We scrambled down to the hiding place, securing the reins, and then, of one mind, we crept back to the road to look. The sound of hooves grew nearer. We lay still in a long patch of slushy growth a few feet from the edge. The front of my clothes grew damp and muddy, but it was too late to move. Round the curve came a black horse, a destrier of many hands, and on it sat a large man dressed in a monk's robe of fine, heavy woollen. His pectoral cross proclaimed him an abbot, but his hood slipped back to reveal untonsured red-gold hair. His face was set in stern concentration; the high cheekbones and firm mouth spoke of purpose and authority, but his eyes made me afraid. I drew in my breath sharply, so that Will, beside me, laid a finger to his lips. Behind the leader, coming up quickly, rode several other clerics looking more martial than meek; these, presumably, were the abbot's flock. After them rode two men-at-arms looking what they were, without device or livery. The whole group passed by our hiding place in the space of a few moments and disappeared down the road in the direction of Clipstone.

"Whew!" Will said, pushing himself up on his hands. I brushed myself off with relief; in a few more minutes I would have been wet through and frozen to the ground. "That was close. Churchmen or no, they looked like bad business to meet on the road. That abbot could curdle your liver with a look, as my mother used to say," he said cheerfully. "I must admit, he didn't look like the usual greedy cleric who runs after the Prince. Maybe they aren't headed for Clipstone after all. Still, it's best to take no chances and get going." He held out a hand to me to help me over some fallen branches and saw my face. "What is it?" he asked.

I hardly knew how to tell him. "The abbot . . . that was . . . Richard."

"Richard who?"

"Richard Plantagenet." I was finding it difficult to speak. "The King."

"Right, and I'm the Pope's grandson. Come on, Marian, what *are* you talking about?"

I said nothing, thinking.

It sank in at last. "Mother of God! Are you serious?"

I nodded.

"The King? Here, at his brother's lodge? It doesn't make sense. You must be mistaken."

"No. He is much changed, of course, but he is definitely the King." Will still looked doubtful. "You may not know that I attended Queen Eleanor for some time. I have good cause to remember his face," I told him. It was odd, but

I had quite forgotten until that moment that he was my half-brother as well. All that seemed as distant and bloodless as a minstrel's song.

"Even if you're right," he said, "that still doesn't explain why he's dressed as an abbot and riding right up to his brother's door, as if there's no more between them than some argument over knucklebones."

"I've been thinking," I told him. "What was it he was doing when Duke Leopold kidnapped him in Austria? You've heard the story: he was making his way overland in disguise. It's just the sort of thing that appeals to him; he likes to live dangerously. As for Clipstone, no one's been seen there for a month. Supposing he's planning to attack Nottingham Castle. That makes sense. It's John's capital and most of his supporters are gathering there. We've heard that for ourselves. Maybe Richard's using Clipstone as a base to spy out the land and gather support. It's the perfect hiding place — no one would think of looking there for him. And it is a royal lodge, after all, so it belongs to the crown, not to John."

"That's a lot of 'ifs'," Will said judiciously, untying his horse.

"True," I admitted, "but I'd like to see what Robin makes of them. At least there's hope, Will. The King is back!"

"Damn, damn, and blast," he said, bent over the horse's leg. "Windrider has a shoe loose. I'm sorry to take the risk, but we'll have to stop at the smith's. We can't afford to let any of the horses go lame." There was a forge at the edge of Edwinstowe, where the smith worked for us for whatever we could give him. He had known Robin when he was the forester's foster son, and he had defied the ban on succouring outlaws many times out of loyalty to their old acquaintance. Still, even friendship in such troubled times was a risky business. We did not like to show our faces in Edwinstowe except in dire need. However, there were no forges in deepest Sherwood.

"All right then, practical thing first," I told him. "But I refuse to be discouraged. Now I'm sure everything is going to turn out all right!"

I could tell Will was not quite convinced, and in his place who could blame him, but I knew I had not made a mistake. My heart, which I had thought lightened on the journey out, now seemed weightless with relief and happiness. Robin would not fail. He would get Locksley back. My marriage to Guy would be annulled . . . Beyond that my fantasies were more speculative but no less exciting.

As we neared Edwinstowe, circling round the main approach to the village so we could not be seen entering it, I was filled with gratitude and an overwhelming desire to visit the church. Of all the forest's deprivations, this, next to outright starvation, was the keenest, and in safer days everyone had slipped into Edwinstowe now and then to hear services. We hadn't tried it lately, since the Sheriff had been pressing us so hard. But now that we had come so near, I could not keep myself from going in. Will advised me to keep my face covered but did not seem overly concerned. It was certainly true that I no longer looked like a person of consequence.

The little church was dark and quiet, much as it was on the day I had first met Robin there. Through closed eyes I conjured him kneeling before the altar, his grey eyes full of life and purpose, his body barely controlling a passionate energy that had been tempered but not beaten by the harsh life he had lived. Oh God, I thought, don't let him have to live like that again. Let it be all right. Even in such a prayer were the seeds of selfishness. I knew he would never come to me as he was now, dispossessed and without a man's estate, so it was my own happiness I prayed for as well as his.

I wondered what he would be like as a lover. I had known only my husband's embraces, if they could be called that, but I had begun to suspect there was much more to it than that, like a gift one knows is coming, but must wait for. I wondered what he wanted, if anything, from me. There had been other women, I knew, but they counted as nothing beside the other forces that drove him on. Well, we would see.

I looked down at the church floor, ashamed at my roving thoughts. I said a proper prayer of thanksgiving and for the safe deliverance of the King, and I did not forget to pray for Agnes's recovery. Refreshed and satisfied, I rose from my knees and went out into the thin, brittle air of the winter evening.

Some women had gathered by the fountain and were cracking the ice with stones to draw the water. I paused in the shadows for a moment, waiting to pass unnoticed, when I became aware that someone was standing behind me. I turned slowly, so as not to show surprise or fear. The chances that anyone would recognize me in the near dark were very slim, unless I acted foolish.

A single armed man, one of Guy's retainers whose name I had forgotten, peered into my face. "Ah, I thought so," he said, laying a hand on my arm. "I'm sorry to compel you, Lady Marian, but your husband has offered a substantial reward for your return."

I opened my mouth to scream, but he saw it coming and laid a hand over my mouth so that I could scarcely breathe. I struggled and he shifted his grip a little, dragging me backward all the time away from the village centre. I wondered, fleetingly, what chance had brought him to Edwinstowe.

"Don't fight me, you'll only make it harder on yourself. Do you want me to tie you up?"

I shook my head vigorously, thinking that if my hands and legs were free I should have more opportunity to escape.

He was a decent man, young, and I wished I could remember his name. It was clear that he had no idea of my real reasons for leaving Locksley and regarded the whole matter as a simple one of infidelity and misunderstanding. He kindly did not comment on my appearance or my folly, nor did he handle me roughly when he put me on his horse. He was equally deaf to my importunings and promises to better his reward if he would let me go; I would have sold Blidworth itself rather than return to Guy and Lady Iseult.

I asked him whether my husband had had men out looking for me the whole time I had been gone.

He paused, seeming to consider whether it was safe to answer, and then said,

"Only at the beginning. Now that the King is presumed dead, the Prince's cause demands much of our time. Lately we've just had standing orders to bring you back if we found you, that's all."

I said nothing. Information, when you are its sole possessor, is a weapon you must wield carefully, at the right moment. "Then how did you come to be at Edwinstowe?" I asked him.

I couldn't see his face, but I could almost feel his embarrassment. "I . . . I have a friend there, my lady. I met her one time when I escorted you to the church."

We rode along in silence for a while before I realized we were not heading for Locksley Hall. Fear raised the hair on the back of my neck. "Where are we going?" I asked my captor.

He saw no harm in responding. "Why, Nottingham Castle. That's where Sir Guy is. All the Prince's friends are being called to its defence."

I twisted and squirmed and tried to jump from the horse. He only held me tighter, and refused to let me down for any reason, even to answer the call of nature. So I was borne on to the one place I most dreaded to go, which, if I had guessed correctly, would soon be the site of the King's full-scale assault. And I would be within, a seeming traitor to both sides.

13

A S usual, I had overestimated my own importance. The sheriff was not there at the castle gate to greet me with a noose. In fact, I was conveyed with much politeness and little ceremony to a chamber in the high tower, near the Sheriff's rooms. It was normally occupied by attendants of his lady, but she and her household had been sent for safety to a more distant estate. There were few women about, except within the village itself, and the castle had become a bristling stronghold once more, filled with armed men. I opened the tower window and looked out over the flat Trent valley, the water meadows, and the forest and woods stretching on and on. Far below there were men digging trenches at the base of the walls. A train of mules and carts was winding slowly up the hill to the main gate. Even with no expertise in military matters it looked obvious to me that Nottingham could withstand a lengthy siege. King Henry had built it that way himself.

Though I tried not to think of it, intending to prepare myself for my interview with my husband or the Sheriff or both, I let myself wonder what Will would think when I did not meet him at the smith's. Were there any witnesses to my abduction? He would tell Robin I had identified the King on the road; would Robin think I had run off to Nottingham with the news? I was fairly sure we had gone beyond that, but here I was, undeniably housed within the castle walls. The thought, nasty and biting as a fishhook, could not be dislodged. I told myself sternly that in a short time I might be beyond what anyone whatsoever thought of me, and tried to concern myself with that. In all probability no one knew I was here except my captors, and I had only myself and God's providence to rely on for aid.

I saw no one, except guards and a page who brought me food, for three days. I doubt if this was a deliberate torment but it was effective nonetheless. The Sheriff was understandably busy and Guy was absent from the castle; as the time wore on increasing dread wore down my resistance. The page was sullen, but I did glean from him the only good news so far, that Prince John was not in residence and was not expected. I wondered if the Prince knew, after all. It would be just the thing; his supporters could fight the battles, and if the tide turned against them, he would not be there in person to face his brother's justice. John had the knack of slipping and sliding out of the hands of danger into safety, like some greased pig at a country fair. It was a talent I could envy. Guy came at last, on the fourth morning, while I was at prayer.

My senses had been straining after the sound of his step for three days, so of course I heard it when he entered the room. I did not turn or rise from my knees at once, even after the last fervent supplication was finished. I had not made a study of Queen Eleanor for nothing, though the rituals and subterfuges of court were overlaid with the rougher tutelage of Sherwood.

It seemed that Guy too had learned

something from women. He had dressed with as much care and finery as he had for our wedding, in a dark blue tunic and surcoat of soft wool that shone in wonderful contrast to my own coarse, much-mended garments which were, despite whatever care I could give them, frankly dirty. The effect was to put us on unequal footing from the outset. If I had not recalled Lady Iseult's preparation for our first encounter at Locksley, I might have wondered where he learned the trick.

I met his eyes with an effort and said, calmly enough, "Greetings, Husband."

A spasm of irritation, no more, flashed across his face. "You can call me that?" he asked, raising his brows. He spoke without heat, as if he were performing a necessary but unpleasant public ceremony. I had expected to see him angry; this coolness chilled my blood. "I couldn't believe it when I heard you'd been found. And that they brought you here," he added, as if it were as much a matter of inconvenience as anything else.

"Didn't you order it?" I asked him, incredulous.

He seemed unsure. "Yes, certainly, but after so long I thought you were dead." He meant he hoped I was.

"Like the King?"

He didn't react. Perhaps he really believed it. He frowned and seemed to look at me with attention for the first time. "My God, you look terrible. What have you done to yourself?"

I had rehearsed this. "I have been living with a peasant family near Edwinstowe. I didn't tell them who I was, only that I had left my husband and needed shelter." I gestured downward at my grimy clothing. "They were very poor."

He folded his arms. "Apparently. Yet you preferred their discomforts and company to staying on at Locksley. I wonder why."

"You had accused me of betraying you, and your mother was determined to prove my guilt whatever the facts. You threatened me. What else could I do but leave?"

"I know perfectly well why you left, Marian. Do you think me a fool? Don't weary me or yourself with protests. It doesn't matter now."

"I don't know what you're talking about." I would admit nothing; he might well have been bluffing. "And since it no longer matters, I take it I am free to go?"

He didn't bother to reply. "The Prince was angry about the loss of his treasure, but he doesn't know anyone in my household was connected with its disappearance. He thinks outlaws broke in and stole it. He blamed me for a while, but he knows I am loyal. When he is crowned, he will reward me with a new title, and more land. And I have also asked him to give me a richer wife."

Now I understood, or thought I did. I lifted my chin. "I too would like a different husband. But Richard is King, not John. What will *he* give you?"

He stared at me as if I were a simpleton. "Richard is dead, or as good as. The Prince has said so."

It was on the tip of my tongue to tell him I knew better, but if I took it upon myself to reveal the whereabouts of the King before he was ready someone might take it upon himself to make the Prince's prophecy come true. "I think you are wrong," I told him. "But as you say it does not matter. Let me go back to Blidworth and live quietly, and I will agree to an annulment. I'm sure there are grounds enough."

He said, in a voice sharp as a sword, "I'm keeping Blidworth."

"What do you mean? Blidworth is mine by dower right! You can't keep it."

"Ah," he said softly, "but you have no heir."

At last I truly understood him. He meant to have me killed. The Prince would never discover Guy could not even answer for his own wife, and my husband would punish the affront I had given to his name and consequence. He had promised as much. I looked at him with horror and revulsion. He no longer cared how he got what he wanted, and that certainty of purpose gave him the coldness I had noticed. I tried to keep a steady voice. "You do not dare to harm me, Guy. You have no grounds for any action against my person. You have no right."

He flicked his thumb against his fingers

598

and did not meet my eyes. "I have every right. I am your husband. You have dishonoured me. You have committed the sin of fornication. It is my intention to bring you to trial, but I doubt there'll be anyone to object if I avenge my honour . . . privately . . . afterwards."

I stared at him open-mouthed. It was a pretext, of course, the only one that would serve his purpose. "You have proof, I suppose? With whom am I said to have committed this sin?"

He flashed a look at me, glittering and assessing. My mouth felt very dry. "Robert Fitz Ooth, who was Earl of Huntingdon."

In spite of my best efforts to prevent it, a wave of red passed over me, leaving me sick and shaken. I had to answer him, but my tongue felt thick. "The outlaw? You're raving!"

"You were once almost betrothed to him. You sinned with him before we were married." He smiled, producing his best argument. "He was recognized near Locksley, not once but several times. You were meeting him in secret. I think you will find that the story has already reached the ears of the Prince, and Queen Eleanor. As for proof, if it is needed, it will be supplied."

"You'd perjure yourself?" I was relieved, at least, that he seemed to know nothing about my recent dealings with the Queen.

He was silent.

"If you are willing to go to such lengths to be rid of me," I asked him bitterly, "why worry about the trial at all? Why not just do it privily like the murderer you've become?"

He looked offended. I suppose he still had some illusions about himself. "The Sheriff will see it done with justice," he said.

"If it is done with justice, it will not be done at all," I retorted. "As for Fitz Ooth, if he was seen near Locksley, have you stopped to think that it might be because you stole it from him by vile means? Agnes's brother died because you and the Prince connived at it. What about that, Guy? When the screaming skull is shrieking over your mortal remains, what will happen to your soul?"

"My God," he said shakily. "The cat's

a tiger after all. Mother warned me you knew more than you were saying. Well, guess at whatever you like, and say what you please. It won't do you any good now." He made a little, mocking bow. "Madam, I must take leave of you. Forgive me if I do not express my regrets. He turned back and said seriously, "You will be given a little time to prepare, but don't leave it overlong." Then he was gone.

For a while after he left I was simply numb. I imagined what it would be like to die: a terrible jolt, maybe, like a very bad fall, and then darkness. The worms doing their work on my body, myself unmourned and little remembered, without even a child to carry on. I wondered why, in face of the promise of immortality, man found the idea of physical death so terrifying. I found myself no exception and without consolation, despite my years at Fontevrault. It is only to the old that Death comes as a friend. I remembered, when I got round to it, the scruples I had harboured about betraying Guy. I felt none now. I was all alone, and bereft of philosophy.

The Sheriff, on the other hand, seemed possessed of a great deal of it. He had aged a lifetime since we last met; he looked as if all his physical defences had tumbled down. His flesh was pouchy and grey, with a pallor that indicated he had not been much out-of-doors. He also looked profoundly tired. I could almost pity him. This was the King's First Agent in Nottingham, and the King would not forgive him for turning to John. Small wonder if he hoped the rumours were true.

In spite of the more weighty matters pressing upon him, he berated me roundly for my infidelity to Guy. I had requested the audience, knowing him to be more just and less involved than my husband. I also believed him ignorant of my real association with the outlaws of Sherwood, the mere mention of whom was said to drive him into a frenzy of rage. He was only mildly worked up now, taxing me with ingratitude when Guy had given me wealth and position, with dangerous modern ideas, with faithlessness to my convent upbringing, and with a lack of respect for his own position as my former guardian. He even blamed himself for not suspecting I was a wanton when he had to coerce me into accepting the betrothal of Guy in the first place, and as for an illicit association with Fitz Ooth, if I had truly done such a thing, no further degradation of my person or my reputation could be imagined. The man had become not only a common thief but a traitor of a higher sort who betrayed both the law and his rightful rulers for his own greedy gain. The Sheriff grew very red and slapped the table top with his large hand. Then he pressed me hard to give him the name of the family who had sheltered me in Edwinstowe.

"That I cannot do, my lord," I told him. "It would be a poor way to repay the kindness of people who took me in when I had nowhere else to go. Besides, you mean to have my life anyway, or Guy does. I have nothing to lose by silence."

I thought the Sheriff looked somewhat embarrassed. "I confess I would not

. . . that is to say, he does insist on the full penalty, if . . . ”

He straightened, regaining his pride. “Be assured you will have every opportunity to present your defence. A husband's word, even if that man is Guy, is not enough.”

“Thank you, my lord. Since you say you are concerned that justice be done, will you believe me when I tell you that I left Guy not to sin with another man, which I swear before God I have not done, but because of a matter touching my own honour and conscience?”

He was silent some time, studying his hands. Then he cleared his throat. “If this matter of ‘honour and conscience’ is what I suspect, then I won't permit you to proclaim it in public, not even to save your own life.”

“That's clear enough, sir,” I said coldly. “Might I then ask for a trial by combat?”

He looked startled. “You want a champion?”

I took a breath. “I was thinking instead of casting my lot with the outcome of a more general combat. You are preparing for one now, aren't you?"

I could see he thought me impertinent and was about to dismiss me, so I added desperately, "I have reason to believe the Prince's forces will make a stand against the King's here at Nottingham, and soon. I am content to let my fate rest with the winner."

He said, as if he were explaining it to a restless child, "The King is dead. The Prince will become the new king as soon as the crowning can be arranged. Those who would attack are followers of Longchamp or the justiciars in London who dispute the succession. We hope the matter can be settled without bloodshed."

"And if the King is not dead, and has returned?" I said quietly, into my lap.

"Then he would certainly lay siege to Nottingham Castle, and if I did not defeat him he would have my head in a noose," he said briskly. "But don't lay your hopes on that, Lady Marian. My sources, and I have cause to believe them, say the King will not come back. I take it you personally have no reason to think otherwise?"

I looked at him wide-eyed and shook my head. "No, my lord."

"Good," he said, rising from his chair. "It is enough that I have to see you tried for adultery. I don't want to have you tortured as well. You may go, for the present."

I wondered if I should risk everything and tell him I knew Richard was back. In the end, though, he would not believe me, because he could not. If the King came crowned and in state before the walls of Nottingham flying the Plantagenet lions he would still deny it with his last breath. He had made his choice, and his honour and safety lay in keeping faith. He had already foreseen that Richard would have his life in any case, if Richard lived. Therefore, Richard did not live. Yet, as I had perceived long ago, the Sheriff was not a bad man, and in some ways his choice had been forced upon him. Truly, Prince John had a lot to answer for.

14

ON a morning not long after, the siege of Nottingham began. The wind, sharp and damp with a trace of rain, rattled the branches. The spring sun, still mild and new, rose out of the forest and warmed the mist. The first sound I heard was hammering, distant and insistent. I ran to the window and rolled back the covering, straining to see. At first it was hard to tell where the noise was coming from, but by craning my neck I could finally make it out. On a low hill just below and outside the walls, some men were building an enormous gallows. Arrows flew from the crenellations, and every once in a while one of the workers fell over and was replaced, with as little ceremony as if he were a fallen ant. Just beyond the gallows the tents were pitched, showing the banners of Canterbury and York. I did not see the royal standard. I drew back, shivering. How could anyone doubt he was there? The crusader who had slain a thousand unarmed infidel prisoners was on the hilltop, thumbing his nose at the castle and brandishing the means of its defenders' execution. I remembered his eyes on the road and thought it would not be remarkable if he unleashed the frustration of more than a year's captivity and humiliation in the battle to come. The thought filled me with terror, and I was innocent. I wondered how the Sheriff and Guy were feeling.

A horn blew. Archers appeared out of the woods, and men in armour. It was time to come away from the window. I dressed hurriedly and looked about. My chamber guards were gone. I ran into the neighbouring solar and pulled an old shield off the wall; the bands were rotting away, but the wood was still whole enough. This I dragged with some difficulty further up the staircase to a small projecting antechamber whose window slit was just the right size to be covered with my shield and still permit visibility. I thought the opening was too high up to be useful to the defence or in danger from the attackers, but I was not taking any chances. Crouching, I could make out a little of what was happening below.

The noise was terrible, even from so far. Men and horses screaming. Arrows hissing. Swords clanging on armour, hacking against shields. Shouts like animals, harsh, spontaneous, dreadful sounds. I looked directly below me and saw a fair-haired man, his helmet gone, twisting and shrieking under the hooves of a horse. I tried to pray, and understood why prayers for victory were made before and not during a battle. My mind was white as fog. *Keep evil from me* was all I could manage, over and over.

Bodies were piled and tangled outside the walls. The battle surged in knots and waves all round; it was impossible to tell one side from the other. The sun, reflecting off the metal, made everything a glittering confusion. I could smell smoke, and see it rising. Perhaps the attackers had fired the gate.

I don't know how long I crouched there, waiting. After a while I could no longer watch and came away; it seemed obscene. At long length it grew quieter and I brought myself to look out again. What I saw made the gorge rise in my throat, so that I swallowed bile. The engagement on the field was over, for the time being. But now the movement was on the gallows, where bodies twitched and twisted in the rising spring wind. This was the King's swift sentence on traitors, for all the world to see.

I can't say what it must be like to fight in a battle. But I wonder if it could be more terrible than watching powerless, inaudible, unseen, the dreamer of a particularly ruthless nightmare. I felt sick with remorse when I remembered how I had wanted Robin to meet the Sheriff on the field, without having any idea of what that really meant. Well, I knew now, and I prayed with all my strength that he had not been part of it.

In the grip of a formless dread of what would happen next, it gradually dawned on me that my own danger was specific and probably immediate. I came out of the dream and woke to anger. Whoever found me, it would not be crouching, dazed and frightened, at his feet. I ran back to the room where I had found the shield and went rummaging through all the chests in search of a weapon. There was nothing but a small dagger, mostly ornamental but sharp enough. I think if the King himself had entered the room at that moment I could have used it on him. It would be quite easy. You just had to get close enough, and thrust it in, under the hauberk at the neck. Just that one instant and Guy would be dead, or the Prince, sliced out of life forever in less time than it took to extinguish a rush light. It didn't occur to me that this would be a momentous act, or an evil one. I stood there clutching the dagger hilt till my fingers were white and nerveless, but no one came.

Outside, on the field, a horn sounded, I had never seen a stone thrower, but there was no doubt that one was being wheeled out now, facing the castle walls. The horn sounded again, close by. Two horsemen rode toward the King's encampment.

The wind, shrill-sounding now and full of rain, tore at the tents and banners. It blew out of the forest, scraping the battlements. Dusk, thick with water and clouds, fell dark as night. No one came to light the torches.

Lightning flashed in the distance, promising a storm. The noises began again, closer this time and different. The creaking and clanking of portcullis and chains, the thud of feet on wood, muffled shouts. The wheel of fortune had turned, then. The castle had surrendered. Soon the victors would be beating the coverts, to flush out the game.

I considered going down at once to entrust myself to the safety of numbers rather than the loneliness of the tower room, till I remembered how few women there were in the castle, and that I might be considered the legitimate spoils of war in the aftermath of battle. It might be better after all to let things cool down and hope to stay concealed a little longer. Even as I was debating this, I saw it was too late. Someone took the staircase turning at a run, and lunged into the room, sword drawn. I stood quiet in the shadows, holding my dagger behind me. I could hear his breath, ragged and harsh. "Who's there?" he called, peering at me in the gloom.

I stepped out so he could see me but said nothing.

He was a big man, and swarthy, but luckily not yet drunk. "Well," he said slowly, lowering his sword and hooking his thumb in his belt, "what's this?"

I drew in a breath. "I am Lady Marian Fitz Walter," I said, summoning as much dignity as I could muster, since I was aware I scarcely looked the part. For the sake of prudence and other reasons I would not name myself Guy's wife. "I have been a prisoner in this castle. Can you tell me what's happened? Who won the battle?"

He advanced on me grinning, with a loose mouth and a jaw shadowed with black. "It looks like I won, doesn't it?"

"Stay away from me," I told him. "I am warning you."

He checked uncertainly. "Come, sweetheart, I'm here to rescue you, after all," he said plaintively.

He stood poised to grab me, so I cut in coolly, to hide my own fear, "Have you no shame to come scraping against women like some pig on a stone? What would your wife say, or your sister? If you touch me I will try to kill you. That is a promise." I really meant it. After such a day I didn't think I could stand any more.

He looked taken aback, then angry. He puffed out his large chest and glared. "Your name means nothing to me. For all I know you're a traitor like the rest of them in this castle. Orders are to put everyone in prison, till they can ransom themselves out. When you find yourself rotting in the damp caves under this great barn, you'll wish you'd been nicer to me!"

I had no wish to go anywhere with him, much less into the dark caverns beneath the castle. He took my wrist and jerked hard, trying to drag me after him back down the stairs. I resisted, and tried to swing round on him with the knife. He pinned my arm behind me, cursing as the blade grazed him. I could smell his rank sweat. "You little she-cat," he said, between clenched teeth. "I'll teach you . . . "

A light appeared on the stairway, dazzling after the near darkness. The torch slid neatly into the wall sconce, and a black shape filled the doorway. We stopped dead in our struggle, frozen like moths before the flame. The shape advanced two steps into the room and lifted its sword.

"Please take your hands off the lady," said the apparition.

The cold feeling left me, and I wasn't afraid any more. I let my body sag against the wall when my would-be captor released me. "She is my prisoner," he said sulkily, like a little boy. "I'm taking her to the dungeons to await ransoming."

"Step into the light, both of you," said the other.

I pushed myself off with my hands and obeyed him. At the same time I pulled off my head piece, so he could see my face.

I heard a sharp intake of breath, no more. "She is under my protection." A pause. "We are betrothed."

"How was I to know that?" said the soldier, in an aggrieved tone. "She said nothing of it to me." He eyed the stairs with hope. "I'll be going then, since you claim her." His tone said plainly he thought it a bad bargain.

"You have leave," Robin said, lowering the sword point.

From where I stood, in the flickering light, I could see that his face was streaked with dust and blood. He had, however, washed his hands. His muscles slumped in weariness. I reached out for him. "Are you all right?" I asked him.

He did not answer.

"Well, I'm not hurt, as you see," I said lightly. "But what are you doing here?"

Even through the exhaustion, I could hear the slight lift of amusement in his voice. "Did you miss the battle? Nottingham has surrendered to the King."

My eyes went unwillingly to the window. "I guessed that. But . . . "

"How did I come here, you mean? I was looking for you, of course. It was lucky that ass brayed out his plans so loudly or I might have missed you altogether. I've been through quite a bit of the castle already."

"Will told you?"

"Yes, but he didn't know where you'd gone. Fortunately, your young knight had a friend in Edwinstowe he wanted to impress." The levity, such as it was, died from his voice. "He couldn't wait to get back there and tell her and everyone else how he'd restored Lady Gisborne to her husband."

"He didn't know, Robin. He thought that was all it was."

"Yes."

He had not yet touched any more than my hands, but the certainty that he would do so gave a special weight to every word. I felt as if I wanted to both spin out and shorten the moment at the same time. The air was full. Soon the rain would come. "Have you thought," I asked him, "what Alan will make of this when he hears about it? The Fall of Nottingham and the rescue of the Lady Marian from the jaws of death and dishonour! But for you I might be rotting in some terrible dungeon . . . or rotting somewhere more final."

"Don't joke about it," he said fiercely. "Death can always come unlooked for and too soon." He paused. "There is something I must tell you, something you may have to face. Sir Guy . . ."

I leaned forward and laid a hand upon

617

his lips. "Dead?" I whispered.

He nodded. "I'm not sure. I think so. I . . . saw him fall. But . . . " He sounded perplexed. "I looked for his — for him afterwards, and I'd swear he wasn't there. Perhaps one of his men took charge of his body."

"No more then, please. Not yet." Time enough later to tell him what my husband had planned for me. "Hold me."

The metal rings on his hauberk pressed into my flesh with a sharpness that would probably leave a bruise on the morrow, but I scarcely noticed. His face was rough and cool but the inside of his mouth was warm. Beneath the salty scent of his skin I thought I could detect the spice of the wild grasses of Sherwood.

Below, in the castle courtyard, came shouts and the sound of revelry. On the hill across the meadow, cook fires blazed. "It's the victory celebration." My voice sounded odd in my ears, husky and breathless.

He spread his fingers through my hair, lifting it up and away and tilting my head gently backward. It was too dark, in the shadows, to see his face clearly. "I saw you dead," he said softly. "I was sure he would have you killed."

I placed my hand against his heart, which I could feel beating even through the leather and metal. My own seemed to be hammering in my ears. "He wanted to. But you came to save me."

"But I might have been too late. All I could see was a grey morning full of despair, with all the summer and autumn wasted. I'd wanted to use you, to hurt you the way I was hurt, and now there might never be a chance for anything more."

"Robin — " I began.

"No, let me say this." His voice held a note of bleak apology. "You asked me once if I remembered that time we met as children, and I cut you off. Did you think I'd forgotten it? I think I've wanted you ever since I saw you, a brave and beautiful little girl, standing up to that bully. And then when I was given Huntingdon I wanted to marry you, but you chose Guy, the man who had stolen Locksley from me. You were a stranger to me then, but I wanted to hurt you because you wrecked my dream. I told myself it was only fair to use Guy's own wife to bring him down. But the truth was I wanted to make you suffer the way I had." His hands tightened their grip on my shoulders. "Can you forgive me?"

"Hush," I said, my mouth almost touching his. His breath was warm on my cheek. "That's over now." I could hear the rumble of the rain outside, and the drip and patter of the eaves. "I am here."

"You want me?"

"Yes."

* * *

We could not be still. We moved like swimmers in a stream, touching, testing, gliding over each other as we possessed and explored. I was delighted by how good it was, how well our bodies seemed to fit together without borders or edges, dissolving . . . His body, hardened by forest life and strung up by the day's emotions, was drawn tight as a coil, but his love-making was full of a tenderness that surprised me. I found myself responding, shyly at first, and then with abandon. The force of pent-up love fuelled it, but the future too touched at our shoulder. I wanted to squeeze every drop of joy and pleasure out of our time together. And after joy, peace . . .

★ ★ ★

Some time later, I watched the objects in our attic room — the chest hastily pulled against the door, the cast-off pieces of armour, a clothes pole standing empty — take on their familiar shapes in the grey light of a full moon. The rain had stopped. We lay in a tangled heap of clothing wound round our feet in a rope. Mine were sticking out from under the edge of Robin's mantle and were very cold. I was sleepless with happiness. I lay without moving so as not to disturb him if he dozed, feeling the comfort and pleasure of his body next to mine. He stirred and turned toward me, and I saw the faint light of the room reflected in his own eyes. He smiled, and I thought how much I liked his smile, and how little I had seen it lately. I smiled back, and he reached out gently with his hand, sketching just a trace of a familiar caress on my tenderest flesh. Already our love had its habits and its history.

After a time, he said, "We should get up. It's late, and we can't keep them out forever," and I began to remember that I had had a life before the night began. I asked him to tell me how he had come to be in the battle, and in armour, and on what terms the peace was concluded. He said he had gone to Clipstone, with some of the others, to offer his services to the King. "I told him who I was, and asked for the armour and sword so I could fight as a knight instead of as an outlaw." He shrugged. "But I would have come in a cart, like your Lancelot, if I'd had to."

I knew that he had wanted to come as Guy's equal if they met on the battlefield. I wondered if they had, and if it was Robin who had killed my husband. But I would not ask him now, nor for a long time to come.

He told me that after the first sally against the castle, in which the attackers had set fire to its gates, the defenders had sent out two envoys, scarcely believing that it was really the King in person who demanded their surrender. When they were brought before him, they insisted they had thought that he was dead. Richard charged them to tell what they had seen and sent them back within the walls. A short time later, Nottingham surrendered.

"And the Sheriff?" I asked him.

"Found dead, when we entered the castle gates. With a swordstroke across the back of his neck." He sounded disgusted. "It was a present to the King, to buy his favour."

I shivered. "He deserved better than that." I felt sorry for him, even though he would have abetted in my death to save Guy's face and his own neck. Then I told Robin what had happened since I came to Nottingham.

He swore, queer, half-articulated oaths in Saxon and French under his breath. He went on with it for some time. The effect was so unlike him it made me want to laugh.

"Are you hysterical?" he asked me, on a pause.

I shook my head.

"I'll not forgive myself soon for getting

you into this," he said. "And to think that villain dared to use *me* as a pretext for your death."

I looked at him sitting upright with indignation, naked on top of a heap of my clothes. "If you think about it, it's not entirely inappropriate."

"Well." That smile again, which loosened all my limbs at the joints. "In any case you are now either a wealthy widow or wife to a dead traitor, and this is no place for you to stay. One thing that oaf was right about: the King is imprisoning everyone in the castle until he — or she — ransoms himself out." He shook his head ruefully. "I wouldn't wager on my own position being any too secure, either. We should leave here at once."

Something in his tone caught my attention. "What do you mean? Surely you at least are safe now. Didn't Richard promise to give you Locksley back if you fought for him?"

"My love, the gratitude of kings is notoriously unreliable," he said. "And anyway, I didn't ask him for Locksley."

I was taken aback. "Why not?"

"Because when I mentioned the matter of the, ah, deflected ransom money he pretended never to have heard of the matter, though I could see perfectly well by his eyes that he had. I was afraid that if I asked him too soon, while all his attention was on the coming battle, he could just say no, and then I might never get it back." His own eyes, at that moment, looked very grey and clear. "Besides, you and I know I didn't fight in the battle just for the King or for Locksley."

"Oh, Robin."

"Don't even think about it," he said, getting to his feet and clutching his tunic to him in an inadequate fashion which displayed rather obviously that he had not taken his own advice. "We have to get going. Now."

"But where shall we go?" I asked him. Locksley and Blidworth were still in Gisborne hands.

"If you can bear it, I think it would be safest to go back into the forest. Officially, I am still an outlaw and a fugitive. The King will hold a Grand Council here at Nottingham, and then

625

he goes to Clipstone. We'll meet with him there."

I thought of sharing a blanket next to a campfire smelling of resin and bark beneath a clear sky glittering with frosty stars, of Renard, who would build his fox's earth with his chosen vixen, and of spring coming bud by bud, branch by branch to Sherwood.

"I can bear it," I told him.

"That's my girl. Finish getting dressed, and I'll go down below and see what's happening. The celebration should be over by this hour. With luck we'll pass out unnoticed before we're missed. I have the King's leave to be here, but I'd prefer not to take any chances. You'll be all right by yourself for a few minutes till I come back for you?"

I was glad he couldn't feel the sudden jerk of my heart. I nodded. I put my hand up to his chest and his own closed on it, warm and comforting. "Take care, my love."

"You can be sure of that. Now don't worry. John's watching out for us outside the gates."

"Robin! It's been hours!"

He grinned. "I told him it might take some time to find you." His arm dropped from my shoulders and he turned away, dwindling away into the empty darkness like a ghost.

I hastened to put on my mantle and veil, and I was just putting on my shoes when I heard him coming back. I pushed aside the hangings and stepped eagerly into a pool of moonlight. Something stirred in the shadows and I whirled. A black-cowled figure blocked my path; a hand shot out and fastened hard on my wrist. I took a breath to cry out and saw the silver gleam of a knife's blade at my throat. My own, I remembered with sudden regret, was still lying on the floor in the room behind me. The hood came back. I froze. "Ah, the grieving widow, I see. So I was right all along."

"I . . . I th — thought you were dead," I stuttered.

"I can see that," said Guy, quite pleasantly. "I'm sorry to disappoint you, but all I got was a ringing blow on the head that put me out of things for some time. When I came to I found someone had dragged me off the field, or I might be dead yet. By that time it was obvious that things weren't . . . going my way, so I decided to wait and see how events fell out. After dark, a monk giving help to the dying very kindly . . . lent me his robe, and here I am."

He had not lowered his dagger. He looked very tired, but keyed up with a feverish excitement. "What do you want from me?" I asked him. "It's madness for you to be here. You've lost, Guy. King Richard is here in the castle."

His teeth gleamed in the dark. "The King is not here. I watched him leave for Clipstone myself, not long ago. Do you think he'd spend the night here, till the castle's been purified of traitors?" He spat the words out. "But your concern for me is touching. I could almost believe you if I hadn't been a witness to your little scene with Fitz Ooth. I'd like to have killed you both then and there, but unfortunately I couldn't think of any plausible reason for a monk to be carrying a sword into the castle." He shifted his grip on my wrist and twisted my arm behind my back. "Now walk ahead of me, and hold your tongue. I'll use the knife if I have to."

"But where are we going? I'm no good to you now, Guy. I told you, it's finished."

"Oh, I don't suppose it's finished yet. I might need a hostage to get back to Gisborne safely, or to leave England. And then someone, the King, or Fitz Ooth, should want to ransom you. I think I'll ask that Fitz Ooth bring it to me himself. After that — well, I have a score to settle with both of you." He shoved me forward, hurting my arm. "Move now. I want to be out of here before your friend comes back."

I didn't see how we could leave without meeting Robin on the stairs. We stepped down carefully in the darkness; for obvious reasons, Guy would not light the torch, and the moonlight did not reach the stairwell. When by my reckoning we had descended about half way, he turned aside and pulled back a hanging on the wall. I could only dimly see it, but I heard it scrape. Then he raised a bar and pushed open the wooden shutter. I felt a cold blast of outside air. "This way," he hissed, in my ear.

I stepped out onto a narrow walkway, which seemed to lead along the side of the upper storey of the castle itself. The main exterior stairway, which led up to the entrance of the Great Hall from the bailey below, lay on the other side of the building. I had not known this walkway existed, but Nottingham Castle was a vast warren of passages and chambers.

The moonlight was hard and brilliant. The rain had dried up, and only a few clouds went scudding across the night sky. The courtyard was empty enough, though I could see the flare of the rushlights flickering far below, where the watchmen guarded the victors' sleep. If I had screamed my lungs out they were too far away to hear. Guy dropped my arm and sheathed his dagger. "It's tricky footing here, so we'll go single file," he whispered. "You first. And don't try anything. It's a long drop down."

Below my feet were darkness, empty space, and hard ground somewhere out of sight. I shrank back against the wall, pressing my damp palms against its cool surface. I have never had a head for heights. Guy nudged me forward. The wooden walkway had fallen into disrepair and some of the planks shifted beneath my feet. They were still damp from the night's rain. Before I had taken too many steps I came to a place where two of them had rotted away altogether, leaving a great gaping hole.

"Step over," Guy ordered.

I clutched at the wall with slippery hands, but I couldn't bring myself to do it. The hole seemed to suck at my feet like a drain. I was afraid to move. I clung there miserably, feeling the courage and hope spill out of me, leaving me spent. Death lay ahead and behind me, and at my feet. I had to fight the urge to give in to it, to let it take me. "Robin," I whispered, into the cool surface.

Behind me, Guy swore under his breath. His hand shoved me flat against the wall, and he pushed past me on the walkway, his back hanging out over the edge. He leapt lightly over the gap in the planking, and extended his hand to me from the other side. "Take my hand," he said tersely. "I'll pull you across."

I stayed where I was.

"Take it," he said, "or I'll shove you

over here and now."

I stretched my hand toward him and he grabbed it, hauling me across the gap as roughly as a sack of grain. Some of the rotten wood gave way as my feet left it and fell with a clunk to the ground. We stayed still, listening. Nothing stirred. We were far from the occupied rooms of the castle now, and practically invisible in our dark clothing in the shadow of the walls. "Come on, then," said Guy at last, giving a little jerk on my arm. "You — "

The walkway vibrated suddenly beneath our feet. I saw Guy look over my shoulder, heard him gasp. At first I could see nothing in the blackness of the shadow along which we had come. Then I saw him.

I knew who it was straightaway, though he was little more than a shadow himself. For the second time that night he had come, against all hope, to save me. My heart leapt in my throat.

"Let her go, Gisborne," he said. "It is you, isn't it? I should have known." He had his sword extended, but I was between him and Guy. I could hear him struggling to get his breath. He must have come running, and running hard.

"So you can run me through? If you come for me I'll send her over the edge, so back off, Fitz Ooth!"

But it was Guy who was giving ground. He took one slow step along the walkway, and then another, pulling me with him. Robin came after us, at a distance, his sword glittering in the moonlight . . . Of a sudden, I realized what Guy was doing. "Robin!" I called. "There's a gap in the planks."

But even as I cried out I heard him slip. I heard, with relief, his startled oath, and then the noise he made catching himself on the edge of the wood, and hauling himself back to his feet. Far below, I saw a long, silver flash, and then his sword clattered on some hard surface in the courtyard beneath us.

Guy dropped my arm and whipped round me once more on the walkway, lightly as a cat. I couldn't see whether Robin had regained his feet or not, but I saw the dagger in Guy's right hand, poised . . . Forgetting fear at last, I ran after him down the narrow ledge, as carelessly as if it were wide as the London Road. There was nothing to stop him with but my fist, so I raised my arm and hit him as hard as I could on his right shoulder blade, to make him drop the knife.

He staggered, still clutching the dagger, and caught himself on the wall with his left hand. At the same time Robin leapt forward in a kind of flying motion that knocked Guy backward with a thud. The knife dropped from his fingers just as Robin came in with a savage chop at the throat. Guy jerked his head aside in time and lashed out with a foot, and then the two were locked together, heaving and rolling in a tangled heap that looked particularly nightmarish in the harsh moonlight. The wooden planking shuddered violently, groaned, and then gave way with a terrible splintering sound. One second I was standing on the ledge, and the next I was sliding feet first toward oblivion.

I clutched wildly at the rotting wood, my hands scraping against its rough surface as I fell. My fingers slid further, gripped, and held me. My feet were dangling over open air. I could feel the blood running down my wrists.

Above my head the two men still thrashed and heaved, but I could no longer see what was happening. Each movement seemed to loosen the precarious wooden structure even more, and when I tried to pull myself up it made an ominous ripping noise. All I could do was cling desperately with my aching, nerveless hands and wait for the last jolt that would send me plunging into the dark courtyard below . . .

I hung there scarcely daring to breathe, every tremor from the struggle above grinding pain into my weakening hands and fear into my body. As I watched, dangling, a head appeared on the edge of the walkway, the upper body extended over empty space almost as precariously as I was. The other man lay uppermost, clamped on top. In the stifling shadows I could not tell which was Robin. The man on the bottom made a desperate heave to rid himself of his attacker. I heard the sick sound of flesh and bone smacking together, then felt a violent shaking so forceful I could not keep my grip and slid another few inches along the wood. There was a cry, a dreadful sound that plunged like a meteor into the night and then ceased on a thump on the ground below. I was trembling myself, now, the wood slipping surely from my hands despite my clawing and scrabbling for a hold. I could hear the survivor panting and struggling for breath. "Good-bye, Robin," I said, to the man above me, or to the man on the ground below. Now I would never know which was which . . . My hands loosened, opened, and came away from the wood.

Something caught my wrist with a jerk, almost wrenching my arm out of its socket. My free hand, thinking for me, flailed until it found a hold again. My arms were a jelly of pain. His hand kept a firm hold on mine, though I could hear the breath sob in his throat from exertion. Bit by bit he hauled me up toward the solid ledge, till I could take some of the terrible weight off his grip by finding a foothold on the planking. Next minute I was in his arms, holding him tight enough to smother him.

"Oh, love, oh, love," was all I could

say, over and over . . .

After a time, he said, "If you hadn't made him drop his dagger, I might be dead."

I said, in a kind of harsh whisper, "I would have killed him, if I could. He meant to kill us both. He . . . Oh, Robin. You *came*. You found me. I thought . . . " I'd thought I'd never see him again.

I shivered, and his arm tightened around me. "I almost missed you altogether," he said. "I went back, and I couldn't find you anywhere. After a while I thought of Gisborne. I told you I was troubled when no one could find his body on the field. But I didn't see how he could have taken you without passing me on the stairs. Luckily, when he closed the entrance to this walkway, a corner of the hanging caught in the door. Otherwise, I might never have found it."

Such a little thing, the mercy that had saved us and given us another chance at happiness.

"Robin," I said, not wanting to ask, but feeling I must, "you don't think there's a chance he's . . . " I looked down into the abyss below.

He shook his head.

"Then could we go, before they find us here? This place . . . all the deaths . . . I want to go back to Sherwood."

He smiled and got to his feet, and put a hand down to me.

And so, after talking our way out of the castle with the King's pass and hints of the King's business, we made our way across the meadows and fields to the edge of the forest, where John stood waiting. "Well that took you long enough," he said peaceably.

We turned and followed him into Sherwood, where the trees stood like sentinels, pale grey in the waning moonlight.

15

THE Council at Nottingham lasted four days, and had far-reaching consequences. In the presence of his mother (still firmly in possession of the title of queen, for at least as long as her daughter-in-law was out of England), Chancellor Longchamp, the Archbishops of York and Canterbury, the present Earl of Huntingdon (the prince of Scotland), and other nobles, the King confiscated all the principal offices and land holdings of England again and sold them off to the highest bidders, repudiating all his former concessions. To raise additional money to finance the inevitable war with King Philip for control of Normandy and pay off the remainder of the ransom, he also instituted a land tax. After some haggling, wayward Prince John, who was not present, was allowed to keep his English holdings and was ordered to appear before the Court by the 10th of May, on pain of banishment. Many of those who had served the Prince in a lesser capacity were permitted to make their peace with the King by paying a hefty fine. Others, even those who had not taken sides, lost their estates and titles and their fortunes.

If I had known any of this, it might have cast some shadow over my happiness, or at least given me pause. But I was far too busy enjoying Sherwood the way a captive surveys a cage he knows he is quitting. Agnes was my only present sorrow; she had survived the illness but looked thin and wasted and full of melancholy; Alan had not come back. I did what I could for her and promised her a place wherever I lived.

True to my other promise, I let Renard out of *his* cage for the last time. Agnes said he'd begun sleeping in it with the door open most of the time, so I took it away and burned it so he could not come back. That brought on my own attack of melancholy, and I had to stay away from the spot where it had stood until I was sure he would have given up and gone. I hoped he found his vixen soon, and that she deserved him.

On All Fools' Day, Robin and John and Will and I, along with those who hoped for pardon because they had fought for the King, went to an audience at Clipstone Palace. Richard and Eleanor had just come from dinner and the All Fools' festivities, garlanded and bowing backward and doing all the other ridiculous things one does at the feast. They left the Lord of Misrule's chair empty, someone said, because only one person belonged there by right and he was absent. I saw at once that the merriment had not touched the King's mind or heart. Captivity had changed him. He was thinner, of course, and more pale, but something in him had hardened, and not to anyone's good. His voice had a bitter edge and his eyes were cruel in a calm face.

Eleanor too had changed, but she seemed more herself than before, vain and calculating and much more light-hearted, now that her son was back. She had, I think, a deep reserve of strength she had not even now exhausted, but once there was nothing left to strive for she would permit herself to grow old at last. Though I knew from experience she could be callous and malicious, I would, of the two larger-than-life figures seated before us, much rather have thrown myself on her mercy than her son's. However, her eye passed over me without acknowledgement.

Richard stood, consulted for a moment with a scribe, and then said wearily, "I am mindful that I have cause to be grateful to you all for your help in the siege of Nottingham. I therefore grant everyone under the rank of knight or clerk a free pardon from outlawry, though at the same time I warn you that the Forest Law will be enforced to the same degree of strictness as before, and any offences will be punished without regard to what was done here today. The slate between us is wiped clean. You are free to go back to your homes or whatever lives you had before the crimes were committed."

I looked at Robin. His lips were drawn in a thin line and his face wore that closed-down expression I'd hoped never to see there again.

"There are two cases I shall consider apart," the King went on. "Lady Marian of Gisborne, née Fitz Walter."

I stepped forward.

"Your husband was one of a group of greedy nobles who tried to manipulate my brother and use him for their own selfish plans. It is only just that he should not be allowed to keep these ill-gotten gains, even in death. Furthermore, you yourself left Nottingham without paying the ransom I required. What do you say to this?"

I could have laughed at the construction he had invented for his brother's behaviour, if I hadn't felt so frightened. Robin took my hand, squeezed it, and held it by his side. I swallowed. "I say, Your Grace, that as soon as I became aware of what my husband was doing I did everything in my power to undo it." I hoped this was saying enough, since I could hardly be explicit about the Prince, who had already been officially 'forgiven'. "And that when Sir Guy discovered my intention, I was forced to flee to . . . to Sherwood to save my life. As for Nottingham, I was a prisoner there myself, under threat of death from the Sheriff and my husband. I did not think the requirement for ransom would apply."

The King shrugged. "Well, I will waive it. You don't look as if you could afford to pay it anyway. However, the Gisborne holdings are forfeit. They will be sold, and the proceeds will go to the crown. With respect to — "

"Wait." The Queen spoke for the first time, though I had felt her eyes on me throughout my part of the interview. "This lady and I have some unfinished business, don't we?" Her voice didn't sound old at all, but dry and hard as spice.

I turned toward her with relief. I was on surer ground here. "Your Grace was very kind to me last year when I came to you with . . . with the ransom to plead the case of the outlaws."

She frowned. For a moment I wondered if she would play her old game of forgetting my name, but what she said was, "You've changed a great deal, and not for the better."

I repressed a sigh. Everyone I met lately seemed to begin conversations with unfavourable comments about my appearance. "I spent the winter out-of-doors, in Sherwood, madam. I fear it did little to improve my complexion or my apparel."

She smiled, not kindly. "And why didn't you spend the winter in the convent where I arranged a place for you? At considerable trouble and expense to myself, I might add."

"Your Grace, I am very sorry I took your money gift and then used it for another purpose. I intend to pay you back out of my estates as soon as they are restored to me. But as for why I went back to Sherwood instead of the convent — " I looked her full in the face and told the simple truth — "I couldn't leave him."

"Ah," she said, a sigh of deep satisfaction. So the young Duchess of Aquitaine was there still, with the old woman. "'Him', I take it, is Robert Fitz Ooth, the outlaw, and doubtless the reason you were so eager to annul your marriage, though you seem to have found a more permanent solution to *that* problem. The very same man who refuses to relinquish your hand throughout this audience, if I'm not mistaken." She looked triumphant.

Robin's mouth twitched, but he said nothing.

"That is correct, Your Grace."

The white eyebrows lifted like a gull in flight. Even the King looked amused. "And are we to understand that you wish to marry him now, without prospects?"

"We should both prefer it *with* prospects, madam, I do assure you. But even without, yes."

"Hmmph. Your season out-of-doors doesn't seem to have done your wits much good either." She leaned over and whispered something to her son, who looked annoyed. She whispered something more. He shrugged.

"My mother has convinced me that I should make some additional provision for you both." He sounded as if he would sooner part with a tooth. Well, he had had a hard time of it, but no doubt he had never been hungry or frozen or really sick for the entire time

646

of his confinement. "Fitz Ooth."

"Sire?"

"I hereby revoke the Articles of Outlawry drawn up against you. You can have it from the clerk in writing." He cleared his throat. "I regret I cannot restore you to your former titles and estates as well, but you have said you understand that. However, to reward your loyalty, in addition to forgiving you for your attack on one of my agents and for all of my game you've consumed in the past years" — he smiled thinly — "I will give you and the Lady Marian, free and clear, the manor house of Blidworth, with taxes and scutage reduced by half for the next five years." He sat back restlessly in his chair, looking about him.

Robin, however, stood quite still. "You are very generous, Your Grace," he said calmly. "But may I respectfully point out that Blidworth already belongs to the Lady Marian. It is hers by dower right. I would petition you for the return of Locksley Hall, which was my home from boyhood and was taken from me by force and deceit. Besides the hand of this lady, it is all I would ask."

The blue eyes narrowed. "Then you ask too much, Fitz Ooth. Half the nobles in the kingdom have had to bid for their properties, including my own half-brother York. The other half of the estates will be put up to auction after my second coronation. Damn it man, I need money to fight the French King, and Locksley will bring a good price. I already have a bid for it, from another man I need to reward. Of course," he said, with a small gesture of amusement or contempt, "you are free to try to match his offer, but I think you will find it dear. Take what I have given you, and count yourself lucky to have that."

It was the King speaking, cold and unanswerable. I felt sick with rage and shame.

Richard made a half bow of dismissal and turned away.

Robin stood where he was. "Pardon me, my lord, but it is not right."

The room grew very quiet. The Queen laid a restraining hand on her son's arm. Unbidden and unwelcome, the thought crossed my mind that this man had slaughtered a thousand people in the

648

space of a morning, and boasted of it afterwards. The hair rose on the back of my neck. Suddenly Richard burst out laughing, a loud hoarse sound that was no more reassuring than his anger. "You're mad," he said pleasantly. "Too much stolen meat has cracked your brain. You still think like an outlaw even though I've offered to make you respectable again." The smile was frosty. "Well, I wash my hands of it . . . Take it or leave it, we are quits now. You have no more claim on me."

After the chill, anger rose in me like a sea surge. I felt as I had while I waited in the tower room with a dagger in my hand. I didn't wait to see what Robin would say or do. I stepped forward. "Lord King!" My knees were shaking, but with anger, not fear. "He may not have a claim to press, but I do." The King looked at me with astonishment and the Queen, I thought, with pity. "I would rather speak of it in private," I told them, "but I have an object of great value I would offer you which will support it. I will give you this treasure and" — I drew in a breath for courage — "Blidworth, if you will permit Robert Fitz Ooth to retain Locksley."

"No, Marian!" Robin cried. "You're not to give up Blidworth. It's your security."

"We've seen how much security counts for," I told him between clenched teeth. "Let me do this. For my own sake more than yours."

"What is this treasure?" asked Richard, leaning forward.

"It would be better not to speak of it until I bring it to you, Your Grace, and then you can judge for yourself how valuable it is. But it lies hidden, and I will need a day to collect it."

"Oh, bother." said the King. "I'm going hunting tomorrow and after that we travel to Southwell. Am I never to be allowed any free time?"

I bowed my head, so he could not see my expression. "I could be back after supper tonight, Your Grace, if that would be convenient."

"Very well, but this 'object' had better be as valuable as you suggest. I'll send an escort with you to make sure it gets back here safely." He tapped his thumb to his lips reflectively. "And I think Fitz Ooth will remain here, too, for surety. If it works out as you say, then I will consider your request."

★ ★ ★

Outside, in the shaded courtyard, Robin took my arm and swung me around to face him. "Now would you like to tell me what that was all about?"

I shook my head. "Don't ask me, at least not yet. It's something to do with the past, something I'll be glad to get rid of. But in case it doesn't work out, it would be safer for you not to know."

He passed a hand over his eyes and hair. "Whatever it is, you should not have brought it up. Did you see his face? God help you if you disappoint him now. It's almost sure to cost you Blidworth, and then where will you turn if something happens to me? You've thrown away your future."

He looked quite bleak. "I don't think so," I told him. "I still have the French lands, after all. Besides, how can you worry about me after" — I lowered my voice — "what he did to you? What about Locksley? Is that the King's justice?" I was so angry I could scarcely form the words. "Where is his honour? Does he think a King has no responsibilities or obligations? We fought for him, we saved the ransom, people *died* because of him, and this is how he treats us. If I were Richard I would die of shame."

"It is only children who expect life to be just," Robin said. "Some day there may be a reckoning, even for kings. But in the meantime, even if he gave me Locksley with open hands, how long do you think it will be before fortune's wheel turns again? One year? Ten? You've seen how much his commitments count for when it's a question of money. And what if he dies, in one of these interminable fights with Philip? Prince John almost took the throne while his brother lives. What do you think could part him from it after Richard dies? How long do you think we would keep Locksley then? I think your claim to Blidworth would be easier to defend." He rubbed his eyes in a weary gesture. "I want to keep you safe, but I don't know how."

I took his two hands in mine and kissed his cheek. "Don't think that way," I told him. "Who was it who was lamenting the lost summer and autumn, when we met in the tower room at Nottingham?" I looked up smiling into his eyes. "We have what we have. That is enough."

★ ★ ★

It was a long time since I had been at Blidworth, but I saw less of it than a passing pilgrim on the way to a shrine. The bailiff came out to meet us, but he was one of Guy's men and looked at me with fear and dislike. I would have liked to sack him then and there, but my future authority was uncertain, and there was no one I could appoint in his place on the spur of the moment. I wanted to look the house over, but the escorts were restless and hurried me through, though politely. I found it had changed, but as I have seen it seldom since that day my present memories are all in accord with my early ones; it is reality that has dimmed. I have found this is one of the few pleasant aspects of increasing age.

We dug up the cedar chest I had buried in the orchard without difficulty, and I opened it to make sure the chalice was still intact. It was there in its wrappings, as beautiful as it was when I first saw it at Fontevrault. I stared at it for a moment, reliving the day and waiting to see if it spoke to me at all. I'm not sure what I expected, but the chalice was mute. Now it was just a beautiful object, the means to an end. In fact, I was relieved to be getting rid of it and felt a lightening like a blood-letting. As I suppose in a way it was. I closed the lid carefully, handed up the chest, and mounted for the ride back to Clipstone.

Robin and John were sitting in the courtyard when we rode in. They leapt to their feet, but we swept past them on orders from the King. I began to see what Robin meant about not disappointing him. I'd had little else to think of on the ride back besides how he would deal with the chalice and me, but I couldn't begin to predict Richard Plantagenet.

He received me alone, without the

Queen, to my enormous relief. One of the guards carried in my casket, set it at his feet, and left it. Feet shuffled all round, but we were the only ones in the small solar. He took the only chair, and left me standing. I bowed. "My chalice, Your Grace," I said, and gestured toward the casket.

He lifted it deftly from its wrappings, turning it around in his hands so that the jewels caught the winking torchlight. It was not full dark and I could see the pleasure on his face as he handled it. Then he tipped it upside down and saw the inscription. Silently, I handed him the scroll that accompanied it, and watched him read. I heard his breath catch. For the first time he looked at me. "How did you come by this?"

"Your father gave it to my mother," I said evenly.

"When?"

I explained how it had been left in trust for me at Fontevrault.

The shadows came and went over his face from the flickering brazier. It was impossible to tell what he was thinking. It looked as if he were lost in memory.

"Do you know what this means?" he said at last.

"I can guess. But it is no more than that."

"Then what do you want?"

"Because of what it may mean? Nothing."

"You said you would press a claim on me."

"My lord, I only said that to claim your attention."

He turned it over in his hands speculatively. "Women always say they don't want anything from you, but they lie." He raised his head. "Locksley. That was what you wanted."

"In exchange for the chalice and Blidworth," I reminded him.

"And your silence?"

"Your Grace may be assured I will be silent in any case."

"By God you will!" His veins stood out angrily on his forehead. "Do you think I want my mother to hear about this? She's old, and she's had enough to bear. When I think of what she suffered at that man's hands . . ."

I was becoming alarmed. He seemed

to think I might be blackmailing him, and Richard would be a bad enemy. Sister Beatrice had warned me a long time ago. I said quietly, "I think you misunderstand me, sir. There is no proof of anything that need distress the Queen. I don't think of it now and haven't in years. I just want to be rid of the chalice and marry Robin and find a little happiness. I thought you might like this piece because your father had it made, that's all. For all I care you can melt it down at once."

He sighed. "And you don't want me to find you a prince to marry or acknowledge you as my sister, or anything of that sort?"

I had to struggle to suppress a shudder. "No."

"Very well, then. You and Fitz Ooth can have Locksley. But no remission of taxes or scutage. And I don't want to hear anything about this again."

"Oh, *thank you*, Your Grace," I said, and burst into tears.

16

THE little church at Edwinstowe stood open to the daylight. A soft breeze brushed the tree tops and stirred the lilacs on the porch; the air was full of the drift of their scent. The meadows too had kindled into spring. A popinjay hopped along the path, bold and watchful, hoping to catch the grain as it fell in a shower over our heads.

"At last," said Agnes, looking wistful.

"Long life and much happiness," said John, smiling.

"And many adventures," added Will.

"Not too many, I hope." I laughed. "I think we've all had enough to keep us for the rest of our days." I reached up, a little shyly in that circle of friends, and brushed some grains from Robin's hair. His smile crinkled down at me in the sunshine. "It isn't only misery that lengthens time," I said. "I hope the peace and happiness of this day lasts forever. For all of us."

"If God wills," said Father Tuck. "His blessings be on you both."

"Let's go home," said Robin.

The wind sang in the branches, and deep in the forest the oaks roared. We stepped out into the clear day, and went home to Locksley.

Epilogue

ALL that is as clear to me as yesterday, brightly pictured in the colours of springtime and new love. It is yesterday that I forget, the propers of the seasons, the devotions of the Hours, the name of the new sister in our house with eyes like Cecily's. In spite of my duties and observances, I have too much time for remembering. Through the window of my mind I can see the small white scar on his shoulder as he lay next to me, his warmth nestled into the curve of my flesh, his back strong and smooth beneath my hands. It is strange how, after a time, every line of his body and skin became as familiar to the touch as my own. I know I should not indulge in such thoughts, not, as the Reverend Mother would say, because they are sinful (though I am pledged to obey her now), but because they occasion too much pain. But memory — and desire — are all I have left of him, and I will

660

endure what I have to to preserve even that. Love is Suffering. Yes.

There is wisdom in endings, and in knowing where they rightfully fall. We should have lived on at Locksley, raised children, ridden Dun Crump and his successors to the Goose Fair and market days, and grown old and quiet by the fireside, entertaining our grandchildren with long ago tales of Robin Hood and the outlaws of Sherwood. The King too should have come home from the wars with France, begotten an heir, and settled down to rule his realm. That is what should have been, but as Robin said, it is only children who expect life to be just.

We had five years. Five years I think of now as perpetual spring: the daffodils growing right up to the foot of the cherry trees, a snow of pink petals in the breeze, the bees buzzing round my hives beneath a sky blue as lapis. We spent our days like new-minted coins. Happiness comes and moves on. It is lost the moment we touch it, and it can no more be stayed than one can stop the stream's flowing with a hand.

All that came afterwards was winter. One day in mid-March, 1199, King Richard heard about a fabulous treasure buried at the castle of Chaluz near Limoges, and was hit by an arrow while trying to persuade the castle's defenders to turn it over to him. So far as I have heard, the treasure never existed, but on the 6th of April Richard died and shortly thereafter John was crowned at Westminster. Soon after that the new King made a tour of his lands and began to settle up his accounts. As in some terrible recurring dream, we were fugitives again, but this time there was no hope to fill our emptiness. Locksley burned. I caught the plague and nearly died of it, and Robin brought me to this house, the same shelter Eleanor would have sent me to all those years ago. Here the sisters nursed me back to a health I could scarcely welcome, when I learned he had gone.

The tale of his death has a dozen versions, and I need not recount it in detail. Some of the variations even reach me within these walls, since few now have any idea of who I was, or what we were to each other. (Alan made the song, but he would not sing it for me. I could not quite forgive him for Agnes's early death and his own marriage, so soon after, to a bishop's ward. We saw each other seldom, and now he too is gone.) It is enough to confirm that Robin was badly wounded in a skirmish with French pirates off the Yorkshire coast, trying (I believe) to get enough money to buy a small estate somewhere beyond the reach of King John. You need not go far these days to do that.

All this trouble, and more, I lay squarely at the King's feet. But who is to blame for what happened afterwards, for Will Scarlet's remembering with reverence and kindness the girl he had been betrothed to, who had healed me when I was sick with childbed fever? She was Prioress of Kirklees, made so some years after my money gift made it possible. Did Janet still bear me malice for who-knows-what twisted pattern in our past, and was Robin the instrument of her revenge? Or was it just an accident that, in bleeding him, she cut an artery and let the life flow out of his body onto the infirmary floor? I shall never know the truth of it. John and Will buried him, and even they do not know.

Since then I have pulled the monastery walls around my head like a blanket and shut out the world and all the madness of the dark years of King John: the loss of Normandy and Poitou and the Aquitaine to Philip (luckily I had sold my lands in France to dower my keep here, or I might be homeless still), the wars with the Holy See over Steven Langdon, and the wars with the barons over their privileges which resulted in the Magna Carta, a doomed document if I ever saw one. Everything the King touches turns to dross.

Just yesterday he passed by here on his way to the Abbey of Swineshead. I could not answer for what I might have done if I had met him face to face, brother and monarch or no. I was spared that encounter, but all of us, from the novices up, were turned out under orders in the dark of night to look for remnants of the royal baggage train, which had overturned in the Great Wash. It seems he was carrying his private collection of plate and jewelry, as well as the institutional regalia of the crown of England, and it was all lost.

I stood barefoot on the edge of the marshes, in the autumn chill. An unseen bird made weird, disembodied cries from a distant branch, but otherwise all was silent except for the lapping water. A salt tang was in the air, heavy as incense. The surface was smooth and undisturbed. I did not think the King would get his treasure back. There was a story, old as the barrow mounds, that a water god lived there, who demanded a life every year. Perhaps he had altered his tastes. I wondered if my own chalice, which had passed in due course from Richard to John, had been part of the lost treasure. I certainly liked to think so. The water god was welcome to it, from me.

The night's bright necklace of stars glittered in the pool at my feet. I saw, in the reflection, the wood-wose capering in silvery leaves. I shut my eyes, and when I opened them he was gone.

The bards sing, and the children remember. There is wisdom in ending, but it is not ended yet.

Afterword

A SUMPTUOUS gold chalice, popularly known as 'King John's Cup', was dredged up out of the fens some time before the end of the seventeenth century. The splendid workmanship suggests the cup was made for royalty, and tradition holds that the piece was part of the baggage lost by the King while crossing The Wash, just before he died in 1216. The chalice is now in the possession of the King's Lynn Corporation in the Guildhall of the Holy Trinity, King's Lynn, Norfolk.

FATAL RING OF LIGHT
Helen Eastwood

Katy's brother was supposed to have died in 1897 but a scrawled note in his handwriting showed July 1899. What had happened to him in those two years? Katy was determined to help him.

NIGHT ACTION
Alan Evans

Captain David Brent sails at dead of night to the German occupied Normandy town of St. Jean on a mission which will stretch loyalty and ingenuity to its limits, and beyond.

A MURDER TOO MANY
Elizabeth Ferrars

Many, including the murdered man's widow, believed the wrong man had been convicted. The further murder of a key witness in the earlier case convinced Basnett that the seemingly unrelated deaths were linked.

THE WILDERNESS WALK
Sheila Bishop

Stifling unpleasant memories of a misbegotten romance in Cleave with Lord Francis Aubrey, Lavinia goes on holiday there with her sister. The two women are thrust into a romantic intrigue involving none other than Lord Francis.

THE RELUCTANT GUEST
Rosalind Brett

Ann Calvert went to spend a month on a South African farm with Theo Borland and his sister. They both proved to be different from her first idea of them, and there was Storr Peterson — the most disturbing man she had ever met.

ONE ENCHANTED SUMMER
Anne Tedlock Brooks

A tale of mystery and romance and a girl who found both during one enchanted summer.

CLOUD OVER MALVERTON
Nancy Buckingham

Dulcie soon realises that something is seriously wrong at Malverton, and when violence strikes she is horrified to find herself under suspicion of murder.

AFTER THOUGHTS
Max Bygraves

The Cockney entertainer tells stories of his East End childhood, of his RAF days, and his post-war showbusiness successes and friendships with fellow comedians.

MOONLIGHT
AND MARCH ROSES
D. Y. Cameron

Lynn's search to trace a missing girl takes her to Spain, where she meets Clive Hendon. While untangling the situation, she untangles her emotions and decides on her own future.

NURSE ALICE IN LOVE
Theresa Charles

Accepting the post of nurse to little Fernie Sherrod, Alice Everton could not guess at the romance, suspense and danger which lay ahead at the Sherrod's isolated estate.

POIROT INVESTIGATES
Agatha Christie

Two things bind these eleven stories together — the brilliance and uncanny skill of the diminutive Belgian detective, and the stupidity of his Watson-like partner, Captain Hastings.

LET LOOSE THE TIGERS
Josephine Cox

Queenie promised to find the long-lost son of the frail, elderly murderess, Hannah Jason. But her enquiries threatened to unlock the cage where crucial secrets had long been held captive.

THE TWILIGHT MAN
Frank Gruber

Jim Rand lives alone in the California desert awaiting death. Into his hermit existence comes a teenage girl who blows both his past and his brief future wide open.

DOG IN THE DARK
Gerald Hammond

Jim Cunningham breeds and trains gun dogs, and his antagonism towards the devotees of show spaniels earns him many enemies. So when one of them is found murdered, the police are on his doorstep within hours.

THE RED KNIGHT
Geoffrey Moxon

When he finds himself a pawn on the chessboard of international espionage with his family in constant danger, Guy Trent becomes embroiled in moves and countermoves which may mean life or death for Western scientists.

TIGER TIGER
Frank Ryan

A young man involved in drugs is found murdered. This is the first event which will draw Detective Inspector Sandy Woodings into a whirlpool of murder and deceit.

CAROLINE MINUSCULE
Andrew Taylor

Caroline Minuscule, a medieval script, is the first clue to the whereabouts of a cache of diamonds. The search becomes a deadly kind of fairy story in which several murders have an other-worldly quality.

LONG CHAIN OF DEATH
Sarah Wolf

During the Second World War four American teenagers from the same town join the Army together. Forty-two years later, the son of one of the soldiers realises that someone is systematically wiping out the families of the four men.

THE LISTERDALE MYSTERY
Agatha Christie

Twelve short stories ranging from the light-hearted to the macabre, diverse mysteries ingeniously and plausibly contrived and convincingly unravelled.

TO BE LOVED
Lynne Collins

Andrew married the woman he had always loved despite the knowledge that Sarah married him for reasons of her own. So much heartache could have been avoided if only he had known how vital it was to be loved.

ACCUSED NURSE
Jane Converse

Paula found herself accused of a crime which could cost her her job, her nurse's reputation, and even the man she loved, unless the truth came to light.

BUTTERFLY MONTANE
Dorothy Cork

Parma had come to New Guinea to marry Alec Rivers, but she found him completely disinterested and that overbearing Pierce Adams getting entirely the wrong idea about her.

HONOURABLE FRIENDS
Janet Daley

Priscilla Burford is happily married when she meets Junior Environment Minister Alistair Thurston. Inevitably, sexual obsession and political necessity collide.

WANDERING MINSTRELS
Mary Delorme

Stella Wade's career as a concert pianist might have been ruined by the rudeness of a famous conductor, so it seemed to her agent and benefactor. Even Sir Nicholas fails to see the possibilities when John Tallis falls deeply in love with Stella.

CHATEAU OF FLOWERS
Margaret Rome

Alain, Comte de Treville needed a wife to look after him, and Fleur went into marriage on a business basis only, hoping that eventually he would come to trust and care for her.

CRISS-CROSS
Alan Scholefield

As her ex-husband had succeeded in kidnapping their young daughter once, Jane was determined to take her safely back to England. But all too soon Jane is caught up in a new web of intrigue.

DEAD BY MORNING
Dorothy Simpson

Leo Martindale's body was discovered outside the gates of his ancestral home. Is it, as Inspector Thanet begins to suspect, murder?

LARGE PRINT
Todd, Catherine J.
  Marian

DATE DUE

12/93